The
HEART
of the RITZ

Also by Luke Devenish

The Secret Heiress
Den of Wolves
Nest of Vipers

The
HEART
of the RITZ

LUKE DEVENISH

SIMON &
SCHUSTER

London · New York · Sydney · Toronto · New Delhi

A CBS COMPANY

THE HEART OF THE RITZ
First published in Australia in 2019 by
Simon & Schuster (Australia) Pty Limited
Suite 19A, Level 1, Building C, 450 Miller Street, Cammeray, NSW 2062

10 9 8 7 6 5 4 3 2 1

A CBS Company
Sydney New York London Toronto New Delhi
Visit our website at www.simonandschuster.com.au

A catalogue record for this
book is available from the
National Library of Australia

Cover design: Lisa White
Cover image: Mark Owen/Trevillion Images
Typeset by Midland Typesetters, Australia
Printed and bound in Australia by Griffin Press

The paper this book is printed on is certified
against the Forest Stewardship Council®
Standards. Griffin Press holds FSC chain
of custody certification SGS-COC-005088.
FSC promotes environmentally responsible,
socially beneficial and economically viable
management of the world's forests.

To Dad, who loves his books.
Always my best encourager.

PROLOGUE

1 April 1922

Hans told himself he had no less right than any man to enter the Ritz. At twenty-five years old, he was a fellow of fine looks and high education: two attributes alone which surely meant he belonged there. He had fought in and survived the World War and had received the Iron Cross for his valour. By these and any other measure he was exceptional. Yet now that the Ritz signage, so discreet it was unreadable from the other side of the square, had become impossible to ignore because he was standing beneath it, his nerve failed him. It had never failed him once in the trenches.

To his horror he found that he simply could not go inside the Ritz. Disgraced by this cowardice, he made to move on – until he took hold of himself. He stood so that he might be thought to be viewing Napoleon's column, but of course, he was not. He was viewing the famous Hôtel Ritz and dreaming of the elegant life that was lived at the heart of it; a life as secure and serene and as comfortable as a life lived curled in the womb; a life that didn't belong to him, Hans Metzingen, the handsome nobody from defeated, humiliated Germany. But it could be his, if only he would go inside.

Hans lit a cigarette, one of three that remained in his crumpled packet. He had no money for more. He had set precious francs aside for weeks to pay for the drink he fantasised buying from the bar; a drink he could almost taste now. A chauffeured car pulled up to the curb while he smoked, steeling himself to try again. Uniformed men spilled from the hotel entrance to see to the car's occupants. The rear passenger doors opened and feminine feet, clad in silk stockings and high heels, connected with the pave-stones as the men took hold of their gloved hands, helping each lady emerge. There were four women in all, weighted with jewellery and furs; chic cloche hats bowed in a huddle while they lit cigarettes in holders.

There was a willowy blonde, effortlessly soignée; an aristocrat. Next to her, a shapelier red-head, blousy and loud; American perhaps. Then a tiny brunette, coarse-mouthed and cheeky; so quintessentially Parisienne. And finally, an elegant older woman, nominally in charge of the others. She was a woman Hans recognised: a soprano from the Palais Garnier, and not a French woman either. What was she, Hans wondered, English? Or something else still?

The women regarded him with practised eyes, as women everywhere will regard a good-looking man, even a German one. Hans' masculinity was all that he had to offer them; his handsome face and his Teutonic size. He stood that little bit taller, stronger, holding his cigarette just so. He did not look away from them. What would they take him for, he wondered. A guest? A gigolo? He could be either if they asked. The four pairs of feminine eyes appraised him slowly, appreciatively. Then they looked right through him to the doors.

The Ritz men brought the luggage around while the women moved as a group to the entrance, aware of Hans following them with his eyes. First one, then two, then three of the women passed through the doors, lit by the chandeliers' glow from the lobby. Only the cheeky Parisienne lingered; she had dropped something. Before he could even give thought to it, Hans had the door for her, and then the dropped object, too. It was a little lip rouge encased in gold. Hans gave it back, his hand a giant German's hand and hers a precocious Parisienne child's. She smiled at him, brilliantly; a film star's smile. He felt a stirring in his gut and knew that his desire was returned.

Hans caught his reflection in the door: his shabby evening suit, bought fully two years before the war, ill-fitting on his frame; his too-worn shoes that no amount of polishing could restore for the holes; his bluntly hacked hair, cut fast and uncaringly and cheap; his expression of shame that he ever thought such an adventure possible.

'Monsieur?'

A Ritz man was standing behind him with a trolley of luggage.

'I'm sorry – what?'

The man winced at his despised accent. Hans watched the Parisienne move further inside.

'Are you a guest here, Monsieur?' The Ritz man didn't smile because he knew the answer.

Hans saw the little brunette become enveloped by her friends, as others called out to her from the bar. She belonged here. She spun around a last time to flirt with him over her shoulder, one eyebrow raised in a pantomime of the Ritz man's shattering question.

'*Are you a guest here, Monsieur?*' The man had a badge pinned to his lapel. Hans read it: Claude. He looked no older, no better than Hans himself, and yet his question said otherwise. 'You are not, are you, Monsieur?'

'No,' said Hans. 'I am not a guest, no . . .'

Hans did not imagine the contempt he saw in the other man's eyes, and with it the unspoken response: '*And you never will be, kraut.*'

Hans was holding the door for a servant and was thus made lower than the low. The trolley of luggage rolled past him as Hans stood aside. His dream was just like any other dream.

At the point of awakening, it was gone.

PART ONE

Intuition

1

22 April 1940

Polly's first suspicion that something was wrong came when she returned from the lavvy. The door to the first class compartment now wouldn't open to let her inside again. She stood in the corridor, confused, with the French Riviera rushing past the train windows while she rattled the door. 'Aunt Marjorie? Have you locked this?'

'Is that you?' Her aunt's voice from within sounded anxious, on edge; a different Aunt Marjorie from the one Polly had left minutes before.

'I'm back from the loo, do let me in again.' Polly thought she heard the compartment window being hauled open.

'Just a minute, dear,' called her aunt.

Polly looked up and down the empty passage, as if someone might come along with an explanation. 'What are you doing in there?'

'Nothing. I won't be a moment . . .'

Yet Marjorie *was* doing something because the door stayed closed. Polly took a step back as if contemplating taking a running kick at it. 'Is there someone in there with you?'

'Don't be silly, of course there isn't,' Marjorie assured her. Yet she still sounded stressed.

'Then let me back in. I feel silly out here.'

Polly heard the window fall shut again with a thud. Then her aunt opened the compartment door, flushed in the face and wiping dust from her eye, but otherwise smiling as if nothing was amiss. Her Marcel-waved hair had come loose from its pins. 'What on earth were you doing?' Polly asked, astonished, coming inside. 'Sniffing the sea breeze? Your hair looks like a chimney brush, Auntie.' She laughed, resuming her seat on the banquette opposite Marjorie's and picked up one of her aunt's fashion magazines.

'What's the fuss, can't I open a window if I want to?' Marjorie objected, adjusting her silk day dress where it had bunched. She patted at her hair. 'I was hot. And then I wasn't. So, I shut it again.'

This disingenuousness rang false. Polly frowned at her.

'Polly,' said Marjorie, evenly, before her niece could say it, 'nothing is wrong – we're on our way to a lovely long stay in Nice, and I know you'll adore it.'

Yet she locked the compartment door again, firmly. Then she poured herself some chilled champagne from a bottle she had clearly ordered and opened while Polly had been gone.

Polly blinked, finding this indulgence theatrical. 'But why do you want us shut in here so suddenly? You didn't before.'

Marjorie seemed on the verge of forming a particular reply before thinking the better of it. She sipped her champagne.

Polly tried again. 'Did someone come in here and upset you?'

Marjorie shifted in her seat. 'Why in heaven would anyone come in without an invitation?' She fiddled with her green Hermès handbag, slipping her fingers inside.

Polly felt herself at a loss. This was only her second day in the company of her beloved aunt – the aunt who had hitherto only existed in cherished letters sent from exotic locales to Polly's decidedly unexotic locale in Sydney, Australia, where she had lived her whole life until Marjorie had sent money for her passage to France. With every hour in Aunt Marjorie's presence, Polly was becoming more aware that the aunt she had thought she knew well from her letters didn't quite match the woman of reality. She was funny and glamorous, certainly, just as she had always seemed in her letters, but she was also harried and secretive, as if Polly's arrival from Australia was inopportune, even though it had been Marjorie who'd arranged the journey when Polly's father had died.

'I'm not a child anymore,' Polly ventured, tentatively. 'You can tell me when there's something making you uneasy, Auntie.'

'You're sixteen and still very much a child,' Marjorie responded. Then she softened. 'Nothing's making me uneasy, dear, and I know it's good fun, but you must stop being so dramatic.'

But Polly could see something was making Marjorie very uneasy indeed. She held her aunt's look, peering into her depths, but the older woman simply held her gaze. 'Is it Hitler?' Polly wondered, for want of anything else.

Marjorie actually laughed at that, which Polly would have found comforting ordinarily. 'Who's been saying such silly rubbish to you?' her aunt asked her.

'No one. The war is in every newspaper headline.'

Marjorie grew annoyed again. 'We're perfectly safe from Hitler all the way down here on the Riviera.'

Polly remained firm. 'If it's not the war, then it's something else.'

Marjorie chose to gaze out the compartment window. Her hand grasped and ungrasped something hidden in her bag. Then she turned back to her niece and said, 'I've had a *life*, Polly.'

'Well, of course, you have.' Polly smiled. 'And I've so enjoyed reading about it in all your wonderful letters.'

Yet Polly was thrown by a flash of fear in her aunt's eyes before Marjorie suppressed it. 'And it's been a very good life,' her aunt went on.

'A marvellous life. You have always inspired me.'

'Quite a lot of it couldn't be put in my letters . . .'

Polly couldn't conceive why Marjorie was telling her this. The shadow of her aunt's fearful look stayed in her mind, making Polly feel fearful, too. Then an image of her late father came unwelcome to replace it and she picked up the magazine to force away her old grief at his loss. 'You drive me mad, you really do,' she said, making an effort at lightness.

Marjorie smiled, brightening again. 'Appalling words to hear from one's own blood.' She laughed.

'It doesn't mean I don't love you, Auntie.'

'I know.'

Polly idly thumbed the magazine. 'And I'm very grateful for everything you've done since Daddy left us.'

Marjorie reached out and patted her hand.

Aunt and niece fell silent under the rumble of the Riviera train. After a minute, Polly glanced up from the pages to see Marjorie looking from her own silk dress to Polly's childishly pretty ensemble.

'What is it?' said Polly.

'I should have let you wear something more sophisticated,' Marjorie said. 'You're growing up very fast, Polly.'

'*Let* me?' Polly scoffed. 'This is what I chose to wear, Auntie, from a very limited wardrobe, I assure you. And I'm sixteen, remember, not twenty-six.'

Marjorie squinted at Polly in the reflected Mediterranean glare from the window. 'It's a lovely cardigan, of course it is, but still. And then there's your hair.' She mused, 'Perhaps it's time to wave and colour you.'

'If you think I look mousy and plain,' said Polly, feeling sensitive, 'then please say it.'

'That's not what I meant at all. You're really very pretty.' Marjorie got up from her banquette and sat next to Polly, and as she did, with a jolting shock, Polly saw what her aunt had been clutching inside her handbag. Made of ugly, black metal, the sheer

10

incongruity of such a thing being in her aunt's possession at all caused Polly to miss the implication of it. It was as if she couldn't process the very idea of Marjorie owning a gun, and so she didn't, at least not at first.

Marjorie, oblivious, kissed Polly on the forehead. 'I know from your own lovely letters how badly you long for adventures, Polly. I felt just the same when I was your age, you know. It's why I left Australia. I wanted fame and fortune on the stage.'

Polly stared, then blinked, trying to glance inside her aunt's bag again. But the bag had closed now, and somehow the shock stopped Polly even putting it into words. 'Were – were we even talking about me longing for adventures?'

'We should be,' said Marjorie. 'We have certainly talked about it in our letters.'

'Perhaps I should go to a school here,' said Polly. She felt as if she had bizarrely become two people: the one who had not seen the gun and could carry on with the conversation, and the one who *had* seen it and who now couldn't say anything at all.

'Life is your school now,' Marjorie told her.

'Are we just going to travel through France?'

'Oh, so you don't like France now – after barely two days?'

'I love it,' said Polly, and she meant it. 'I've studied the language and history since I was eight – I believe in everything France stands for.'

Marjorie raised an eyebrow. 'And what's that?'

'That you should even need to ask, Auntie,' said Polly, incredulous. 'Liberty, equality and fraternity, of course – the foundations of modern democracy.'

Marjorie smiled at her niece's romanticism.

'I'm very happy to live here with you so long as I might do something that has *purpose*,' Polly told her. She looked around at the excessive comforts of the first class compartment. 'Does all this have purpose? I don't think it does very much.'

Marjorie seemed to be thinking.

Polly tried to remind her of what she'd expressed so often in her letters. 'I want to do something meaningful. Something positive. Especially with the war. Oh, I know nothing terrible has happened to France yet, but it might – otherwise why call it a war at all?'

Marjorie's fingers hovered at the catch of her bag again as Polly watched.

'What you're saying, I think, is that you'd like a career? Just like I had.'

Polly considered this. 'Yes, I very much think that I would like a career. I would like to *be* something, just like you were when you sang at the Paris Opera. It could be the perfect way to do good.'

Marjorie fell quiet once more and Polly made to return to the magazine. But when she glanced at her aunt again, the older woman was gazing upon her with a look of deepest and most profound love.

Marjorie sniffed, emotional. 'My heavens,' she whispered, 'we're so very alike, aren't we?' Marjorie cleared her throat. 'Of course, I've long known that we are peas in a pod from our letters. How could we not be? The women in our family have always been the ones to wear the trousers.'

Polly didn't know what to say.

'Here's a proposal then,' said Marjorie. 'Once we're settled in Nice, I promise we'll solve you.'

'Like a crossword puzzle?'

'We'll turn your dreams into some proper plans. You could become a journalist perhaps? You're so articulate for a girl your age.'

Polly felt her excitement rise a little. 'Could I do that, Auntie?'

'Why not? I have friends who work at magazines.'

Polly looked doubtful. 'Fashion magazines?'

'Is there any other kind? They could give you advice.'

Polly regarded the frivolous cover of *L'Officiel* in her lap. 'Do you really think it's me?'

'Perhaps not right away, but in time. Anything's possible when you're young and impassioned. Let's listen to your heart, dear.'

Polly went to say yes, that of course she appreciated the idea of this very much, but then she realised that she was being distracted. The schism that had divided herself ended. 'Why do you have that gun in your handbag, Auntie?'

Marjorie froze at the question, exposed. Then she managed to say, 'You mustn't worry about that.'

'No?' Polly wondered, disbelieving.

Marjorie shut the bag tight at the clasp and placed it on the banquette at arm's-length. Then she took a second glass from the drinks shelf and poured some fresh champagne in it, before handing it to Polly. 'Here's an adventure for you,' she told her niece. 'Why don't you take a little sip?'

'Is that all you're going to say about it?'

Marjorie looked at her levelly. 'For the moment, yes. Now, try some champagne.'

Polly couldn't help but stare at the tall, tulip-shaped glass of gold in her hand, with the beads of bubbles erupting from the bottom and winding all the way to the surface, reminding her of a game of snakes and ladders.

Polly sipped. It was neither sweet nor sour, and weirdly dry in a way that left no remnant of itself once it slid down her throat. The champagne tasted nothing like she had expected.

'Nice?' Marjorie asked.

'I'm not sure . . .'

This was clearly a good answer.

'Champagne never is at first. Don't be in such a hurry to grow up, child.'

'I'm not in a hurry,' said Polly, putting aside the glass. 'Please tell me about that gun.'

But Marjorie wouldn't. 'The things we want most never come soon enough,' she said, wistful, 'and then when they do, they're gone all too soon . . .'

This just made Polly cross. 'Why don't you want to answer me?'

Marjorie kissed her again and finished her own glass. 'I'll tell you everything tomorrow, I promise. When we make proper plans.'

Marjorie cupped her cheek. 'You really mustn't worry. I'm taking care of everything. You'll see.'

'But what's "everything"?'

'*Tomorrow*,' Marjorie repeated.

Polly gave up. 'That sounds lovely, Auntie.'

Marjorie decided then that she wished to visit the powder room. She unlocked the door and stepped warily outside into the first class corridor, looking both ways. To Polly, it seemed like she shivered, as if caught by a draught.

'Are you *sure* nothing happened while I was gone?' Polly asked her for the final time.

Marjorie clearly wanted Polly to believe that she was sure. 'I'll be back very soon.'

The green leather Hermès remained on the banquette. 'But your bag, Auntie?'

Marjorie held her niece's look for the longest moment. 'Will you look after it for me, dear?'

Polly kept the compartment door open, so that she might watch who came and went along the corridor while she waited for her aunt to return. She found herself in a less anxious frame of mind. Perhaps she was drunk, one sip having been enough to send her giddy. She knew this was unlikely, though, and that her aunt's responses had simply reassured her that nothing was really wrong, even though instinct told her otherwise. Perhaps it was the inexplicable presence of the gun that made her feel better. The knowledge that such a deadly weapon lay hidden in soft green leather mere inches from where she sat forced Polly to concede that she did not really know her aunt at all.

From her spot just inside the compartment door, Polly became aware that she was not invisible to others. There were quite a few handsome, uniformed young men among the first class passengers – French Army officers, Polly assumed – and in succession one, then another, and then a third glanced her way while making the trip to the dining carriage. Polly reacted with the same awkward surprise when she locked eyes with each of them, which broke whatever spell might have been at the point of being woven. None of the young men returned a glance in her direction again. It was like being dismissed. Marjorie's comments about her appearance replayed in Polly's head. She felt a stab of loneliness, thinking again of her poor father, and of how he had died.

A woman entered Polly's periphery next and, with a start, Polly recognised her. This petite brunette was sultry and glowering, at least upon first impression, before the earthy humour behind her darkly made-up eyes flashed, and let it be known she was someone who did not take herself seriously. When this woman spoke, it was with the parigot accent of a Parisienne guttersnipe. 'The Riviera,' she tossed her curly dark hair at the wide azure sea that stretched to the horizon through the windows, 'is not worth the shit on my soles, if you ask me, puss.'

Polly shot out a giggle before she realised it.

The woman smiled in a way that was more pursed lips and knowing looks than an actual grin, before her lips gave way to a blinding show of pearl white teeth that didn't look real. She was a film star, a famous French one.

'That was Zita . . .' Polly said in amazement, to herself. Marjorie had sometimes spoken of this woman in her letters.

'You bet it was, baby,' said another woman, American, red-headed and curvy, who had materialised in the corridor while Polly had been lost in the encounter. 'Best goddamn lay in Pigalle.'

Polly's eyebrows shot skyward at this and the expensively, if blowzily dressed American screamed with mirth. 'Oh, don't mind me – *I* didn't say such a distasteful thing. I only read about it on a pissoir wall.'

Polly couldn't think how to reply.

The woman frowned. 'At least try looking like you're having fun, honey,' she admonished her. 'For your Auntie Marj's sake. Don't let the old team down, okay?'

Polly was startled. 'Do you know my aunt, too?'

'You bet your patootie I do.' She winked at Polly. 'Better than most.' Then she went on her way to the dining carriage.

A short time later, a willowy, fair-haired woman of quite extraordinary chic drifted along. She appeared to be wearing the very same dress on the open page of *L'Officiel* magazine that sat in Polly's lap. The black and white photography failed to do justice to what was standing before Polly in the deepest, most luscious royal blue. The woman caught Polly staring because she was staring at Polly in turn.

'Is – is your dress by Lanvin, Madame?' Polly stammered at the coincidence, before she thought to stop herself.

The woman responded with a smile of such effortless grace and then pronounced in cut-glass French, 'You're Polly Hartford.'

'Why, yes, Madame,' said Polly, answering in the same language, even more surprised.

'Will you permit me to join you?'

Polly sat up straight on the banquette, shocked. Then she remembered her manners. 'Please do.' She got to her feet to be polite and was dismayed to find herself a good head shorter than her visitor. 'How do you know my name, Madame?'

'Because I am Madame Alexandrine Ducru-Batailley,' the woman told her, taking a seat on the banquette opposite, and presenting a hand in a white kid glove. 'The *Comtesse* Alexandrine, if such a rank means anything today.'

Polly had encountered this woman's name in Marjorie's letters, too. 'What a pleasure to meet you, Madame Comtesse,' said Polly, meaning it. She took the woman's hand and gripped it. There was no resistance, no hint of strength to the other at all, and yet she could tell it was there.

'What a lovely bag,' said the Comtesse, indicating Marjorie's Hermès on the seat next to Polly, 'is it yours?'

It was as if the secreted gun had started throbbing inside it. Unaccountably, Polly lied: 'Yes, Madame.' She picked up the bag and placed it in her lap.

Polly took another moment to take in the Comtesse's elegant appearance. Alexandrine was flawless. 'You are my aunt's friend, Madame?'

'One of several on board who are among her very best friends, darling, and honoured to call ourselves such.'

Polly found this confounding. 'But – but does she even know you're on the train?'

'Of course.'

'You've spoken to her?'

'When you were in the powder room, I believe.'

Polly felt a shiver up her spine.

She undid the catch of Marjorie's bag and slid her fingers inside it, just as her aunt had. She felt the handle of the gun. She knew she mustn't panic or lose her head. 'Tell me, Madame,' she started, evenly, 'did it seem to you that she's not quite herself today?'

Alexandrine said nothing, her lovely face expressionless.

'Did it feel to you as if she's dealing with something awful – something she's keeping quiet?'

The Comtesse tut-tutted at this idea.

'You see, awful things have been kept from me *before*,' said Polly, frankly. 'I have a sense for these things. When my poor, late father –'

Alexandrine interrupted her with a look that was deeply, unexpectedly sympathetic. 'I know about your poor father, darling.' She left her banquette and sat next to Polly, gently lifting the handbag from Polly's lap and placing it on the seat between them, so that she could take hold of Polly's hand. 'It was dreadful what happened to him – dreadful for you. You've known too much pain for someone so young.'

The bag was open. All the Comtesse had to do was glance inside and see the gun for herself. Polly felt her mouth turn to chalk. Yet Alexandrine projected an aura of trustworthiness. Polly began again, 'Do you think my aunt is not quite herself because of the war? I want to try to understand it all but people just fob me off.'

'There's no reason to worry, darling,' said Alexandrine, frowning. 'Hitler won't get past that lovely row of forts all along the border with the Boches. They're Monsieur Maginot's cleverness.'

Polly had heard this certainty about the French defences before but there was something effortless in the conviction with which the Comtesse spoke. 'I see,' she said.

'Do I sound like I am "fobbing you off"?'

'No, Madame.' Polly considered. 'You sound very confident.'

'As should you be.' Alexandrine's attention had wandered to the window. She stood and stared out at the sun-drenched scenery.

'I do like your dress,' said Polly, for want of something else to say. She went to show her the magazine. 'It's quite a coincidence, really –'

'Thank you,' said Alexandrine, automatically. Her brow was creased and she raised the window, admitting a gust of warm air.

'Perhaps Auntie might take me to Madame Lanvin,' Polly mused above the din of the train and the wind through the window. 'It says here she does mother and daughter fashion. Wouldn't that be much the same as auntie and niece?' She was trying to look at her own clothes differently since Marjorie's remarks.

Alexandrine's gloved hand flew to her mouth. 'Oh my God!'

Polly craned to see what had taken her companion's attention.

The Comtesse had her arm out the open window, pointing at something they'd passed. 'Oh my God – stop the train!'

'Madame?' Polly stood up. 'What is it, Madame?'

'It's Marjorie!' Alexandrine cried. 'It's Marjorie out there!'

Polly threw herself at the window. The body of her aunt in the Mainbocher silk dress lay sprawled on her back in the long, dry grass beside the railway tracks, rapidly receding as the train sped away.

Somehow, she had fallen from the train.

'Auntie!' Polly's scream became deafening, overwhelming, drowning all other sounds as someone unknown, somewhere else on the carriage, pulled at the emergency cord and the luxurious Riviera sleeper began shrieking and grinding to a halt.

2

25 April 1940

In the rented Nice villa's sunny sitting room, with its windows looking out onto a vine-wrapped courtyard and rooftops beyond, the warm, morning air was wreathed in cigarette smoke. At the centre of an odd-bod collection of comfortable chairs, a low table was host to a clutter of cocktail paraphernalia. Ten o'clock in the morning was not too early to toast a departed friend.

Two gold medals were lifted from their satin-lined case and placed in Polly's cupped hands. Emotionally fragile, she stared at them, uncomprehending. 'But whose are these?'

'Your aunt's,' said Alexandrine, simply. 'And now they're yours, darling.'

Polly tried to make sense of them. 'But these things are for soldiers – for men.'

Alexandrine cast an appeal for assistance to the shapely American woman occupying the chair next to hers, now greedily drinking a martini. Her name was Mrs Huckstepp, but to her friends she was Lana Mae. She was the same American woman Polly had met briefly on the train. She, too, was another best friend of Marjorie's.

'We girls get 'em too, honey, it ain't the Middle Ages,' Lana Mae told her. She pointed a lacquered red nail at the first medal. 'That's the *Croix de Guerre*.' Her pronunciation of French, which was what they were speaking, was rather rough around the edges, filtered through a Mid-western twang. She pointed out the medal's features. 'It's what they call a square cross – very la-di-da – and those are crossed swords. Your aunt got this at the end of the Great War.'

'But I don't understand,' Polly said, softly.

'What's to understand?' Lana Mae said. 'This other one's the *Légion d'honneur*. Ain't it a pretty peach, though? Just about the biggest gong you can get in good old France.'

Polly was still uncomprehending.

Petite Zita, another of Marjorie's grieving best friends, was curled in an armchair to Polly's right. 'Puss, she earned them. Don't have us think you can't get *that* idea inside your head. She was a heroine to France.'

'But she was from Australia?'

The three other women cast looks at each other and then burst into laughter; Zita and Lana Mae matching each other with full-throated guffaws; Alexandrine laughing rather more elegantly, a gloved hand to her smile.

'God, what she did to try to wash that stain from her cami-knickers,' Lana Mae chuckled. 'It never did come out, and I should know. I used the same damn soap on my own drawers.' She looked around her, mock-conspiratorial. 'Do you think they can tell I'm from Kansas?'

Alexandrine composed herself. 'The medals were awarded to your aunt in recognition of her relief work,' she told Polly. Her eyes were shining at the memory. 'She was completely tireless through-out the conflict. Devoted thousands of hours, and thousands of her own precious francs to the war effort.'

'The gas-burn cases broke her heart,' said Zita. 'All those poor, pretty boys. She was nice to them. And generous.'

'And, baby, you'd better believe this when I tell you,' Lana Mae chimed in, 'she was as Frenchy as these two stuck-up broads right here.' She threw a many-ringed hand towards Alexandrine and Zita, who enjoyed the insult. 'She was an inspiration to me, your Auntie Marj,' Lana Mae added, sniffing back a tear.

'An inspiration to us all,' said Alexandrine. She took the medals from Polly's hands and placed them in their little satin-lined case. 'God rest her soul.'

'God rest her soul,' the other two echoed. They sipped their cocktails, contemplating the loss of their friend.

'So, then . . .' said Zita, after a minute. She weighed up grieving Polly through heavily kohled eyes. 'You must know about *us*?'

'I know your names,' said Polly, 'from my aunt's letters.'

'And?' said Zita.

'I know you're a famous film star,' Polly tried to offer.

Zita was dismissive. 'Every idiot and her pimp knows that, puss. What about what Marjorie *did* for us when nobody else gave a pigeon shit?'

Polly had no idea.

The three women looked among themselves again and seemed to wordlessly come to the agreement that this lack of knowledge wasn't a bad thing. They relaxed a little.

'I do know she was an opera singer, of course,' Polly gave them. 'She was a great soprano.'

Zita chuckled. 'You're not a total cretin then,' she said. She fluffed her curly hair.

'She was very famous in Paris,' said Polly, 'before the Great War. My father kept a scrapbook about her.'

'Your father who died.' Zita made this a fact, rather than a question. 'Your mother being dead already, which is why Marjorie sent for you here.'

'Yes.' Polly felt hot tears threatening. She'd held them off all morning, but these women were making the task hard. 'Yes . . .' she said again. But no other words followed, for it was only now occurring to her, three days after Marjorie's shocking death, that she had no family left. She tried to make her best effort. 'I suppose it wasn't an extensive scrapbook,' she conceded. 'And I suppose I didn't look at it as closely or as often as I might have . . .'

The three older women were united in looks of disapproval again.

This pushed Polly over the edge. 'I'm so sorry,' she whispered. She gave in to crying.

'Oh, darling girl.' Alexandrine was at her side with a handkerchief. 'No more of that. We've all cried enough. Stop being so harsh with her, Zita.'

The film star bowed in apology. 'It's tough to lose someone who loved you, puss,' she said softly. 'Don't mind me.'

Polly nodded, blowing her nose.

'What you didn't know about Marjorie's life was not your fault,' said Alexandrine. 'It's Marjorie I blame. We're all brought up as girls to think of modesty as a virtue, but really, Marjorie sometimes took it to extremes.'

'But she wasn't modest at all,' said Polly, bewildered by this. 'At least not in her letters to me. She was so colourful – so extravagant. She couldn't help dressing lavishly, and always in haute couture. She always insisted on the highest of fine dining. She always went everywhere accompanied by so much music and art.'

She caught the three women passing looks with each other again.

'Darling, that was Marjorie being *French*,' said Alexandrine.

'Even nuns shop for their rosaries at Cartier,' Zita added.

But Polly had succumbed to tears again. When she stopped, she found the women changed in their approach to her. As one, they were tender.

Alexandrine seemed to be grappling with how to broach something delicate. She glanced at the others. 'There's something else you don't know. Marjorie was living on borrowed time, Polly.'

Polly stared at her.

'You see, baby, something went bad with her heart,' said Lana Mae, gently, 'just lately, don't ask us to explain, that's just how it was. The quacks told her it could burst any time.'

'Any time at all,' said Zita. She shifted in her armchair. 'That's what happened, we think, on the train.'

'The police think it, too,' said Lana Mae.

'And the doctor,' said Alexandrine. 'She must have been passing between carriages – that's when her heart burst. That's why she fell.'

Polly's face creased with her terrible grief again and they waited until it was past.

'But – but why didn't she tell me if she was so very ill?' Polly asked them in time.

The women were uncomfortable.

Bewildered, Polly tried to look back on her aunt's recent actions, seeking to equate what the women were telling her with what she'd witnessed. 'I knew something was wrong on the train,' she whispered, 'but I didn't know it was that.'

'It is possible,' Alexandrine ventured, looking for support from the other two, 'that Marjorie wanted to spare you the truth of her condition.'

Lana Mae agreed. 'You'd not long lost your pa, baby. Maybe she didn't want you getting all worked up with the idea of losing her, too?'

'But I did lose her, didn't I?' said Polly, heartbroken. 'At least if she'd told me she was sick I could have prepared myself for it. But now . . .' she gestured at the sunny, comfortable room with despair, 'I'm prepared for nothing.'

Alexandrine took a long, deep breath through her aristocrat's sharp nose. 'That I very much doubt.' She looked to Zita. 'What was it that Marjorie always used to say?'

'The women in her family wear the pants,' said the film star.

The three women looked at Polly meaningfully.

Lana Mae drew herself up in her armchair. 'Take a good long look at this Temple of Venus you see here before you,' she said to

Polly, indicating herself. 'I come from a town so goddam hick that if we'd *had* a set of tracks I would have been born on the wrong side of 'em. Did it stop me? No. Did it stop your Aunt Marjorie? God no! That dame just had way too much talent and style.'

'Do you know,' Alexandrine addressed the other two women in the room, 'that afternoon, on the train, when one by one we made our way along the corridor to see what Marjorie's celebrated niece actually *looked* like, she knew my dress was by Madame Lanvin – and she told me so as well?'

'Did she now?' said Lana Mae, taking a sip of her second cocktail.

'It was only because it was the same dress as the one in the magazine I was reading,' said Polly, self-conscious now.

The confession seemed to disappoint Alexandrine.

Lana Mae squinted at her. 'How old are you again, honey?'

'Sixteen,' said Polly.

'I'd already hitched and ditched my first husband at sixteen,' sighed Lana Mae, polishing a ring on her dress. 'It's a perky age and I miss it.'

'At sixteen I made a pass at a priest in Pigalle and got a full fifty francs for it,' Zita declared.

'And I took a bribe to marry my Jew,' said Alexandrine.

Polly gawped at all three of them.

'At sixteen years old, you can no longer let yourself be treated as a child, puss,' Zita told her through a fall of cigarette ash, 'you must demand the world treats you as a woman.'

'Marjorie would have told you the same, surely,' Alexandrine wondered, 'in all her long letters?'

Polly thought about the things that Marjorie had said to her on the train. She thought about that first ever glass of champagne. She nodded. 'I see now that she did.'

Alexandrine smiled at her kindly again. Then she looked to the other two, before receiving their resigned nods. She got to her feet, moving to the bureau in the corner of the sunny room.

Alexandrine opened the drawer and took out a lavender-coloured envelope. She laid it upon Polly's knee.

The envelope had a single typewritten word on it: *Polly.*

'What is inside it?'

Alexandrine didn't quite meet her eye in answering this. 'Your instructions, darling.'

Polly opened the envelope. It contained a letter, also typewritten, and wholly in French.

Dear Polly,

You've been given this letter, so that means that I'm dead. That seems a very melodramatic thing to type upon the page, but there it is and I'm sorry. Quite possibly you are angry with me, too.

It is such an awful shock to be told that one might die at any time. It sends a person a little silly. I know I've been silly, but in my head, I've been trying to do my best with it all. To me, what I've done in the time that I have been given since the doctor broke the news to me makes sense, but to you perhaps it doesn't. There's such a lot to take on and consider, you see, before death happens, especially if you don't know precisely <u>when</u> it will happen, only that it <u>will</u>. It causes one to try to make decisions only on what's important. And so, I have tried.

There are many things I hope to do with you, and for you, Polly, now that you're here with me in France. I have been so looking forward to them. These are things relating to your growing up and becoming a woman. I cannot know here, writing this letter to some unknown date in the future, whether I will have done any of them yet, or if I have, just how many. I can only hope that I will have started on the path, and made a good start, before the time comes.

But when it comes – which it must and will – you will not be left on your own. We are each other's only family, which makes my dying more painful for you, I know, but I also want you to know there are other families to love.

I have another family. A good one. Alexandrine, Lana Mae and Zita. I call them the Girls.

Those three darlings have been like daughters to me, at times. At other times, more often really, they've been like sisters. Having you to take care of has filled me with purpose, Polly, something I've not had for such a very long time. You mean more to me than the life I led before you came here and I'm grateful. Yet all the same, that life should now become yours.

If God has been kind, then you are already embarked upon it, with me by your side, and you will have already met the Girls, making what I write here superfluous. But if not, and if God has asked for me sooner, then this is what you should know:

The Girls will look after you and look out for you. I have set aside a good deal of money for them to do so in my will. Listen to what they say.

The Girls are my gift to you: the gift of my other family. Think of them like your guardian aunts. Think of them as being just like me – only three.

The Girls are exemplars of womanhood. They are standards of how a modern woman should live and be in this world. I mean you to learn from them. From their lives. From their experiences. From their independence. Write down what they say. They are teachers. They have been given the task of giving you lessons, but not like school.

You will get lessons in Fashion.

You will get lessons in Fine Living.

You will get lessons in what being a modern woman means.

Trust in the Girls. Believe in them. Let them be your aunts. They will never lie to you.

Aunt Marjorie xxxx

Polly had another cry when she had finished reading. The three women – the Girls – comforted her, avoiding platitudes and simply being *there* while she wept.

Afterwards, feeling numb, and cradling a cup of tea, Polly said, 'I never even knew she could use a typewriter.'

Alexandrine shifted awkwardly. 'Well, I suppose there's a lot you never knew.'

The Girls waited for further comments from Polly, but she just stared at the letter in her lap. Why was it typed, she wondered, and not handwritten, as every other letter from Marjorie had been? And why was it in French, when between themselves they always wrote – and spoke – in English?

'Haven't you got any questions for us, honey?' Lana Mae wondered, worried.

Polly looked up at her. 'You say I didn't know my aunt, Mrs Huckstepp. Well, this letter proves I didn't. And do you know what else it proves?' Polly took a deep breath. 'She didn't know me.'

The three women were stunned.

Polly tried hard to swallow the confusion she felt. 'I'm sorry – I'm just very shocked by this. Forgive me. I didn't mean to say such a dreadful thing.'

'You're upset. After everything that's occurred, that's to be expected,' said Alexandrine.

'We're going to look out for you, puss,' said Zita. 'Marjorie's left you plenty of cash. Everything's taken care of.'

'You'll *like* us, honey.' Lana Mae smiled. 'We're fun, you'll see.'

Polly did her best to be encouraging back. 'I already like you. And I can see that you're fun.'

'Then what is it, darling?' Alexandrine asked her gently.

Vivid in Polly's memory was the final conversation she'd had with her aunt where they had talked of Polly's future as something meaningful and good. Yet where was this in her final letter? Had she really been willed to these women like a lapdog?

Something wasn't right about the letter – about any of it. Marjorie's shocking death; the coincidence of her three best friends travelling on the same Riviera train; the gun in the green

Hermès handbag. Facts were being kept from her; secrets were being held. Yet Polly had no one else.

'It's nothing,' she said, eventually. 'Nothing at all. I'm sorry.' She smiled at them, forcing herself to present the attitude that they – and Marjorie – apparently wished for. 'I feel very grateful for everything my aunt put in the letter,' she said. 'I feel very protected and loved.'

'Good,' said Alexandrine. 'That's so good, darling. We're all very pleased.'

But the uncertainty in her eyes didn't match her words.

'Oh God, I feel guilty,' said Lana Mae, picking the olive from her empty glass.

'Shhh!' said Alexandrine. She made sure the sitting room door was tightly closed, before returning to the sofa. Polly had gone to her bedroom, leaving the three women alone.

'Well, what have we *done*?' said Lana Mae. 'How will we ever live with it?'

'We did what we had to do, and we'll live with it as we do with any of our other secrets,' said Alexandrine, firmly, with a particular look to Zita. 'What choice was there?'

Zita grimaced. 'Too late to go losing it now, puss,' she said resignedly to Lana Mae.

'Oh God,' wailed Lana Mae. 'What if she finds out?'

'She won't,' said Zita. 'We'll play our parts.'

'You're the actress, honey, not me.'

'How hard can it be? "Guardian aunt." We could do it in our sleep.' Zita looked to the other two. 'Couldn't we?'

'Why don't you just give the part its proper name, honey,' said Lana Mae. '*Mother*.'

Zita's face fell. 'Oh Christ,' she said. 'Who are we fooling?'

'*Polly*,' said Lana Mae. 'We're fooling that innocent girl. Which is why we oughta be ashamed of ourselves.'

Alexandrine was not having any of this. 'I can't believe these cold feet from you. We looked high and low for a letter among Marjorie's things, or have you forgotten?'

'You know what I think?' said Zita. 'She never wrote one at all.'

'Oh, she wrote one,' said Alexandrine. 'She told me she'd written one months ago when she got involved in all this –' the words caught in her throat, '– in all this "business" again.'

'This "business" got her dead,' said Lana Mae, bleakly.

'We don't know that,' Alexandrine hissed.

'Sure, we do, we just don't want to admit the possibility of it,' said Lana Mae. 'Whether she fell or was pushed, it amounts to the same.'

'Pushed?' Alexandrine turned on her. 'She wasn't *pushed*. Don't say something so ridiculous. Who do you imagine would push Marjorie from the train?'

Lana Mae fixed her with a look. 'She was caught up in something she shouldn't have been – just like she was in the last war. She couldn't help herself. Not even French and yet she acted like Saint Joan herself.'

Alexandrine opened her mouth to say something and then closed it again. She looked to Zita who had fallen conspicuously, guiltily quiet. A look passed between them that was missed by their American friend. The Comtesse collected herself and began again: 'Marjorie was worried about her heart condition,' Alexandrine insisted. 'She was worried about what might happen to Polly, because she was worried about how much time she had left.'

Zita closed her eyes.

'She was worried that whatever secret "business" she was doing for France wouldn't get done before her ticker got her,' said Lana Mae. 'That's why she wanted us here at the Riviera, isn't it? She wanted one of us to finish off the job.' Lana Mae swigged her drink. 'Well, it turns out she had a higher opinion of us than we deserved. Let's face it, girls, courageous we ain't. Our answer to

Marj would have been a big fat no.' She turned to the film star. 'Ain't that right, Zita?'

Zita cast another glance at Alexandrine. 'Sure, puss. Whatever you say . . .'

Lana Mae frowned. Zita's reply had rung hollow. 'That *is* the reason Marjorie wanted us here, right?' she asked her. 'I mean, you took the call, didn't you, honey?'

Zita said nothing.

Lana Mae looked to the Comtesse. 'Or was it you, Alexandrine?'

Alexandrine cleared her throat. 'I made the call. I told Marjorie it was essential we see her . . .'

Lana Mae was thrown. 'Is there something you're not telling me?'

Alexandrine gamely took the conversation reins and returned to the original topic. 'Lana Mae, enough of this nonsense, Polly is what is important here and nothing else. That poor child has suffered. More than anyone should at her age.' She looked emotionally at the other two. 'You *know* her mother died giving birth to her – and you *know* her father killed himself.'

They did know.

'Poor woman,' said Lana Mae, softer now. 'She never lived to love her own child. And she's such a sweet child, too.'

Zita nodded. 'What an idiot *he* was. Lost all his money and blew out his brains for it.'

'A cowardly act,' said Alexandrine. 'He left nothing for his daughter. Polly had no idea of anything.'

Lana Mae wiped another tear from her eye. 'That kid's had lousy luck.'

'We found Marjorie's will,' reminded Alexandrine. 'Thank heavens the money side of things is clear.'

'Just not the moral side,' Lana Mae despaired. 'They're not Marjorie's words that Polly read, honey, they're *ours*.'

'But they're *like* Marjorie's words,' said Alexandrine. 'The sort of thing she might have said.'

'But she didn't say 'em, did she? How do we know what she would have wrote down? It could have been something different. Oh God, can we really *do* this, girls?' Lana Mae pleaded. 'With this stupid damn war? We don't even know what the future holds.'

'Yes, we do,' said Zita. Then, bleakly, 'The future holds krauts . . .'

Lana Mae stared at her. 'Oh my God, you *are* keeping something from me – I can see it in your face. What is it, Zita, tell me right now.'

Zita looked desperately to Alexandrine.

The Comtesse shrugged, grim, before steeling herself. 'Zita *is* keeping something from you and when you hear what it is you'll know why.'

The American looked shocked and then vindicated as the film star shrank into her chair.

'In our long years of faithful friendship,' said Alexandrine to Zita, reassuringly, 'we have always shared our very worst secrets – and always we've been glad that we did. I can't carry the burden of this one alone anymore. Lana Mae needs to know now, too.'

Zita held her American friend's eye, vulnerable.

'Spit it out then,' Lana Mae told her.

Bitterly ashamed of herself, Zita did so. All of it.

Afterwards, when Lana Mae had recovered as best she could from the shock, she asked, 'And what is Polly gonna know about this?'

'None of it,' said Alexandrine, emphatic.

Lana Mae was sceptical. 'You think we can keep it from her? She's Marjorie's niece. You can bet your patootie she inherited more than money from her aunt. I think the kid's got her smarts.'

Zita had been left exhausted by what she'd confessed. She looked up from her armchair, fragile. 'If Polly is smart and she guesses what I've done, then good luck to her, puss,' she said. 'A woman needs smarts if she wants to get by in this shithole

32

world. And if Polly's got enough to see the truth of me, then maybe she'll be smart enough to see *why* I did it, too.'

'It won't come to that,' Alexandrine was hasty to reassure her, 'we won't let it, darling. We're your friends, aren't we? We keep each other's secrets to the bitter end. That's what we've always done. We won't do otherwise now.'

'We're *women*,' Lana Mae said. 'Wars are different for us than for men. Men start wars, and they finish 'em, while we girls just go along for the ride.'

'Wars are for women to *endure*,' agreed Alexandrine. She reached out and took Zita's hand across the little table and squeezed it. Lana Mae took her other hand and did the same.

Zita's eyes filled with tears as she clutched at her two dearest friends. She was made humble, as ever, by their wellspring of love for her – their love for each other.

'What men fail to understand is that, for us, endurance means compromise,' said Alexandrine, taking a deep breath. She let her lungs fill with air, then released it, purging herself. 'If Polly should learn of your actions, darling, then perhaps enough of our good influence will have rubbed off on her before she does – enough for her to understand what compromise for a woman really means in war . . .'

3

10 May 1940

A hired, chauffeur-driven Rolls-Royce Silver Ghost met the four of them as they alighted from the first class sleeping carriages at Gare de Lyon. The breathtakingly beautiful capital of France stood at the centre of the Girls' shared cosmos. It was Paris that Marjorie had always called 'the life', and now it was to be lived by her niece.

'Where are we going again?' Polly asked, trying to gain a better view of the splendours that passed the window from where she sat in the Rolls, squeezed between Alexandrine and Zita. She had the Hermès handbag on her lap – Marjorie's handbag. The gun was still inside. Polly had almost come to believe that her aunt had intended her to have possession of the gun all along – as bizarre as this idea was, it made more sense to Polly than the words in Marjorie's last letter.

'We're going home,' said Lana Mae. 'Home sweet home, honey. There's no place like it.' She had popped a champagne bottle, its contents unchilled but by no means unpleasant. She passed the crystal glasses around, liberally filling them, not thinking twice about including Polly in the celebration. Not one of them batted

34

an eye when Polly took what was only her second sip of bubbles in her life. No one even asked her if she liked them, which made her feel a little sad.

'They're not as bad this time,' she whispered, somewhat surprised. Then she asked, 'What is the address again?'

'The Place Vendôme,' said Alexandrine, as if that answered everything. 'Sit back and relax, darling.' She cast a smile at her friends. 'In a little while, you might even start to recognise a few things.'

Zita chuckled, knowingly.

'The Eiffel Tower?' Polly wondered.

'Plenty of time for that ugly thing later,' said Alexandrine, dismissive.

'You forget I've never been here before,' Polly said.

'We know you haven't,' said Alexandrine, sagely, 'but all the same, just see.'

Polly caught a glimpse of one of the white-on-blue street signs fixed to the walls of buildings they glided past. 'That sign,' she said, pointing. Their rented Rolls had entered a narrow and otherwise nondescript street. 'Are we on the rue du Faubourg Saint-Honoré?'

They'd been waiting for her to notice.

'Paradise!' Zita saluted her, raising her champagne glass.

'Oh, it's the haute couture district,' said Polly. 'Oh look, there's Houbigant Parfums – and the House of Hermès.'

'Where your lovely bag comes from,' said Alexandrine.

Polly subconsciously checked that the catch was still closed. Then she realised they were looking at her as if they expected a rather greater level of excitement. 'Just like Aunt Marjorie's magazines,' Polly offered. She pointed out the window again. 'There's Fabergé.'

She was unconvincing, and they deflated.

'Those gaudy eggs are over-priced and over-rated,' Zita said.

'You only say that 'cos I've got three of 'em,' said Lana Mae.

'Did I say gaudy, puss? I meant hideous shit.'

35

Lana Mae laughed, taking a swig from her glass.

Polly feared she'd disappointed them. 'Lanvin!' she cried, in what she hoped was the desired level of enthusiasm, pointing at the other side of the narrow, busy street. 'And is that Chanel down there?'

'We'll be popping along to see *her*, later,' said Alexandrine, mysteriously.

'The lousy, snobby cow,' Zita sniffed. 'Still, her dresses, puss.' She pinched Polly's chin. 'Sublime. You'll want to wear them all together at once.' She sniffed again. 'But she's still a cow.'

The street, full of shop after shop of milliners and fabric merchants and enticing designer ateliers, now spilled into a vast square. The graceful, seventeenth-century façades of the Place Vendôme were, at first glance, identical on all sides. Then, as the Silver Ghost glided out in a wide and beautiful arc, passing an enormous Roman column with a statue of Napoleon on top, it became apparent to Polly to which of the façades they were headed. One was marked with a single, identifying word, so discreetly placed that an unknowing eye might miss it.

Ritz.

On either side, generously spaced, were two more words:

Hôtel.

Restaurant.

The great car drew to a graceful halt at the curb, and behind them a second vehicle, another Rolls, hired to ferry their staggering amount of luggage, halted too. A gloved male hand was on the rear door of the women's car before the chauffeur had even finished with the brake. The door was opened, and Lana Mae was out first, still with her champagne, breathing in gusts of traffic-choked, Place Vendôme air.

'Smell it, girls. It's poisonous today! It's the little things you always miss most.'

'*Bonjour*, Madame Huckstepp,' said the elderly footman who had opened the door.

36

'*Bonjour* to you, too, honey,' she handed him the not quite empty champagne glass. 'Go ahead and finish it. I've got my eye on a hot bath and a bite of baguette and blue cheese. Travelling gives a girl a real appetite, don't you find?'

Polly had emerged from the car, along with Zita and Alexandrine, and she stared up at the full five stories of the beautiful façade with its little balconies and awnings and high Mansard roofs aglow in the afternoon sun. 'Are we dining here?' she asked Alexandrine.

Alexandrine gave that special smile of hers that said volumes without needing to utter one word. Then she made her way up the short flight of steps towards the hotel's glass front entrance. The door was opened by another similarly aged footman, and Alexandrine entered first, followed by Polly at her heels, then Lana Mae, and then, taking her own good time, Zita, who seemed to know the first footman intimately.

'Pierre. Nothing ever changes with the Ritz – or with you.' She laughed, squeezing his arm. 'Let's thank the stinking Virgin for it.'

If Polly had expected to find herself standing within some impossibly grand, palace-like lobby, she would have had reason to be disappointed. The room beyond the hotel entrance said nothing – and yet everything – about the extraordinary character of this celebrated hotel. It was *not* a palace, and yet, for those who lived in palaces it most definitely *was*. Any visiting royalty, perhaps in Paris on a shopping whim, would feel instantly, reassuringly at home here. It was not about making a vulgar display. It was all about being the recipient of a quiet, sequestered entitlement.

The Ritz had no real lobby. What it had instead was a welcome hall, as one might find in a stately mansion, and yet there was nothing fusty or ancestral about it. The un-grandiose reception area was but one of a whole series of decisions made to make the hotel feel intimate and cosy. It also discouraged loiterers who might otherwise behave as voyeurs. The ample chairs and little side tables were exclusive and expensive; reproductions in the styles of French kings. Thick carpeting; rich upholstery; tapestries hung here and there. Abundant masses of flowers in chinoiserie vases were on every table. To the left, through an arch, was the suggestion of the first of several exceedingly discreet bars, this one called The Vendôme. A second bar, a little further down the hall and through an alcove, was called the Petit. There were hardly any other people in evidence; guests or staff. Ascending heaven-ward was a sweep of magnificent, exquisitely carved marble stairs.

There wasn't even a reservations counter. Instead there was a simple, elegant desk, holding no more than a white telephone and an open, cloth-bound ledger. Behind this desk had been seated a small, moustachioed gentleman when they'd arrived. Bedecked in a blue pinstripe suit, spats, and patent leather shoes, he was now advancing upon their little group, screwing a monocle into his right eye and beaming at them.

'Mesdames. Mesdames,' he greeted them collectively in French, spreading his short, stout arms as wide as his tight suit jacket allowed him.

Alexandrine presented her cheeks to be kissed by him and received two pert pecks placed like gunshots in the air, that didn't actually touch her skin.

'Madame Comtesse Ducru-Batailley,' he intoned, each syllable of her name rolling from his tongue with pleasure.

'Darling Monsieur Auzello.'

'You have returned at last.'

'How we've missed you.'

He went next to Lana Mae, kissing the air at her cheeks with the same little explosions. 'Your bath has just now been drawn, beloved Mrs Huckstepp.'

'Claude, you little cutie!' cried Lana Mae. 'You knew just when we would arrive?'

He tapped his nose. 'I have my spies at Gare de Lyon.' His eyes were twinkling. 'And we have added a certain something to the bath water . . .'

'Not my favourite bergamot bubble bath?'

Monsieur Auzello chuckled; a mischievous boy.

'I'm taking these clothes off already,' said Lana Mae, yanking her gloves from her hands.

He turned to Zita. 'My lucky eyes. Can it be credible they be rewarded just by the sight of you, Mademoiselle Zita?'

Zita barked out a guffaw and threw both her arms around him, kissing him squarely on the moustache. 'You smarmy bastard,' she told him, warmly, 'if your Blanche gets to hear you say that it won't be the bubbles I find in my bath, but the toaster.'

Auzello laughed. 'A telegram came for you this morning, Mademoiselle.' He handed her a little envelope.

For the tiniest moment, the three women faltered. Zita didn't open it. Then she stood aside and presented Polly.

'So, this is she?' Auzello marvelled.

To Polly's dismay his eyes filled with emotion. He unscrewed his monocle and took a handkerchief from his top pocket, dabbing at his cheeks.

'Monsieur Claude?' said Alexandrine, tenderly. She laid her hand at his shoulder and he rested his own upon hers for a moment.

He composed himself, addressing Polly. 'You must forgive me, Mademoiselle. The resemblance between yourself and *la femme divine* is uncanny . . .'

'Who is the "divine woman"?'

Before Polly could phrase any more of what would only have brought fresh exposure of her ignorance, Alexandrine stepped in: 'That was Auntie Marjorie's famous *sobriquet*,' she said. Then she turned to Auzello. 'Far too young to have ever seen *la femme* perform, if you can credit it, Monsieur.'

This only pricked his eyes again. He blinked it back, studying Polly's face like a painting. 'Ah. Yet there she is in the brow – and in the turn of the mouth. Remarkable.'

Polly had never heard it said before that she bore any resemblance to her aunt. Then the unguarded way in which the little man looked at her changed. She ceased to be a painting to him and became fully flesh and blood; a guest. He stood back and paused, expectantly. Polly was confused.

'Your hand, darling,' Alexandrine whispered.

Polly held out her hand a fraction, and Auzello, who had been waiting according to the rules of French politeness, picked it up and kissed it.

'I am Monsieur Claude Auzello at your service, Mademoiselle Hartford; I am General Manager of the Hôtel Ritz.' There was a sharp report as he clicked his patent heels together. 'I have anticipated this day, and all is ready for you, Mademoiselle.'

'Ready for *me*?' said Polly, further surprised.

He waved his hand to the stairs. 'All is prepared. An exquisite suite. You will only know comfort here.'

Polly turned to the other three. 'So, we're staying here, then?'

Her three guardians looked amused.

'Staying, *living* – these are the same words, surely?' pondered Claude.

The elderly footmen were now engaged with taking the considerable collected luggage towards an elevator.

Lana Mae hooked her arm through Monsieur Auzello's. 'Claude, baby, just how many nights' bed and brioche does Marjorie's little legacy get for our Pol?'

'One thousand and one nights' deluxe accommodation, Mrs Huckstepp,' he replied.

Polly's jaw dropped. 'Excuse me, Monsieur?'

'One thousand and one nights' accommodation most precisely, Mademoiselle. Fully paid for. Including gratuities. Although you may be so moved as to express your own generosity once you have come to love our exceptional staff . . .'

Polly turned to Alexandrine, who of the three, seemed less likely to try fooling her. 'This is really true?' she asked. 'Aunt

Marjorie paid in advance for a thousand and one nights' stay for me?'

'In the most famous hotel in all Paris,' said Lana Mae, finishing the sentence for her.

'Only all *Paris*?' Monsieur Auzello wondered under his breath.

'It's true, darling,' said Alexandrine, although she didn't quite look at Polly as she said it; an avoidance Polly had by now encountered not infrequently from her. 'Monsieur Auzello is well across everything, as you just heard.'

Polly regretted the champagne, feeling she needed a little lie down. 'But why?'

'Because we live here,' Zita shot at her, getting bored with all the standing about. She held the unread telegram in her hand.

'And we're your guardian aunts now, baby, so you'd better believe we ain't kidding around,' said Lana Mae.

'And how else to keep our eyes on you,' said Zita, 'if you're not under the same stinking roof?'

'But why a thousand and *one* nights?' Polly asked. 'It seems such a strange number to choose.'

Alexandrine gave her enigmatic smile again. 'There was always something of Scheherazade about your lovely aunt, darling.' She looked at Polly in the eye as she said this, but held her gaze just a little too intently.

Polly frowned. Once again, she was left with the impression that she wasn't being given the entire story regarding Aunt Marjorie's legacy. But a distraction arrived before she could pursue it.

'Ah, look, see who it is!' Monsieur Auzello's little cry took Polly's attention to the sight of an elderly woman making her way down the magnificent stairs, accompanied by the clatter of claws from two little dogs.

'It's Mimi!'

'Oh *bonjour*, Mimi!'

It occurred to Polly then that for all the contrivance to cosiness and intimacy here, those who lived in this establishment still

41

needed to make an entrance. This was how things were in high society, where so much depended on delivering a pitch-perfect performance. This was the reason for the staircase. A lady, dressed in finery, could descend in the knowledge she was being appreciated by every eye.

Zita, Alexandrine and Lana Mae moved forward to embrace the splendidly dignified old woman as she reached the bottom stair. Her two little dogs spilled at their feet.

'The Sirens have returned to wreck us upon the rocks,' the lady announced in Swiss-accented French as she received their air kisses.

Taking her hands, they led her to where Polly had remained with Monsieur Auzello.

'Look, Mimi, here she is,' Zita said, as Polly stood awkwardly before them.

Just as Auzello had before her, the woman was suddenly brought near to tears.

'Oh, Madame, now, now,' said Auzello, producing a fresh handkerchief from a different pocket.

'Forgive me, Mademoiselle,' said the lady, pressing at her eyes. 'You must hear it spoken too often of your great resemblance to your aunt.'

Given this was only the second time such a thing had ever been said to her, Polly cast a glance at Alexandrine, who gave a little nod.

'Yes, Madame,' Polly replied, not wanting to seem rude.

'So, you know who I am?' the woman asked her, kindly.

Polly had to shake her head. She had no idea.

'Ah,' said the woman, not offended. 'Then, this is a wonderful day for each of us.' She paused again, just as Monsieur Auzello had done, and this time Polly had the wit to present her hand. The older women didn't kiss it, but gripped it lightly in her own. 'I am Madame Marie-Louise Ritz,' she revealed, 'the owner of this hotel, and known as Mimi to my friends.' She brought her other hand to Polly's cheek. 'Just as your brilliant aunt has achieved an immortality within your lovely face, when the time comes I shall receive an immortality of my own.' With an expansive gesture she indicated the hotel all around her. '*This* will be my immortality,' she told her, warmly. 'Welcome to the Ritz family, my dear.'

Lana Mae, with her bubble bath calling her, disappeared towards her accommodation, the Imperial Suite, which was, Polly learned, the largest and most expensive suite in the entire hotel. Zita and Alexandrine each peeled away towards their own suites leaving Polly, having waved goodbye to Monsieur Auzello at the reception desk, in the dignified company of Madame Ritz.

Polly kept Marjorie's Hermès handbag held tightly under her arm.

'At the Hôtel Ritz, we are the very last word in elegance, hygiene, efficiency and beauty,' Mimi began her tour. 'Please allow me to show you, Mademoiselle.'

Polly quickly discovered that the hotel existed in two, somewhat imbalanced halves, like unidentical twins, that the harmonious Place Vendôme façade gave no hint to. There was the Vendôme half, which faced the square, and behind it stood the Cambon half, with no view of the square at all, and named for the rue Cambon it gave onto beyond. The two halves of the hotel were connected by a long corridor.

'This was my husband César's last, great creative contribution before his untimely death,' said Mimi of the corridor, as they traversed its plush carpet. The two walls were lined with polished brass vitrines offering for purchase an enticing assortment of luxury items from the same shops Polly had seen on the rue du Faubourg Saint-Honoré.

'The need for such a corridor was unavoidable when we made the expansion to the rue Cambon,' Mimi informed her, 'but it was my husband's suggestion that beautiful things should be displayed

43

here, so that a walk along this otherwise functional passage might be made an exercise in pleasure.'

Polly supposed it was pleasure she was feeling as she passed the scarves and jewellery and handbags on display.

Mimi observed her. 'You like beautiful things?'

'I don't really know,' said Polly, 'I mean I can appreciate how lovely they are, of course, but it's not like I have such things of my own.'

'No?' Mimi looked at the Hermès bag.

Polly felt caught out in her lie and wanted only to qualify herself. 'This belonged to my aunt.' She knew the old woman would never require her to open it.

'Ah,' said Mimi, appreciatively.

'But I've never really thought of myself as a "luxury" sort of person,' Polly told her.

'How interesting,' said Mimi. 'And yet what is Paris if not a city filled with beautiful things?'

'That is something I'm beginning to realise, Madame.'

'I find there are two types of guests among our Ritz family,' Mimi went on. 'The first are those for whom this Parisian beauty is everything, and the pursuit of it the single most abiding passion in their lives.'

Polly wasn't sure if she was meant to feel an affinity with this type of guest. 'And who are the second, Madame?'

'Ah, they are somewhat rarer, Mademoiselle,' said Mimi, enigmatically.

They reached the corridor's end and entered the Cambon side of the hotel. There, among the highlights, was the Ritz's grand dining room, *l'Espadon* – The Swordfish – which featured large windows overlooking further gardens, the attractiveness of which was enhanced by the reflection of enormous mirrors throughout the room. There was another bar, called simply the Cambon. 'Do go in and see Guy later, when you're feeling refreshed,' Mimi told her.

'Guy?'

'Monsieur Martin. In the Cambon bar. We won't go in now, he'll be busy. But please go in later. It will give him much pleasure.'

'I will then, Madame,' Polly said.

Mimi now took Polly up a different set of stairs to her suite of rooms, which was on the Cambon side. On the way, she explained something of the Ritz philosophy regarding guest rooms, building Polly's anticipation of what her own suite would be. 'My late husband had such a horror of disease,' said Mimi, 'a horror I shared, naturally. And so, when it came to the design of this hotel, all heavy carpets and drapes – most especially drapes – that did nothing more than gather dust and germs were excluded from the *décor*. Here the curtains are made from only the finest muslin, the very lightest of fabrics, so that they can be easily washed, you understand?'

'Yes, Madame,' said Polly, as Mimi led her along a bright, high-ceilinged passage.

'It was also decided that every room should have only built-in closets – much more discreet,' Mimi went on. 'No ugly cupboards jutting out.'

'I see.'

'And most radical of all: a bathroom. Private and plumbed. For every room.'

'Why was that radical?' Polly wondered, as they continued along.

'You are very young.' Mimi smiled. 'How could you be expected to have any memory of the Nineties? For all the gaiety of the *Belle Epoch*, things were not nearly so modern. But at the Hôtel Ritz, we were determined to be ahead of the times. Another innovation from my husband was that every room would have a clock – Swiss, of course, for that is our nationality – which would keep the time exactly. After all, if a woman chooses to be late, she should time the length of her lateness down to the very last second, don't you agree?'

Polly was amused, enjoying the commentary.

'We have a zeal for precision, we Swiss,' said Mimi. 'Ah, see, we are here.' They had reached a door, much like all the others in the light-filled passage. 'You will find what awaits you inside reflects a feminine taste,' Mimi told her. She opened the door. 'I hope it will suit a young woman on the cusp of her first romance.'

There were so many lovely details to take in upon entering that Polly didn't quite process that statement, which if she had, would certainly have made her blush. Her eyes wide, she was over-whelmed at first, trying to make appropriate noises in apprecia-tion of everything she could see. The room was big – the biggest room she had ever had cause to call her own – and blessed with windows that diffused the afternoon sun through opaque white curtains made from the muslin Mimi had extolled. At the far end there was a large, high bed with little tables on either side, and closer to the door, a sitting room set comprising two reproduction armchairs and a sofa. One armchair had a small brass hook on the outside of its armrest, so that a seated lady might hang her purse. 'Convenience and efficiency,' Mimi said.

Polly learned now that the Ritz adhered to specific colour schemes. Blue, white and grey were applied to all rooms facing south, where the sun was brightest; champagne yellow was applied to rooms facing north, making amends for the absence of sun. Polly's room, facing north-west and the rue Cambon, had its yellow set off by the upholstery, which was equally light in spirit, being patterned in feminine Watteau pink. The walls were covered simply with flat Dutch paint, in the eighteenth-century tradition.

Mimi indicated the walk-in closet, and upon opening the door for Polly to peek inside a light came on within. There was no visible switch for it. 'It's automatic,' said Mimi. 'My late husband's demand for efficiency and convenience again.' The sole item hanging inside the closet was a towelling robe, divinely soft, and coloured peach. 'It is complimentary,' Mimi said. 'There is no better shade than peach to enhance a woman's complexion.'

46

The room's light fittings were covered with pleated lamp-shades and lined with pink silk. They gave off a wonderful, flattering glow. 'The hours of thought he gave to these fittings,' Mimi said, wistful. There was a fireplace with a mantle, upon which stood two fine Japanese vases. The famed Swiss clock, decorated in bronze and pearl, hung on a wall. The room's light switches were in the shape of tiny violin handles. The taps in the bathroom resembled golden swans.

'You said before that there were two types of Ritz people,' Polly said, watching the water flow. 'There is the one for whom the pursuit of beauty is everything. What is the other type of guest?'

'The second guest has no need for beauty – no need for it whatsoever,' said Mimi.

Polly was surprised. 'And why is that?'

'Because they already have it – in *here*.' She pressed a palm to Polly's chest. 'A hidden beauty, deep inside, that depends for nothing upon appearances, which so often deceive. We cannot always see it, those of us who might lack it, but when such inner beauty makes itself known to us, ah, it is blinding. The very best kind.' She brushed a little tear that had formed at her eye. 'My husband had this special type of beauty, Mademoiselle.'

'I can see that he did,' said Polly, looking about her at the gorgeous suite. 'He placed it into every part of the hotel.'

'That he did,' said Mimi. 'Yet, do you know who else shared this beauty from within?'

'Who, Madame?'

Mimi took Polly's hand. 'Your aunt.'

It brought a lump to Polly's throat to hear that. It took her a moment before she could speak. 'I – I loved her so very much,' she told Mimi, softly. 'Wherever Aunt Marjorie was, she always took time to write, sending her words all the way to me in Australia. And then, when my father died, she sent for me here, so that I'd not be alone . . .' Polly forced back the sting of emotion. 'She was everything to me, and now she's gone, too. I fear I never told her how much I loved her, Madame . . .'

Mimi kissed her cheek. 'She knew it, little one,' she whispered. 'Marjorie carried you with her in her heart.'

When Mimi made to leave, she opened the door to find Monsieur Auzello waiting patiently in the corridor outside. 'What is it, Claude?'

'There has been news, Madame.' He gave her a little envelope, serious.

She opened it, withdrawing a folded telegram. 'Ah,' was all she said, once she had read it. She stood still for a moment, contemplating. The little dogs took a seat at her feet. 'We shall of course reply,' Mimi said, finally, 'and offer commiserations from all at the Ritz.'

'Already composed, Madame,' Auzello told her.

'Then send it at once in my name.' She saw that Polly lingered behind her at the door, curious. 'It is from our dear friend Charlotte, the Grand Duchess of Luxembourg,' Mimi told her. 'She says her reservations at the hotel will not be required. She and Prince Felix have decided to go instead to a château in the Dordogne.'

The apparent banality of this arrangement seemed starkly at odds with the seriousness with which it had been received.

'Has something happened to the Grand Duchess?' Polly wondered.

'Well, yes,' said Mimi. 'The German forces have commenced an invasion of her country. Charlotte and her family have fled.'

Polly was shocked to the core.

'You must not be concerned,' Mimi told her. 'Luxembourg is such a tiny place, and while it is very unpleasant for Charlotte and her family, life here in Paris will go on as before.'

'Because of Monsieur Maginot's concrete forts?' Polly asked.

'They are impregnable,' Mimi pronounced.

'That's what people say.' Polly looked long at the majestic old woman. 'Madame, if I asked you a very important question, would you answer me honestly?'

Mimi looked startled. 'Of course, I would, child. Is there something that troubles you?'

'Yes,' said Polly. 'Are we deluding ourselves that the Germans won't come?'

Mimi drew herself up. 'What a thing to ask.'

'I think my aunt feared that they would,' Polly said. Ideas had been forming in her mind, building a picture of Marjorie that was at odds with the one that the Girls had provided – yet it fitted what Polly had witnessed. Polly clutched at the bag, finding comfort in what was hidden there. 'I think she was taking precautions.'

Auzello had gone very still.

'You said you'd answer me honestly, Madame, so do,' said Polly.

Mimi regarded her appreciatively. 'I like you very much,' she said. 'You are a forthright young woman, I can see that.'

But Polly was waiting for her answer.

'If the Germans *should* dare to show such aggression against France, which I do not believe they will,' said Mimi, 'we will never know anything of it *here*.' She stamped her foot on the floor, startling the Belgian griffons.

'And why is that?'

'Because we are the *Ritz*,' Mimi declared with a flourish. The dogs became animated again as she headed up the hallway towards the stairs.

Polly wanted to feel more reassured, just as she had when Alexandrine had expressed not dissimilar sentiments, but she found the task harder this time. She noticed Monsieur Auzello, the hotel's esteemed general manager, whose faith in the Ritz should have been the surest, looked unsure.

The handbag slipped from her arm before Polly quite realised it, dropping to the floor with a thud. The catch sprung loose, and the black steel muzzle of Marjorie's gun poked from the bag, unmistakable.

Polly and Claude stared in surprise at it for a moment. Then Claude stooped to the floor to pat the nuzzle back inside, before picking up the bag and returning it to her.

Polly was flabbergasted.

'Is it loaded, Mademoiselle?' Claude asked her, quietly.

'I – I don't know.'

He indicated the bag. 'If you please, let us see then . . .'

Polly found herself numbly taking the gun out by the handle and pointing it at him.

Claude winced at the *faux pas* and showed her the correct way to pass a gun to someone. 'Always grip it by the barrel, Mademoiselle.'

'I'm so sorry.'

He held it like an expert, inspecting it minutely. 'This is a *Modèle* 1935 pistol,' he said, 'an excellent French weapon, semi-automatic and requiring a standard 7.65-millimeter *Longue* cartridge. It's French Army issue.' He handed it back to her. 'And yes, it is certainly loaded. That is fortunate.'

Awed, Polly felt the weight of the weapon anew.

'You've never fired it?'

Polly shook her head.

'I see – well, that is the safety catch.' He showed her. 'It is presently on.' He clicked it. 'And now it is not.'

Polly didn't know what else to say. 'Thank you for the lesson, Monsieur.'

'It belonged to your aunt, I assume?'

It seemed pointless to lie. Something about Claude made her feel she could trust him. 'It did.'

He nodded. 'Then you were correct in your estimations,' he told her. '*La femme divine* was indeed taking precautions – she wanted you to defend yourself, I think,' Claude reassured her, 'should the worst ever come.'

Polly swallowed the fresh lump in her throat and nodded at him. 'Or perhaps defend France, as she might have done?'

Claude held her look, a meeting of equals. Then his face acquired its mask of pleasantness again as he moved down the hall in Mimi's wake.

Stepping dripping out of her bath, Polly answered the internal telephone in her room to be told by Alexandrine to meet her, Zita and Lana Mae at the rue Cambon entrance to the hotel in fifteen minutes.

'Wear suitable shopping clothes, darling. Something comfortable, yet chic.'

Polly looked at her well-worn outfits brought all the way from Australia, already unpacked and hung in the built-in wardrobes by a maid. She was doubtful which of them, if any, might fit that bill.

'We shall visit Mademoiselle Chanel before cocktails,' Alexandrine told her. 'Her premises are in the rue Cambon, and they are so worth appreciating from inside. I know we shall find you some very nice new things.'

'For me?' Polly said, with astonishment. '*Me* wearing Chanel?'

'Why not? Don't you remember what Marjorie wrote? You are to have lessons in fashion. Think of this as your first.'

'But – but I don't need anything so extravagant.'

'Extravagant?' said Alexandrine, astonished in turn. 'This from the girl who reads her late aunt's *L'Officiel*?'

Polly looked at the cover of the fashion magazine she had read in the train, now unpacked for her by the maid. She hadn't known why she had kept it, only that she couldn't bring herself to throw it away. 'That's because there was nothing else to read,' said Polly.

Alexandrine rejected this. 'Then I cannot believe you haven't read somewhere that to embrace Chanel is to embrace simplicity itself.'

Polly had never encountered such a sentiment.

'As I thought,' said Alexandrine, wrongly taking her silence as confirmation.

'But the cost,' said Polly.

'Your wonderful aunt did not leave you her money for *that* sort of comment to be made,' said Alexandrine. She hung up.

Polly picked up the magazine half-heartedly, wondering if any of this could really be *her*.

Alexandrine and Lana Mae arrived in the Cambon lobby – smaller than the main one off the Place Vendôme, and thus even more intimate – just as Polly came down the stairs in what she hoped was the most suitable of her clothes. She clutched the green Hermès handbag – it now being unthinkable not to carry it with her everywhere. Polly wondered what people would say if they knew what the bag contained. It was comforting that Auzello now shared her secret. It struck Polly as wonderful that her being armed and dangerous at the will of her late aunt was the most acceptable thing in the world to the General Manager of the Ritz. She was beginning to think that she would like it here.

Polly had a few moments to glance further inside the Cambon bar while they waited for Zita. In stark yet not displeasing contrast to the rest of the Ritz, the bar was sensationally of the *now* in its ambience, being shiny with glass and steel and chromium plating that epitomised the Art Deco style. Outside a Fred Astaire and Ginger Rogers picture, Polly had never seen such an exuberant display of slick modernity. She rather liked it.

'We'll have a pick-me-up in there later,' said Lana Mae, 'and introduce you to Guy.' She glanced at Alexandrine. 'It occurs to me, honey, that we'll need to decide what Polly's signature drink will be.'

'That's true,' said Alexandrine. 'Guy will insist on committing it to memory.'

'It won't matter about my age?' Polly wondered.

Alexandrine's facial expression was all too clear, mirrored by Lana Mae.

'*What* did we say about that?' said Lana Mae.

'I think I quite like champagne,' Polly ventured hastily, not wanting them to know that the glass she had been given in the Rolls-Royce was only her second.

'That's not a *drink*, honey,' said Lana Mae, 'it's no different than water.'

'Perhaps in the way that you consume it,' Alexandrine quipped.

'You can have a glass of bubbles anytime,' Lana Mae added, dismissively. 'No, you want to find a *real* drink, something distinct – a cocktail. They're Guy's specialty. He wrote a whole book about 'em.'

'What's your signature drink, Mrs Huckstepp?'

'Call me Lana Mae, remember, baby, you make me feel old. And I'm mighty fond of martinis. A good clean poison. If you spill some on your blouse it doesn't stain.'

Alexandrine made a little signal at the arrival through the street entrance of another woman, expensively dressed and attractive, just as they were, but without quite the same attention to her maquillage and hair. She was accompanied by a teenage girl, who was pretty if somewhat pouty, and wearing dark glasses. The girl was younger than Polly by a year or so and was likely the woman's daughter. Her arm was hooked protectively through the older woman's, who looked unsteady on her feet, dishevelled, as if she'd just come inside from a gale.

As the two entered, Polly and her guardian aunts heard the tail end of the popular song the two had been singing as they'd walked up the street:

'*Attends-moi dans ce pays de France*
Je serai bientôt de retour garde confiance . . .'

The girl, in particular, had a wonderful voice. Polly translated the words in her head:

'*Wait for me in this country of France*

I'll be back soon, keep confident . . .'

'Speaking of drinks,' Lana Mae muttered, affectionately. 'Speaking of fond.'

Alexandrine called out to the new arrivals. 'Good afternoon, Blanche darling, how's the weather out there?'

The woman and her daughter seemed to take a second to work out where the question had come from. 'Oh hi,' Blanche said. 'We've been at lunch.' Her accent, like Lana Mae's, was American.

'We can see that, honey,' Lana Mae laughed as she kissed her, 'was it nice? Or was it just long?'

'Both,' said Blanche. 'And who is this?' She met Polly's eye with a friendly smile.

'Darling, let us introduce you,' said Alexandrine, pleased. 'This is Polly Hartford – dear Marjorie's niece.'

'Ah. Well then,' said Blanche, adding nothing more. The sympathy on her face showed that she fully understood and respected Polly's loss.

Polly held out her hand and Blanche took it.

'This is Madame Blanche Auzello – Monsieur Claude's lovely wife,' Alexandrine completed the introduction. 'She and her daughter lately live here in the Ritz.'

'Freeloaders!' cracked Lana Mae.

'Pleased to meet you, Madame Auzello,' said Polly, keeping Marjorie's bag securely under her arm. Blanche's hand felt damp in its glove.

'I'm Odile,' said her teenage daughter. She held out her hand at an angle that was slightly awkward for Polly to shake. Polly realised then why the girl was wearing dark glasses: she couldn't quite tell where Polly was. She was blind.

'Hello, Odile,' said Polly. 'How old are you?'

'Fifteen,' she said. Her accent was French. 'How about you?'

'Sixteen,' she told her with a faint air of superiority.

'Oh?' Odile said, surprised. 'You sound younger than that.'

Polly wasn't sure how to respond.

'Have you heard what's happening right now?' Blanche asked them.

'Where, darling?'

'At the Maginot Line, for God's sake.'

Polly caught the loaded look that passed between Blanche and Alexandrine and realised that Alexandrine was harbouring a hidden anxiety.

'Oh honey, we ain't paying any mind to that,' said Lana Mae, who didn't notice this.

Blanche looked cock-eyed at her fellow American. 'Why aren't I surprised, Lana Mae?'

'Look around you, honey. Does anyone else look worried?'

'Sometimes I think you live with your head in the sand.'

'No, darling, we live here at the Ritz.' Alexandrine smiled warmly. Yet Polly saw there was an unspoken understanding between her and Blanche.

'As do you, baby,' Lana Mae told Blanche. 'So, don't go claiming some highfalutin knowhow that's better than ours. The war is all the way over *there*, not here, so why lose sleep over it?'

Zita made her belated arrival on the Cambon stairs and was delighted to spot their mutual friend. 'Oh Christ, send that stinking soak to the bar, puss,' she called out, 'a blind idiot could tell how badly she wants another drink!'

Only Polly was mortified by this seemingly insensitive crack. Flinching, she mouthed a distinct 'I'm sorry' to Blanche.

Yet the latter accepted Zita's words with a good-natured smirk, before turning to regard the film star. 'Screw you, Zita,' she rejoindered, gaily. 'Did you get your little telegram?'

This caused the other three women to pull up short.

'You're reading my mail now?'

'Oh sure, because you're *so* interesting,' Blanche teased.

'*Mama*,' said Odile, warningly. 'This is no place for a fight.'

'Who's fighting? These girls are our good pals.'

Yet Polly saw that the comment had thrown Zita – along with Alexandrine and Lana Mae.

'She tell you what was in it?' Blanche asked the others.

'*Mama*,' said Odile again.

But her mother was in too good a mood to stop. 'I'll give you a clue, so you'll know what she's hiding from you.'

'*Blanche* –' Zita looked stricken.

'It came from the krauts.'

Surprise rippled through Polly alone. The others didn't flinch.

'Good luck figuring that out,' said Blanche, laughing, thinking she'd dropped a bombshell. In truth, only Polly had felt the impact of it. The others' lack of response was telling in itself.

Odile was shaking her head.

Polly could see that Blanche was a little intoxicated, certainly, but beneath it she seemed vulnerable and scared.

'Perhaps we will see you in the Cambon bar when we return from our shopping, Madame Auzello?' Polly said.

Blanche looked at her blankly for a moment, as if she'd forgotten Polly was there. 'Sure, why not,' she said. 'You and Odile should make friendly.'

'I'd like that,' Polly said to the other girl. 'It was very nice meeting you.'

'You, too, Polly,' Odile said, and then in a stage whisper she added, 'Good pals are thin on the ground around here – I don't know if you've realised it but everyone is so damn *old*.'

Polly had to smile. 'Surely you can't mean any of the lovely ladies here?'

'Well, not Mama, *obviously*, because she's so beautiful,' said Odile. 'But these other hags . . .'

Lana Mae hooted, and Polly had to put a hand over her mouth to stop herself laughing outright.

They watched Blanche head off on the arm of her sightless daughter, swaying down the corridor that led to the Vendôme side.

'Before she was Auzello's wife, she was Auzello's *mistress*,' whispered Lana Mae, wickedly to Polly. 'They were both of them married to somebody else and it's anyone's guess who fathered that naughty girl – so don't go giving Blanche any class she don't deserve.'

Polly turned to Zita. 'But what was Madame Auzello talking about?'

Zita gave an insouciant look. 'How do I know?'

'A telegram from the Germans?' said Polly. 'Was she joking?'

A loaded look passed between the Girls. Zita then appeared to cave. 'Unfortunately, no, puss. You can read it if you like. Maybe it'll make more sense to you than it does to me.' She took the opened telegram from her purse. 'It's some stupid riddle.' Zita unfolded the little sheet of paper and showed Polly the tele-grammed message she had received. The others said nothing.

I will bring you a gift from little Lotti. H.

The words seemed innocuous to Polly. 'Who's little Lotti?' she asked.

'You tell me,' said Zita.

'Then who's H?' said Polly.

'A mystery,' said Zita. 'Or maybe someone's idea of a gag.'

Alexandrine was watching closely as Polly puzzled at this. 'Someone sent this to you from Germany?'

'Maybe it was meant for someone else?' said Zita, shrugging.

'Maybe,' said Alexandrine.

Zita screwed it up into a ball. 'Who cares. We're going shopping.'

As they exited the Ritz, the incident nagged at Polly's conscience. While Zita had been open, letting her see and read the strange telegram, Polly had been left with the impression that the film star – along with her two closest friends – had in fact been tightly closed.

*

Once they were outside in the rue Cambon, where the afternoon air was warm with a light breeze, Polly took up the matter of the German invasion of Luxembourg and what it all meant. The others knew about it but no one seemed very much alarmed by the news. It was true what Lana Mae had said; looking around at the well-dressed men and women, most especially the women, with the extraordinary confections that were the season's best hats perched upon their heads, it was hard to find any other attitude than indifference in their manner.

'Well, whichever way you skin it and no matter *what* happens,' Lana Mae mused, 'this ain't gonna be the worst thing for us girls.'

'How is that?' Polly wondered, as they made their way down the bustling street.

'Keep in mind I was practically a *child*, honey, when the last war happened, and my memory ain't what it could be, but I do remember things weren't as lousy as you'd think.'

'It's true,' said Zita. 'Doors opened for us then. Like magic.'

Alexandrine agreed. 'Of course, we were all *very* young, Polly,' she said, furthering Lana Mae's conceit, 'but for women like me, with so few servants left to help at home, and the dreadful lack of coal for the fires, well, we had to give up the tradition of hosting weekly salons. So, instead, we went to the Ritz. It was still heated.'

'It's what started it all,' said Zita.

'It's what changed things for girls like us,' said Lana Mae.

'But hadn't the Ritz already been here for years?' Polly was trying not to be too distracted by the astonishing things she saw in the shop windows they were passing.

'Until the Great War, hotels like the Ritz had only been places to stay on vacation,' said Alexandrine, 'when one had a respectable excuse. For a woman to visit such an establishment when she was not on holiday, well, it was as good as admitting to sin.'

'Because it *was* sin – one of the good ones.' Zita laughed.

'Hotels were where a girl went if she wanted some happy time with her beau,' Lana Mae spelled it out. 'A fabulous French tradition.' She sighed, nostalgic. 'I miss those days. That all went away with the fighting.'

'Women were left to themselves,' said Alexandrine. 'With the men at the Front some of the bolder, more confident ladies began to appear at the Ritz. They met other women of their own daring kind.' She gave her secret smile. 'Oh, when I think of it . . .'

'We headed straight to the hotel bars,' said Zita. 'They'd been forbidden to us once, but now they were as friendly as could be. The Vendôme was pretty nice all right, but the Cambon, now that was where the action was.'

'A woman could speak directly to the barman there,' said Alexandrine. 'And order her own drink. That never happened before the Great War.'

'Such low-lifes we could meet. Bohemians. Actresses!' cried Zita.

'I met an atheist politician once,' said Lana Mae, 'I was electrified.'

'I met my very first *parvenu*,' said Alexandrine, looking at the other two, meaningfully. 'And then I met another one.'

All three of them laughed.

The penny dropped for Polly. 'Is that where the three of you first became friends?'

'The four of us, darling,' said Alexandrine. 'It's where we met your dear aunt.'

Polly felt the urge to cry sneak up on her. Sometimes she managed to keep her grief for Aunt Marjorie to the back of her mind, but at other times, moments like these, it came back.

Zita saw it first. 'Oh puss, no more tears.'

'I'm sorry . . .'

'You made it through Claude and Mimi telling you how much you looked like her. Why now?'

'I know.' Polly had a thought as she sniffled. 'Do I really look like her? You didn't tell me I did.'

The three of them passed their usual glances at each other.

'That's because you don't, puss,' Zita said, flatly.

Polly's grief stopped with the surprise. 'I didn't think so either. But they seemed so sure.'

Zita shrugged. 'Maybe they just wanted to see a resemblance?'

'Maybe there *is* a resemblance,' said Lana Mae. 'If you squint a little . . .'

'Perhaps the resemblance will be clearer in time,' Alexandrine suggested, tactfully.

Polly studied them quizzically. 'But how *old* were you all when you met at the Ritz?'

The three of them looked vague.

'Somewhere around your own present age, I'm sure, darling,' said Alexandrine, with a flutter of her hand. 'But who counts?'

Their short walk along the rue Cambon had taken them to the front of Chanel's grand boutique at Number 31. The four of them stood staring for a moment at the window displays: sumptuous gowns that were miracles of stunning simplicity.

'Oh God. I think it's time to start living beyond my means,' said Zita.

'*Start* living?' Lana Mae queried.

'We're here for Polly,' Alexandrine reminded them. 'It's all about her this afternoon. And tomorrow afternoon. And most likely the afternoon after that. We're here for dear Marjorie's wishes.'

'She wanted to do this with you herself, you know, baby,' Lana Mae told Polly.

'When would she have done it?' Polly wondered.

'When you turned seventeen, eighteen, who knows? But as sure as eggs are eggs, she'd have done it. She was planning on it. Why else put it in her last words to you?'

Alexandrine gave Lana Mae a warning look.

'But let's not overcook it too much,' Lana Mae added, hastily. 'It's just shopping. As normal as breathing.'

Polly's tears had dried up, but the grief behind them remained. 'I feel like she's with us,' she whispered, 'and that she's feeling pleased.'

This made the Girls fall silent for a moment as they remembered their lost friend.

'*Yes*,' said Alexandrine, eventually. 'See anything you like?' She was looking up at the windows.

'I really can't imagine what they might look like on me,' Polly said.

'I think you'll be pleasantly surprised,' said the Comtesse, smiling.

As they went to push open the heavy glass door, a jewelled hand on the other side turned a little sign. What had formerly read 'Open', now read 'Closed'.

The four of them stood reading the word for a moment in puzzlement.

'But it's not the right time for closing,' said Lana Mae.

They saw through the door who had turned the little sign: it was Coco herself.

'Mademoiselle!' Alexandrine tapped on the glass. 'You have the time wrong. There's at least another hour.'

The door opened a crack. Polly got her first glimpse at this legendary figure of fashion: she was rail thin, with barely a bust; her curled, bobbed hair was as black as jet; she was dressed in deep navy blue, and her signature pearls swung in two long strings from her neck. 'Can't you read?' she asked them, abrupt.

'Coco, honey, you should try to get your watch fixed,' said Lana Mae. 'Or buy a Swiss one, they keep better time.'

'It's not the closing hour,' said Zita, frowning at Coco. Polly remembered her calling the famed designer a 'snobby cow'.

'It is today.' Coco looked Zita up and down in return, radiating condemnation.

'But we're here to buy clothes,' said Alexandrine. '*Lots* of clothes.' She indicated Polly. 'This is Marjorie Tighe's niece. Do let us inside, darling, it's a very special day for Polly.'

'I told you,' said the designer, 'we're shut.'

'But why, I don't understand?'

Coco stepped out onto the front step, folding her arms at them, disgusted. 'Where do you three fools live, under a rock?'

Alexandrine was mortified. 'We live at the Ritz,' she reminded her, evenly. 'As do *you*, Mademoiselle.'

'You live with your heads in a hole.'

Embarrassed, Polly heard the echo of Blanche's teasing words.

'What do mean by that, puss?' Zita demanded.

'Why don't you buy a newspaper?' Coco suggested. 'Read more than a menu for a change?'

'The gall of you!' cried Lana Mae.

Alexandrine was the diplomat. 'Surely, Coco, you can't mean the Luxembourg trouble?'

'Mother Mary,' said Coco, shaking her coal black head. 'The "trouble", as you call it, Comtesse, is the German invasion.'

'Well, yes, possibly, but not here. This is France.'

'God above. You're all incredible.' Then she caught Polly's eye and had reason to pause. Something unspoken seemed to pass between them. 'Except for *you*,' she said quietly. 'Because you *get it*, don't you, girl?'

Clutching Marjorie's bag, Polly was taken aback.

Coco shook her head at her, pityingly. 'So, what did you do wrong to get stuck with these featherheads?'

Alexandrine bristled. 'All right then, Mademoiselle, you're closed,' she said, 'but for how long?'

'Indefinitely,' barked Coco. Then she thought of a better answer. 'For the duration.'

'For the *duration*?' Alexandrine parroted.

'It's my patriotic duty,' Coco spat at her. 'This is no time for something as frivolous as selling fashion. Why don't you three fools put some thought into what *you* might do as your patriotic duty? Or are ideas like "duty" and "thought" beyond you?'

She shut the door on them. And locked it.

*

On the initially silent walk back to the Ritz, the three older women would have had Polly believe that nothing so dreadful had been said to them at all, and that the purpose of their excursion had not been shopping but exercise. Polly kept quiet, but she knew her three guardians had been publicly belittled in front of her, and that such an affront had been deeply humiliating for them.

Finally, she decided to break the ice. 'Well, as Lana Mae might say, I've never heard more horse-hooey in my life.'

This stopped the three women in the street.

'Mademoiselle Chanel was a perfectly horrid woman,' Polly told them. 'What appalling rudeness. It just goes to show that all the lovely clothes in the world can still do nothing to dress up a bad character.'

Lana Mae broke first with an explosive guffaw.

'The stinking piss of her,' said Zita, joining in. 'What did I say she was, Polly?'

'A snobby cow.'

'God, when I think of the money I've spent there,' said Alexandrine.

'That all three of us have,' said Lana Mae.

'Money that she has never accepted gracefully,' said Alexandrine, '*ever*.'

'The nerve to judge us,' said Lana Mae.

'When hasn't she judged?' said Zita. 'We only put up with it for the frocks.'

'Aw, the frocks . . .' said Lana Mae, sadly.

Alexandrine made a stand. 'Chanel's offerings this season are well below standard.'

Polly was pleased with what she had started.

'You're right, puss, *L'Officiel* said as much.'

'All this troublesome politics,' Alexandrine said, 'it's the perfect excuse for her.'

'Excuse to do what?' asked Zita.

'To close down, of course. She's exhausted creatively. She's wrung the well dry.'

'Oh honey, now it all makes sense,' said Lana Mae, warming to this theme. 'She's probably broke.'

'Up to her fanny in debts – of course she is, the stinking sow,' Zita agreed.

'And now Hitler's marched on Luxembourg and suddenly it's manna from heaven for her,' said Alexandrine. 'A face-saving way out.'

Zita sparked a cigarette. 'To dress it up as "patriotic duty"? It's disgusting.'

'She oughta be ashamed,' said Lana Mae.

Together, they felt mollified enough to continue walking, heads held just a degree higher than they had been five minutes before. Polly couldn't wipe the smile from her face.

'Tomorrow,' said Alexandrine, turning to Polly as they walked, 'we shall go to Lanvin. She understands the importance of fashion in these upsetting times.'

'That would be lovely,' said Polly, trying not to laugh.

Walking the Paris street in the warmth of the afternoon sun, Polly felt a sudden, quite unexpected wave of affection for her three guardians. This rush of feeling was as surprising as it was also welcome. She was beginning to make sense of these women. They were ridiculous, certainly, and exceedingly frivolous, too. They were also secretive, deliberately keeping things from her, if not from themselves, which made Polly suspect that their superficiality was in fact a collective mask. If anything frightened them it was the threat of a loss of face, yet nothing bonded them tighter in defiance, either. Together, they were formidable.

Polly envied the bond between them. She was not a friend in their eyes, but a pet. Until these women saw her otherwise, how could she trust them like they trusted each other? They *were* keeping things hidden, Polly reminded herself. This meant they didn't trust her, either.

Polly only now noted how appreciative masculine eyes lingered long at the Girls – taking in their enviable figures, their perfectly coiffed hair, their marvellous hats, their stylish and comfortable clothes. But when the same men's eyes moved towards Polly they soon flicked away. On the Paris street, she was as dismissed as she'd been on the train by the soldiers.

Polly felt the old hurt before she bit it back hard with a resolve: no more should she let herself feel stung by such male disregard, she told herself, not when she was at the cusp of such an exciting new life. She should take herself down a path where rejection was irrelevant in the face of purpose. This, Polly imagined, is what Marjorie might have done – or the Marjorie of her letters, at least.

Her late aunt had given her a loaded gun, after all, and one day – perhaps one day very soon – Polly intended to fire it.

4

10 June 1940

Polly as good as skipped down the Cambon stairs. It was extraordinary to her how quickly she'd come to feel at home in the Ritz. Not even a month had passed and yet she could have convinced herself she'd been living here far longer. At her elbow swung a somewhat bizarre, cylindrical-shaped box in the most startling shade of red. It was an impulse buy she'd purchased that morning from Madame Lanvin and she was keen to show it off.

'*Bonjour*, Madame!' Polly called out, spotting Mimi.

The two griffons barked, and Mimi looked up from the Cambon lobby, where she had been running a finger along surfaces for dust. '*Bonjour*, Mademoiselle Polly. You look quite delectable. Like a blood orange sorbet.'

'Do I, Madame?' Polly was wearing another recent purchase, this one from Jacques Fath. It was a dress she particularly liked because, like the cylindrical box, she had chosen it on a shopping expedition unaccompanied by her guardians. It was an afternoon dress in a colour called *bois de rose*, with short puffed sleeves, a corselet waist, and a straight skirt, and it had a plain bust line that buttoned up through the centre. She had teamed it with a little bolero jacket. While it was true Polly didn't feel wholly herself in clothes of such style and expense, she knew they helped her fit in this strange new world she now inhabited. Polly tried to make the cylindrical box hang just so at her elbow, but Mimi didn't take the bait.

'How have you been sleeping, my dear?' the Ritz owner enquired.

Polly considered this. 'I suppose a little lightly, Madame.'

This was like an axe blow to Mimi. 'I shall order the mattress changed this very instant. Monsieur Claude!' she called out, knowing that Auzello was at his desk all the way on the other side of the hotel.

'It's not the mattress – the mattress is lovely,' Polly reassured her. 'I've been sleeping restlessly because of all that's going on. I can't help thinking about it. Sometimes it keeps me awake.'

'You make me confused,' said Mimi. Then another thought occurred to her. 'Are you in love, Polly?'

Polly regretted what she'd started. 'Of course, I'm not, Madame. The very idea.'

'Hmmm,' muttered Mimi, not entirely convinced. 'At your age, you should be trying love on for size, you know. Just to see if you like it.'

Polly stuck to the resolve she had made on her very first day in Paris. 'I *don't* like it and I know it already. There are too many other things of far more importance.'

Mimi smiled. 'More important than love?'

Polly wanted to move on. 'I mean the war, Madame.'

Mimi pooh-poohed this. 'Tell me, where are the bombs we were dreading? Where are the rampaging armies in the streets? There is nothing of war to be seen at all. It is simply posturing. And what have I said about the Ritz?'

'Nothing changes,' said Polly, by rote now.

'Exactly. Now you *will* have a fresh mattress and I won't be told otherwise.' Mimi made her way with a wave towards the corridor of vitrines, and Polly went, somewhat gratefully, into the Cambon bar.

'*Bonjour*, Guy!' she called out as she entered.

'*Bonjour!*' he called back as she took up position, leaning her elbows on the chrome-heavy bar. 'The usual, *chérie?*' he asked.

'Oh, well, I'm not sure.' She glanced at her little wristwatch. 'Isn't it still a bit early?'

Guy gave her a very droll look and started assembling the ingredients.

By now, Polly had been thoroughly introduced to Monsieur Guy Martin, Head Bartender at the Cambon bar, and a font of much wisdom and fun. He was a Cambon bar fixture, and rather handsome for a man of fifty, but he was not, Polly suspected, using a phrase once employed by her aunt in her letters, 'the romancing kind'. Although she wasn't entirely sure quite what was involved, she knew this was a code for being homosexual. According to Lana Mae, Guy was thought to have an Algerian lover called Baptiste, who ran the Dress Circle bar at the Théâtre du Vieux-Colombier. Polly couldn't help feeling sophisticated with this knowledge.

It had been decided between them that Polly's signature drink would be a Brandy Alexander. It came in a champagne glass – the wide, Marie Antoinette kind, not the flute – which meant it looked elegant when held in a feminine hand. It was a mixture of cognac, something else that sounded like 'cocoa', and cream. It was certainly delicious although Polly couldn't get used to the idea of drinking cocktails in the way that the other guests drank them, as a preferred refreshment over coffee or tea.

As Guy set to making the cocktail, he clocked the new red Lanvin box. 'The shape of that thing's unusual, *chérie.*'

'Isn't it?' said Polly, pleased that someone had noticed her impulsive purchase. 'And what do you suppose it is for?'

'Your fancy little feminine bits and pieces, just like your Hermès bag?'

'Wrong, Guy.' She opened the cap at the top and then, with faux ceremony, tipped a gas mask onto the counter. The bag had been designed to fit it perfectly. 'What do you think?'

'Ingenious,' said Guy. And then, somewhat slyly: 'So, how much was it?'

'Guy!' Polly protested. 'That is something one never asks.'

He waited.

'One hundred and eighty francs,' whispered Polly, in due course.

'Including the gas mask?'

'I'd already been given that by Monsieur Auzello.'

'Extortionate.'

'That's very unfair,' Polly protested. 'It's by Lanvin. And gas masks are so ugly to carry around.'

'Exclusively extortionate. Madame Lanvin must have seen you coming, *chérie*.'

'Oh you,' Polly said, as if dismissing this. 'My late aunt's instructions were very clear that I should be suitably wardrobed. I'm simply obeying her wishes.'

'Let's have a proper look at what you've got on today then,' said Guy. 'Give us a little twirl.'

Polly stood back from the bar so that Guy could better see her, and duly spun on her heel.

Guy whistled. '*Ooh-la-la.*'

But he didn't quite convince her, because she didn't convince herself. Polly felt the clothes didn't sit on her properly. It was like she was playing dress-ups.

Polly watched him work. 'This afternoon I thought I'd visit the French Red Cross,' she said.

'To volunteer?'

'Yes, to do something worthwhile for the war effort. I can't spend my life shopping and reading magazines – it's an absurd way to live. What do you think?'

Guy wrinkled his nose. 'Can't see you driving some ambulance in that little ensemble.'

'Don't be silly. This is only what I'll wear for the interview. I don't want to look too *young*.'

Guy let that slide.

'While I was outside earlier this morning, I saw a newspaper headline that said men aged over forty are being called up now.'

'Did you?' said Guy, apparently not much interested.

'Will that mean you get called up, too?'

Guy paused, and then brought a hand up to pat at imagined tresses at the back of his neck. 'It's at moments like this I regret having told you my real age.'

'You mean fifty's still too old to be mobilised?'

Guy narrowed his eyes, arch.

To Polly's mind it only sounded like he'd had a lucky escape if it was true. 'People were being quite emotional on the street,' she went on. 'The crowds were almost chaotic around the metro stations. First at Concorde, and then, when I walked down the rue de Rivoli, just the same at Palais-Royal.'

Guy was as indifferent to war worries as Mimi had been. 'It'll all blow over, *chérie*, you shouldn't fret about it. You should be out enjoying yourself.'

'There were lots of men carrying suitcases,' she added, doggedly. 'Wives and children were making goodbyes.'

Guy just shrugged.

'Oh, and the Louvre was still closed. It was so disappointing. I'm still yet to see any of the art. There were big lorries at the entrance. I think they might have been putting the paintings inside them.'

'Want me to take you down to the hotel's air raid shelter then?' Guy said. 'Just in case the Boches show up?'

'I didn't realise there was an air raid shelter?'

'Oh, it's very chic,' said Guy. 'Monsieur Auzello's made the *chaises longues* more comfortable for longer stays by adding sleeping-bags purchased especially from Schiaparelli.'

Polly wasn't quite sure whether to believe him or not, yet knowing the Ritz, the existence of such a facility did not seem beyond the realms of possibility. 'Maybe some other time.'

Guy finished mixing the drink. 'Here.'

She longed now for a nice cup of tea instead. Yet she didn't feel she could say so. 'I shall have it at my table, thank you very much.'

'Of course, you will,' said Guy, before adding, under his breath, but not so far under that Polly wouldn't hear it: 'Anything for Mademoiselle de la Muck . . .'

Polly just laughed.

She took a seat at a little table in the corner that Guy had told her Cole Porter had once occupied, for days at a stretch, in 1934, where he wrote 'Begin the Beguine'. Given that Polly had also once heard from another quarter that the lively Mr Porter had written the hit song when travelling on an ocean liner, she took the story with a grain of salt. Still, it didn't hurt any to know that the famed American had occupied the same chair as her.

As she sipped her cocktail, Polly became aware of a new staff member she'd first glimpsed a day earlier. A boy of around Polly's own age, he was being 'given' to Guy at the bar. Blanche Auzello, sober today, was spending time carefully explaining what she wished him to learn in Guy's care. Given Madame Auzello had no role in the hotel's management, this was odd. Polly only picked up one or two words. The clearest was 'nephew'.

She observed the exchange as covertly as she could from her little table in the far corner. The young man was dressed in the hotel's standard uniform for males who fell low in the hierarchy: black upon black, apart from the blinding white of his shirt, which was starched so much that it crackled. He wore it with a crisp white bow tie.

It was his hair that most struck Polly, magnetic in its attraction, being almost impossibly blond, as if bleached in the Sahara, or by a life lived entirely at sea. It was not the sort of blond one often saw among the darker-haired men of Paris. If a woman of the city had sported such a hair colour, people would think she had dyed it. It was the hair of someone from another country.

It was German hair.

Blanche departed, and the young man was left looking expectantly at Guy, his hands placed behind his back. Guy at once corrected this and gave him a long white napkin which he was required to drape across his left arm, in which he would also carry a small tray. An apron was found, also in white and he was sent to clear tables.

Polly realised with some astonishment that he was actually aware of her. She had seen him glance once in her direction, when he had first been brought into the bar, and Polly expected that to be the end of his interest. Yet he'd glanced at her again while Blanche had been talking, and his eyes had lingered upon her. He'd done a funny little head toss then, almost as if he was greeting her. This only left Polly confused.

He now made his way around the room, picking up empty glasses and enquiring of patrons whether they wanted something more. One or two of them spoke to him, but not much. He was awkward and seemed out of his depth. Polly suspected that one of the things Guy had been asked to instruct him in was 'charm'.

Eventually, he came to her table.

He picked up her empty Brandy Alexander glass and placed it on his tray.

'Would Mademoiselle like something else?' He did the head toss again.

Before Polly thought to stop herself, she gave the same head toss back. This made both of them smile. Polly was free to look at him properly now. He was decidedly handsome, perhaps not conventionally so, for his looks weren't those of a matinée idol's, but he was striking all the same. His eyes were a soft, rich brown, which was slightly surprising, given that Polly had been imagining the sharpest of blues to go with his very blond hair. He was also quite tall – taller than the average French man – and lean. He looked to Polly as if he might do well in a running race.

'Mademoiselle?'

Polly realised she had let rather a lot of time slip by while she pondered him. 'Sorry. I don't know. I don't think I should. It's not even eleven yet.' She made a confession. 'I'm rather new to all this. I still don't know if I'm a cocktail sort of person at all.'

He blinked. 'As you wish.' He made as if to leave her and then didn't move at all.

Polly's confusion increased. Was he seeking a conversation? 'Who are you?' she asked him, for want of anything else.

'I'm Tommy, Mademoiselle.' He waited and smiled at her.

Polly had learned enough about French politeness to know that no hand may be shaken unless the other person offers it first. She did so, although she wasn't sure if this was the done thing between a hotel guest and a member of staff who was not of Monsieur Auzello's rank. She felt unexpectedly captivated at pressing her skin to his. His hand was wide and long-fingered, soft, and very clean.

'And who are you?' he asked.

Polly quite liked his disregard of formality. Such a question had never been asked of her by any member of staff, either because they already knew who she was, or because they couldn't expect to know. 'I'm Polly,' she told him, 'Polly Hartford.'

'You're not French?' he asked, even though they were speaking it.

'No,' she told him. 'I'm from Australia.'

'Oh?'

She could see him thinking that he'd never met someone who wasn't from the same hemisphere as himself. She suspected it made her exotic.

'I don't think you're from Paris either,' said Polly. 'Is that a slight accent you have? Alsatian perhaps?' She had heard that Frenchmen from that region often seemed foreign to other

French ears. To ask if a person was 'Alsatian' in these times was a better word to use than 'German'.

'I am sort of Hungarian,' he told her, uncomfortable. 'My full name is Tomas Harsanyi.'

It was her turn to be struck by the exotic. 'Sort of?'

He didn't elaborate. 'I'm fully a French citizen.'

'I see.'

She glanced to the bar and saw that Guy was glancing back at her. Any second, she knew, he would order Tommy to stop gossiping with guests and start working again. Yet, the order didn't come. Guy went back to mixing cocktails for other patrons.

He clearly wanted her and Tommy to talk. She couldn't ask Tommy to take a seat with her, however, for that would have been a step too far in staff–guest relations, if not for her, then certainly for Claude Auzello, should he have walked in. So, she remained in Cole Porter's chair, while Tommy remained standing.

'You've not been called up?' she asked him.

'Not yet,' said Tommy. 'I'm still seventeen.'

'Oh? I'm sixteen,' she told him. 'I had my birthday in March.'

'Yes?'

She almost wondered if he'd wish her a late happy birthday, but he didn't. Yet he seemed to want to continue the conversation. 'Have you worked at the Ritz very long?' Polly asked, already knowing the answer.

'No. This is my second day.'

'You're doing very well,' she said, encouragingly. 'It can't be easy, learning so many new things. I'm sure I'd be quite hopeless at it.'

'I am Madame Auzello's nephew,' he told her, without having been asked. 'She is an American, but she also has Hungarian blood.'

'I see.' She wasn't sure why he wanted her to know this specifically.

He now seemed to be searching for something else to say. 'Your clothes,' he said, finally, 'they are very new on you.'

'Oh! How nice.' Then it occurred to her this wasn't exactly a compliment.

A blush came to his face. 'I'm sorry,' he told her. 'I didn't mean to say something like that.'

'But you did say it.' She decided she wasn't offended, as she smoothed her skirt in her chair and adjusted her bolero jacket. 'I don't feel very comfortable with haute couture yet, and I don't know if I ever will. Honestly, you wouldn't believe what people are expected to pay. And apparently, I must expect to make some terrible fashion mistakes to begin with. That's according to my guardian Alexandrine.'

He reacted to the name.

'She's the Comtesse Ducru-Batailley,' said Polly, 'perhaps you've served her here?'

'No,' said Tommy, emphatic.

'Oh.'

Whatever composure he had gained now evaporated. 'Your new clothes are not a mistake,' he said.

This didn't much sound like a compliment either and Polly was again grateful for her recent resolve not to let male disregard upset her. It made dealing with awkward situations like this far easier. 'You mustn't be put off by people with titles,' she offered him. 'My guardian has her faults but she's really very nice.'

'That will be all, Mademoiselle.' He spun around so quickly he nearly lost the Brandy Alexander glass.

'Wait,' she said.

He faced her again.

'What do you think about everything that's going on?'

'Going on?'

'The war,' said Polly.

He looked taken aback that she should ask him such a thing, and Polly resigned herself to another non-answer. 'No one here seems to take it seriously,' she complained. 'Or at least they don't take *me* seriously when I raise the subject. I wondered if it was because I'm only sixteen, and if maybe you receive the same treat-ment at seventeen?'

He looked at her blankly for a moment, then seemed to weigh her up, as if he wanted to tell her something that was important to him. 'When I talk about the war, people do not ignore me or patronise me – but perhaps this is because I only talk about it with people who understand what this war means.'

Polly sighed. 'I don't seem to know anyone like that.'

'Well,' said Tommy, 'now you know me.'

The simplicity of that statement made her insides feel fluttery. 'Do you think we will be safe here?'

He paused, and then, lowering his voice as if he feared being overheard, he said, 'We will not be safe anywhere. Some Parisians think they are living in the clouds, but when the Germans come the shock will be terrible.'

Polly considered this for a moment. 'And they will come?'

'Of course. The Germans hate the French too much not to.'

'But what about the French Army? Won't they hold the Germans back?'

'What about the Maginot Line?' Tommy countered. 'The Luft-waffe bombed it while the Wehrmacht came through the Ardennes.'

'Yes, well,' Polly found herself stumbling. The blitzkrieg attack on the concrete forts after the fall of Luxembourg had been very shocking, as had the folly of thinking the Ardennes Forest was 'impregnable'. Once the news had broken of both catastrophes, the French Government had still continued to reassure people there was no cause for despair.

'I saw some of the newest army recruits being marched down the Champs-Élysées,' he continued. 'They didn't have enough boots for them all. Some of them were wearing their carpet slippers.'

Polly let his sobering words sit with her for another moment. She would definitely make the effort to visit the French Red Cross office later, she decided. 'Thank you, Tommy,' she said, 'for being so honest with me. I never hear such things from anyone else.'

'If people are not being honest with you, it is because you are a girl, not because you are sixteen,' he told her.

She frowned, not appreciating that insight at all, even though she knew it was likely true.

Tommy returned to the bar and Polly returned to staring into space. She was conscious of him moving about in her periphery, visiting other patrons, picking up spent glasses. The unwelcome fluttery feeling in her stomach continued and made her feel slightly breathless. After another minute of it, Polly got up from the Cole Porter chair.

'*Adieu*, Guy,' she said cheerily, as she passed by the bar.

'Thanks for helping me break the lad in, *chérie*. He needs proper working on his nerves.'

'Tommy?'

'Ah, very good,' said Guy, knowingly. 'You're at first names already.'

Polly wondered if she'd got Tommy into trouble somehow. 'He was very polite. And friendly.'

'He's a gormless lump who stands for everything that's wrong with the world these days,' said Guy, crushingly.

Polly felt very aware that Tommy, who was taking a drink to someone at the other side of the room, was at risk of hearing these words. 'That seems a little unkind,' she told Guy.

Guy shrugged. 'We can't get the staff anymore, *chérie*. We've been reduced to recruiting from high schools.'

'He was really very polite,' Polly reiterated.

She saw Tommy trying not to seem like he was craning his ear to listen to them.

'He'll turn out in the end, I suppose,' said Guy.

'Of course, he will,' said Polly, 'under your good training.'

She was just making to leave again when Guy added: 'He give you that line about him being the "nephew"?'

'Well, yes,' said Polly.

Guy rolled his eyes. 'Please don't be the one little fool who believes it.'

Polly was shocked. 'What do you mean?'

For once, the barman chose discretion. 'You're the one for the "observations", *chérie*, I'm sure you'll work it out in good time.'

Feeling suddenly disheartened, although she couldn't have said why, Polly was almost reluctant to look in Tommy's direction again as she departed the Cambon bar. Yet as she stepped through the threshold to return to the lobby, she found herself unable to stop from giving him another glance.

Tommy caught her eye from where he was in the act of delivering a drink, and gave her his head toss again, not as a greeting but goodbye. This time she didn't return it, less certain of him. Tommy held her gaze for barely a moment before he looked away. Yet it was more than long enough for Polly, who had come to know she had reason to put stead by her intuition, to be left feeling sure of something.

Just like her, and just like her guardians, Tommy was keeping something secret from the world.

It was a lovely afternoon to go walking and was made even lovelier for Polly by the fortifying knowledge of what remained hidden in the Hermès bag. It was empowering. The Paris streets, pulsing with people before war was declared ten months earlier, had become gradually denuded of men. Those not called up for the military were either too young, too old, too crippled and sick, or in some other way deemed useless. Everywhere Polly looked there were always women, and being Parisiennes, they were as spectacularly turned out as they ever were, and perhaps even more so. Given there were so few men about to impress, this left only the most exacting fashion critics to dress for: other women. To stroll along any of the Haussmann boulevards was to participate in a sumptuous, unending, open air fashion parade. Polly knew she was being found badly wanting by the many pairs of female eyes that judged her. And yet, the *Modèle* 1935 in her handbag made something as shallow as looks seem completely irrelevant.

Perhaps twenty metres ahead of where she was walking in the direction of the 8th arrondissement French Red Cross office, Polly saw a flash of blond hair – quite possibly German blond that was 'sort of' Hungarian. She walked on her toes to see better.

Weaving his way through the pedestrians, the blond was a good head taller than most, and hatless in the sun, which was why she had spotted him. It was surely Tommy. Keeping up with his pace, although she was some way behind him, Polly found that she liked the way he moved, Tommy being lithe in his gait and quite purposeful. He looked very different out of his Ritz uniform.

The afternoon air was warm, but Tommy had on a well-worn, black leather flyer's jacket, like an antique from the 1914 War. It was belted at the waist and too big for him, but his shoulders were broad, and he could carry it. Tommy's trousers were a pair of thin, baggy tweeds, easily two decades old as well, and yet they went with the jacket perfectly. On his feet he wore canvas tennis shoes in a grubby off-white. His hair captive to the breeze, Tommy's hand kept scraping it back from his forehead.

If Polly hadn't been additionally fortified by her resolve to be impervious to male disregard, she might have said he looked marvellous. She had never met a boy – who was almost a man – who had such an effortlessly casual style to him. He may be sort of Hungarian, Polly thought to herself, but in what he wears, and wears so well, he could only be Parisian.

Up ahead, Tommy veered onto the street itself, where he dodged past oncoming cars and made it to the other side. He then continued in a new direction, heading south towards the Seine. Polly stopped on her side of the street in surprise, watching him go. It was almost as if he'd known she'd been somewhere behind him, watching. Then, in a move that surprised her more, Polly dashed into the traffic herself, to a clamour of horns, and started following Tommy properly.

Within a moment she had lost him. Baffled at herself for taking such an uncharacteristic action – darting into traffic after someone she'd spoken to precisely *once* – Polly pretended her course had been this one all along, and that Tommy had nothing to do with her taking an unorthodox route to get to the French Red Cross office. She found herself on the narrow rue Saint-Florentin, which took her to where the rue de Rivoli met the Place de la Concorde and the huge stretch of manicured green that was the start of the Tuileries Gardens on the other side. That was when she saw Tommy again, now entering the park. He showed no awareness of her as he made his way under the trees.

Polly felt her heart race, whether from exertion or frustration at being forced to wait at the busy rue de Rivoli for the crossing signal, she couldn't have said. She lost sight of Tommy again but told herself she didn't care. She knew he was now in the Tuileries somewhere, but it was only as the signal came and she dashed across the road to enter by the gate that it occurred to her she had no idea what she'd say if she came face to face with him. This caused her to slow down. Polly entered the gate at a leisured pace and declared to herself that she had come to view the extensive array of statuary.

A meandering walk through the gardens revealed how many statues the Tuileries actually contained; in every direction, down every gravel path, there were more and more. She visited Theseus and the Minotaur, then the monument to Waldeck-Rousseau, and then the statue of Laocoön and his sons before it occurred to her that all these statues were male nudes. A blush came to her then that her private thoughts had been translated into a too-revealing selection of art.

Determined to view some female nudes to counter this, Polly was in the act of looking about for a figure to intrigue her when she spotted Tommy in the distance. The sun struck his hair anew as Tommy seemed mesmerised by a sculpture of a man in great anguish, pressing his face to the palm of his hand. The sight of such pain, and Tommy standing beneath it gazing upwards in deep contemplation, was very moving to Polly.

Then Tommy walked away.

Polly decided not to pursue him; it now seemed unforgivable that she had observed him in such a moment at all. She let herself lose sight of him as he went under the trees, but then felt drawn to the statue that had captivated him.

The statue was, she discovered, a representation of Cain from the Book of Genesis. The lesson of Cain had seemed as much of a tragedy for him as it was for his brother; Cain was marked by his crime, cursed to wander, unloved and alone. Polly had been the only one in her Sunday School class who had felt this. Even the teacher had mocked her for it.

When Polly looked from the statue to the plinth she saw a note.

Folded up very small, it had been squeezed into a gap in the masonry, at the point where the plinth met the ground. Polly blinked at the sight of it, innocuously placed, where it might be seen by anyone, and yet was unlikely to be seen by anyone at all.

Instinctively, she knew it had been placed there by Tommy; he'd known she had followed him and he wanted her to know. The note was for her.

Polly prised it out with her fingers, which wasn't easy because it was jammed in tight. Once removed, it was revealed as an ordinary scrap of thin notepaper, but the sight of Tommy's hand-writing – messy and rushed – seemed thrilling for being so male.

Polly smoothed the thin paper and began reading what Tommy had written to her.

Beloved Grand-mère

You mustn't worry for me, I am safe. Madame has kept her word and taken good care of me. She has been clever in how she's solved it. I do not need school, so please don't fret anymore about that; life is my school now. I promise I will learn from whatever is ahead and become as good as I can in everything. You know me, I am <u>determined</u> to do good in this world, and I will not leave it until it has become a better place. You will never be less than proud of me, I promise that too. I am listening to my grand-mère's good sense, however, and trying not to take risks. When things go bad, as we fear they will, I will take none at all – I swear it. I will leave all my messages to you here, one every week, for as long as I can. I love you very much – you and Papa. Tell Papa this.

Your grandson,

Tommy

Polly folded the letter and returned it to the gap in the stone, feeling painfully ashamed that she ever could have thought herself the recipient. Tommy led a life of his own – a complicated life, where such communications were necessary – and she had made herself privy to it through underhand means that spoke of a lapse of character. She, who had longed to do good in the world, had proven inadequate to such an ideal. It was with humiliation that Polly compared herself to Tommy, who had expressed the same longing, and yet was so better suited to actually achieving something. Tommy, Polly knew, would never have done what she had just done.

He would never have abandoned a resolve so easily either.

On her way to the French Red Cross again, Polly noticed there were many more cars speeding in the capital today. Drivers seemed to be taking great risks in turning corners, as much with themselves as with the pedestrians who leapt back from near-death moments.

Halted at a crossing, Polly looked up the Champs-Élysées towards the Arc de Triomphe in the distance when she heard the shattering impact of a car crash, followed by an unceasing horn and a great deal of shouting. She couldn't see what had happened but she knew it couldn't be good. Unnerved, she made the decision to abandon her Red Cross visit until tomorrow and walk back to the Ritz.

Heading in the reverse direction, she was struck now by the sight of people running in every which way. People were panicking. Something was happening, somewhere unseen. Polly started walking faster, infected by a fear which no one was naming.

Stepping up to a curb at the rue du Colisée, she tripped and fell, landing badly on her knee and tearing her stocking. There was blood on her skin.

People continued rushing past and no one helped her. Polly tried to get up but realised she had lost the Hermés bag. She saw it lying on the pavement just as a woman's foot kicked it into the road.

'My bag!'

She tried to get up again, but the rush of people was too great.

'Please, someone get my bag!'

A man trod on her hand. Another woman gave her shin a sharp kick. There were no apologies. No one could even see her. They were all looking up in fear. She could hear the sound of a loudspeaker nearing, horribly abrasive, but as to what was being announced she couldn't tell in her distress and embarrassment.

From among the faces blind to her difficulty, she saw the one face that was not. A shock of blond hair was scraped back from a forehead by a broad, long-fingered hand.

'Tommy!'

He was on the other side of the road. He looked scared for her.

He made to dash out into the traffic, just as a car swept around the corner from the Champs-Élysées, going too fast.

It nearly collected him. Tommy disappeared among the faces again.

The green Hermès bag had been crushed under the car's wheels.

Broad hands were at her shoulders and Tommy was suddenly above her.

'We've got to get you to your feet.'

Tommy managed to help right her again and Polly somehow stayed standing. Her knee throbbed badly. Tommy wouldn't let go of her hand.

She stared in anguish at the road. 'I lost my bag.'

He seemed to implicitly understand what it meant to her.

'Wait a moment.'

She watched with a knot in her stomach as Tommy took a moment to gauge the oncoming traffic. Then he ran out and snatched up the bag from the road, mere feet ahead of the next vehicle, before dashing back to where she was.

She took the bag from him gratefully.

'Is anything broken?' he asked, panting.

The catch had come open, but she had no intention of looking inside to examine the gun while he was there. 'Nothing important, I'm sure. Thank you, so much.'

He seemed to accept this.

'The streets are a nightmare today,' said Polly, 'what is happening?'

He didn't answer. 'We've got to get you back to the hotel.' He was scared for her still.

He helped Polly to walk. She was limping with the pain.

Several times, as they made their way back, Polly looked to her side to see Tommy's face. He was determined, his mouth set in a grim line.

In the clamour and fear, Polly felt ridiculous at being so pleased to see the front side of him. She had wanted to know what he was wearing beneath his flyer's jacket and she had been rewarded. Tommy wore a white cotton undershirt, rather tight, and not as clean as it might be, yet it was a perfectly in-keeping fashion choice.

The image of him burned into her mind, sustaining her when she wasn't casting more sideways looks at him through the tumult around them. She now felt triply ashamed that she'd ever followed him to the Tuileries.

When they neared the Place Vendôme, their progress difficult through the surging crowd, they encountered a French military vehicle to which a loudspeaker was fixed at the roof.

'The French Government has this morning left Paris for Tours. The people of the capital are advised to make all arrangements necessary in the face of a rapid enemy advance. It is expected that the forces of Hitler's Germany will enter the city within days.'

'No!' Polly stopped dead.

'Watch out, don't fall again.' Tommy held her up by the arm.

But it was too great a shock. 'There – there has been no word of this before now,' she stammered, staring at him. She felt sick with it. 'No hint of this at all. The newspapers said the war was going well.'

She remembered then what Tommy had told her in the Cambon bar of soldiers wearing carpet slippers.

'I don't think the newspapers have been telling us the truth for months,' said Tommy. 'I don't think anyone has.'

Her face had gone white. 'What will happen when they come?'

He looked at the rushing people around them. 'Panicking doesn't help anyone.'

She was struck by how calm he seemed. 'You'd already heard the announcement, hadn't you? Why didn't you tell me back there?'

She had embarrassed him. 'I didn't know what you'd do. You were already upset.'

This made her see red. 'Because I'd fallen down and hurt my knee, Tommy. I still would have appreciated being told what you knew.'

'Come on, let's cross the square.'

But she shook loose from his hand. 'I thought you were honest with me?'

Caught, he didn't know what to say.

'You say panicking never helps anyone – well, I'm *not* panicking, am I? Being cosseted and mollycoddled doesn't help a person, but I'm not doing that either – *you* are. To me.'

He tried to take her arm again. 'I have a duty to get you to safety.'

'What duty?'

'As an employee of the Ritz.'

'Oh, I see. Well, we're not in the Ritz now, and you're not even on duty. I can look after my own safety perfectly well, thank you, Tommy.'

She made to limp directly across the square to the hotel before she looked at the traffic and thought better of it, instead taking to the periphery to go the long way around.

'Wait!' he called out.

She turned and glared at him.

Tommy walked to where she stood. He lowered his voice so that only she might hear it. 'You think you're so brave walking around Paris with a gun in your purse?'

Polly gasped.

'Yes, I saw it. And if someone else sees it, they might not be so respectful of your stupidity.'

Polly held the leather tight against her chest. 'What I choose to carry in my handbag is my business.'

He tossed his head with contempt. 'You're just a silly little rich girl playing kids' games.'

She drew herself up straight. 'Tell me then, if you hadn't so manfully saved my bag from the cars, do you think you would have guessed what's inside it?'

He didn't have a reply.

She smiled with disdain. '*No*,' she answered for him. 'So, you can call me a "little rich girl" all you like, but when the Germans come, which of us will be better prepared to stop them?' She turned on her heel.

Tommy watched her go, angry now, too. 'Leave Paris!' he called after her.

Polly looked over her shoulder at him.

'*Please* leave Paris,' he implored her.

She stopped again. 'Why?'

'Because neither of us knows what they'll do.'

Each looked long into the other's eyes. Polly thought then of how he'd written to his grandmother, promising he wouldn't take risks. She felt ashamed anew for reading what he'd said. 'I'm sorry –' she called back to him, 'I don't know what's wrong with me, Tommy – I'm so sorry for what I did.'

He was still looking at her, and Polly wondered, had he actually understood what she'd meant?

Tommy turned without a further word between them and fought through the rushing crowd.

With her sprained knee now bandaged by the hotel nurse, it felt indescribably unreal to Polly to be sitting down to late luncheon at *l'Espadon*. Seated with her at the central table in the beautiful mirrored dining room were Alexandrine, Lana Mae and Zita. They were joined by two others: Mimi Ritz, who had entered the room spectacularly hatted, gloved, and para-soled, while every man in the room rose from his chair to nod at her; and a middle-aged gentleman, Doctor Paul Mandel, a respected Canadian surgeon. He was wearing a rumpled coat with his grey hair uncombed, looking sleepless and distracted, and saying little.

Mimi was leading a conversation on the *l'Espadon* cuisine that to Polly's ear seemed almost insane in the face of all that had happened. And yet, she felt stunned into silence, unable to speak of what was so obvious outside the Ritz walls.

'Oh, yes,' Mimi was saying, 'it is essential to avoid a too-rich cuisine. A meal ought to be transparent, one must not mask the ingredients.'

'Like haute couture,' said Zita, sparking another cigarette while she ate. She alternated between bites and puffs at every meal.

'Indeed,' said Mimi. 'As with a fine gown, when it is kept simple, one can see the beauty so clearly.'

'And when it's stuffed full of ruffles you can hide the horrors underneath,' said Lana Mae, through a mouthful of fish. She winked at Doctor Mandel, who didn't respond.

Polly kept trying to catch Alexandrine's eye, but the Comtesse, who was rather pale, seemed to be avoiding her looks.

Polly fell to staring at the other tables in dismay. All the luncheon regulars seemed to be there, as if nothing out of the ordinary had occurred. The eccentric Mr Wall was at his table facing the garden, dining with his chow dog, Pepe, who was wearing a canine tuxedo specially made by Charvet. Monsieur Guitry, the flamboyant playwright, was at his usual table; as was Serge Lifar, the Russian ballet star; and Monsieur Cocteau, the fashionable poet, said to dabble in drugs. The dining room's chilly sommelier, Monsieur Lefèvre, was in place, striding to the table of a gentleman who had risen in his chair, making to remove his jacket.

'But it's too warm,' the man tried to explain.

'Not *here*, Monsieur,' said Lefèvre, remaining by the man's chair until he sat down with his jacket secured again.

In the far corner there was the wife of the French industrialist who had once sent a Ritz footman to London to retrieve a forgotten key. Near another of the windows was the portly Arab gentleman who told the same anecdote about how he once requested a meal of elephant foot from the Ritz kitchen, and they duly purchased a beast from the Jardin des Plantes and served up one of its roasted feet for his delectation.

Polly snapped, slamming her knife on the table. 'We have all been played for fools!' she announced to the room, angry.

Her companions paused from eating but made no immediate response.

'Well, we *have*,' said Polly, 'For weeks we've all been taking comfort from patriotic idiocy. When the Germans invaded the Netherlands, we were told that France would hold fast should our turn come next. When the Luftwaffe bombed the Maginot Line, we were told that our safety was secure in the hands of the glorious French Army.' She looked around the table. 'Why aren't you all as furious about these lies as I am? Or as worried about what is coming next? The French Government has fled!'

'Polly,' said Alexandrine, sternly, dabbing her lips with a napkin, 'there are ways of expressing anxiety that are better favoured by persons of breeding and poise.'

This only made Polly angrier. 'You would have had me believe these terrible things would never happen,' said Polly. 'Were you just lying to me like Aunt Marjorie lied about her illness?'

She saw the sharp stab of guilt this struck in Alexandrine, Zita and Lana Mae equally.

Alexandrine met her eye at last. 'There are ways of making accusations that are better favoured by persons of breeding, too.'

But Polly could see the Comtesse was fearful and ashamed. Polly turned to Mimi. 'You told me lies, as well. Everyone did! Well, almost everyone.' She thought of Tommy and felt guilty that she'd lost her temper with him, even though he'd discovered the gun.

'That's no way to speak to Mimi, baby,' Lana Mae rebuked her.

'*Please*, Lana Mae,' Polly implored, 'I was just on the Champs-Élysées and people started panicking when they learned the government had gone. And now here we are having a lovely late luncheon as if nothing has changed.'

Mimi, seated next to Polly, placed a hand on her wrist. 'My dear girl, everything has changed and of course we are aware of it.

And if you feel I somehow misled you in my opinions upon this war, then I apologise. But remember this: nothing can change so much as to preclude us enjoying fine cuisine.'

Polly wanted to scream.

'Plans have already been made for you, puss,' said Zita. 'Eat your slops and calm down.'

'What plans? Why don't I know anything about them?' Polly demanded.

Seated on her other side, Alexandrine deliberately resumed eating.

'Alexandrine called up that old bitch Suzette,' said Zita, taking a long drag of her cigarette. 'She's meeting us at the Cambon doors with a car.'

Polly turned to the Comtesse in bewilderment. 'But who is Suzette?'

'Suzette is my husband's housekeeper,' said Alexandrine, as if it explained everything.

Polly was incredulous. 'You're *married*?'

'I am quite sure that I told you I am.' Alexandrine placed her fork on the plate. 'And Suzette is Eduarde's old retainer, wonderfully capable. Now, please stop speaking to me in that highly accusing tone, Polly. I have said I am sorry.'

Fury raged anew. 'No, you haven't. Only Mimi did, and it wasn't much of an apology at all.'

'*Puss*,' said Zita, warningly.

'But what will there be in this car?' Polly went on.

'*Us*, honey,' said Lana Mae, 'we're going on a picnic to the seaside.' She winked at Doctor Mandel again.

'To Brittany,' said Alexandrine, 'Monsieur Auzello has made reservations for us at a lovely hotel in Saint-Malo.'

Polly's hands clenched into fists. 'This is crazy – we've got to fight!'

Doctor Mandel cleared his throat. 'My dear young woman, if you would cease your interruptions for one moment you would see that your guardians have made an excellent provision for you. You're being taken to safety.'

'Just until it's all sorted out, baby,' said Lana Mae. 'No one wants to be away from things for too long.'

Polly pushed her chair back from the table and looked at each of them coldly. 'So, we're going to run like cowards?'

Doctor Mandel turned to Alexandrine. 'I see there was indeed little point informing the girl in advance of these measures.'

Alexandrine shook her head.

'She is prone to hysterics?'

'She is still so very young, Doctor,' said Alexandrine, apologetically. 'We must remember how it is at her age.'

'What disgusting hypocrisy!' Polly exploded at that. 'What happened to being treated as a *woman* at the age of sixteen?'

Alexandrine blanched. 'Polly!'

'No. I'm telling you right now that I'm not going anywhere. I'm going to *fight*. Along with everyone else who still has a shred of courage.'

The Comtesse stood and slapped Polly hard in the face. 'You'll find it very hard to fight when you're busy being raped.'

In the awful silence that followed, Polly could do nothing more than sit down again.

Mimi picked up the threads of conversation. 'Doctor Mandel has been so very helpful in his advice to me,' she told them.

'Oh yes?' said Lana Mae.

He smiled at her.

'Before we came down to luncheon I asked him whether I, along with my fellow investors, should strive to keep the hotel doors open with the Germans so likely to be imminent,' said Mimi.

Zita looked appalled. 'You mean you're thinking of closing? Christ, it's not the end of the world. So what if we have a few krauts in the lobby? They'll still want a cocktail like the rest of us, won't they?'

Mimi was reassuring. 'In business one must always be pragmatic, Zita, despite the ties of family. However, Doctor Mandel has convinced me that closing the doors would not be in our best interests.'

'Thank God for that,' said Zita.

'If Mimi closes the hotel, it will only be requisitioned by the Reich,' said Doctor Mandel.

'You mean they'll just take it?' said Lana Mae, shocked.

Mandel wrinkled his brow. 'Why wouldn't they? They'll be the victors, and the Ritz is internationally celebrated.'

'But this is horrifying!'

'You mustn't concern yourself. As an American citizen you have your neutrality, Mrs Huckstepp. Your own property will be safe – as will Madame Mimi's.'

'The dear doctor has reminded me,' Mimi told them, 'that I, along with my fellow investors, are citizens of Switzerland, and likewise neutral in this war. This means the Ritz is also neutral. The Germans will not take the Ritz from us because they cannot under international treaties. And so, we have no reason to close.'

The others at the table considered this for a moment.

'As you always tell us, Mimi,' said Alexandrine, 'nothing changes at the Ritz.'

But Mimi looked uncomfortably at her plate.

'Make no mistake, Madame Comtesse,' said Mandel, sipping from his glass of wine, 'the hotel will most certainly be *occupied* by the Germans, once they arrive.'

'Like I said before, puss,' Zita chimed in, 'so what if there's a few krauts in the lobby?' But she looked uneasy now.

'They better not be asking for the Imperial Suite,' said Lana Mae, with a look of warning to Mimi.

The Ritz owner resumed eating. 'The Germans will be accorded the same white-glove service extended to all our guests . . .'

*

Her cheek still stinging from where Alexandrine had slapped it, her bandaged knee still sore from the fall, Polly hurled random items of clothing into a suitcase, not caring to fold them, not caring how they might be ruined or crushed. She didn't care what she left behind either. None of it meant anything to her now, all of it was false. Her hatred for her guardian aunts throbbed in her head like a migraine. She'd already been sick with it, meaning her lunch had been wasted. Her eyes were red from the tears she'd shed, alone, well away from the women whose controlling two-facedness would only see them accuse her of being a child for crying.

Polly's eyes fell on Aunt Marjorie's old issue of *L'Officiel* and her useless fury found its focus in the woman who had willed everything upon her.

'I hate you for not telling me you were sick!'

She kicked the magazine.

'I hate you for leaving me with them!'

The issue flew across the floor, where Polly now stamped on it, twisting her soles so that the glossy cover ripped apart, and the lying, doe-eyed model was left as belittled and powerless as Polly felt.

Something flew out of one of the pages: a scrap of white paper, with a message in English written in Marjorie's unmistakable hand.

Polly stopped and stared.

She stooped to pick it up.

It was just a note; scrawled words meant as a personal reminder perhaps – or an affirmation of something Marjorie profoundly believed.

We are women when the world is men's. To live through their wars, we concede – and we compromise

If you do not forgive her, then the cost of being female is unbearable for all of us

Wouldn't <u>you</u> like to think you'd do anything for Polly?

Polly read and re-read what it said. When had Marjorie written this? The magazine had been new when Marjorie had purchased it on the train, which meant she could only have written the message on the train, too. Polly tried to think of when Marjorie might have done so and could only conclude it had happened while Polly had been in the powder room. Alexandrine had visited her aunt in those same short minutes. Had Marjorie written it before or after she'd come?

Whatever Polly's aunt had intended by the words, the meaning seemed hopelessly lost now. Yet was it? The words remained, untethered to context, wanting only to attach themselves where they might fit.

Concede. Compromise. Forgive.

Polly folded the piece of paper and looked again at what she had thrown into her suitcase. She took everything out and folded each item of clothing with care, mindful of what it had cost, and of the respect that should be due accordingly.

The last item she packed was Marjorie's medal box. Polly opened the case and ran her finger along the satin lining.

She knew it for certain then: her aunt had understood her all along. It was she, Polly, who owed understanding to her aunt.

The rue Cambon was more chaotic than Polly had seen it. To the metallic accompaniment of iron shutters being pulled down on shopfronts and cafés along every street, Parisians were endeavouring to leave the city by whatever means were available. It felt to Polly, stepping through the hotel's glass doors and onto the pavement to be met by a clamour that was deafening even by Paris standards, that every last citizen had chosen the rue Cambon as their escape route.

Impossibly, amidst the sea of honking, fuming, barely moving cars, the elderly and deeply wrinkled Suzette was standing by the door of an enormous black Mercedes, which she had driven all the way from the Comte's grand home near the Parc Monceau. She wore an ancient pair of driving goggles, as if the car was open to the elements. The housekeeper had mounted the vehicle halfway onto the curb, at a forty-five-degree angle, creating an additional hazard for the cars trying to squeeze past on the narrow street.

A man rolled down his car window to abuse Suzette directly for this lack of consideration. The tiny, wizened old woman answered him with an obscene hand gesture.

'Suzette, darling, you're perfectly on time,' said Alexandrine, gliding through the hotel doors to kiss the servant.

Suzette swatted her lips away. 'When have I not been? And you look like a tart, Madame. Have you gone raving mad with the rest of the city?'

Zita, at Alexandrine's heels, barked out a laugh at this least servile of greetings.

'You look no better,' Suzette told Zita in turn, 'but at least you've got the excuse for it.'

'And what's that, puss?' asked Zita.

'It's your fucking vocation.'

Zita only laughed louder. But there was anxiety in her eyes.

Alexandrine gave Zita's arm a little squeeze. 'And so then, what of the Comte?' she asked Suzette.

Suzette threw out her hands. 'Where else? At home with his nags. Said he wouldn't leave 'em to the krauts, didn't he?'

Polly could see that the hurt this caused Alexandrine was real. She covered it with a wry look to Zita. 'His thoroughbreds have always meant rather more than his wife.'

'That's not true and you know it, puss,' Zita said, gently.

'Ah, quit whining,' Suzette dismissed Alexandrine. 'He let you have the car, didn't he? And *me*.'

'Mixed blessings have always been my favourite kind, darling.'

Suzette fixed a hard eye on her. 'And what of you know who?'

'*Don't*,' said Alexandrine.

The old woman was angry. 'Madame, please –'

'*Don't*,' said Alexandrine again.

'I won't if you show some good grace about it,' Suzette pleaded.

'It's taken care of. I've done my part, it's enough,' said Alexandrine.

The old woman had tears in her eyes. '*Have* you taken care of it, Madame? Or have you just washed your hands of it?'

'I have done exactly as my husband asked. Did he ask for more?'

Suzette conceded. 'He did not.'

'Well then.'

Suzette pulled a handkerchief from her blouse and wiped her eyes with it. 'Heartless cow,' she said under her breath. 'You've got ice for feelings.'

Alexandrine ignored this.

Polly glanced to Zita, who would have had the world believe she was as in the dark about this coded conversation as Polly was.

Suzette now took in the sight of Polly. 'And who's the tarts' apprentice?'

'Suzette, this is Mademoiselle Hartford,' said Alexandrine, trying to brush the unpleasantness away.

Polly, still in shock from the rapid escalation of events, had lost her anger in the wake of discovering Marjorie's note. She was willing to leave with her guardians now, more so for knowing she had the means to defend them in the Hermès bag. She held out a hand, which Suzette glanced at suspiciously and then ignored. 'English?'

'I'm from Australia, Madame,' said Polly.

'Poor little bitch.'

Polly would have been offended ordinarily, but she caught a twinkle in the old woman's eye and guessed this abrasive manner was largely put on.

'Polly is Marjorie Tighe's niece,' Alexandrine told the servant.

Suzette's face softened. 'Ah. She was one of the good ones. I'm sorry for the loss of her, Mademoiselle,' she said to Polly, and then to the others, hardening again: 'She was better than you two tarts put together.'

Alexandrine just smiled. 'Suzette is quite a deplorable servant, as you can see, Polly. She's scaldingly rude, completely offensive, and when I first married the Comte I could not begin to understand why he employed her.'

Suzette cackled, showing smoke-blackened teeth.

'But after a while I started to draw my conclusions.'

'It's because I know where the corpses are buried,' Suzette said to Polly with a leer, tapping the side of her nose, and then to the others again: 'Get your luggage in the car. Don't you know Hitler's coming?'

'Maybe you could help us with it?' Zita suggested. There were no footmen to be seen.

'Not with my fucking back,' said Suzette. 'Do it yourself. It'll be practice for when they throw you in the prison cell.'

'They'll throw you in long before me, puss. Open the trunk at least.'

Suzette did so. Already inside the Mercedes' capacious hold was a little crate of Dom Perignon champagne, plus a wicker food hamper.

'Provisions!' cried Alexandrine. 'Darling, you always think of everything.'

'Bribes for the Boches to stop them raping me,' said Suzette, sourly. 'And you're right, I always do.'

The three of them started squeezing their cases inside, which is when they saw the other item that had been placed in the trunk. Wrapped in a quilt for protection, it had the size and shape of a painting.

Alexandrine gave a little cry. 'Suzette?'

'Yes, it's your precious Renoir. Don't turn on the waterworks.'

But Alexandrine's eyes were already wet. 'Thank you, darling.'

'It wasn't me wants thanking,' Suzette said. 'If I'd had my way, I'd have chucked it in the Seine.'

'Eduarde put it there?'

Suzette shrugged. 'Still blubbing that he never loved you?'

Alexandrine frowned and brushed a tear from her cheek. She loosened the quilt so that Polly could see. 'Look,' she said. 'It's my beautiful mother.'

Polly saw the innocent face of a ten-year-old girl, dressed in the fussy clothes of the 1880s. Her hair was a halo of golden ringlets. What little remained of Polly's ill-feeling towards Alexandrine now fell away completely. 'It's lovely,' she whispered.

Alexandrine brusquely nodded, covering the canvas with the quilt again.

'What if we can't fit our cases in?' said Zita.

'See these two titties of mine, tart?' Suzette responded, puffing out her scrawny chest. 'They're *tough*.'

'The champagne's going in the back with us then,' said Zita, flatly. Polly helped her pull out the little crate.

'You mustn't mind the crone's tone,' said Alexandrine to Polly. 'While it's heartening she's retained her ability to drive the car at her age, rather more of her faculties have fallen to dust.'

'It's true,' said Suzette, 'I shouldn't be allowed out in public. I took a piss in the back seat before you got here.'

Zita barked with laughter again.

Assaulted by the clamour of the street, Claude Auzello slipped out through the Cambon doors. 'Ladies, ladies, before you leave –'

'Claude, darling, we've already said goodbye,' said Alexandrine. 'And it was not goodbye, remember, but *adieu*.'

There was an unspoken steeliness to her manner with him now, Polly saw. It suggested yet another tacit understanding. So much was said while staying unsaid between the Ritz people. It was as if the entire hotel was constructed entirely of secrets. Would it take her a thousand and one nights to discover them all?

'But of course, it was *adieu*, dear Comtesse. You will return to the Ritz in no time,' said Claude, with his polished professionalism, 'but this has come for Mademoiselle Zita.'

There was another little envelope containing a telegram in his hand.

Zita's jaw clenched. She cast a glance at Alexandrine. 'I don't want it.'

'I'm sorry?'

'It's another one of those stupid jokes. I don't want it,' said Zita. 'Throw it in the street.'

Claude was lost. 'But Mademoiselle, that is irregular?'

'Or give it to Blanche to read. She enjoyed the rest.'

Claude was horrified.

'*Zita, please.*' Alexandrine looked severe. Yet she didn't contradict her friend. 'You heard what she said, darling,' she told Claude.

Zita snatched the envelope from his hand and tossed it high in the air and into the traffic. Polly saw it vanish under car tyres in dust.

'You've done your duty now,' said Zita. She embraced Claude, kissing him on the moustache. 'You're a good one, puss.' She kissed him again. 'I didn't get to see Odile before I had to go, so tell her she's a good one, too. And tell her I'll take her along to my next film set just as soon as we're back again and all this has died down. Then she can meet all the *lesser* stars.'

'I will. Take care, Mademoiselle.' Claude pulled the handkerchief from his pocket. He turned to Polly and at first had no words for her. Then he said, 'You are properly packed, Mademoiselle?'

Polly held his look, more confident than the gun alone could have made her feel, now that she had Aunt Marjorie's words. 'Yes, Monsieur. I have forgotten nothing.'

With a pat to her cheek, he returned inside.

Polly kept looking about her, half-hoping she might see Tommy among the hurrying pedestrians. The image of him in his tweeds and flyer's jacket stayed in her mind.

'Where's the fat American tart?' Suzette demanded.

'She's coming now,' said Alexandrine, as Lana Mae came out the glass door. 'Darling, where is your luggage?'

99

Lana Mae looked uncooperative. 'Honey, please don't blow a goddamn fuse.'

Alexandrine's temper flared. 'Don't tell me you couldn't decide what to pack?'

'You're the living end!' said Zita. 'Just throw in some rags. It's only for a week at the most.'

'That's not it, girls . . .'

Alexandrine glowered at her. 'Don't tell me you're not coming now.'

Lana Mae squirmed. *'Girls . . .'*

Suzette frowned as if her every prejudice about these women had just been confirmed.

'How could you?' Alexandrine demanded. 'The Saint-Malo arrangements have been made for all of us.'

'I know they have, baby, but the banks have all closed and I can't get any of my jewels out.'

'Screw your jewels,' said Zita.

Lana Mae eyed Zita's handbag. 'I bet you've got all yours.'

'Because I'm not the idiot who shoves them in a bank!'

'Oh girls, it's not just the jewels, there's my furs, too.'

'It's summer,' said Alexandrine, 'this is not the season for sable.'

'But I've got a whole closet of 'em hanging upstairs in my suite. Seventeen at last count. You can't make me leave those. They're like babies to me.'

There was a chilling silence from the women.

'And I've come over poorly!' Lana Mae claimed. 'I've been feeling a pain in my belly since lunch.' She indicated the spot. 'Right here – it's murder!'

Alexandrine pointed a gloved finger at her. 'This is not about you, me, the furs, the jewels, or your over-eating, Lana Mae,' she said warningly, 'this is about *Polly.*'

Lana Mae flushed with guilt. 'But you'll both be there with her . . .'

'Our ward Polly, to whom we have shamefully lied and treated with such contempt,' Alexandrine went on.

100

Zita and Lana Mae's mouths gaped, surprising Polly with their strength of reaction.

'Oh my God!' cried Zita.

'Honey, what are you *saying?*' gasped Lana Mae, mortified.

Polly watched curiously as Alexandrine paused for emphasis before answering. 'All along Polly has suspected the truth about the ineptitude of France's men in this war.'

There was a visible wave of relief from the other two women.

'Oh that,' said Zita.

'Oh that, indeed,' said Alexandrine. 'Polly is no fool. She knew she was being lied to – and she knew we were all just playing along in order to spare her our own fears. Well, look where it's left us.'

To hear this said by Alexandrine was not only vindicating but moving. Polly stepped forward, wanting only to be peacemaker now. 'It's all right,' she reassured them. 'I understand why, and I forgive you for it. You were only trying to protect me and none of that matters now.'

'It does,' said Alexandrine. Her face folded with shame. 'I hit you, darling . . .'

As one, they became aware of Coco Chanel standing a small distance from them on the rue Cambon pavement, a suitcase in her hand. The upset evaporated as Polly's three guardians instantly took a unified stance in the face of her.

'Well, hullo, puss,' said Zita, smiling with her teeth, but not with her eyes. 'Waiting for trade?'

It was plain to Polly that Coco Chanel was markedly less haughty today.

'Oh, good afternoon, ladies – yes, I'm just waiting on my car.'

'Oh yes?' said Alexandrine. 'Your lovely Rolls?'

'That's right,' said the famed designer. 'I sent my little maids to fetch the chauffeur for it earlier.' She glanced at the dainty timepiece she wore at her wrist. 'I can't think what's become of the maids or the car. It's been more than an hour now.'

'That ugly thing keeps shitty time,' said Zita of Coco's watch, 'you'll find it's two hours.'

The designer frowned.

'What'll you do if Germaine and Jeanne don't come back for you, honey?' Lana Mae wondered with false regard.

They all enjoyed the longing glance Coco gave the black Mercedes.

'I'm sure it won't come to that,' said Chanel, convincing none of them.

Alexandrine turned to Lana Mae. 'Fortunately, my husband's car is such a *roomy* vehicle,' she told her.

'And without your fat ass inside it, it'll be roomier still,' said Zita to Lana Mae, picking up on the theme.

They smiled at Coco, who smiled back with transparent expectancy.

'All the more space for us then,' said Alexandrine, 'I do like to stretch my legs.'

With that they turned their backs on the hapless designer.

'Take care then, darling,' said Alexandrine to Lana Mae, meaning it. 'I feel like killing you for it, but I know we'll cope somehow.'

'I'll stick to my suite and stay fixed to the phone,' said Lana Mae, relieved. 'Don't worry, girls, I won't try to fraternise or do anything stupid. I'll take every meal in my bed.'

'I thought your guts ached?' said Zita.

'I've got a bottle of pink bismuth for that.'

'Don't knock yourself out,' said Zita, kissing her. 'We'll be back in a week.'

'You bet your patootie you will,' said Lana Mae, 'I'll keep you clued up on the krauts and let off a flare when we've got the all clear.'

Lana Mae turned to Polly. 'I know you're mad at me.'

But Polly wasn't. 'You're neutral, Lana Mae, just like the Ritz. I think it's a jolly good idea you stay behind. We need a spy in our camp.'

'See?' said Lana Mae to Alexandrine, triumphantly, before hugging Polly. 'The kid understands. I'm doing what Marjorie asked for *and* I'm looking out for my furs.' She fished inside her handbag. 'Here, baby, I want you to have this.'

She removed a jar of face cream.

'Cosmetics?' said Zita, incredulous. 'You shouldn't give those up too lightly, you need all the help you can get.'

Lana Mae gave Polly the most meaningful look in her repertoire. 'For a rainy day, baby.' She winked.

Polly was surprised. She already had face cream of her own and had packed it. 'Thank you, Lana Mae,' she said all the same.

'Can you fucking tarts get your twats in the car?' said Suzette, well sick of standing there. And then to Polly she said: 'I don't mean you, Mademoiselle, you're not a tart. I'd call your late aunt a saint if I believed in them, which I don't, being a Jew, so let's just say she was one in a million.' She pinched Polly's cheek. 'I'll get you out of here safe. I owe it to her.'

The foul-mouthed, aged housekeeper took her driver's seat on the edge of a pile of cushions so that she could both reach the pedals with her feet and see past the hood of the car. As she steered the massive black Mercedes down the rue Cambon towards the rue de Rivoli, and from there to the first road that would lead them out of the capital, Polly spotted Tommy in the street. His hair was unmissable.

He was still in his flying jacket and tweeds, now accompanied by Blanche Auzello.

They were walking very closely together in the direction of the Ritz, their heads bowed in conversation. They looked troubled, serious. Just as the car passed them, for the second that Polly could see them both clearly, Blanche reached out and took Tommy's broad hand.

Polly had wanted to call out, or at least wave goodbye, or do something, anything to show Tommy that she'd seen him and was sorry that they'd quarrelled. Yet the unexpected intimacy between Hungarian nephew and American aunt stopped the words in her throat.

They disappeared.

Turning back inside the car, Polly realised that Alexandrine had been looking at Tommy just as intently. When she saw Polly had noticed this, she covered. 'Was that Blanche Auzello in the street?' she wondered. She had kicked off her high heels and was duly stretching her legs in honour of the despised Chanel.

'Where?' said Zita, who had opened one of the bottles of Dom Perignon.

'We've passed her now,' said Alexandrine.

'Poor old drunk,' said Zita with affection, sipping the champagne.

Alexandrine saw that Polly was watching her closely. 'She had that barman with her, the very blond one.'

There was the sliver of a pause before Zita responded. 'The one who looks like a kraut?' The line felt unnatural.

Polly couldn't help herself. 'He's Hungarian, sort of,' she clarified. Then, unable to help herself further, she added: 'His name is Tommy Harsanyi. He's seventeen, practically the same age as me.'

Zita apparently processed this. Alexandrine was very still. Then Zita asked Polly, 'Friends, are we?'

Polly's relief was indescribable at managing not to blush. 'I'm friends with all the nice staff,' she said, 'I'm friends with Blanche, too.' She gave Zita a supercilious look. 'You tease her that she's a drunk, but I've never seen her drink any more than you do.'

Zita gave a look of such supreme superciliousness it put Polly in the shade. 'What is *Tommy* to Blanche Auzello?'

'What do you mean? He's her nephew – she's his American aunt.'

'Oh, *puss*,' said Zita, falling back in the seat.

Polly was dismayed.

'She is not his aunt,' said Zita.

Alexandrine didn't move – and Zita didn't look at her. 'Take it from me,' she went on, 'I've loved Blanche since the old days when she hung around film sets giving stagehands the pox. That blond young man who is sort of Hungarian is her *lover*. She's notorious for her cradle-snatching. When Auzello wakes up to it, she'll be out on her fanny.'

This was a shock to Polly. Yet Alexandrine almost seemed to relax. Polly deciphered what she imagined was the truth: Zita believed the gossip, Alexandrine did not. Polly quietly decided then that she didn't believe it either. She looked to Suzette, perched on her cushions in the front.

The old woman had heard everything, of course. Her grim mouth was twisted with the words she, too, was stopping herself from saying.

5

11 June 1940

The dreadful scenes made Polly think of what it must have been like to have lived ignorantly, if uneasily, in ancient Pompeii. Having somehow got used to the threat from Vesuvius, each Pompeiian must have reached a point in those final days when the rumblings became unbearable, and then terrifying, which is when they finally fled. The unknown hazards of the open road would have seemed preferable to the horrors of staying at home. Each person on the narrow, poplar-lined road that Polly and her companions now found themselves travelling on, deep in the French countryside on such a clear-skied, warm summer's day, had fled in terror of a different kind of Vesuvius. Instead of lava and pumice stone, they were running from Germans.

Most of those fleeing were women, children and the elderly. The men were in the army. Schools had been closed and exams had been postponed. Polly had observed that it wasn't just French refugees congesting the roads but desperate families from as far afield as Belgium and Holland. Some of those who fled used private cars. Others had taken to bicycles, or simply walked, sometimes pushing wheelbarrows or prams in front of them, cradling aged relatives as if they were babies.

Polly and her guardians were luckier than many. They had a car. And thanks to Suzette's considerable foresight, they also had spare gasoline. Unlike so many of the other vehicles with which they shared this nightmare journey, however, they did not have a mattress roped to the roof.

'Perhaps we should try to find one from somewhere?' Alexandrine was saying.

'From where?' said Zita.

Alexandrine looked out the window on her side. 'Perhaps from a farmhouse?'

'We're not stopping,' said Suzette, perched on her cushions in the driver's seat.

'But people seem to think they're essential.' Alexandrine looked hopefully at the mattress tied to the roof of the car in front of them. 'Perhaps we could offer to buy that one?'

'Sleep sitting up if you're so fucking weary,' said Suzette, 'although how you might be wearier than me I don't know, Madame.' She flexed and cracked her swollen knuckles at the steering wheel.

Polly stirred from a doze. 'They're not for sleeping on,' she said, yawning, 'although that would be rather nice.' The pace of advancement was so slow that the Mercedes was travelling no faster than those walking, and she had heard the mattresses explained by someone alongside the car window.

'What else is a mattress for then?' said Zita.

Suzette was droll. 'That such a question should come from *your* lips. What sort of prostitute are you?'

'Shut up, you old prune.'

'They're for protection from the bombs,' said Polly.

This silenced them.

After a while, Zita said, 'I don't know if a mattress would do much good if it comes to that then . . .'

Polly didn't think one would either and they let the subject of mattresses drop.

Thanks to the forced confines of the journey, Polly had become privy to some marvellous details of her guardians' lives.

'Tell me the story again,' Polly said, prodding Alexandrine.

The Comtesse groaned.

'Go on. I love hearing it,' Polly pressed. Of the guardian aunts, it was Alexandrine who came from the most 'establishment' of circumstances, Polly had discovered. 'You were born Alexandrine de Pelletier,' she started her off, 'the only daughter of Catholic aristocrats from the Burgundy region.'

Alexandrine fluttered her eyes to Zita, making a panto-mime of indulging Polly in such inquisition, even though she enjoyed it.

'Your ancestors include a mistress of Louis XIV, a cardinal, and a general who served Napoleon,' Polly went on. 'And your beautiful mother, when still a ringleted girl, was the subject of the celebrated portrait by Renoir.'

'Should have tossed it in the Seine . . .' Suzette muttered from the driver's seat.

'Hush, you,' said Zita, who was happy to share tales.

'And you fell in love at fourteen,' said Polly. 'Tell me about that again.'

'I thought I'd spoken of it rather expansively as it is.'

'I want to hear it all again. I love the way you tell it.'

'As you wish,' Alexandrine acquiesced. She shifted her position in the big back seat and began. 'His name was Philippe, the sweet-faced second son of a Burgundian Vicomte. He came with no title, but he would have made a kind husband.'

'And why didn't your families encourage the match? You were of the same class.'

'Her family were broke!' Zita cackled. 'Happens to the very best of 'em, puss. That's how they get to be the worst.'

'My prospects were constrained,' said Alexandrine, with dignity.

'And what happened when you turned sixteen?' Polly asked. 'My age?'

'With her poor heart broken by what could never be with the Vicomte's boy, Alexandrine was "sold" into a profitable marriage, weren't you, puss?' teased Zita. 'Profitable for the de Pelletiers.'

'Who was your "buyer"?' Polly prompted Alexandrine.

'Unexpectedly perhaps,' said Alexandrine, 'he was no Bluebeard, darling. And Eduarde *was* the heir to a title – his late father was then still the Comte Ducru-Batailley – and with this came an absolutely splendid fortune.'

'Was he nice looking?' Polly wondered.

Alexandrine seemed to let the image of Eduarde fill her mind. 'He was darkly handsome, yes, and very dashing, too. He was – and still is – an exceptional equestrian.'

'You should see him riding on his steed,' said Zita. 'Make a girl's heart flutter.' She sighed. 'But then he was also a Jew.'

Suzette pressed her fist to the car horn for no apparent reason.

'You say that like it's something awkward,' said Polly to Zita, as they blocked their ears.

Zita regarded her dryly. 'Don't be naïve, puss.'

'I am naïve,' said Polly, 'as you like to remind me.'

Zita looked at Alexandrine to furnish the details.

The Comtesse inspected her nails. 'My husband's family are Jewish in the way that the Rothschilds are Jewish – or the Ephrussi family. Or the Camondos.'

'You mean – famous?' Polly wondered, slightly at sea.

'Famous for being *rich*, maybe,' said Zita.

'The Ducru-Batailley family's Jewish faith was something from a century ago,' said Alexandrine, 'when they'd been given their title by King Louis Philippe.'

'*Bought* their title, don't you mean?' said Zita.

Alexandrine gave her a chilly look. 'You were there were you, darling?'

Zita laughed. 'The Jewish thing's as good as forgotten now, puss, stop banging on about it.' She looked at her own nails. 'Practically forgotten, anyway.'

'I didn't know Catholics could marry Jews?' Polly asked Alexandrine.

Alexandrine made light of this. 'I was expected to convert to Judaism first, darling.'

'Which you did?'

She was vague. 'In that regard, rather more effective than the boring old rabbi were the jewels and the haute couture that accompanied the process. All those Hebrew words he muttered at the Synagogue de la Victoire were quite meaningless to me, darling, and very soon forgotten, I promise you.' She looked at Zita. 'I certainly never went inside there again.'

Zita shrugged.

Yet Polly was left with the distinct impression she'd been privy to a face-saving line that Alexandrine had used before. Was it easier, she wondered, for Alexandrine to let others believe the conversion meant nothing, than let them discover that the opposite might be true?

'Did you love Eduarde?' Polly asked.

'Darling, your questions!'

'I'm sorry, was that rude?'

'No, it wasn't, puss,' said Zita.

Alexandrine gave Zita a narrow look but answered Polly. 'I did love him. It wasn't very difficult.'

'Did Eduarde love you?'

Zita chuckled. 'You're learning all the right stuff to ask fast.'

'I'm sorry, was that rude, too?'

'No,' said Alexandrine, 'it was very sensible. Of course, that is the very question you would want to know, and the answer is: he *said* that he loved me. Passionately.' She touched the back of her hair. 'But then he also said that to his mistress.'

Polly was somewhat shocked.

'Ah,' said Zita, appreciating this reaction. 'Now she's getting the full picture.'

Alexandrine gave Polly a teacherly smile. 'Men are intemperate creatures, darling. The sooner you emulate them in all that you do – just as *we* have – then the happier you become in your independence.' She looked at Zita. 'What a good lesson for today.'

Polly thought of her own resolve to stay above male disregard. 'Are you saying you have no need for men?'

'No one's saying *that*,' said Zita. 'But what Alexandrine is saying, well, it'll make more sense to you in good time, puss.'

Polly found that it was making sense already.

'Let me summarise everything else that you need to know about my husband and I,' said Alexandrine, bringing this part of the conversation to an end. 'He was compulsively promiscuous, a shameless womaniser who freely admitted as much when I asked him. And I wished I hadn't asked him. By the time I knew the extent of his unfaithfulness I was pregnant – and taking far too many pills to get to sleep at night because of him.'

'You have a child?' Polly asked. 'I didn't know.'

Alexandrine shook her head, and Polly saw then a glimpse of a desperate pain the Comtesse carried. She was mortified. 'I'm so sorry, Alexandrine – I've been very insensitive.'

'I gave birth to a daughter,' Alexandrine said simply. 'Louise. She was severely disabled.'

It was Polly who found her eyes welling now.

'She survived two days,' said Alexandrine. 'By then our marriage was dead. My husband knew that I blamed him entirely for the tragedy.'

'Oh, Alexandrine, I'm so sad to hear that,' said Polly.

The Comtesse elegantly rearranged herself in the seat again. 'Don't be, darling, it happened so long ago, and while I would give the whole earth to have my little daughter with me again, in so many ways what happened proved the making of me. My marriage was dead, yes, but Eduarde and I did *not* divorce.

That wouldn't have suited either of us. We are French, after all, and born of the upper-class, and thus we are exceedingly civilized. What my husband and I have now, if not conventionally a marriage as others might think of it, is something that those in our circles infinitely prefer: we have an *arrangement*.' Alexandrine gave Polly a secretive wink. 'And I recommend it highly, darling.'

Polly fell into contemplative silence again.

It seemed that none of the thousands of refugees along the road really knew where they were going. South or west seemed to be the general direction, in preference to north, which is where the Germans were known to be advancing from. Polly's group were ostensibly headed to Saint-Malo, but the road they were on, which went west to Dreux, was simply where they had found themselves as they were swept along with the multitude.

What other women had chosen to wear for the flight from the capital had been much commented upon by those in Polly's group. Some women, it was noted, given the summer heat, had daringly put on shorts, perhaps in the belief they would not be on the road for long. Others, thinking longer term, had ignored the hot weather entirely and had chosen to wear a large portion of their wardrobes upon their backs. They were dressed in layers of clothes: winter coats over spring jackets; blouses over shirts, dresses over skirts; bizarre ensembles topped off with scarves, gloves and hats. Polly's companions admired this practical attitude.

'See, Polly,' Alexandrine said, 'the dress codes for women of fashion must never be ignored, even if the wearer becomes itinerant. Parisienne elegance must always be maintained, regardless of cost. These women are *prepared*.'

Polly thought it was madness but didn't say as much.

Zita had identified a recurring style she christened 'refugee chic'. This involved the teaming of a shirt with narrow trousers and as much make-up as if heading for an evening at the opera.

One fashionable woman travelling on foot had tapped at the window of their Mercedes and asked if she could take a cupful of their gasoline to use as nail varnish remover. The colour of the hat she'd snatched from her boudoir when she'd fled didn't match the colour of her nails. Alexandrine gave her a cupful of their precious spare fuel without even a moment's hesitation.

There was a line of trudging people on either side of the road. Ancient old ladies, more wrinkled and withered than Suzette, lay sprawled on the roadside, exhausted and unable to go on, lying next to families who were taking advantage of the sunshine to bring out picnics. Mothers breastfed in the ditch. Flirty girls in heels somehow found the energy to dance, catching the attention, and then a ride, with dubious men in a truck, who tossed cigarettes at an old man who scrabbled on the road to retrieve them.

When Polly stirred from her doze again, she saw the others had their attention caught by something outside, beyond the windscreen. The long, poplar-lined road stretched before them, rolling down a hill towards distant Dreux. The line of cars, trucks and walking refugees stretched the full distance, disappearing into the summer haze. From that same haze came something travelling in the opposite direction, headed to where the Comte's big, black Mercedes moved little faster than a crawl.

'My God, what is that?' said Alexandrine.

The object wasn't travelling along the road but flying not very far above it.

'It's a plane,' said Zita.

'Is it one of ours?'

None of them could tell.

'It's getting closer,' said Alexandrine.

'Why is it flying like that?' said Polly. 'It's down too low.'

The crowd around them rippled as if rocks had been cast in their pond. From the distance came the unmistakable sound of machine-gun fire.

'It's shooting!' Zita cried out. 'It's shooting at the people on the road!'

Those on foot began to scream, abandoning prams and wheelbarrows. Some began diving into the ditches; others broke from the road and ran into the wheat fields.

'It's killing people – we've got to get out of the car!' shouted Zita.

'I'm not going anywhere,' said Alexandrine.

'We're sitting ducks in this big ugly thing!'

'They won't shoot *us*,' said Suzette, eyes fixed on the approaching plane.

'Of course, they will, they're shooting everything else. Look!'

'That's why I took the Mercedes,' said Suzette, tapping her nose. 'It's a kraut car. They won't harm one of their own.'

'You crazy old bitch, as if that'll matter to them!'

'I'm staying put,' said Suzette. She looked to Alexandrine. 'Just like Madame.'

'Puss, *please*,' said Zita to the Comtesse.

'I refuse to abandon my dignity by running into a ditch,' said Alexandrine. 'I refuse to abandon my dignity by running at all.'

'This is insane!'

Polly felt trapped between Alexandrine's elegant refusal and Zita's angry panic. 'What should I do?'

'You're coming with me.' Zita grabbed her by the arm.

'Ow, you're hurting me!'

'Bullets hurt more.' She sprang the handle and kicked the door open, pulling Polly outside with her.

'My handbag!' Polly managed to grab the Hermès purse. On the road, the roar of the approaching plane's engine was near deafening, as were the screams of those still trying to find cover and safety.

'You crazy cows!' Zita shouted into the car. 'Get out and save yourselves!'

But Alexandrine was unmoving. In the driver's seat, Suzette placed an unlit cigarette at her lips.

'Any last words?' the old servant asked Zita, with a wink.

'Quick – run for God's sake!' Zita cried to Polly, pushing her forward.

'Where?'

'The ditch – there's nowhere else to go.'

They fled towards the roadside, where a shallow trench was already choked with others trying to save themselves.

'There's no more room!' someone yelled at them.

'Screw you!' Zita yelled back. She forced herself among them, making way for Polly to squeeze in beside her. The ditch was no cover at all. They were completely exposed.

'They're not gonna shoot you, they're *not*,' Zita swore, hugging Polly tight against her. She tried to cover Polly's head with her thin arms, but Polly could still see everything. She'd lost hold of her handbag again in the rush. It had fallen open onto the road, some of the contents strewn about. She saw the little jar of face cream Lana Mae had given her, standing on its lid, unbroken. Amazingly, Marjorie's gun was still inside the bag. Polly looked sideways at Zita and saw that her guardian's eyes were on the sky. Polly tried to reach out and grab the green leather.

'What are you doing?' cried Zita, pulling back her hand.

The plane was so close they could make out the markings on the wings: square black crosses edged in white. It was a German Messerschmitt.

The bullets seemed to hit the ground before Polly even heard them, or at least that was how it seemed as she shrank into the weeds, as hopelessly vulnerable as everyone else. The screams of the refugees became one with the plane's shrieking engines, before all sound melted away entirely. Polly could hear nothing at all, she could only see. Abandoned prams and makeshift carts began to lurch and jump about as if someone was still there controlling them. Then they began to disintegrate. Car tyres popped, windows shattered. A man who had carried nothing but a mattress with him all the way from Versailles had taken cover beneath it in the middle of the road. The bullets ran up the length of the cushioning in eruptions of wool and springs. A spray of blood shot out from the blue striped ticking.

Polly could see directly into the Mercedes: Suzette still in the front, Alexandrine in the spacious rear. The Comtesse leant forward to rest on the old woman's shoulder. Suzette placed her hand on Alexandrine's own. They were tenderly saying something to each other that no one else would ever know.

The snaking trail of bullets smashed the Mercedes' windscreen into shards that exploded glittering all over the road. The hood punctured, emitting steam in geysers as liquids gushed from underneath. Projectiles tore up the sleek, black roof. There was blinding dust everywhere and Polly began to splutter. She went from seeing everything to seeing nothing at all.

She couldn't tell whether she was about to live or die.

When Polly found herself able to make out her surroundings again, the plane had passed overhead, continuing its rain of destruction upon the hundreds more who filled up the road behind them. And then it was gone.

Zita was no longer there.

Polly wasn't in any pain. She sat up in the ditch and saw her handbag with the jar of Lana Mae's face cream. She was just putting it inside her bag again when she remembered what had happened to the Mercedes. She leapt out, screaming Alexandrine's name. She made no sound and neither did anything else. Polly realised she'd lost her hearing. At the shot-up car, Zita was pulling the rear door open.

Inside, the spot where Polly had been sitting was ripped into shreds. Stuffing had burst from the seat obscenely. Two bullets had passed cleanly through a book she had brought with her. From inside, the roof of the car looked like an upturned colander. Alexandrine, impossibly, was quite unscathed, apart from the dust that caked her entire body. She showed Zita the bottle of Dom Perignon she'd been about to open before the plane came along. It was open now. The cork had been shot off.

In the front seat, just as impossibly, Suzette was unhurt. The old woman took a deep drag of her cigarette.

Polly saw Zita mouthing the words: 'Are you all right, puss?' just as her hearing came back to her.

'Depends what you call all right,' said Suzette, sniffing the air. 'I reckon Madame's gone and messed herself.'

The old woman went to get out of the car, which was when she looked at her other hand. Two of her fingers were gone.

Polly found herself feeling dizzy then and lost her balance and hit the ground, vomiting, just as Suzette did the same.

6

14 June 1940

Clutching to her entitlement as a means of suppressing her guilt, Lana Mae threw open the doors of her Imperial Suite and stuck her henna-red head into the hallway. 'Help me! Is anyone there? Help me!' Her voice echoed down the corridor, bouncing off the ceiling and walls. She waited, panting, for several seconds. The Ritz was so silent she could hear the roof creak. 'Help me!' she called out again.

It wasn't quite seven o'clock in the morning and yet incredibly, *impossibly*, there was not one person to answer her.

'This is not acceptable!' Lana Mae screamed into the nothingness, feeling the panic in her throat rising now. 'This is not what I pay good American cash for!'

She flew back into the suite, leaving the doors open, passing the first salon and re-entering the second, where for the past five minutes she'd been trying to raise someone – *anyone* – on the internal telephone. She picked up the receiver again, striking the cradle over and over with her fingers as if that would somehow solve everything.

'Hello? Hello! Are you there? I need help!'

Just as she was thinking of throwing the phone at the window someone answered at the other end.

'This is the Vendôme lobby.'

'Monsieur Auzello!'

'Ah, Mrs Huckstepp.'

'Where is everyone? I've been screaming for hours! I need help up here. Right now!'

'You must forgive me, dear Mrs Huckstepp, but we are presently unable to assist you.'

'What!' Lana Mae couldn't believe such words could ever come down a telephone receiver at the Ritz.

'It is regrettable, but true,' said Auzello from the lobby. 'Our hands are full.'

'Have you lost your Frenchy mind?'

'I'm sure Mrs Huckstepp is quite correct,' said Auzello. 'Will that be all?'

'No, that will not be all!' Lana Mae roared down the phone. 'Where's that goddamn Mimi? Is she down there, too? Put her on the line, Auzello, I wanna remind her just how much I pay for this highfalutin set of rooms.'

'Madame Ritz is right by my side, but as I said, our hands are full.'

'And why the hell aren't they full of *me?*'

'Because new guests are about to arrive.'

Lana Mae felt an arctic chill. She flicked the muslin curtain at the window and peered out onto the Place Vendôme. What she saw made last night's dinner repeat itself at the back of her throat. With an effort she fought back the urge to be sick. 'I – I can see *Germans* in the square,' she rasped into the receiver.

'Then you have the full picture,' said Auzello. He hung up.

Lana Mae started to shake. 'This is what I deserve for letting the girls go without me,' she berated herself, 'for letting Polly go, like I didn't give a damn . . .' She appealed to the ceiling. 'Can you forgive me for it, Marjorie?' The nausea became a stomach twinge. She fumbled for the bottle of pink bismuth she kept in her purse.

'Can I help you, Madame?'

Lana Mae spun around with a mouthful of bismuth, spluttering a scream.

The tall, lean, impossibly young, impossibly blond assistant barman had come into the room. It took her a moment to place him – and remember what it was about him that she, along with Zita, had been sworn not to tell anyone. Secret-keeping was second nature to her. 'I know you, don't I?' Lana Mae pointed at him, wiping the pink from her mouth.

'You look upset,' Tommy said gently, with a smile of concern, holding her stare with his soft brown eyes. 'How can I help you, Madame?'

Lana Mae felt herself slipping again. 'Oh God, I let Polly go . . .'

He raised an eyebrow, recognising the name.

'How could I? How the hell *could* I?' Lana Mae wailed.

Tommy took her gently by the hand, not caring for guest protocol. Lana Mae quieted almost at once, struck dumb by the surprise of feeling her skin enclosed within his. He felt warm. Clean. He led her to a chair, looking through the door to the master bedroom as he did so. A huge rosewood armoire was out of place, showing evidence of having been dragged along the carpet.

He helped her sit down.

'I think I want to kiss you, kid,' she muttered, dazed.

'Madame?'

Lana Mae flushed. 'What the hell's wrong with me?' She started crying again. 'Oh Jesus, they're *here*.'

'The Germans?'

Lana Mae's face was full of fear. 'They're outside in the square. Dozens of them. Just standing around their motorbikes taking photographs.'

Tommy nodded. He'd already seen them.

'What the hell will they do?'

Tommy didn't know. He indicated the master suite. 'Were you trying to move the furniture, Madame?'

She remembered then. 'Oh, yes, oh God – there might still be enough time – will you help me, kid?' She shot up from the chair, pulling him across the salon's carpeted floor into her bedroom.

The doors to the built-in robe were wide open.

'*My furs,*' said Lana Mae. 'All seventeen. I can't let 'em fall into Fritz hands, I *can't.*' She indicated the armoire. 'You see. I was trying –'

Tommy did see. 'You thought if you moved it in front of the built-in robe?'

'Yes! Maybe it'd hide 'em? Make it look like there's no built-in at all? What do you think, kid? Good idea?'

'A very good idea, Madame. I helped Mademoiselle Chanel do the same thing.'

Lana Mae frowned. 'Oh, you did, did you?'

'Your furs are much nicer, Madame.'

She smiled. 'Once I've hidden 'em safe, maybe I could get away from here somehow – follow the girls to Saint-Malo, make it up to 'em.'

'Are the furs all you wish to hide?'

Lana Mae looked around the scattered contents of the room. 'Oh God. I don't know. I mean, I've gotta leave myself something to wear . . .'

He pointed at the bed. 'Will you wear that?'

A huge French flag, big enough to unfurl from the Imperial Suite's windows, had been balled up in Lana Mae's frenzy.

'Oh hell – I must be crazy!' She snatched it up and was about to toss it inside the built-in before she teetered on the edge of breaking down again. 'I love this flag – I love France. Is this the end of it all, kid?'

He gently took the flag from her hands and kissed it, before placing it on the floor of the built-in. 'France is eternal, Madame,' he told her, simply.

Lana Mae blinked back the tears in her eyes.

Tommy got behind the armoire and began to push. 'This will take two of us.'

She joined him in the effort. Positioned next to him, straining to shove the huge piece of furniture in front of the built-in doors, it seemed to Lana Mae that the nice young man, impossibly blond, was also very comfortable in the company of a sophisticated older woman.

She was actually sorry when they got the armoire in place.

Mimi endured an apprehension so overwhelming that all she could think of was the cognac bottle. It was not even 7 am and here she was, shaking so badly her jewellery rattled, until Claude made her sit down. All she wanted was one little nip to calm her. She loathed herself for such disgraceful weakness; she was surely no better that Claude's wife, Blanche. Yet still all she wanted was cognac.

She tried to focus on the crisis at hand. 'What are they doing out there now?'

Auzello was near the glass front doors, peering into the square. 'The same, Madame. Taking photographs of Napoleon's column. They are posing in front of it.' He looked to Mimi over his shoulder. 'Apart from the Germans the square is empty. No other people or traffic at all. I've never seen it like this . . .'

They had both been awake since well before dawn, when, with those who remained of the staff, they had listened to a radio broadcast announcing the fall of Paris. They had clutched each other and wept. The sky on the horizon had been lit by artillery fire. The streets outside, unnaturally silent, had gradually filled with the sounds of the first of the German motorcycle patrols entering the city, followed by the rhythmic feet of soldiers marching in formation. Then had come loudspeakers, demanding in French that citizens surrender all private arms.

Mimi made to get up again but Auzello was onto her. 'Please do not rise, Madame, you are not looking well.'

'I am perfectly all right.' She struggled to her feet, only to feel weak at the knees.

'Madame!'

She fell back in the chair.

'Oh, Madame.' He took her hand. It was hot and damp.

'Please, Claude,' she whispered, 'perhaps a little cognac?'

He went to ring for service until he remembered there likely wouldn't be any. Easily half the staff had fled the city in recent days, along with many of the guests. The Ritz had been left with a skeleton crew of rusted-on retainers and long-term guests already marked for their obstinacy, self-delusion or bad luck. And then there was himself, Mimi, and Blanche and Odile, who together wouldn't be leaving the Hôtel Ritz even if Hitler's bombs were dropping on top of it. Mercifully, it hadn't come to that yet.

Just as his mind wandered to Blanche, out for the count upstairs in their bed, the boy with the shock of blond hair appeared on the stairs. Her 'nephew'.

'Tommy?'

'Monsieur Auzello?'

'You're still here?'

'Where else should I be, Monsieur?'

Claude felt an onset of emotion at the simplicity of such an outlook. He pulled himself together. 'But of course. Madame Ritz is feeling faint. Will you bring a cognac bottle and glass from the Petit bar?'

Tommy saw Mimi, weak in the chair. The grand old woman looked tiny, exhausted. 'Of course, Monsieur.'

'Wait – the key.' Claude fumbled at his waistcoat pockets. He couldn't find what he sought. 'It's at the desk.' He went to look in the drawers.

'Claude . . .' Mimi croaked.

'In a moment, Madame.'

'Claude,' she repeated.

'I will find it.'

'Claude, *please* –'

He looked up. Two German officers were entering the lobby from the square. They loomed like giants, as tall as the doors, densely muscled and unexpectedly tanned, as if part-way through a summer holiday; a duo of fair-haired, blue-eyed Teutonic tourists in Wehrmacht steel grey. The younger of the two had a camera hanging from a strap around his neck.

The older man needed no camera; he was committing it all to memory. He looked about him as if the act of stepping inside the Ritz had a near-religious significance to him. 'Like returning to the womb . . .' he muttered reverently in German.

Claude guessed the older German had visited before; he was not making memories, so much as refreshing them. Yet he still had the manner of a stranger – or of one of those pathetic unfortunates who had looked through the doors without ever gaining the courage to enter. He almost pitied him.

Despite it, decades of experience delicately dealing with guests of every imaginable temperament and persuasion asserted itself. '*Bonjour* Messieurs, welcome to the Hôtel Ritz.' Claude beamed, his arms expansive in his usual gesture of greeting, 'And how might we help you on this exquisite summer morning?' It was only when he'd finished these words that he realised he'd spoken to them in French.

The older of the two men replied, also in French. '*Bonjour* Monsieur. It is indeed a magnificent day. And in reply to your offer of help perhaps you might answer me this: how should we treat the inhabitants of a city that have not lifted a finger against us?'

The senior officer then burst into a peal of laughter that was loud and deep and immediately echoed by the younger German standing next to him. They ceased laughing and stood smiling at Claude, disarmingly open-faced and happy. This question was, Claude realised, a German attempt at a joke, and yet an answer was still expected from him. 'You must treat them with equal goodwill, I have no doubt, Monsieur,' Claude replied.

The senior German held out his huge hand, pleased. 'I am Oberstleutnant Hans Metzingen.'

Claude went to respond as he would ordinarily, until an impulse held him back. His own hand wouldn't move. He froze on the spot, mortified, knowing how offensive this must be to the German, yet he simply could not shake the hand of the invader.

The younger German flinched, then frowned, his eyes on Auzello's fist where it stayed still at his trouser seam.

Oberstleutnant Metzingen saw Claude's problem for what it was. The hand with which he had intended to shake Claude's own now went smoothly upwards, ending in a Nazi salute. 'Heil Hitler!'

'Heil Hitler!' the younger German echoed, doing the same.

'I appreciate your apprehension, mein Herr,' said the Oberstleutnant to Claude. 'I would no doubt feel the same, were I in your shoes.'

'Monsieur . . .' Claude tried to explain.

Metzingen stopped him. 'Please, there is no need. The truth is, I am not in your shoes. Instead I am the barbarian who is at your gilded gate.'

'Mein Herr . . .' Claude started again.

'Herr Oberstleutnant, I am Madame Marie-Louise Ritz.'

Claude glanced to his side. Mimi had risen from her chair, perfectly calm and poised.

'Frau Ritz, it is an honour,' said Metzingen, bowing to her with a click of his heels.

Mimi did not offer her hand either. 'I am the owner of this hotel.'

'Indeed, I am well aware, meine Dame.'

'And I am Monsieur Claude Auzello,' Claude said, finally, buoyed by Mimi. 'I am the General Manager of the Hôtel Ritz.'

'And of that I am well aware, too, meinen Herr.' Metzingen indicated a manila folder the younger German carried under his arm. 'We have made extensive notes on all the key positions here . . .'

Claude froze at the sight of the file – and yet he was not surprised. He had suspected for months that someone he trusted – someone unknown – had been betraying the Ritz by stealing and copying confidential information. He allowed himself to show no trace of this to the Germans. 'Then perhaps if Herr Oberstleutnant wants nothing more than his question answered?'

'I'm afraid I want far more than that,' Metzingen smiled, good-naturedly. He nodded at the younger German. 'This is Hauptmann Günther Jürgen,' he said. 'We are here to oversee all operations.'

Jürgen clicked his heels.

'In Paris?' Claude asked.

'In the *Ritz*,' said Metzingen. He gestured about him. 'This hotel occupies a supreme position among all the Paris hotels to be requisitioned by the Reich.'

Mimi went pale. '*Requisitioned*, Herr Oberstleutnant? The Hôtel Ritz is to be taken from us after all?'

Metzingen cast a look to Jürgen in embarrassment. 'I must apologise, meine Dame. My command of the French language is not as it was during the last war.'

Jürgen shook his head. 'I disagree. It is exceptional, Herr Oberstleutnant.'

'No, no,' said Metzingen, self-effacingly. He looked to Mimi again. 'The word I meant was "occupy" – the Hôtel Ritz will be *occupied* by us.'

'I see,' said Mimi.

'Only by the very highest-ranking officers of the Reich, you understand.' He looked appreciatively around him at all the elements that comprised the Vendôme lobby décor. 'There is no hotel more sumptuous and yet so *discreet* in Paris,' he said. 'Such exquisite taste, such – to use your good French word – *chic*, Frau Ritz.' He turned to the Hauptmann. 'You agree, Jürgen?'

'Of course, Herr Oberstleutnant,' said the younger man, 'the Hôtel Ritz is quite peerless. There is no other hotel like it.'

'No other,' said Metzingen. 'Even in Berlin.'

Mimi hesitated. 'Thank you, Herr Oberstleutnant.'

'But of course, you thank us, for it is indeed a great honour.'

Mimi said nothing, but her look was enough to voice the question on her lips.

'Reichsmarschall Göring will be resident here,' said Metzingen, as if she'd asked it.

'Indeed?' said Mimi. 'Then, yes, we are honoured.' She formed the words without meaning them.

Metzingen now took the manila folder his subordinate carried and opened it, revealing documents and plans.

Claude's eyes widened at what was there, but he wouldn't allow himself to react.

'*There*,' Metzingen indicated the area immediately outside the glass entrance doors, 'and *there*,' he pointed to the lobby just inside, 'and *there*,' he pointed to the base of the grand hotel stairs, 'will be positioned soldiers ready to present arms to all military officers who enter and leave the hotel.'

Claude acknowledged the directive. 'Of course, Herr Oberstleutnant.'

'The Ritz consists of two halves, does it not?'

'That is so,' said Claude.

But the question was to Jürgen, who was consulting a blueprint. Claude bit back his rage. For the Germans to have such a detailed floor plan meant that the Ritz had been betrayed utterly. Who of the hotel family he so loved could have thrown them to Hitler's wolves?

'Two halves, that is correct, Herr Oberstleutnant,' Jürgen said.

'This side, I assume, is the Vendôme half?'

'Yes, it is.'

Metzingen turned back to Claude. 'Every suite, every room, every corridor on all five floors on the Vendôme side is now forbidden to civilians,' he said. 'Also forbidden for civilians to enter are the salons, the bars, and this,' he looked around himself, appreciatively, 'the Vendôme lobby. No civilian is to enter here, Herr Manager, or enter any of the spaces named on threat of death.'

Claude's mouth had gone dry. 'By "civilians" you mean hotel staff?'

'That would be impractical,' said Metzingen. 'For how would we clean those rooms? No, no, staff will be permitted – *vetted* staff. Hauptmann Jürgen will conduct the vetting process.'

Jürgen nodded to Claude. Then he looked to Tommy, who throughout the exchange had stayed exactly where he was at Mimi's vacated chair. 'I doubt you'll have any trouble, lad,' Jürgen called to him in French, good-naturedly.

'Why is that, Monsieur?' Tommy managed to smile as he asked.

'Aryan looks like yours, you must be German?'

There was a palpable pause as they waited. 'I am part Hungarian, Monsieur.'

Jürgen didn't believe him. 'Mindful of the boss's feelings, are we? Very smart, keep in his good books while you can. Your secret's safe with us.'

Mimi found her voice once more. 'Herr Oberstleutnant,' she said to Metzingen, 'will the occupying forces of the Reich be paying for their rooms at the Ritz?'

'My dear Madame Ritz, of course the rooms will be paid for,' said Metzingen. 'We are quite civilised, you know.'

A wave of relief washed across Mimi.

'We have prepared a list of appropriate room rates for your perusal.' He turned to his subordinate again. 'Is it here in the file, Jürgen?'

It was. The Hauptmann produced a sheet of paper and handed it to Mimi. She read what was there.

Claude watched as the poise she had regained now left her. 'Madame –'

She needed his arm to support her. 'Herr Oberstleutnant . . .' she faltered, 'these rates – these rates represent a discount of more than ninety percent . . .'

'Oh, is that so?' asked Metzingen, concerned.

'Twenty-five francs a night for a room? It is not possible.'

'You'll find that it is,' said Metzingen, reassuringly. 'These figures have been precisely calculated. Each monthly bill must of course be sent to the Government of France. Our accommodation is at their expense, I'm sure you appreciate.'

'Herr Oberstleutnant,' said Claude, 'there is no French Government. At least not in Paris.'

'At least not anywhere!' Metzingen laughed. Then he waved away the concerns. 'It'll all be sorted out. An interim French Government will be assembled. There's a proper procedure to be observed here, you'll see.'

'And what of the Cambon side of the Ritz, Herr Oberstleutnant?' Mimi asked, shaken.

'Meine Dame?'

'The Vendôme, you say, is for high-ranking Germans – what is to become of the Cambon half of the hotel?'

'Well, that must be run quite normally, of course, we are not here to disrupt things. The rooms, the bar and your famous *l'Espadon* restaurant must remain open and available to the public – to the citizens of France and neutral countries. What reason could there be for closing such celebrated amenities?'

Mimi's reply was almost inaudible. 'Thank you, Herr Oberstleutnant . . .'

Profoundly satisfied, Metzingen drew a great gust of air into his lungs, as if savouring and retaining the very essence of the hotel. He seemed entirely nourished by it. 'Ah, Frau Ritz,' he sighed, 'I do so look forward to meeting them all.'

'Who, Herr Oberstleutnant?'

He looked surprised she should ask. 'Why, the denizens, meine Dame. The people your hotel is so rightly famous for. All the artists and playwrights, the film stars and millionaires. The entrepreneurs, the fashion designers, the girls – those famous, fashionable *filles* from the Ritz, meine Dame! So long I have wanted to come to the very heart of your establishment, and now that I have, what a pleasure it will be to spend time in their company.' He glanced once more at Claude, before adding almost as an afterthought: 'And perhaps we shall settle one or two old scores . . .'

It was only as Tommy tried to light a cigarette in the alley off the rue Cambon that he saw how badly his hands were shaking. For the life of him, he couldn't strike the match against the book without dropping it. While he tried again, he heard the lines of a song he half-recognised:

'Wait for me in this country of France
I'll be back soon, keep confident . . .'

He looked to the top of the alley and saw who had sung: Blanche's fifteen-year-old daughter was slouching there.

'What's the matter with you, Tom? Forgotten how to smoke?'

'Odile? Are you crazy? Come in here.'

He went to pull the pouty girl in, but Odile pushed his hands off. 'I can manhandle myself, thanks very much. Is there still something to sit on?'

'There's the crate.'

Odile used the stick she carried to locate the crate. 'Good.' She sat down. 'Been on my feet for hours.'

Tommy fell next to her, stiff in his Ritz uniform.

'Gimme the matchbook,' said Odile.

Odile struck a light in one go and Tommy put two cigarettes to it, giving one to her.

'What are you doing walking around out there?' The cigarette tasted awful, now that he'd lit it. He knew he should just give up on the habit.

'What are you doing needing me to light your cig?'

'Given you can't see anything, I'll give you a bit of news,' said Tommy, 'the krauts have turned up. It's been a shock to people.'

'Old news. When are you going back to school?'

'What's that got to do with anything? Are the schools even open?'

'Not at present,' said Odile, grinning. 'I guess it's a holiday. Answer my question.'

Tommy was glad Odile couldn't see his unease. 'You already know the answer. School's done for me. I work here at the Ritz now.'

While Odile was highly, sometimes bizarrely capable for a girl who was going blind, her descent into sightlessness meant she'd lost touch with how transparent her features could be. Her disbelief in Tommy's story was so plain that Tommy feared someone else seeing it.

'I still don't *get* you,' said Odile, wrinkling her brow. 'I heard you were top of your class in a snooty lycée. What was it again?'

Tommy didn't say.

'Okay, keep it to yourself then, but why chuck in a bright future to come work here?'

'At the best hotel in Paris?'

'Don't give me that, it's just waiting on tables and pouring drinks. You could have been a doctor or something. And don't you have some rich dad?'

Tommy's unease shot higher. 'Did your mama tell you that?'

Blanche hadn't. 'Maybe I was just fishing,' Odile conceded. 'But why should I have to? What's the big secret with you?'

Tommy didn't answer that either. 'Maybe I like working in hotels?'

Odile's expression of disbelief was unaltered.

Tommy changed the subject. 'There's krauts out there with machine guns, you know.'

'Yeah.' Odile grinned. 'I've been watching them for hours.'

'*Watching* them?'

'I still see more than fools like you will ever know,' said Odile, contemptuously. 'When the kraut tanks started rolling in this morning I thought I'd try an experiment while the olds were all losing their breakfast.'

'An experiment?' said Tommy, sceptical. 'Like Madame Curie?'

'Like the poor little blind girl walking the streets with her poor little blind girl's stick and her shades on.' Odile tapped the dark glasses she wore. 'I played it up, Tom, swinging the stick like nobody's business. "I'm blind! I'm so blind!" Krauts loved it.'

Tommy blinked at her. 'Sometimes I think you're off your head, Odile.'

'Krauts thought that, too.' She laughed, while blowing a smoke ring. 'Guess what? They left me clean alone. Didn't touch a hair on me.'

Tommy didn't know whether to congratulate her or pity her.

'For a girl who can't see, I saw a lot of interesting stuff.'

'For instance?'

'They've put their own traffic cops at every big intersection and all the main squares.'

'But there are no cars on the road.'

'Sure, there are: theirs. Kraut army vehicles are everywhere. To help them out more, they're even putting up their own street signs. I didn't know that's what they were – I just heard them banging in the nails – but a bum on the street told me. He said they're all written in kraut language, with black borders around the edge. Think about it, Tom. They came here with all those signs ready-made. They're *organised*.'

Tommy thought about Hauptmann Jürgen's bulging manila file with the detailed floor plans of the Ritz.

'They've set up shop in all the government buildings,' said Odile, 'every building I passed had krauts going in and out of it. There are no more tricolour flags. Just swastikas.'

Tommy gave up on his cigarette.

'And get this,' said Odile, 'down at the Tuileries they're setting up for a big brass band. They're gonna march up the Champs-Élysées *every day*. I asked a kraut and he was excited about it!'

'You really want to get shot!'

'I told you,' said Odile, 'poor little blind girl. The kraut said the big brass band was for the entertainment of other krauts – and Parisians.'

'Any Parisian would rather pull out their fingernails.'

'That's what I told him, too.'

Tommy couldn't believe her recklessness.

She just laughed. 'All right, I didn't, but I sure as hell thought it.'

Tommy's hands had stopped shaking. 'I've got to go back now, Odile.' He stood up from the crate to leave.

'Wait.'

'Monsieur Auzello will be looking for me, there're krauts in the hotel.'

'I *know*,' Odile said, sarcastically. 'And I know Claude's wetting himself.'

'Why did you come here looking for me?' Tommy asked, annoyed with her. 'Go back upstairs to your mama or she'll be crying for you.'

Odile's face was ever transparent. Tommy caught sight of such a sudden depth of emotion, he was thrown by it. He wondered then: did Odile have a crush on him? Whatever she felt, she now hid it beneath anger. 'I'm not a kid anymore, and neither are you,' she told him. 'All the olds have gone placid and *weak*. They let the krauts walk right in here.'

'I've got to go,' said Tommy.

'Is that all you've got to say about it?'

'What else is there to say?'

'How about: maybe it's our turn to take charge?'

Tommy stared at her, incredulous.

'I don't know how it was at your snooty school,' she said, testing him, 'but at mine all we talked about was the war. We talked about what was happening in the newspapers, and then we started to think that maybe those rags weren't even telling us what was real.'

Tommy remembered how he had come to the same conclusion with his own school friends, before he'd been forced to leave them behind.

'Then we listened to the radio from England,' said Odile, 'and we knew as much as the best of them then – and yet where are the best of them now?'

Her words stirred something. The anger Tommy had barely been able to hide in the lobby pulsed at the back of his head.

He thought about the turns his life had taken. He thought about Blanche Auzello, Odile's mother, and what she and Claude had done for him. He thought about what he had to hide.

He kicked the crate in frustration. 'What are you trying to say, Odile?'

'Are you a Jew, Tom?'

Tommy froze with the shock of the question.

'I'll make it easier for you then,' said Odile. 'So am I.'

'My dear Mrs Huckstepp, I must really insist that you admit me to your rooms.' Claude's plaintive voice came through the huge double doors to the Imperial Suite.

Inside the suite, on the other side of the doors, Lana Mae was obdurate: '*No.*'

'But it is a matter of the utmost urgency.'

'More urgent than my throbbing skull?' Lana Mae demanded. 'More urgent than the fact I can't get any goddamn breakfast today? Not even one lousy *pain au chocolat*? I'll let you in when you remember the meaning of service, Auzello, and not before.'

'Mrs Huckstepp, you really must let me in right now,' said Claude.

'Or what?'

'Or I fear there'll be consequences.'

Lana Mae guffawed. 'Like hell, baby. I'll give you one: I go and check into the Hôtel Crillon.'

'Of course, Mrs Huckstepp is welcome to move to another hotel should she so choose.'

'Fat chance!' said Lana Mae. 'Now beat it and leave me the hell alone.'

Claude fell silent. Lana Mae strained to hear what was going on outside. There were muffled voices revealing that Auzello wasn't alone.

'Is Mimi out there? I wanna talk to her instead of you,' Lana Mae spat through the door jamb.

There was a pause. The conversation stopped. 'Madame Ritz is not here,' said Claude.

Her bluster hiding fear, Lana Mae offered a straw. 'Is Tommy out there? Put Tommy at the door, I'll speak to him.'

'Tommy is not here either, Mrs Huckstepp.'

She heard a key being inserted in the keyhole.

'Don't you dare come in here!'

Lana Mae looked for something to throw and landed on the Swiss clock. She pulled it from the wall just as the key turned in the lock.

'You bastard!' She hurled the clock and it struck the edge of the opening door, bouncing onto a side table and hitting the floor, where it landed face up, still keeping time, unbroken.

A supremely athletic, well-groomed man with streaks of grey at his close-cropped temples, in the same shade of grey as his tailored Wehrmacht uniform, entered. 'Ah, Frau Huckstepp, what an unlucky aim,' the German said, pocketing the key and glancing down at the impervious time piece. 'If I didn't know better I would praise this clock as a fine example of German engineering.' He picked it up. 'Not a scratch on it.' He shook it in his hands. 'Nothing loose inside. Extraordinary.'

'Oh my God!' Lana screamed, finding her lungs again.

'Not God, merely his subordinate.' He held out his hand. 'I am Oberstleutnant Hans Metzingen.'

Lana Mae could only gape at him.

'You, too?' said Metzingen, withdrawing his unshaken hand. 'That is disappointing.'

Lana Mae saw Claude hovering behind the Oberstleutnant at the door. He looked like he'd aged ten years in a morning. 'I am a citizen of the United States of America!' she began.

'That's quite correct, meine Dame, we already have note of it in our file. There is no need to shout.'

'That makes me neutral – *neutral*! Just like the goddamn Swiss!'

'Again correct, which is why I had hoped for your courtesy. To shake another's proffered hand is the sign of common civilisation and decency, is it not? Our nations are in no disagreement, after all.'

Lana Mae felt herself deflating. 'That's right. You bet your patootie, we're not. All this has got nothing to do with me.'

'*Patootie*,' Metzingen echoed her, amused, 'how charming.' He clicked his fingers. 'Where are the plans, Hauptmann?'

Lana Mae only then saw the second Wehrmacht officer standing at the door; a younger man, even taller, extremely good looking and no less athletic. Claude seemed to fade into the wall between these two giants.

'Here, Herr Oberstleutnant,' said Jürgen, handing him a blueprint from the manila folder.

'Ah, very good,' Metzingen said, unfolding it. 'Now, what have we here.' He looked around the room, comparing what he saw with the plan.

With sickening realisation, Lana Mae saw it was a map of the entire Imperial Suite. She looked to sweating Claude. 'What's going on here?'

He just shook his head.

'The Hôtel Ritz Imperial Suite comprises three separate bedrooms, quarters for a maid, three connected salons, a dining room, and of course the grand boudoir,' said Metzingen. He looked to Lana Mae. 'A lot of rooms for just one lady?'

'I – well.'

'I'm sure you like to entertain.' Metzingen smiled. He turned to Jürgen. 'Let's examine the suitability of the boudoir first?'

'Yes, Herr Oberstleutnant.'

They walked in the direction of Lana Mae's enormous bedroom and with terror she thought of her furs, hidden or not behind the massive armoire. The Oberstleutnant lifted his eyes from the blue-prints, appreciating the suite's interior. 'Look at the care that is taken with the décor, Jürgen. Such tastefulness abounds.'

'It is very beautiful,' agreed Jürgen.

'Auzello, please, what's happening?' Lana Mae hissed at the general manager.

'I tried to warn you,' he hissed back, but his face was only full of sympathy.

She regretted how she'd spoken to him. 'But you could've told me why – told me in code or something.'

'*How* could I? They are in control, Mrs Huckstepp, they are in total control.'

'Oh, Herr Auzello?' Metzingen called out from the boudoir.

Claude winced. 'Herr Oberstleutnant?'

Lana Mae could see into her bedroom, where Metzingen stood now directly in front of the armoire, the plans in his hand. How long until he wondered where the built-in was?

'Do you know that fragrance by Guerlain?' Metzingen asked Claude.

'Which one, Herr Oberstleutnant?'

'You know the one, it's very famous. Such a charming scent. What is it called?'

'I am not sure which fragrance you refer to.'

The Oberstleutnant's face darkened. 'Please do not imagine I am a fool.'

Claude further paled. 'I – you see I am not so familiar with women's perfume.'

'Is it Shalimar?' Lana Mae offered, her heart in her throat.

Metzingen brightened once more. 'That is the one, Frau Huckstepp! A most heady fragrance. It comes in an exotic bottle?'

'It's awful nice,' said Lana Mae. 'And expensive.'

'No doubt,' Metzingen nodded. He turned to Claude. 'Go to Guerlain and acquire twenty bottles of Shalimar, that should suffice.'

Claude was horrified. 'The House of Guerlain will be closed, Herr Oberstleutnant.'

'Oh, I know it is,' said Metzingen, 'we passed it on the rue de la Paix. Please open it.'

Jürgen started pushing Claude towards the door.

'Thank you, Herr Auzello!' Metzingen called happily as he returned to the blueprints.

Lana Mae looked on helplessly as Claude was treated with contempt by the younger German.

'Just get the perfume,' Jürgen told him.

Claude found himself staring at the incongruous camera hanging from the young man's neck. 'But, how can I? I'm not the owner of the shop.'

Jürgen gripped him hard by the lapels. 'This is how the Reich has walked all over you frogs like dirt. When we say we want something, we get it. Now go.'

'But our Mrs Huckstepp?' Claude pleaded. 'What is to happen to her?'

Jürgen's look was cold. 'The Oberstleutnant will decide.'

Claude caught Lana Mae's sickening fear as Jürgen kicked the doors shut in his face.

Completely alone on the pavement, Claude hurried up the rue de la Paix in the direction of Guerlain, huddled into his suit jacket as if it was late November and not mid-June. He could not stop himself from shivering, and nearly stumbled against a wall with it. He had to halt to calm himself, trying to think of what on earth he might do and say when he got to the perfumery.

'You look done in, Papa.'

He turned with a yelp. The untidy teenage girl with round, darkened glasses and a long length of cane was lounged in a doorway, smoking a cigarette. Blanche's daughter.

'You shouldn't call me that – I'm not your papa.'

'For want of a better one,' said Odile. 'You're still married to Mama, aren't you?'

Claude tried to achieve dignity. 'Your mother led a full life before I came along.'

'Of course, she did, she's beautiful – and so what if it's anyone's guess who my real father was? I don't lose sleep over it,' claimed Odile, 'you're still Papa to me. You brought us here to the Ritz, didn't you?'

'You know why I did that.'

'Sure. So, we'd be safe and sound if the krauts showed up. Turns out they're here.'

Claude's anxiety got the better of him and he had trouble getting his breath.

'You're not well, Papa.'

'I – I'll be all right,' said Claude. He tried to screw in his monocle, but his eye was watering.

'The hell you will. Here.' Odile stuck her arm under Auzello's elbow. 'Lean on me. I'll help you get where you're going to.'

The girl lurched forward with Auzello pinned beside her; she swept the cane from side to side on the pavement like a long magician's wand.

Claude felt his breathing ease. Her presence was actually comforting.

'Where are we going?'

'Guerlain.'

'It's closed.'

'It's fallen to me to open it.'

'We'll chuck a rock through the window then.' She turned her head. 'Oh shit. They're back.'

139

A black German military vehicle was heading slowly up the street behind them. Claude didn't dare look at it.

The vehicle drew up beside them.

'We'd better stop,' said Odile, 'it'll get things over quicker.'

Claude looked with terror to the road. On top of the vehicle was a cluster of shiny megaphones. Inside the car, two young Wehrmacht men were smirking at him. The one in the passenger seat had a microphone in his hand, looking at a typewritten sheet in his lap as he began to read out. His German-accented French was ear-splitting through the megaphones.

'You have been completely betrayed!'

'Tell us something we don't know, kraut,' Odile muttered.

'There is no longer any efficacious resistance you can mount against German–Italian military superiority!'

'Jesus and Mary, are the dagoes turning up, too?'

Claude jabbed the girl with his elbow to shut up.

'It is useless to continue the struggle. Think of your poor children, of your unfortunate wives!'

'He must think we're related, Papa,' said Odile with a laugh.

'Demand that your government end this struggle that has no hope of success!'

'Oh, we will, kraut, if we can ever find them again!'

The Wehrmacht soldier pulled down the window of the car, turning the microphone off. Claude's stomach turned itself into knots. 'You,' said the soldier, pointing right at him.

'Yes, Monsieur?'

'Where is the Boulevard des Capucines?'

Claude had lived in Paris for decades but couldn't think where that street was for the life of him.

'You want to go back the other way, Monsieur,' Odile told the soldier, 'you're heading in the wrong direction. Go back to the Place Vendôme and from there go down to the Seine. You can't miss it.'

The soldier was pleased. 'Thanks, kid.'

'You're very welcome, Monsieur.'

The German driver put the car in reverse and returned the way they had come down the eerily empty street.

It was only when Claude and Odile had gone another ten feet that Claude recalled where the Boulevard des Capucines really was. His stomach knotted twice. 'You sent them in the opposite direction!'

Odile was laughing.

'You stupid girl, you'll get us both killed.'

'Gotta die of something, Papa.'

'What if they come back for us?'

'They'll be too embarrassed now.'

'Embarrassed?'

'Well, wouldn't you be?' said Odile, tapping her skull. 'They just took directions from a blind kid.'

When Lana Mae entered *l'Espadon*, dressed in the best frock she'd been able to throw on in a hurry, her face unmade, her hair unset, and forced, without the order having been given, to take the Oberstleutnant's arm, there had been more of the hotel's regulars in attendance. She had been unable to meet their mortified eyes. One by one, most had melted away. Mr Wall remained, along with his chow, and so did the industrialist's forgetful wife. Most of the dining staff had already fled in the exodus, so waiters were thin on the ground. Monsieur Lefèvre, the chilly sommelier, was still on hand, performing triple duties as *maître d'*, food waiter and wine expert.

Once they were seated, Oberstleutnant Metzingen took the handwritten *l'Espadon* luncheon menu with glee. 'My dear Frau Huckstepp, will you look at the delights the chefs have prepared for us?'

The offerings were more limited than Lana Mae had known in twenty years at the Ritz, but to the Oberstleutnant they were evidence of the hotel's exceptionality. The luncheon menu had been named the 'Victory Menu'.

'*Fillet of sole poached in German white wine,*' Metzingen read out. 'What an excellent appetizer – and so appropriate for the occasion!'

Lana Mae smiled politely without remotely feeling joy.

'*Roast chicken for the principal dish,*' Metzingen read on, 'presumably French, you suppose? *Served with asparagus dressed in Hollandaise sauce.* It is the simplicity of the cuisine that is to be celebrated, is it not? *And cheese and local summer fruits to follow.* French fruits for the picking! There is humour here, Frau Huckstepp, I detect young Jürgen's hand with the kitchen staff.'

Lana Mae gulped at the German wine while Metzingen sat back in his chair expansively. 'Oh, to be here at last at the Hôtel Ritz. They say exceptional planning is its own reward, but truthfully, it is the faultless execution of those plans that brings the greatest joys, don't you find?'

'I – I don't know what to say to that,' Lana Mae told him.

'Really? Yet you strike me as a woman who has planned her trajectory most precisely, Frau Huckstepp.'

'My what?'

'Forgive my French, I would speak in your native English, but sadly it's rather worse. Not "trajectory" then, "career".'

'I haven't had to slave for a living in years,' said Lana Mae, coldly.

'Well, of course you haven't, that's just what I mean. Yours is a career of quite another kind. What was the little phrase I read about you in the file we assembled . . .' He raked his memory. 'Of course: Lana Mae Huckstepp won first prize in the American Cinderella Derby!'

Lana Mae choked. 'They're *my* words! I say that about myself!'

'Well, yes, you must say it quite often, that's why it's in the file.'

'How did you get those words? Who told them to you?' But in her heart she already knew who.

He looked away. 'I've no idea. A discarded lover perhaps?'

Lana Mae darkened. 'Are you calling me a whore?'

The Oberstleutnant was shocked. And then apologetic. 'My French, meine Dame. Cultural differences. We Germans think of the women in Paris as being extremely liberated – highly independent.' He chuckled. 'So, yes, perhaps you were right. A whore.'

Lana Mae stuck her chin out. 'How dare you say that to me.'

'Good!' said Metzingen. 'There's your independence right there! We admire you for it, you know.' He took a sip of his wine. 'But we'd never put up with it at home, of course.'

Lana Mae felt she might weep. She blinked the threat of tears away. 'What else is inside your lousy file?' She dreaded the answer, yet she had to know. It wasn't so much what had been revealed that was distressing, but how the Germans had chosen to interpret it.

'Oh, this and that,' said Metzingen. 'Your life of pointless idleness, for instance. That's in the file.'

Lana Mae winced.

'Your lack of intellect. The fact you contribute so little to anything other than your beautification and comfort – your astonishing self-indulgence. And then there's the staggering extent of your American wealth.' He smiled at her. 'Your decadence is breathtaking, Frau Huckstepp, quite breathtaking.'

Stung anew with shock and shame, Lana Mae tried to pick up her glass from the table but found she could no longer hold it. Her stomach twinged. She scraped her sweating palms against her napkin before reaching inside her purse for the reassurance of her pink bismuth bottle.

'The important thing to remember is that yours is only one of many thousands of files,' said Metzingen, 'files meticulously assembled and kept. The *organisation* behind it, Frau Huckstepp. It's allowed us to know everything.'

Lana Mae crossed her arms and tried to brazen it out with him. 'You could read what you told me in any society column. That's what you Germans call "everything", is it, honey?'

The Oberstleutnant laughed and clapped his hands. 'You are the most delightful luncheon companion.'

Lana Mae managed to take another slug of the riesling. 'I'm waiting.'

The Oberstleutnant's face changed. He levelled a stare of his own. 'There is a file on every significant building, every apartment block, every crossroad, and every Metro station in Paris. Why do you think that is?'

Lana Mae wouldn't let her nerve fail her. 'Because you've got too much time on your hands?'

He didn't laugh. 'It is so that our complete assumption of this city would be instant and tremendous for those who live within it, meine Dame. It is so that we would know before we even arrived which of the crossroads were crucial and must therefore be controlled – which they now are. It is so that we would appreciate which of the so many splendid and beautiful buildings would need to be requisitioned – which they now have been. It is so that we would understand where the most essential of the archives of France could be found, that the information within them could be made our own. It is so that we would know which of the many extraordinary museums have the most desired collections.' He regarded his napkin. 'It is so that we would know which of the art galleries are owned by Jews.'

Lana Mae swallowed.

Oberstleutnant Metzingen pushed back his chair. 'The Führer has a grand vision for Paris, Frau Huckstepp – and accordingly, I have a vision for the Ritz. We are not the barbarians but the shield against those who would undermine centuries of tradition.' He rose from the table, folding his napkin. 'I am afraid I must draw this luncheon to a close.'

'But – but you haven't even eaten yet,' said Lana Mae, frightened of him.

'I am tired. My food will be sent to our suite.'

'*Our* suite?' Lana Mae's tongue felt thick in her mouth.

His lips split into a grin, but his eyes didn't soften. 'I am sorry, my poor French once again. I meant "my" suite. The Imperial Suite is mine as I prepare it for Reichsmarschall Göring's arrival.'

'But – but where will I go?'

Metzingen stopped and considered, before replying. 'That is of no concern to the Reich.' He gave a short bow and clicked his heels. 'I am sure that as a liberated, independent whore you will think of something.'

Lana Mae only managed to lift her eyes from her glass once he was gone. She cast a look of desperate shame around the room. Of the few diners left, every one of them was looking right back at her. She had been hoping for sympathy but there was none. Lana Mae saw all too clearly the expressions of condemnation in her fellow guests' faces. They had heard every word the German had said about her – and, what's more, they agreed with him.

Feeling the wound of this silent denunciation far worse than the German's summation of her character, Lana Mae knew she was on the verge of breaking down. But then at the far end of the dining room, a middle-aged woman sitting alone at a table in a chic summer hat with a flute of champagne in her hand turned and gaily raised her glass in Lana Mae's direction. Her beaming smile, far from condemning Lana Mae, offered only ample encouragement. 'Surprise them,' the woman's warm grin seemed to say, 'show them that's *not* who you are . . .'

With a dreadful jolt, Lana Mae recognised the woman. 'Marjorie?'

She lurched from her chair, tipping backwards, spilling the last of the riesling in a wide, golden arc all around her. Scrabbling ungracefully on the floor to right herself, Lana Mae looked to the far end of the room again.

The table was empty, set for no one.

Lana Mae's emotions overwhelmed her. 'Oh, Marjorie . . .' she sank to her knees. 'How did I ever deserve you as my friend?'

7

22 June 1940

The beautiful Renoir canvas was undamaged, at least, wrapped in its quilt in the trunk. Its frame had been struck by a bullet, however, leaving a long, ugly gash along its gilt. This was the best of the news. The Comte's black Mercedes was immovable. Faced with no option, they retrieved the portrait and abandoned the vehicle, leaving it with all the others that had been shot to uselessness by the Messerschmitt.

With Suzette's bloody hand bandaged as best they could with a scarf, she, Zita, Alexandrine and Polly sat at the roadside, the older women drinking from the shot champagne bottle, while they argued their best course of action. For Polly there was no argument. 'We're going back to Paris,' she announced.

'Darling, please don't be a fool,' said Alexandrine. 'The Germans will be all over the city by now.'

'They're all over here. They'll be all over Dreux when we get there. And Saint-Malo, too. What's the point of us running, Alexandrine? What are we even running to? We need to go home and *do* something.'

'What on earth can we do?'

Having lost two fingers, Suzette was in considerable pain, but she gave no hint of it. 'The kid's right, Madame. I miss my bed. I want to go home. The Comte will be needing me,' she said, as if the worst she'd suffered was a bruise. Then she added, for Alexandrine's benefit, 'And there's others I miss – those we left behind. I can't sleep for worrying these nights.'

Alexandrine's face flashed with anger at this oblique statement. She composed herself and turned to Polly. 'Please, listen to me – we must get to safety.'

'There is no safety,' said Polly. 'But there is still self-respect. Isn't that something that a Comtesse who refused to run even when a plane was shooting at her might know a little about?'

Alexandrine wrestled with this. 'Zita, please say something?'

When Polly looked in Zita's eyes, she saw a flash of the famed insouciance. 'Screw it,' said Zita, tossing her curls. 'If I'm gonna be shot then I'll take my bullet in Paris, thanks very much, and so should you.'

'And what if *he's* there?'

Zita gave Alexandrine a blank look. 'Who?'

'You know very well who . . .'

Polly realised who she meant: the sender of the telegrams.

Zita kept her voice and gaze level. 'That was a joke, remember, puss, some kind of mistake.'

'Was it?' said Alexandrine, with her eyebrow raised.

Polly turned to the film star. 'Who is this man, Zita? A boyfriend?'

Zita was icy. 'If he is, then no wonder I don't remember him. What's one among hundreds? And if he thinks he's got a beef with me then he can go and join the queue.' Her look told Polly she should not risk asking about this again.

'All right then,' said Alexandrine. She gave Suzette a long and steely look. 'If the majority wish to go back to Paris, then that's what we'll do. We must uphold our own example of French democracy.'

'Good,' said Zita. But now she seemed less sure.

'I'm worried for Lana Mae,' said Polly, relieved. 'She shouldn't be all alone.' If they could have read her heart, they would have known she was worried for Tommy, too.

Suzette said nothing more. There was only gratitude in her eyes for Alexandrine.

Yet Polly knew that her guardians' hold on their secrets was loosening. Their efforts made in the name of her safety proved they cared for her. How much longer until they trusted her, too?

They selected new outfits – elegant walking clothes, with appropriate hats and shoes – then, together, the four of them began to walk against the oncoming tide of misery.

Suzette stumbled once, early on, and looked in danger of collapsing again. Zita suggested they put her inside an abandoned wheelbarrow and trundle her home to the Comte.

'My fucking arse, you will,' Suzette replied. She recovered then, spurred by a fear of indignity, although Alexandrine kept her arm firmly linked in hers, holding her up, for every exhausting kilometre.

Polly kept the quilt-wrapped Renoir tightly under her arm, along with the Hermès bag.

While they had all been careful to take just a single suitcase from the Mercedes each, these grew heavy fast. They gave things away to women they met on the road and kept what was left of the food, and whatever else they could squeeze inside their handbags, which, as Alexandrine said, were pleasingly capacious bags this season, as if their trials on the road had been anticipated by the fashion designers.

After two days, Zita was the first to declare eating as unnecessary when the last of their provisions grew low. 'It's a good opportunity,' she said. 'I'll lose ten kilos while this keeps up. I'll walk back into the Ritz to wolf whistles.' But her mind seemed heavy with unspoken thoughts.

Some things were so awful it was better not to acknowledge them. This was how it was when they came across the line of black and stiffened bodies sprawled on the road. These were the corpses of women like them – along with others: children, babies. When these Parisiennes and their families had encountered the Messerschmitt it had deployed an incendiary weapon. They'd been burned to death. No words could describe how it was to view these twisted remains, with the lovely summer wildflowers in bloom just metres away, untouched and uncaring, and the birds still singing in the trees. So, Polly and her guardians didn't attempt any words. The corpses barely stank. The fire that had consumed the women and children had somehow preserved them too – as if the Germans wanted others to learn from such fates.

When the dreadful sight was behind them, Polly asked Zita to tell her of her life again. Polly knew the shared stories gave strength to those who told them, and strength to those who listened.

'This again, puss?' said Zita with effort.

Polly answered with red-rimmed eyes.

'Why should you escape the confessional?' said Alexandrine, too-brightly, forcibly maintaining their progress along the road again.

'I've already told you everything that's fit to write about,' Zita went through the motions of complaint.

'Tell me again,' said Polly, with a wavering voice, 'to clarify things.'

Zita theatrically sighed, as if resigning herself to it, but she took Polly's hand before kissing it, cradling her close.

'You were born very poor,' Polly started her off.

'Yes, puss,' said Zita. She seemed to grow in stature, as if walking a stage. 'I had no mother or any low-life, no-good swine of a father that I can remember. I was raised by my granny, who was a salty old concierge in the shittiest apartment block on the slope of Montmartre.'

'The *lower* slope,' said Alexandrine, in a practised line.

'The *lowest*,' said Suzette, joining in. 'Might as well have been Pigalle.'

Zita sniggered and brushed a tear from Polly's cheek with her finger.

Suzette winked at Polly. 'That's the red-light district, Mademoiselle. Where all the women of ill-repute can be found.'

'Thank you, Suzette,' Alexandrine warned her.

'But it wasn't all brothels and streetwalkers, was it, Zita?' Polly pressed the film star, finding her own feet again.

'No, puss,' Zita said, 'not so far away down the rue Richer was the Folies Bergère.'

'And you had always wanted to *act*,' Polly said.

'*Act?*' Suzette queried. 'Is that what's she's calling it now?'

Zita was unfazed, warming to the routine. 'When they gave me a job it meant posing on stage, smirking half in the nude. And so what? I wasn't ashamed of my beauty. I was only a little bit older than you when I started doing it.'

'Terrible,' said Suzette, 'living proof you can take the girl out of the gutter, but you can't take the –'

Zita reached across and pinched Suzette's nose before she could finish.

'Ow!'

'Stop it, Zita, she'll bleed on my dress,' warned Alexandrine.

They were all starting to laugh now – the kind of laughter heard at a guillotine.

'The Folies Bergère helped me get used to people staring at me,' Zita continued. 'I became a star when I was cast in a half-decent film. I went to Berlin to do it. That was before all the films became talkies, of course. In those days it didn't matter what lousy accent you had because no one could hear it. All that mattered was how you looked. And, puss, I looked *divine*.'

Polly was building her strength again. 'What was the film called?'

'I don't remember but it was set in a hotel.'

'A famous one?'

'Ha!' Suzette started up again.

'Managed to catch it did we, puss?' Zita asked her, ready to pinch again.

'Five times. Only made me cry the first three.'

Zita was delighted. 'Puss!'

'You were shit in it,' said Suzette. 'I kept going back just to see if you'd get any worse.'

Zita predictably guffawed. She turned back to Polly. 'I played a slut. My first and by no means last such part.'

'Zita was electrifying,' said Alexandrine, 'she set all Europe alight with her sex appeal. She was better than Garbo.'

'Just a foot *shorter*,' said Suzette.

'It's true,' said Zita, ignoring the crack about her height. 'That's what made me a star. I'd come from the Pigalle gutter and so did the character they'd written for me. So have all the others they've written for me since. I'll let you into a little secret, puss,' she squeezed Polly, looking conspiratorial, 'I don't act, I just *be*.'

'That's not true at all,' said Alexandrine. 'Zita is so good at her craft she makes it look too easy.'

'I've tied up every part that calls for an insouciant tart,' said Zita, with a smirk.

'What is your surname, Zita?' Polly wondered. 'I don't think you've ever told me.'

Zita sniffed. 'I don't need a surname. When people see my name on posters, they know what they're getting, and they flock to it. I am the mistress of my own creation. Something I recommend to you, puss.'

'Aren't you gonna ask Zita about her men?' Suzette wondered. 'It only seems right.'

Polly turned back to the actress. 'When did you get married?'

Zita gave a dry look. 'I didn't, puss. And won't. As Suzette well knows, I prefer affairs.'

Thrilled at such candour, Polly glanced to Alexandrine, who was making a study of looking away, as if this topic of conversation had not arisen.

'And if my lover of the moment is married, then so be it,' said Zita, shrugging again. 'I always go shopping for absolution at the confessional. I place high value on my feminine independence, puss, which is a value we all share.'

'That's true,' said Suzette.

Alexandrine turned back to Polly and nodded.

'I want to work, I like getting paid for it, and being a star is not only a source of cash, it's liberating,' said Zita. 'It doesn't require any professional qualification, or even better, any class. The perfect career choice for a woman who more than anything else likes being the centre of attention.' Zita smiled brilliantly, showing every one of her unreal teeth.

After several days' walking, sleeping at night in the fields, Polly's little group encountered landmarks they better recognised. They had returned to the outskirts of Paris again. Polly was more exhausted than she had ever thought it possible to be, but she was not yet dead, and for that she was grateful. She was deeply anxious, however, as were they all, although none of them voiced their individual fears.

Paris, initially at least, seemed as it had been when they'd left it. The differences only grew clearer to Polly the closer they came to the centre. There were hundreds – *thousands* – of Wehrmacht soldiers in grey-green uniforms marching in formation up the Boulevard Saint-Michel. Polly watched, stunned, recalling French

Government missives that had made her believe that the soldiers of Germany were weak and incompetent. File after file of sharp, smart, goose-stepping young men made the French Government's lies pitiable. A brass band led the soldiers on, playing an unlisten-able dirge called *'Preussens Glorie'* – Prussia's Glory. Polly felt sick just hearing it.

There were tanks. There were motorcycles. There were military vehicles. There were no cars driven by Frenchmen at all. What Parisians there were in residence were travelling on foot, just as Polly and her companions were, which made their return to the capital seem unremarkable amongst so many others who were covered in dust, stained with sweat, and still wearing perfectly applied make-up.

There was a red and black swastika flying from the Eiffel Tower.

There were red and black swastikas flying everywhere.

The garish symbol of occupation made the beautiful city look vile. The newly hung flags didn't waft in the breeze from rooftops and towers like the colours of a civilized nation should, asking a person to raise their eyes to see them. The gaudy logos of Hitler's hate hung in every line of vision, impossible to avoid, suspended from famous façades like cheap, foreign-made curtains wanting only to be washed.

There were distressing numbers of cats and dogs in the streets, abandoned by owners, left to fend for themselves.

There was not one bird left in the trees; a heartbreaking absence of birdsong. Rotting wads of feathers choked the gutters, providing scraps for the cats. Polly learned from a passer-by that the French Army had set fire to the oil reserves at the industrial edge of the city, just as the Germans entered. The acrid cloud of smoke from the blaze had killed every bird that flew near it.

It was when they crossed the Seine by the ancient Pont Neuf at the western tip of the Île de la Cité that Polly saw the strangest change. Dozens of Germans, handsome and strong, were arrayed in nakedness on the little scrap of park that was the Square du Vert-Galant. Dozens more unclothed Germans sprawled on the quay below that sloped to the river's edge. Unburdened by self-consciousness, some played football, while most just lay in the sun.

'Sweet Mary and Christ,' said Zita.

The Germans knew that Polly and her companions were frozen there, staring at them, and couldn't have cared less. There were a few whistles from the men, some waves, but none of the Germans moved; none of the men tried to accost them. They were orderly, well-behaved.

The reposing soldiers issued a glow of masculine beauty and virile healthiness that was mesmerising to Polly, who had never before seen a man without clothes. Uniformed German bodies that were threatening when marching up the Boulevard Saint-Michel, now displayed naked were desirable, and disturbingly so. Polly made an unspoken comparison with the defeated, emasculated, still absent Parisian men of the glorious French Army.

'They're dirty perverts,' said Suzette, spitting on the pavement at her feet. Yet she couldn't look away either.

'Halt, meine Damen, may I see your identification papers, please?'

A pair of Wehrmacht soldiers, both in full uniform, were stationed at a black and red sentry box that now stood at the northern end of the Pont Neuf.

Polly and her companions had been expecting this and had prepared for it as best they could. But Polly had known there could be no preparation for the Germans discovering what she had hidden in the Hermès bag. She wished she had left the gun behind, her mind filled with images of the black, burned corpses. What would these men do to them all if it was found?

'Of course, Monsieur,' said Alexandrine, handing her paper to the soldier who held out his hand. He read what it said of her details while his colleague looked at all four of them knowingly, aware of what they had until a moment before been gazing upon in the park. Only Zita held his gaze.

The first soldier gave Alexandrine's identification back to her. 'Thank you, Comtesse, all is in order,' he said, polite. He looked to Zita. 'Frau . . .'

'Frau*lein*,' she corrected, handing him her identification.

He saw her name and seemed to be trying to make a connection between it and her haughty face. 'You remind me of someone from the *Kino*, Fräulein.'

'Yes?' said Zita.

Polly realised that whatever name Zita had down on her papers was almost certainly her real one.

'But your name, it is not the same as the woman you resemble?'

'But that *is* my name, Monsieur,' said Zita.

He returned her identification. 'All is in order then.' He clicked his fingers at Suzette. 'Meine Dame?'

Alexandrine feared that Suzette was about to repeat Zita's 'Frau*lein*' crack and pinched her elbow in warning not to try it. Suzette handed her identification over in silence.

The soldier read it and frowned. He showed it to the other man. 'Jewess?' asked the second.

Suzette puffed out her chest. 'I am the housekeeper for the Comte Ducru-Batailley,' she said, 'a very important man. You'll want to watch yourselves, boys.'

There was an almost unbearable moment of stillness during which Polly felt the hard steel of the gun barrel press against her chest through the bag.

The first soldier gave Suzette's identification back to her. 'You will no doubt find that that is already known to us, meine Dame,' he told her.

They came to Polly last, and she realised then, as she tried to stare guilelessly at their unlined faces, that they were barely older than she was. She realised, too, that despite the grime and dust that covered every inch of her, she was actually pretty in their eyes. Their manner was different with her. Their instinctive respectfulness was tinged with a keen frisson of sexual interest that was as arresting to Polly to experience for the very first time from men as it was also confronting. She knew for certain then: they would never think to ask what was in her bag. Zita and Alexandrine placed protective hands at Polly's waist.

The second soldier smiled at Polly, as the other read her identification. This soldier then looked up at her, surprised, when he'd made sense of it. '*Australien?*'

She clutched the covered Renoir on one side, the bag on the other. 'Yes, I was born in Australia, Monsieur.'

The two Germans traded a look. 'British Empire?'

Polly swallowed, but held her ground. 'That's right, Monsieur.'

'Germany is at war with Great Britain,' said the first soldier. 'Not for much longer, but still, we are enemies today.'

'The child is a resident of France,' said Alexandrine.

Ordinarily, Polly would have rankled at hearing the word 'child' used about her, but here she stayed calm.

'I live at the Hôtel Ritz,' she offered them. 'Perhaps you know of it?'

The soldier handed her paper back. 'You are a British foreigner, Fräulein, and therefore you must make yourself known to the Occupation authorities. Please report to your nearest police station to be placed upon the official register. You must return to that police station daily so that your movements can be monitored for your own safety.'

Polly felt a sting of anger but wouldn't let herself give in to it.

It took great effort, but Polly gave the solider her sweetest smile. 'I did not know this was the rule, Monsieur. I will do as you say at once. Thank you so much for your kindness.'

Both soldiers seemed to swim in her smile, beaming back.

'Please return to your hotel first, Fräulein. Refresh yourself from your journey. The police station will still be there for you tomorrow. The formalities can wait until then.'

As the four of them left the bridge, turning to pass the Metro entrance on the Quai de Louvre, they encountered a row of lurid, identical posters pasted onto the walls. Joan of Arc was depicted, tied at the stake, while at her feet, with his flaming torch ready, was the British Prime Minister Churchill. Few of the posters were still legible. Some had been torn to pieces and many more were smeared with river mud. Further along the quay, closer to the Louvre, a band of Frenchmen were pasting fresh posters over the top of the spoiled ones, identical in message. These men, supervised by a group of frowning German soldiers, showed vivid signs of having been beaten for the crime of defacing the older posters.

Zita stopped dead in the street.

'Darling, what's wrong?' said Alexandrine, startled.

'I can't do it, puss. I can't go back to the Ritz, just now. I – I need to do something else.'

'What else?' Alexandrine was clearly thrown. 'Don't be silly, darling. The Ritz is our home. Where else would we go?'

'No. You go on. I'll come back later . . .' Zita stepped into the oncoming traffic.

'Zita!' Polly cried, horrified at the danger.

The film star looked even tinier amidst the flow of German military vehicles and motorbikes that honked and swerved around her.

'I'm sorry,' she called to them. 'I just can't.' She barely made it to the other side of the street in safety.

'Zita, please!' Alexandrine called after her.

But she was already running in the other direction.

When they had recovered enough to continue along the last few blocks to the Place Vendôme, Polly finally insisted on knowing the truth. 'This is about the person who sent her the telegrams, isn't it?'

'I don't know,' said Alexandrine.

Polly looked hard at her.

'*I don't*,' said Alexandrine. 'It could be as she said – that she received them by mistake.'

'I saw you when we talked about it near Dreux,' said Polly. 'You didn't even make a pretence of going along with that twaddle Zita came up with for my benefit. What you implied that day was the truth: the telegrams came from someone Zita once loved.'

Alexandrine tried to seem vague. 'Perhaps there was a man she was involved with when she was making films in Berlin . . .'

'What did he do to make her so frightened of him?'

'You put words in my mouth,' said Alexandrine. 'Zita is *never* frightened.'

Polly gave her a sceptical stare. 'She ran into the traffic. She could have been knocked down. She seemed frightened to me.'

'You misinterpret her,' Alexandrine shook her head. 'And I'm sorry, but that's all I know of it.'

'No, it isn't,' said Suzette, dark.

'*Don't*,' said Alexandrine to her, warningly.

Suzette wasn't having it. 'We're in this together, you said, Madame. All equal. Tell the kid what else there is and stop using all your pathetic excuses to keep her in the dark. If I worked it out, so will she in good time. Why not let her feel trusted by you? Or isn't being Marjorie's niece enough for you cows?'

Alexandrine looked to the pavement, exposed, while Polly waited in astonishment. It was as if Suzette had known exactly what she had spoken of only in her heart.

'If it is the same man, then there may have been a child born to them,' Alexandrine answered, finally. 'Although, I swear to you, Polly, Zita will deny it if you ask.'

'No, she won't,' said Suzette. 'She might even be relieved.'

'Shut up, Suzette, you don't know a thing about it.'

But it was clear to Polly that she did. The old woman scoffed.

'How do *you* know about this child?' Polly asked Alexandrine, quietly.

'You forget I was a mother once – however briefly.' Polly watched her struggle to word her answer, struggle to break her code of loyalty to her friends. 'It is just something I *sense* in Zita,' said Alexandrine, 'a feeling that she understands my pain more than Lana Mae could, because she has known the experience of being a mother herself . . .'

Suzette clicked her tongue in disgust at what she saw as obfuscation. 'I've had enough of this,' she told Polly. 'Zita's kid is called Lotti.' She glared at Alexandrine. 'And there's no getting round it, Madame, she was born a little kraut.'

Anonymous in the evening shadow, Zita felt the alcohol course through her veins as she told herself it made up for the pride she had lost somewhere on the trek from Dreux, along with her suitcase of clothes. She was drunk. Not so far gone as to be incoherent, for she knew she would have need of her words, but drunk enough to face him, if indeed he was there to be faced.

As she rounded the rue de la Paix, the near-empty cognac bottle slipped from her hands and smashed on the pavement. Shocked by the noise it made in the weirdly quiet surrounds, Zita briefly sobered again to consider what she was about to do.

She was returning to the Ritz, the one home she had. Her friends would already be inside, despising her now for abandoning them. Yet Zita knew that if they were ever to truly hate her then it would have come months ago, back when she told them of what she had done. Each, in turn, had been angry then, certainly, and horribly shocked, but in the end the long years of friendship – the long years of secrets shared and kept – had meant too much. Zita's beloved friends – Alexandrine, Lana Mae, and Marjorie – had forgiven her actions because they understood why she had done them, true friends to the end. Then Marjorie had died and left as her legacy, Polly, a parentless girl. It was the thought of Polly discovering Zita's truth that she so struggled with.

German military vehicles were drawn up outside the hotel where once the private cars of the wealthy had parked. Wehrmacht sentries stood guard at the Ritz glass doors.

Zita looked longingly at the cognac dripping into the gutter. She could have done with one last slug for her nerves.

It was time for her to perform.

Pulling herself up to full height, which was more than it might have been, thanks to her heels, Zita stepped towards the two sentries, willing herself not to stagger or slip, and risk giving her drunkenness away. She lit a cigarette.

'Halt!'

'Hello, boys.' She greeted them in German. 'Nice night for it.'

Their manner was polite, but they were looking her up and down like so much horseflesh.

'It is nearly curfew,' one of them said, 'please return to your home, meine Dame.'

'This is my home.' She moved forward.

'Halt!' They drew their machine guns at her.

'What?' said Zita, innocently. 'A woman can't kick off her shoes and run a nice bath for herself now? Look at me, boys, I look like shit on a plate. But you'll love the little show I'll put on for you tomorrow when I come out these doors again.' She fished in her handbag. 'See. Here's my suite key. Now let me in.'

'Civilian guests use the Cambon entrance,' said the first soldier.

'Oh, do they now?' It hadn't occurred to Zita to try the other way first. 'All right then.' She made to go.

'Halt!' commanded the second of the Wehrmacht men. He said something to the first sentry that Zita couldn't quite hear. They regarded her again. 'What is your name, Fräu*lein*?'

Zita considered giving him her real name, until instinct told her she'd do better offering them the name that went with her suite. 'Zita,' she told him. 'Just Zita.' She was thankful the light outside the entrance was rather more flattering than the brighter light within. She gave a long exhale of cigarette smoke from the shadows. 'Perhaps, you've heard of me?'

'We have, meine Dame.'

'How nice,' said Zita, pleased.

'Won't you come this way?'

Zita preened. 'Preferential treatment? Now I know I've come home.' She stepped through the doors held open for her. 'Thank you, boys. I didn't catch your names?'

But the first of the sentries was saying something to a pair of Wehrmacht soldiers positioned inside the entrance. Zita's German was rusty, and she missed what it was while trying to block the glare of the lobby's chandeliers from her eyes. All four soldiers now regarded her.

'Are you sure?' one of the new soldiers queried.

A man from the first pair confirmed it. 'It's her. Look at her. Don't you go to the *Kino*, man?'

The new soldier scratched his head. 'She always plays sluts.'

Zita thought on her feet. 'I've made a career of it, puss.' She gave a little twirl. 'Can't you tell I'm in costume? I've come off the set. Christ, do you think I'd let myself look this rotten if I wasn't getting paid for it?'

This seemed to amuse them.

'This way, please.' The men directed her to the grand staircase, where two more Wehrmacht men stood guard.

Zita glanced around the Vendôme lobby for any evidence of Mimi or Claude, or any other face she knew. But there were only Germans. 'Thank you, boys. Tell your mamas they gave you nice manners.' She took the first stair.

'Escort Fräulein Zita,' said the original sentry to the third pair of men.

'This way, meine Dame.'

'There's no need, I've lived here for years.'

'For your safety, meine Dame.'

'Oh. Well, if you insist on it.'

The two stair sentries fell into position on either side of Zita as she began to ascend. 'Isn't this sweet?' she purred. 'Personal service.' Her head was swimming and she caught her heel on a step, making her stumble. They steadied her under each arm.

'Careful, meine Dame.'

'It's been a very long day on the set, boys,' said Zita, embarrassed. 'Guess I'm more tired than I knew.'

They didn't let her go. Their hands felt like steel.

When they reached the first floor, rather than continuing up another flight of stairs to where Zita's suite was, they turned into the first-floor corridor.

'Not this way, I'm in the cheap seats.'

'This is the way, meine Dame.'

'The way to where?'

'Where you are wanted.'

She tried to plant her feet on the floor. 'Enough now, boys, we've all had some fun. I'm on the second floor.'

They lifted her from the ground and continued walking. She struggled in their grip.

'Please do *not*, meine Dame. There is only shame in being forced to strike a woman.'

Zita went limp.

They were nearing Lana Mae's rooms. 'Stop here, boys. There's an old pal of mine in this one. If we play our cards right, she'll give us all a drink.'

To her surprise, they did stop, returning her feet to the floor in front of the closed doors.

'That's better.' Zita smoothed her hair and dress. 'Christ, let's hope I don't make her bring up her dinner at the sight of me.' She went to press the bell, but one of the double doors opened before she could reach it. Another Wehrmacht soldier stood guard on the inside.

'Fräulein Zita is here,' said one of her escorts.

The new soldier opened the double doors fully, regarding her with interest. 'Please come in, Fräulein.'

Every bone in her body told her not to. 'A good friend of Mrs Huckstepp are you, puss?'

The new soldier waited. Zita stepped inside. The Imperial Suite doors closed softly behind her.

She looked fearfully at the new man, before calling into the rooms beyond. 'It's only me, Lana Mae – your little Zita, back from the grave and looking like the warmed-up dead.'

The doors to the grand boudoir opened slowly and Zita caught a glimpse of the armoire, incongruously blocking the built-in. Then she saw him: a huge, middle-aged German man, still dripping from a bath and wrapping himself in a Ritz peach robe. There was a cigar at his lips.

'Ah, little Zita, you have come home at last. And you look like the dead, you say? Yet to me you have never looked lovelier.'

She gasped. 'Hans?'

The past reclaimed Zita. Her strength gave out and she sank to her knees.

Metzingen took his time approaching her, savouring the cigar. He opened a drawer at the bedside table first and withdrew something from it. The Wehrmacht sentry who had let her into the suite now vanished inside another room.

Zita tried to make words. 'Hullo – how've you been, puss?'

'But my pretty *Liebchen*, why do you look so afraid of me?' said Metzingen, surprised.

'I'm not afraid – I'm very happy to see you. Can't you tell?'

'Yet you are trembling?'

She was. Zita stared at his powerful arms, his enormous hands, remembering everything about him, everything he could *do*. 'Hans, don't – please don't – whatever you're thinking of doing to me . . .'

'But I have not come all this way to hurt you. Why would I do that, *Liebchen*?'

She wanted to believe him.

'Wasn't that clear in my telegrams?'

She raked his eyes, desperate for a sign of sincerity. 'Yes, the telegrams . . .' Now her teeth were chattering.

He shook his head pityingly. 'Zita, you are the love of my life. You know that you are.'

'Listen, Hans –'

'*You know you are.* You have been so very good to me,' said Metzingen, 'so very loyal.'

She tried again. 'I haven't, Hans – not really.' She took a deep breath, squaring up to it. 'I ran away from Berlin. I left you there.'

Yet he seemed only forgiving of it. 'That's old news now. We were both so young and naïve back then. All is forgotten because you have been kind to the Reich.'

She cleared her throat. 'It wasn't kindness, Hans – you *made* me do what I did.'

'Hush now, that's not true.'

'But it is.'

'*Liebchen* . . .' He cradled Zita's face in his massive hands. 'The floor plans, the files, all that we needed to know of the Ritz – what you did, you did for your love of the Führer.'

She closed her eyes at her crime fed back to her. 'You know I didn't, Hans, I don't share your ideology – I *can't* share it. It's why I ran away.'

'That was the reason?'

She opened her eyes again. 'It was one . . .'

He chuckled. 'Hush. You did what you did for your love of me, Zita.'

'Oh God. *Hans, please listen –*'

'And of course, you did it for the love of our child . . .'

Zita stopped, frozen, her face in his fingers. With a twist of his wrists, he could kill her, she thought, like she'd seen him kill others.

Instead, he showed her what he had taken from the drawer. 'I promised you a gift from her . . .'

It was a photograph of a smiling girl, aged no more than twelve. Her hair was cut in blunt bangs. Her dress was simple and shapeless. She was using both hands to eat a hunk of bread in some institutional room. She was innocent and happy; a simpleton.

'And look, see, she has written to her *mutti*,' said Metzingen. He turned the photograph over. On the reverse, in the crayon scrawl of a child far younger, the girl had written her name.

Lotti

'I have kept my side of our agreement,' Metzingen said. His look was tender. 'Our Lotti is well cared for.'

The longed-for sight of her daughter pushed Zita into something like clarity. 'She looks so pretty, Hans . . .'

Metzingen smiled. 'She's a lucky girl, healthy and strong.'

'When did you see her last?'

'Two months ago. Before we commenced the French campaign.'

Was this a lie? Zita wondered. And yet she wanted to believe he had visited her. 'My Lotti . . .' She kissed the photograph before slipping it into her purse.

There was a long moment while Zita and Metzingen regarded each other; he so incongruously effeminate in the peach Ritz robe, she so incongruously ugly in her still filthy clothes from the long walk home. Her fear at seeing him again after so very long fell away. It could have been 1927 once more. Zita saw herself from that time: the rising silent film star in a divinely decadent Berlin. She saw Hans as he was then: the lowly director's assistant and the most beautiful man she had known; a Teutonic god. She remembered the very first words he had said to her: a quaint little story of how once he had held open the door for her at the Ritz, five years earlier, when he had given her a lip rouge which she had dropped on the step. Zita had lied and told him that she remembered it well. He had been transparently pleased. They had fallen into bed. They had fallen into an affair. And then she had learned of his growing interest in something he called National Socialism – something that had come to mean everything to him. Or, almost everything. He had room in his heart for Hitler – and for her.

Metzingen drew on his cigar. 'Well, then,' he said, exhaling a billow of smoke to the ceiling.

'Yes, Hans. Well, then.' She looked at him now knowing all he could do to those who posed a threat to his obscene belief. She looked at him knowing he was still just a man despite everything; a man who had once desired her as no other man had desired her before – or since.

She looked at Metzingen and knew that desire was still raging inside him. There was a chance she could win this, she thought; there was a chance that all those flimsy justifications she had made to her three beloved friends might yet hold firm. 'Is all Paris to learn of it? Is the Ritz?'

'Learn what?'

She couldn't say it.

'Ah,' said Metzingen, understanding, 'you mean your betrayal?'

She hated that word. How could what she had done ever be called a betrayal in the scheme of things? What tiny importance was a single hotel when measured against Hitler's war? So, she'd stolen some floor plans, tattled a few tales. She had done it because no one would really be hurt by it. She had done it to ensure Lotti's safety, the very purest of motives: a mother protecting her child. Who could condemn her for that? Zita well knew: everyone.

Polly.

'Do you wish Paris to know of your brave actions for the Reich?' he wondered.

She swallowed. 'Do *you* wish Paris to know?'

He seemed to consider it.

'I don't think I could bear it if people found out . . .'

'No?'

She shook her head.

'I agree it is too early,' Metzingen conceded. 'When the dust is settled, and Paris has accepted its changed circumstances, then will be the time. You'll be celebrated then, along with all the Führer's spies.'

She shivered, knowing this was a temporary reprieve. She would simply have to make the best of things. 'And what of us, Hans? What are we to be now that you've come for me?'

'To the world or just to ourselves?' he wondered.

'Both,' she said.

He considered again. 'To the world we will be strangers for now,' he told her, pragmatically. 'If your service to the Reich is to remain secret. But in private, away from all eyes, well then . . .' He clearly savoured the prospect.

'Well then, what? What will we be, Hans? Tell me.'

'Oh, *Liebchen*.' He smiled. 'You already learned that script.'

She didn't shift from his gaze, but her fingers found the buttons of her blouse. She undid the first one.

Metzingen let his incongruous robe fall open, so that she could gaze upon him again, as he gazed upon her. Each were as magnificent now to the other as they had been when they were younger.

'On these occasions, Hans, we know that a script isn't required,' Zita told him. She knew what would come next for her, but she knew what she must hear from him before it began. The blouse slipped from her shoulders. 'My friends here. You will not hurt them? Promise me.'

'What friends?'

'You know very well who, Hans. Lana Mae. Alexandrine. And now there's a young girl we look after. Her most of all. *Promise me.*'

He moved towards her, the robe falling to the floor. 'I promise you anything.'

'And our child,' she whispered. 'You will let me see Lotti now – now that I've done all you asked? You'll let me make up for my abandonment, somehow?'

'Of course, I will.'

'*Promise me.*'

His mouth was on hers. 'I told you. I promise it, *Liebchen.*'

He scooped her up and threw her onto the bed, in the sumptuous grand boudoir that was formerly Lana Mae's. He tore off Zita's shoes, her silk stockings, her stained summer skirt; he hurled all of them out the door. Then he regarded her, naked before him, as the smell of her reached his nose.

'I have walked for four days,' Zita told him, embarrassed.

He pulled her from the sheets by her ankles and tossed her bodily into the shower. He turned both taps on full and left her there alone to achieve his scrupulous hygiene standards; a fastidious German to the end.

PART TWO

Interruption

8

7 August 1940

Out of necessity, Polly had conditioned herself to wake up first, ahead of the Girls, just as the first rays of dawn brought a glow to the muslin curtains. Trying not to groan at feeling so stiff from yet another night spent clinging to the edge of her once spacious bed, she was glad she could at least slip out from under the covers and into the bathroom before the others awoke and monopolised it. Once the Girls were awake, the bathroom became a battlefield.

Still under the eiderdown, Lana Mae stirred a little, ceased her snoring, and rolled over to Polly's vacated spot, but didn't wake up. She began snoring again. Next to her, at the other edge, sleeping Alexandrine stayed perfectly, elegantly still. On the Watteau pink sofa, under a mound of quilt, Zita slept curled like a cat. Picking her way through discarded shoes, hats and other apparel that wouldn't fit into the built-in, Polly crept inside the little bathroom and gratefully shut the door.

Since the end of June and their return to the Ritz, the four of them had been faced with no other respectable choice than to bunk in together. Lana Mae, Alexandrine and Zita had all held suites on the Vendôme side of the hotel that were now fully occupied by Germans. Only Polly's rooms, on the Cambon side, had been left alone. It would, they all hoped, be a temporary arrangement; Claude had promised to give them all rooms of their own just as soon as more became free again. Polly hadn't minded being the answer to the Girls' accommodation crisis, despite the imposition it entailed, for as she saw it, there was safety in numbers, and safety was now paramount to them all.

Polly sat on the lavvy before filling the bath, using the time it took filling with water to brush her teeth, while running through her mind the day's intended routine. Today, as with every other day now, Polly would bathe first and return to the bedroom just as the others complainingly yawned and stretched. Then would follow a short burst of recriminations from those (Zita and Lana Mae) who felt that Polly's early rising was somehow a ruse to deprive them of things. Then a knock at the door would see the delivery of coffee, croissants and fresh fruit brought up from the hotel kitchen. Given there were always Germans to be found in *l'Espadon* now, the four of them had abandoned going downstairs for breakfast at all, declaring that their daily fortifications needed to be taken in private if they were ever to have a hope of facing the enemy with élan. So, they ate in Polly's room, strewing the communal bed with croissant crumbs as they planned how best to tackle whatever the morning's particular obstacles might be. This was when the set routine branched into variety.

The four of them had decided, back in late June, when the sudden shift in circumstances had made them look at every aspect of their lives anew, that not only did safety reside in numbers, camaraderie did, too. When they left the Ritz, which they did every day, they went together. Whatever individual appointment each or any of them might have, it was faced in company. Sometimes they split into pairs, but they never went anywhere alone.

When Polly had finished getting ready, she opened the bathroom door to find the others awake and glaring accusingly at her.

'Every morning,' said Lana Mae, with sleep in her eyes, 'every goddamn morning you get up before any of us do, fresh as a goddamn daisy, to turn that perfectly acceptable bathroom into a goddamn sewer.'

'Good morning to you, Lana Mae,' said Polly, affectionately, bending down to kiss her American guardian on the cheek. Lana Mae hugged her tightly, as she did every morning, her guilt at not having shared the ordeal on the road by no means dissipated since her friends' return. 'And what do we have to look forward to today?' wondered Polly.

'I've gotta go see my banker,' said Lana Mae, 'now that he's opened up shop again. It's been too long since I've made that smarmy bastard do a song and dance for me.'

Polly smiled. 'I've got to make my daily visit to dear Gendarme Teissier,' she said, which was how she referred to the police officer in charge of the Foreigners Register at the 8th arrondissement prefecture.

'And I have no plans,' said Zita, fluffing her hair, 'although I should drop in on my heel of an agent. It's time the layabout got me more work.'

'You can do that tomorrow then,' said Alexandrine, neatly swinging her feet from the bed and into a pair of mules. 'Let's try to keep things simple today. I promised I would visit poor Suzette.'

It was agreed.

There was the expected knock at the door. Polly was becoming practised at not letting a sliver of her feelings show as she went to open the door before anyone else thought to. Tommy was waiting in the corridor with their breakfast on a trolley. He gave her the little toss of his head and she gave it back, beaming at him, which was as far as they went in stepping outside protocol with the collective eyes of Zita, Lana Mae and Alexandrine upon them.

'Bonjour, Tommy,' called Lana Mae, yawning and in danger of spilling from her nightgown.

'Bonjour, Madame,' said Tommy, being careful where he put his eyes. 'I'm sorry there is no fruit today.'

'Why not?' said Zita.

'The produce at Les Halles wasn't acceptable when Monsieur Auzello went down there before dawn, Mademoiselle. The Germans have requisitioned the best.'

They collectively grunted.

'At least they've left us the coffee,' said Zita, although she might well have added 'for now'.

Alexandrine didn't even acknowledge Tommy.

As Polly held the door open for him to wheel the trolley into the corridor again, and out of sight of the breakfasting Girls, she tried to catch his eye. 'Hello,' she whispered.

'Hello,' he whispered back.

They stared at each other for a moment, feeling something between them that didn't quite need any words.

Then, for want of anything else to say, Polly asked, 'You're not working in the Cambon bar so much these days?'

'Are you still trying to like cocktails?' Tommy asked back.

'No.' She laughed. 'I've given them up. They didn't quite suit me.'

He appreciated this. 'It's healthier. I've given up cigarettes because they didn't suit me either.' Then he added, 'We're short-staffed these days, I work where Monsieur Auzello puts me.'

'I see. And so, you live here, too?'

She held his look and saw his small reaction of surprise that she had somehow discovered this.

'Yes,' said Tommy. Then he added, 'There are empty attic rooms. They're from the time when more guests travelled with their servants.'

If not for her resolve to remain unaffected by males, Polly might have wondered whether he was telling her where she might find him should she so care to look. Inside the room, the Girls were aware of them talking now. 'See you around then,' said Polly.

'Sure.'

He brushed against her hand, his fingers sweeping the most sensitive part of her wrist. She gave an intake of breath with the surprise of it. Tommy went on his way down the corridor. Polly stayed where she was, her mouth slightly open, watching him go.

'*Darling.*' Alexandrine had an eyebrow raised, warningly.

Polly closed the door and came back inside the room.

Every day that she had seen Tommy since her return to the Ritz, Polly had tried to look for the proof that would confirm he was Blanche Auzello's lover. Always she saw the look in his eye that told her he carried a secret. Yet this look wasn't proof.

When Polly sat down while the Girls began their morning bathroom war, she discovered the tiny, folded piece of paper that Tommy had slipped inside her sleeve. She didn't take it out to read what it said, for fear of her guardians noticing. She kept it exactly where Tommy had hidden it, knowing that it would be something that united them both.

For Polly the German Occupation meant the thing she had most feared had happened, and yet it wasn't as bad as she had feared. Still, Polly knew, this didn't mean she could abandon caution. Leaving the Ritz as one of a foursome, via the hotel's Cambon doors, brought Polly into a city still denuded of Parisian males. Those men who hadn't been killed at the front had been taken captive and were now held in prisoner of war camps. Polly had heard talk that these men would be allowed to return home in stages, yet so far very few had. She had also heard talk that these camps were really labour camps in disguise. Despite the absence of men, the capital was no longer feminised. The women of Paris were now matched by thousands upon thousands of admiring men. The German invaders routinely stood aside to allow Polly and the Girls to pass in the street. French men had rarely done that. The German men did not harass them, and did not call out, unlike the French. The Germans offered seats in cafés, and even when out of uniform, they were equally well dressed, well-mannered and amiable, and most surprising of all, so many spoke French. This was what Polly meant when she said that the German Occupation wasn't as bad as she had feared. Beguilingly, yet disturbingly, Paris had almost become better for all women. Yet Polly wondered how long this would last.

While the city appeared to be functioning as it always had, it wasn't. In addition to the lack of cars driven by French people (the Germans had 'purchased' them all), the clocks had been brought forward one hour so that Paris was the same as Berlin; an unsettling, if not unbearable imposition. Parisians coped with it. They also coped with the night-time curfew from ten o'clock at night until five in the morning. All the lively establishments, including the Ritz, now started their entertainment while still bathed in daylight, in order to be done by the restriction.

This morning, Polly and the Girls headed off as a group. Polly's practice of getting her guardians to share their stories, which she'd honed to a fine art on the road home from Dreux, was now one she continued in Paris. She could see that reliving old times from before the Occupation helped strengthen the Girls' faith, and her own, that such times might return.

'It's your turn today, Lana Mae,' announced Polly, slipping her arm through the American's.

'Me?'

There was a group of Germans ahead of them on the street – uniformed men. Four beautifully dressed women emerging from the Ritz had gained their instant attention.

'The lessons I learn from these stories are very enlightening,' Polly told her, well aware of the Germans, as were her guardians, yet making no mention of it. The four of them started walking towards the soldiers down the rue Cambon, hats held high.

'You were born in Kansas,' Polly started Lana Mae off.

Lana Mae settled into the rhythm of their heels upon the pavement, seeing the Germans but not seeing them. 'That's right, honey. The polite term for what I was back then is "rural poor", but I prefer my own words for it: hick town trash.'

The others laughed, loud and confident; a show of feminine unity.

'That was me,' said Lana Mae, stopping now to perform a little curtsey, 'I started working for a living of my own when I was young, *real* young, and only because I had to. You see, I wanted to eat.' She patted her ever-straining girdle. 'Maybe a little too much, but then I've always loved my food. The very first job I got was as a waitress, and it had one perk: free grits. But everything else about it was lousy. So, I got a job as a telephone operator, and from there, because I had such a charming speaking voice, you understand, I got hired as a receptionist at a very respectable doctor's practice.'

'Which was where she screwed the boss,' Zita crowed.

'Zita, *please*!' Lana Mae complained, covering Polly's ears. She uncovered them again. 'It's where I *seduced* the boss.' She saw Alexandrine frowning. 'Oh honey, *please*. And this from the dame with her la-di-da "arrangement" with the Comte.'

Polly grinned at this grown-up talk while Alexandrine chose to say nothing, dignified.

'She did more than screw the doc,' said Zita, enjoying this. 'Clever puss, she married and divorced him, too.'

'And all before I was seventeen,' said Lana Mae, proudly, wiggling her behind.

The soldiers looked at each other, delighted at Lana Mae's posing, but none called out or spoke. As one, they stepped from the pavement and stood in the road respectfully while Polly and her companions passed. 'Bonjour Mesdames!' called one of them in French. He tipped his cap at them, his smiling companions following suit. They were ravishingly, unsettlingly handsome.

By now Polly and the Girls had well learned it was safer to engage with the Occupiers when they were being friendly than risk making them otherwise by not. 'Bonjour Messieurs,' called Lana Mae in return. There was a moment while the two groups appraised each other, before Lana Mae started her story again. 'The doc thought I was twenty-one,' she said, as the women resumed their walk as if nothing about the encounter was noteworthy at all. 'Gruesome to-do when he found out the truth.'

They laughed again, deliberately feminine and gay. Not one of the four turned to look back at the soldiers.

'Anyhoo, sometime after that,' said Lana Mae, 'as a gay divorcée, I took myself to Cincinnati, which is where I met my beautiful Horace T. Huckstepp.' She became wistful.

'He was your second husband?' Polly sought to clarify.

'Two times the charm,' said Lana Mae, 'and before you ask, yes, I loved him, and yes, with all my heart, and yes, he loved me – we were written in the stars, baby.'

'And in the newspapers,' said Zita, sticking her head between Polly and Lana Mae's linked arms. 'Horace T. was a steel magnate, filthy rich, and thirty years older than little Lana Mae.'

'True love is blind to age,' said Lana Mae. 'Sadly, we were shunned by Cincinnati high society, if you could call it that, and by Horace T's family, which was worse. They wanted nothing to do with us.'

She turned back to Polly. 'I'd had enough of being looked at like dirt, baby, and I was taking no more of it. So, we moved to New York. I wanted to live the high life that was due to the both of us.'

Ahead of them were more Germans appraising them.

Alexandrine stepped in. 'Lana Mae and Horace T. tried to buy entrée into the Manhattan upper crust with several hundred thousand dollars' worth of profligate hospitality,' she said, archly. 'And they *failed*.'

The three women at once burst into more laughter at this, although why it was so hilarious this time Polly didn't quite see.

Still laughing, Lana Mae dabbed at her eye. 'And thank God for it, baby, because without it we wouldn't have come here.'

The new group of uniformed men tipped their caps as well.

'You are beautiful, Madame,' called out one of them.

'Who's beautiful, puss?' Zita cracked. 'There are four of us here.'

The soldier who'd called consulted with a companion. 'You are beautiful, *Mesdames*,' he corrected, grinning, using the French plural.

Zita fluffed her hair. 'That's more like it. Now, next time tell us something we don't know.'

They continued down the rue Cambon.

'But doesn't Paris have snobs?' Polly wondered, apparently innocently, continuing the conversation from before.

This only produced fresh hoots of laughter.

'Oh baby, Parisians are the very *worst*,' said Lana Mae, 'but here no one kids themselves that *any* Americans have pedigrees, let alone hicks like me. And besides,' she added, 'generous hands with a ginormous fortune made up nicely for an oversight of ancestry.' She sighed, suddenly sad. 'But then Horace T's ticker gave out.'

Zita and Alexandrine looked at Lana Mae sympathetically. There was no denying it: their American friend had loved her late husband dearly.

'Widowhood didn't dampen the Mrs Huckstepp sensation any,' Alexandrine told Polly, 'quite the reverse.'

'I started throwing little dinner parties just like we did in New York,' said Lana Mae, brightening again, 'but this time I did it big time. *Real* big. Well, it was only what Horace T. would have wanted. And here in Paris, it *worked*.'

They had reached the end of the rue Cambon. 'This is where I go see my banker,' said Lana Mae, 'I'm running out of cash, and that slimy worm is gonna open his goddamn safe for me.'

'You're the living end,' said Zita, 'We can't fit one more stinking frock in the room as it is.'

Lana Mae looked levelly at her. 'It's not to buy clothes,' she said. There was a new self-respect in her face. 'And maybe when you find out what I'm gonna do with it, you'll think better of me.'

Zita tucked her arm through Lana Mae's. 'Whatever you say. I'll still be your date at the bank.'

But Lana Mae was uncharacteristically serious. 'I'm really gonna surprise you, honey, just wait and see.'

'Yeah, sure.' Zita patted her hand.

Alexandrine and Polly kissed them both.

'You two go then,' said Alexandrine. 'I shall take Polly to see her Gendarme Teissier, and from there we shall visit Suzette.'

Zita and Lana Mae continued to walk, planning a route that would allow them to pass the black and red Wehrmacht sentry boxes that had sprung up everywhere. Long queues stretched from all of them, as Parisians submitted to the Occupiers' endless identification checks.

Polly and Alexandrine decided to take the Metro to get to the 8th Police Prefecture, and took the turn towards Madeleine station.

Exiting the Metro at Opéra, Polly and Alexandrine passed a line of frustrated people queueing outside a bakery. 'Why don't we have to line up for our food?' Polly asked Alexandrine. 'And why do our ration tickets seem to give us rather more than other people's?'

'Because we are paying for it,' Alexandrine whispered, looking around.

Polly wasn't happy with this answer. It didn't seem to her to be in the spirit of France.

At the police prefecture, in a reception thronging with people coming and going, they were required to wait until Polly's name was called by the officer in charge of the Foreigners Register. This was the cheerily pleasant Gendarme Teissier, to whom Polly was obliged to report daily, and whose goal, he would have observers believe, was only to make the unwelcome requirement less irksome where he could. It seemingly pained him that the realities of the busy police station often gave him no option but to keep foreigners waiting while more pressing matters were dealt with. This morning, after ten minutes of waiting, Alexandrine found she had need of a lavatory. Because the police prefecture provided no such amenity for women, she was obliged to seek out another one.

'But I'll be breaking our rule if I leave you alone here,' said Alexandrine, conflicted, although badly in need.

'I'll be perfectly safe. Please go, Alexandrine.'

The Comtesse did, providing Polly with the first opportunity she had to read the tiny folded piece of paper Tommy had slipped into her sleeve. She hadn't dared take it out earlier, for fear it would be snatched by one of her guardians and read out aloud. Whatever Tommy's words, they were meant only for her.

The paper was thin, unusually so, and therefore fragile, but once unfolded it proved larger than she had thought it would be.

She hadn't known what to expect from Tommy's words but with the ghost of his fingers brushing at her wrist she had allowed herself to expect all the same. Yet now that she had the note open before her, she didn't think they were Tommy's words at all. The sheet was crudely printed, and the ink was purple, the result of a mimeograph stencil.

Tips for the Occupied

Don't be fooled, they are not tourists, they are conquerors. Be polite to them, but do not exceed this correct behaviour to be friendly. Don't hurry to accommodate them. In the end, they will not reciprocate.

If one of them addresses you in German, act confused and continue on your journey. If he addresses you in French, you are not obliged to show him the way. He is not your travelling companion.

If, in the café or restaurant, he tries to start a conversation, make him understand, politely, that what he has to say does not interest you. If he asks you for a light, offer your cigarette. Never in human history has one refused a light, even to the most traditional enemy . . .

The guy you buy your suspenders from has decided to put a sign on his shop: MAN SPRICHT DEUTSCH (we speak German). Go to another shop.

You complain because they order you to be home by 22:00 hrs on the dot. You are so naive; you didn't realise that it's so you can listen to English radio?

You won't find copies of these tips at your local bookshop. Most likely, you only have a single copy and want to keep it. So, make copies for your friends, who will make copies, too. This will be a good occupation for the Occupied.

Continue to show an elegant indifference, but don't let your anger diminish. It will eventually come in handy . . .

Polly was transfixed.

She had allowed herself to expect something playful, something personal from Tommy, but what he'd given her was far more significant. Someone, somewhere, had written this list of tips, that, while being ostensibly ironic, betrayed an underlying defiance. These words were an act of resistance.

The writer and the people who had distributed the sheets, and the other people again with other mimeograph machines who had made more copies and distributed them further, these people had all done something, however small, to fight back against the Germans.

Tommy was one of them.

Perhaps he had wanted the means to make amends for patronising her.

If so, he had found it. Tommy had let Polly glimpse a grown-up's life that had nothing to do with fashion, or fine living, or the insulating effect of money.

It was a grown-up's life with *purpose*.

'Mademoiselle Hartford?'

Polly looked up. The friendly, flabby face of Gendarme Teissier was craning from the reception counter to smile at her. 'Yes, Monsieur Gendarme?'

'It is your turn to sign, my girl – would you like to come forward?'

The mimeographed sheet burned hot in her hands. She scrunched it into a ball, stuffing it inside the Hermès handbag, and it was then that something registered as being profoundly, shockingly wrong.

'Mademoiselle Hartford?'

Battling disbelief, Polly tried to process what she had just discovered.

The gendarme was in danger of becoming less polite.

'Good morning, Gendarme Teissier,' Polly greeted him brightly as she hurried to the counter.

'Good morning, Polly.' He smiled at her. 'You look so very sweet today.'

'Thank you. It is such a nice summer's day, isn't it?'

'If already very warm,' he said, sighing.

As Polly went to sign the register book, the gendarme moved it from her reach before she could put the pen to it. Already thrown, Polly was slow to comprehend. She went to move the book where she could sign it again.

Teissier held it from her grasp. 'This is an awkward matter,' he said, 'but you are to be interviewed today. It is just a formality. Will you come inside for a moment?'

Teissier pressed an unseen button beneath the counter and a little door unclicked, giving access to the rooms beyond. Polly felt her heartbeat race and looked around in the hope Alexandrine had returned. 'But why?' She fought to keep her cool. 'Is something wrong today?'

'Of course not,' he said, 'it is just a formality, my girl, nothing more.' He smiled expansively. Polly guessed that this statement – and his smile – was not so much for her benefit as for those eavesdropping. He mopped his jowls with a handkerchief. 'It's what they expect, you know.'

'They?'

Teissier lowered his voice. 'All we have to do is let them *believe* we're listening to them.'

He meant the Germans. 'Of course,' said Polly.

He nodded at the door. 'Let's keep them happy. It's always better in the end.'

Polly did as she was told just as the Comtesse returned. Polly tried to convey her a look that told Alexandrine not to worry, even though Polly herself was desperately worried as the door clicked shut behind her.

Polly found herself in an interview room with no windows. The only light was from a harsh, bare bulb. The heat was stifling.

'This is a very depressing room, I apologise for it,' said Teissier, shutting the door behind them. 'I wish there was a better one, but we will rise above it. Take a seat, my girl.'

There was only one to be had: a hard, wooden stool. Polly sat uncomfortably on it while the gendarme remained standing.

'Please, can't I sign the register, Monsieur?' she asked, clutching the Hermès.

He was a picture of apology. 'I'm afraid I cannot – or rather, I cannot for now. This is very unpleasant.' He mopped at his brow. 'Would you open your bag for me?'

Polly's tongue felt dead in her mouth. 'My handbag is private.'

He gave her an indulgent look. 'Ordinarily, I would not ask something so importunate of a young woman. But nothing is ordinary nowadays.' He scraped his handkerchief across the flesh of his throat again. 'Please give me the bag. I saw that you tried to hide something in there.'

Polly was robbed of words. She gave him her bag. Teissier opened it wide at the catch. The screwed-up sheet inside was obvious. What was also obvious to Polly alone was what the bag did not contain: Aunt Marjorie's gun. Someone had taken it.

'Ah.' Teissier looked saddened. 'And what is that?' he asked, nodding at the screwed-up sheet.

Her mind was molasses. She struggled to make words. 'I – I don't really know, Monsieur. I found it.'

'Will you show me it, please.'

Polly reached forward and took the crumbled ball, smoothing it out to show him, all the while thinking only of the missing gun. When had it gone? Who had known it was there to take it?

'Ah.' The gendarme already knew exactly what the sheet of paper was. 'It is as I feared. This is awkward indeed. You say you found this?'

'Yes,' Polly lied. 'On the Metro. It was left on my seat.'

'And why did you pick it up?'

'I don't know,' said Polly, 'I just did.'

'And why did you keep it?'

'I – I don't know, Monsieur le Gendarme.'

'You just did?'

'Yes . . .'

'The writer of that leaflet has committed treason under French law, do you understand that?' he asked her.

Polly opened her mouth to reply but couldn't say anything. Her heart thumped dully in her chest.

'When he is discovered,' Teissier went on, 'which he will be, he'll find himself imprisoned for it – or worse. Do you see how things are, my girl?'

Polly managed to nod.

'These are changed times.' Teissier shook his head. 'I have seen the most respectable of British men placed behind barbed wire fences – and their respectable British women placed with them. They have all been interned, and we, the gendarmerie, are powerless to free them. So many of these fine people lived in Paris for years – for decades, some of them – leading the most blameless of lives. You live at the Hôtel Ritz, my girl, so you would have seen who is gone from your home. The Canadian Doctor Mandel, for instance, I'm sure you knew him. A respected man. But orders must be followed. I arrested the doctor myself, you see.' He stuffed his handkerchief into a pocket. 'If your aunt were still with us, she would have been among the first to go herself.'

Polly swallowed.

'Still, I find it helps to remember things as they were before this war,' said Teissier. 'You're far too young to have taken notice, so let me tell you how it was. The government couldn't run itself. France was a shambles.' He took a breath, contemplating the memory of it. 'There are those who don't much like the Germans for turning up as they did, but I say this: the Germans have got things running properly again, so perhaps they deserve some credit for it?'

Teissier took the flimsy sheet from Polly and neatly folded it. Then he returned her bag. 'So, please understand me, my girl, you can only remain free at my discretion.'

Polly nodded but could no longer hear him. How could any Frenchman find the actions of the Occupiers acceptable, she asked herself. How could any Frenchman equate what Hitler offered with liberty, equality and fraternity?

'Are you listening to me?' Teissier asked her, sharply.

Polly snapped out of her thoughts. 'Of course, Monsieur.'

'Presently, a teenaged girl like yourself is not seen as a threat to anyone, however non-French she might be.'

'Or non-German?'

He looked at her blankly. 'I stress *presently*,' he said. 'That could change at any time. Please do nothing more that would provoke such a change.'

Polly bowed her head. 'I won't, Monsieur le Gendarme.'

Ushered from her banker's office, Lana Mae had a sudden need to steady herself against the wall. The sweep of stairs that led down to the atrium of the opulent Société Génerale building loomed before her, stretching and receding.

'Are you all right, Mrs Huckstepp?' the silver-haired banker, Monsieur Lacaze, asked her, concerned.

'Yes . . .' She feared she might be sick. 'No . . .'

'I appreciate it's been an unpleasant shock. Do you require a brandy?'

Lana Mae stared at him until she remembered her anger. 'Promise me you'll tell no one about this, Lacaze.'

'Mrs Huckstepp?'

'*No one.* Say it.'

'At this bank we stake our reputation upon discretion.'

'Just say it, you goddamn eel.'

The banker maintained his dignity. 'No one will hear of your predicament from me, Mrs Huckstepp, or from anyone else at the Société Génerale.'

'How many know already?'

He cleared his throat. 'I am the only one here who knows anything of what has happened, because only I handle your funds.'

Lana Mae felt her heart snap in two. She was devastated. 'I was gonna *do* something with my money, for once, do you understand me, Lacaze?'

'You planned a new fashion purchase?' he asked, sympathetically.

She bit back the sting of the reminder of how everyone, without exception, thought about the way she lived. 'I've got enough damn frocks.'

'A purchase of jewellery then?' said Lacaze. 'I am very sorry for the disappointment, Mrs Huckstepp. The Société Génerale is distressed to see any longstanding client such as yourself unable to enjoy the rights of their wealth.'

She felt like choking at his words. 'What about the rights of those who don't have any wealth?' she challenged him. 'Do the wealthy have a right to look out for them?'

He didn't seem to comprehend this notion. 'Mrs Huckstepp?'

She could see no more point to the conversation and began to tackle the stairs. 'Good day to you, Monsieur.'

Monsieur Lacaze bowed after her, embarrassed.

When Lana Mae reached the bank's vast lobby she found to her dismay that Zita had been joined by the last person either of them wished to see: Coco Chanel.

'Look, who it is!' purred the designer, her legs crossed elegantly in a club chair. 'Our dear Mrs Truckstop.'

Lana Mae shot a murderous look to Zita who cast a look of matching fury back. She'd been suffering Coco's company for some time.

'Mademoiselle Chanel, how charming,' said Lana Mae, grimacing.

The designer turned to Zita. 'Did you know our dear Herr Metzingen gave Lana Mae that naughty name?'

Zita went still at mention of Metzingen.

'They shared luncheon together on his very first day at the Ritz,' said Coco.

'He did not, and we did not,' said Lana Mae, rewriting the unpleasant recent past.

Zita narrowed her eyes at Coco. 'The krauts are "dear" now, are they? That's patriotic.'

'We must all try harder to get along,' said Coco. 'The Germans are not at all as we feared. The Oberstleutnant is perfectly decent to talk to should you ever dare show yourself at *l'Espadon* again.'

'Why shouldn't I show myself?' said Lana Mae.

'Well,' Coco flinched regretfully, 'that little "Truckstop" name.'

'That is not what he called me.'

'Oh heavens. I must have it all wrong. You know what the Ritz is like for Chinese whispers. What *did* he call you, dear?'

Lana Mae said nothing. Zita glanced away, ashamed for her.

Coco tittered. 'We really mustn't tease our dim American friend – should we, Zita?' She smiled, as if the film star had been equal part of this.

'No.'

'Not when she's doing such *good* for once . . .'

Lana Mae shivered, thinking of the news that Lacaze had broken to her.

'That's right,' said Zita, who had no idea what Coco might be referring to but didn't intend letting on.

Coco waited. After a moment she said, 'If I'm not mistaken, Lana Mae, your poor little Folies Bergère chorine knows nothing of what you've been up to.'

Lana Mae drew herself up straight. She looked at puzzled Zita. 'You know how I said I'd surprise you one day, baby? Well maybe that day is today.'

Zita blinked, waiting.

'Lana Mae has started a charitable organisation,' said Coco, grinning, 'with some of her American friends.'

'Really, puss?' said Zita, indeed surprised.

'With Babs Hutton and Flossie Gould,' said Lana Mae, and then for Coco's benefit, 'and the Duc de Doudeauville.'

'*Really*, puss?'

'None of whom would have a scrap to do with her if it wasn't for all her money,' said Coco.

Lana Mae felt sick. 'Lucky that's not a problem. I've got more money than you.'

Coco chuckled.

'What is the charity for?' asked Zita.

'For wounded French soldiers,' said Lana Mae. 'We're gonna make care packages to send to all the hospitals.'

'Oh, Lana Mae . . .' said Zita, standing up suddenly. Her kohl-black eyes sparkled with emotion. And then, because she could think of nothing more appropriate to say, she whispered: 'Like Marjorie would have done.'

Lana Mae's own eyes sparkled as she nodded. 'I thought, if a pair of snooty broads like Babs and Flossie ain't going home, despite the Germans, then I ain't going home either. I'm sticking around to *do* something – something good for France.' She looked at Coco with a sneer. 'Something better than shutting up a lousy, stinking store, anyhow.'

The designer had chosen not to hear her. 'Ah, Monsieur Lacaze, so long you have kept me waiting.'

Lana Mae winced as the banker appeared at the top of the stairs, ready to meet the designer. She shot Lacaze a blistering look to remind him of his promise to her.

Coco stood up from the club chair, arranging her pearls. 'Well, good luck with it all,' she said to Lana Mae. 'I know I like to have my fun, but really, you *are* doing good, and who knows, perhaps one day people will even respect you for it?'

Lana Mae held herself together all the way out of the Société Génerale building and onto the Boulevard Haussmann. Then the shock grew too much. She began to sob in the street.

Zita, who had been quietly marvelling that her friend had kept her activities quiet, was stunned to see her abruptly overcome. 'Puss! Puss, what is it?'

They had to sit at a café table, while Lana Mae held a handkerchief to her face as she cried. Eventually, she could put enough words together to tell Zita what had happened.

'The American government, they've put a stop on my funds.'

'They've what?'

'They've frozen my money. They won't let me transfer one more nickel to the Paris bank.'

'But they can't do that – it's *your* money!'

'They say there's too much chance it'll end up going to the Germans.'

Zita clutched her friend's hand. 'Does this mean you're broke?'

Lana Mae nodded, in agony.

'Just as we were both thinking of good Marjorie . . .'

Lana Mae closed her eyelids. 'I saw her.'

Zita blinked. 'What?'

Lana Mae opened her eyes again to stare at her friend, imploringly. 'I *saw* Marjorie. When the krauts came to the Ritz, I saw – I don't know what it was – a vision, a ghost, you tell me, all I know is that I saw Marjorie sitting at a table, smiling. And she thought well of me, baby, she knew I was *good*.'

Zita was bewildered. 'Well, of course she did, you *are* good, Lana Mae.'

Lana Mae shook her head. 'If you'd heard what the bastard said to me . . .'

'Who, now?'

'Metzingen.'

Zita's guilt reached crescendo.

'He told me what he's got inside my file.'

'It's just stupid bits of paper,' Zita pleaded with her, 'meaning-less. Don't take it seriously – please don't. They've got a stinking file on everybody now.'

'Maybe,' said Lana Mae, 'but what he's got on me, it's true. Everything he accused me of, every terrible thing that he said, it was *right*.'

Zita closed her eyes, willing away her self-loathing. 'I never said anything bad about you, puss, I swear it. I never gave him anything that would hurt you.'

Yet Lana Mae wasn't blaming her. 'It did hurt me, but it wasn't what you'd told him – it was how he twisted it. And you know what? I'm glad it hurt.'

191

Zita's eyes filled with tears, mortified. 'Oh, Lana Mae, how can you forgive me?'

But the American had forgiven her months ago. 'That's why Marjorie came to me,' she said, softly, 'and that's why I *have* to do good, don't you see? I called myself Marjorie's friend for over twenty-five years but I never followed her example, I never did anything to help someone other than me.' She scrubbed the tears from her cheeks. 'And now here I am as some phony mother to her niece? Polly should mother me.' She considered this, and suddenly laughed. 'God, it's like she actually does. No, honey, no. I'm ashamed of what I must seem like to that sweet, lovely girl.'

Zita's expression was stark. '*You're* ashamed. Oh Christ, the irony. Next to what I've done, you're an angel – a saint.'

'You did what you did for Lotti.'

'Or for love . . .'

Lana Mae stared at her. 'Do you mean to tell me you still love that bastard?'

Bleak, Zita wouldn't – couldn't – say that she didn't.

Lana Mae's face fell, sad and dismayed for her. 'Well, I guess he's good looking . . .'

'It's much more than that. You don't know how it is between us.'

The American was resolute. 'Well, I'm no saint either.' She wiped her cheeks a last time and put her handkerchief away. She signalled to the café waiter. 'Can you bring me a glass of water, honey?'

The man nodded.

When the water came, Lana Mae drank long and in silence. She put the empty glass on the table and opened her handbag to fossick for a coin.

Zita's eyes popped at the bag's bulging contents. 'Are you crazy?' She looked around in alarm. 'Shut your bag for Christ's sake. I'll get the tip.'

Lana Mae closed her bag again. 'Sorry,' she said, 'I'd forgotten about those. I got the rest of my jewels out of the vault.' She patted the leather. 'That's all of 'em now.'

Zita placed a coin on the table. 'I know I said you were dumb for keeping your jewels in the bank but ignore me. It's safer than carrying them around.'

Lana Mae was untroubled. 'I won't be carrying them for long.'

'What the hell are you going to do with them all?'

The shapely, red-headed American had found a new poise. 'I'm gonna do what Marjorie would have done.'

Polly erased all mention of the 'Tips for the Occupied' pamphlet when she told Alexandrine what had happened. Erased, too, was any mention of the missing gun, although it filled her thoughts totally. Polly knew she had been very lucky. The gendarme had accepted her lies and she had nearly cried with relief when he let her sign the register book to receive her week's ration tickets. 'This has made me wonder just whose side the gendarmerie are on,' she claimed to Alexandrine, as they emerged from the Metro at Monceau.

'They are on the side of the Government of France,' said Alexandrine, adding: 'the government that is really the Boches.'

This had now become all too clear to Polly as well. The new French Government, led by the Great War hero, Marshal Pétain, along with the government's instruments of enforcement like the gendarmerie, was not governing for France at all, but Hitler's Germany, and was doing so *willingly*.

They were walking along the Boulevard de Courcelles, towards the home of the Comte Ducru-Batailley. With every step, Polly ran through her mind the names of those few who could have had access to the Hermès bag – and thus to the gun: Zita; Lana Mae; and, of course, Alexandrine. Added to this very short list were the names of those who knew that the gun had been hidden there: Monsieur Auzello and Tommy.

Polly's account of what had happened at the prefecture was giving Alexandrine doubt. 'Are you sure you didn't provoke him?'

While she hated suspecting Tommy, Polly was also fearful for him. If it was revealed that Tommy had given the pamphlet to her, he could be deprived of his job. Polly's lies grew into further lies. 'Perhaps I did provoke the gendarme a little . . .'

'Polly! What on earth did you say?'

She pulled a fib from the air. 'I complained about the outrageous price hikes in fashion.'

'Oh my God.'

'Well, it is outrageous,' said Polly. 'Lancel raised the price of a lovely suede bag from 950 francs to 1700. We women of Paris are being priced out of buying our own wardrobes.'

Alexandrine looked at her in a way that Polly hadn't seen before.

'What is it?' Polly asked, worried she'd exposed her untruth.

'Nothing, darling.' She was a little wistful. 'You're growing up. I wish Marjorie could have seen what I did just then.'

'What did you see?'

The Comtesse couldn't put it into words. 'I suppose we must expect as much from the war.' She gave her a little sideways squeeze.

'Well, yes,' said Polly, not sure if she'd got away with it.

'You were right to speak your mind, if that's what you did. It's true about these price hikes.'

'Yes,' said Polly, ashamed of herself now for being believed. 'I merely pointed out that the police are supposed to be investigating these sorts of abuses, and yet where were they at Lancel? Gendarme Teissier may have felt I was saying he was incompetent, but I didn't mean him personally, of course.' She trailed off. The loss of the gun made her feel small and vulnerable.

Alexandrine's attention was further along the boulevard. 'That's a Boche car.'

Polly looked ahead. A long, black Daimler-Benz was drawn up at the side of the avenue. Polly and Alexandrine had lately become too familiar with such vehicles at the Ritz. 'It's someone important,' said Polly. 'But I can't see any soldiers.'

'There's only a driver,' said Alexandrine.

The window down, a Wehrmacht soldier smoked a cigarette behind the wheel, his eyes on a newspaper.

'The arrogance of him,' said Polly. She thought of how the pamphlet had told her not to let her anger diminish. 'He must think he's untouchable, just sitting there like that.'

'He *is* untouchable,' said Alexandrine. She gave her a warning look. 'Speaking your mind to the ugly gendarme is one thing, but never do something so bold when the Boches might hear you.' She increased her pace. 'Hurry. We must see Suzette.'

The graceful façades along the Boulevard de Courcelles were beautiful in being identical, as façades were in so many Parisian streets. Polly didn't know which one hid the Comte's residence.

'It is not one of these,' said Alexandrine, 'it is this one.'

They had reached one of the few buildings in the street that had been specifically constructed to stand out. It struck Polly for its resemblance to one of the little palaces in the grounds of Versailles.

'This one is older than all the other houses?' Polly wondered.

'Actually, it's rather younger,' said Alexandrine. 'My husband's late father built it just before the Great War. He would have been pleased to hear your remark, however – he wanted people to think it had been here for centuries. Come inside, where the illusion continues. There's not a single item of furniture to be found that dates later than the Revolution.'

They reached the threshold of a pair of heavy green doors. The Comtesse cast an uneasy glance at the Daimler-Benz, parked level with them at the curbside. The Wehrmacht driver looked up from his newspaper but showed no interest in getting out. He dropped his cigarette butt into the gutter. Alexandrine went to press the bell when she realised the right-side door was ajar. She pushed it open, revealing a spectacularly gilded entrance hall, filled with eighteenth-century paintings and sculptures, and bathed in the reflected glow from long French windows that opened to a garden at the rear.

'What a wonderful room,' said Polly, awed by the first impression it made.

Alexandrine went very still. 'I think we should leave . . .'

A German-accented voice called out from somewhere above them. 'Ah, look – look! You have more visitors, Herr Comte!'

Looking down at them from the top of a palatial staircase stood a group of three men. A dark-haired gentleman, perhaps in his forties, and exceedingly handsome, casually styled in an oriental dressing-gown that only a man of the aristocracy would acquire, raised a muscled arm in greeting.

'Lecki. This is a nice surprise. You should have called first.'

His bonhomie failed to hide the strain in his voice. Alexandrine didn't move.

Polly guessed this was the Comte, but he was not the man who had called out as they'd entered. This was a man they already knew from the Ritz: Oberstleutnant Metzingen. At his side stood the young and capable Hauptmann Jürgen. In the shadows behind them, as tiny as a bird, was Suzette.

It was the first time Polly had seen the old housekeeper looking frightened.

'Come in, come in, my dear Comtesse,' called Metzingen, delightedly. 'We were just now viewing that exquisite Renoir. It is a portrait of your late mother when she was a girl, the Comte informs me?'

They were seated now in a first-floor salon that had once been Alexandrine's morning room, before she and Eduarde had come to the arrangement that had seen her move into the Ritz. Alexandrine was seated next to her husband, on a wide, white divan. Polly, dismissed by the Germans as a child, had been allowed to sit where she pleased. Only the aristocrats were of interest to Metzingen, who strode with pleasure around the room, examining furniture and ornaments.

'Such exquisite beauty to be found in this room, Herr Comte, I congratulate you.'

'Thank you, Monsieur,' said Eduarde, evenly.

Metzingen paused at a four-leaf screen. 'Is this by Boulard?'

'I believe that it may be, yes.'

'Extraordinary. From the mid-1780s, I assume?'

Eduarde deferred. 'Monsieur knows more of such things than I do.'

Studying the German from where she was being ignored at the wall, Polly guessed that this was the impression Metzingen intended to convey.

Jürgen had disappeared. Suzette had been sent to bring them coffee.

'And this tea table,' said Metzingen, rubbing his hand along another polished piece. 'Quite magnificent. By Molitor, surely?'

Alexandrine was growing angry. 'What is happening, Monsieur? I am extremely confused.'

The Renoir portrait, still bearing the scar on its frame, looked over them all from where it hung above the mantle. 'Confused?' Metzingen said, turning to her.

'Why are you here in my husband's home?'

'Dear Comtesse, such a tone. Please remember we are all civilised.' He reached into his uniform and withdrew a packet of German cigarettes, lighting one from a matchbook. 'Do you know, it puzzles me that you have never taken the courtesy to introduce yourself to me at the Ritz.'

Alexandrine was cold. 'In France, a woman does not introduce herself to a man.'

'No?' said Metzingen. 'Nor in Germany, too, thank God. All the same, I have been expecting it from *you*. Aren't you cut from the same cloth as the charming Mrs Huckstepp?'

'Please explain why you are here,' said Alexandrine.

He turned to Eduarde. 'Why don't you inform your wife, Herr Comte?'

A look passed between Comte and Comtesse that Polly, watching in fear from her chair near the wall, tried in vain to make sense of. Eduarde was a polished diplomat, a man of effortless charm, and in every sense Alexandrine's equal. On the face of it, they were a splendid match. Things were being said between them that were not being put into words.

'Lecki, darling, I'm sure I told you all about it,' said Eduarde 'you're such a silly-head at times.'

Alexandrine didn't smile. 'Of course, you did, darling, you always tell me everything, but you know what I'm like.'

'I do.' He glanced at Metzingen, before turning back to her. 'I'm sure you remember that Monsieur Metzingen has such an interesting job.'

'Bullying us all at the Ritz? I'm sure that can only be so interesting.'

Metzingen chuckled but allowed Eduarde to go on.

'I believe it's rather more than that,' said Eduarde. 'He has been charged with nurturing the artists and patrons who will continue to keep Paris so culturally vibrant. The Ritz will be central to this.'

Alexandrine looked at the German with faux interest. 'How lucky we are then.'

'The Comtesse teases,' said Metzingen. 'Perhaps she doubts my qualifications? If so, I do not blame her. For what could a German know of the decorative arts?'

'What indeed?'

The Comte gave her a look of warning. 'The Oberstleutnant was a student at the Sorbonne after the Great War,' said Eduarde. 'His time spent in Paris gave him a deep love of our city.'

Alexandrine said nothing at that.

'Which, in a roundabout way, is what gave me my fine idea,' said Eduarde.

'And what idea is that?'

'That I would gift our Courcelles home to France.'

Alexandrine didn't allow a glimmer of alarm to show. 'Gift it?'

'As my present to the nation.'

'*Our* present.'

'Of course. We've given it to France together. Wasn't that a nice idea?'

'The whole house and everything.'

'And everything. You recall it now.' He touched her hand and left it there. Polly saw the tightness with which their fingers gripped and released each other. 'Our magnificent gesture,' said Eduarde. His eyes bore into his wife's. 'Our great act of largesse.' He looked back to Metzingen. 'Or perhaps, to use a term the Oberstleutnant might enjoy: our *insurance payment.*'

'Yes, yes!' Metzingen clapped his hands, cigarette in his mouth. 'That is good, I like that very much.'

Alexandrine looked to the Renoir. There were tears in her eyes.

Suzette entered the room, bearing a tray of rattling coffee things. Polly automatically stood to assist her, but the old woman shot her such an ugly look that Polly sat down. Suzette moved to a table, placing the tray, before she began to pour and distribute the coffee cups.

'It is a sorry fact of modern life that still we must deal with Jews,' said Metzingen, drawing on his cigarette.

No one said anything.

Suzette served Polly because she was nearest, but as Polly brought the cup to her lips, Suzette pressed her on the arm. Polly returned the cup to its saucer.

'But still, this is the twentieth century and we are not monsters,' Metzingen went on. 'We are not *Russians*, God forbid, living at behest of the tsars. We are civilised people, here in a civilised place, living in so much more civilised times.'

Suzette was before him. He accepted the proffered cup from her and sipped it.

'Pogroms, imagine? What must it have been like?' He shook his head. 'No, no. We abhor such Slavic barbarism.'

Suzette moved back to the table.

'If our advanced civilisation has allowed us the evolution of anything,' said Metzingen, 'it is this modern idea: there are Jews and there are *Jews*.' He sipped the coffee again, swirling the liquid around in his mouth. He regarded the cup with some interest for a moment, before returning it to its saucer.

'Two types of Jews?' said Alexandrine quietly from the sofa. 'Perhaps you might explain it, Monsieur?'

'With pleasure, meine Dame!' He leant his elbow on the grand marble mantlepiece, his fingers idly brushing the Renoir's damaged frame. 'First there are Jews who are stubbornly unrepentant, unembarrassed by their crimes, and so happily unashamed of the conspiracies they have masterminded for centuries.'

Nobody looked at each other. Nobody moved.

'Then there are the other Jews,' said Metzingen, '*Paris* Jews, dear Comtesse, and let's make a paragon of them, shall we? These are Jews like the Rothschild family – such an elegant clan; such exquisite taste. Or the Ephrussis perhaps, I'm sure you must know them intimately, and then the Camondos, of course. All very sensible Jews. No wasted emotions there, no hysterical scenes. These are Jews who can recognise superiority, and negotiate in light of it, and in excellent faith.'

Alexandrine looked at her husband. In the depths of his eyes, he was broken. He looked away. 'And which Jews are we?' she asked.

'*We?*' said Metzingen. 'My dear Comtesse, since when are you a Jew?'

Alexandrine slipped her hand inside her husband's again. 'I'm sure you know when.'

Metzingen rejected this. 'You mean your conversion? Do not trouble yourself with it. We know you didn't mean it. You married the Comte for the money – and the title, such as it is. No one in authority imagines that you ever actually cared for this man's faith.'

Frozen in her chair, Polly remembered what Alexandrine had told her of her 'bribed' conversion for jewellery and clothes.

The Comtesse's version had seemed like a too-easy dismissal, the means of diverting attention from something rather more awkward and embarrassing – like the conversion had actually meant something profound to Alexandrine; profound because it was real.

'That isn't true,' said Alexandrine.

'*Lecki* . . .' Eduarde pleaded with her softly. 'Trust what I have done.'

She ignored him. 'I love my husband. I became a Jew happily. I am still a Jew.'

'No. *No*,' said Metzingen. 'That is not how it is. You see, Comtesse, it's all there in your file.'

Polly saw Alexandrine flinch.

'Our informant was most specific about that,' said Metzingen. 'They had no cause to lie.'

'And who was this informant? Perhaps I know them.'

To Polly, glued to this exchange, it felt as if Alexandrine was testing the water for something.

Metzingen smiled at the Comtesse. 'The informer's identity is none of your concern.'

Alexandrine sniffed. 'A shame. Your informant is wrong. I might have recommended a more reliable one to you.'

The German shook his head, pityingly. 'Herr Comte, please remind your wife.'

Eduarde remained holding Alexandrine's hand. 'You remember, darling. Your conversion was fraudulent.'

A tear slipped from Alexandrine's eye. 'That's not how it was,' she whispered.

'And all my family wanted was respectability,' said Eduarde.

'Your family was ten times more respectable than mine.'

'*No*,' said Eduarde. 'My family were Jews.'

'*Are* Jews,' Metzingen reminded them. His fingers, still on the frame, began to pull at it. 'How does this thing come down?'

Alexandrine stood up. 'Monsieur Metzingen –'

'What is holding it to the wall?'

Suzette stiffened at the table as Metzingen used both his hands to grip the painting.

'Please, Monsieur, it is very fragile,' said Alexandrine.

Hauptmann Jürgen came into the room from the landing. 'The car is ready for you, Herr Oberstleutnant.'

'Good, good. Get this thing down.'

Jürgen joined him at the mantle. The painting was snagged by its wire at the hook. They tried to twist it free. The frame creaked, the canvas crinkling. Plaster crumbled where the hook met the wall.

'You'll fucking wreck it!' Suzette shouted.

She rushed forward as the Renoir pulled free of the wall, escaping the Germans' grip to fall forward into the room, where Suzette stopped it, her old, maimed hands catching expertly at the frame and not on the priceless canvas.

Metzingen had dropped the cigarette from his mouth. He took a moment to steady himself, getting another from his uniform pocket. He couldn't find his matchbook.

Jürgen had one and lit the Oberstleutnant's cigarette.

Metzingen took a deep drag. Exhaling, he waved his hand at Suzette. 'This insolent kike.'

Jürgen delivered a blow that took Suzette to her knees. His second took her to the Comte's Indian carpet.

'Look there at her hand, Jürgen,' said Metzingen, noting Suzette's missing fingers. 'And still she managed to catch the thing? Incredible really.'

Polly was at the window in time to see the Comte's red Delage, a magnificent touring car, pull out into the Boulevard de Courcelles with Metzingen at the wheel, the roof open to the late-morning sunshine, the seats at the back and to the side of him crammed with the best of the Comte's famous wine cellar. Immediately behind, in the Comte's dashing town car, a yellow Simca coupe, was Jürgen, with more of the cellar's best vintages.

Bringing up the rear, in the Daimler-Benz driven by the Wehrmacht soldier, was the Renoir portrait of the pretty little girl in blonde ringlets, strapped to the lid of the trunk.

Inside the morning room, Suzette had been helped into a chair. Eduarde held some chipped ice wrapped in linen to her face while Alexandrine tenderly wrapped her legs in a rug.

'Why wouldn't you let me drink my coffee, Suzette?' Polly asked the old woman, gently.

Suzette met her eye; her voice feather soft. 'It was just for the krauts.'

'Why?'

'Because she urinated in it,' said Eduarde. He stroked the old woman's cheek with love. 'You're as predictable as night becomes day, aren't you, Suzette?'

Suzette kissed his hand.

'You'll be safe from them now,' he whispered to her. 'This agreement ensures it.'

Alexandrine stood up. 'You're a coward,' she spat at him.

'Ah, here it comes then,' said Eduarde, resigned, with a look to Suzette.

'*Coward*,' she repeated. 'To have given them everything – *everything* – before they even asked.'

'They don't ask,' said Eduarde.

'Not even a fight from you then?' said Alexandrine.

'But why would you have expected something so courageous from me, Lecki?' he wondered, standing up to face her. 'With my pathetic track record? No, I thought I'd roll over first like a cur.'

Alexandrine was cold. 'What about your precious thorough-breds? Are the Boches taking those?'

'Every last one,' said Eduarde, lightly. 'As insurance premiums go, this one has proved dear.' The love that had shone in his eyes for Suzette was just as clear in the look he gave his wife. 'And it was worth every franc.'

'Tell me what this "insurance" has bought you *exactly*,' Alexandrine demanded.

'Safety,' said Eduarde. 'For you and Suzette.'

'You heard what he said – I am not even a Jew!'

'You were until I paid for it.'

She flung out her hand, striking his face.

'Don't!' Polly cried out.

Eduarde smiled at Polly, kindly. 'Mustn't worry, kitten, this is well overdue.'

Alexandrine struck him again and again.

Suzette tried to rise from the chair. 'Madame, please –' she said, distressed.

A gesture from Eduarde made her stay where she was. 'Lecki must do this,' he said.

Alexandrine kept striking him until she started to weep, and her arms fell limp by her side. Polly went to her, holding her close.

'And what about your bastard, Eduarde?' Alexandrine spat out the word.

There was a brief silence. 'As informants go, they are rather ill-informed,' Eduarde told her at last. He adjusted his silk robe. 'It would seem there is nothing of the child in their file.'

Alexandrine looked at him searchingly. 'I can't believe it.'

'What child?' Polly asked, startled.

They didn't answer her.

'To the Germans the child doesn't even exist,' said Eduarde.

'That's very nice,' croaked Suzette from her chair. 'The child has never existed for Madame either.'

Alexandrine turned on her, eyes blazing.

'That's the way,' said Suzette, 'why don't you hit me where the kraut got a punch in?'

But Polly saw the tears in the old woman's eyes. Suzette was heartbroken.

'Shut up, Suzette!' Alexandrine shot at her. She turned to her husband. 'I've done everything you asked of me.'

'I know you have.' Eduarde moved towards a bureau at the far end of the room. 'And you know I am grateful for it. The child is hidden and safe, and that is all that I hoped for. If I didn't know that, I could never have been certain of what *I* must do.'

'Who is this child you are talking about?' said Polly. She looked to Alexandrine in bewilderment.

The Comtesse gave her a fierce look.

Only Polly saw Eduarde now take something from the bureau and slip it into his robe.

'Why don't you and the kid pop along now, Lecki? It must be well past luncheon at the Ritz.' The Comte cast a longing look around the room. 'You know I'm very sorry about your mother's portrait. Take something else to make up for it, before they return. Something small, perhaps, that you can hide in your bag?'

'I'm not taking another thing from you,' said Alexandrine. She bent down to kiss Suzette on the cheek. 'I'll send a car for you, darling,' she told the old servant. 'I'll arrange a room at the Ritz.'

'You won't,' said Suzette. 'I'm not moving, Madame.'

'You have to now, don't be a fool.'

Suzette shook her head. '*No.*'

'I bought Suzette a little retirement apartment years ago,' said Eduarde, 'she'll take herself there when I ask her.' He winked at the old woman in the chair. Then he opened a door that led from the morning room to a study. 'Now please run along, Lecki, there's a good thing. Best you're not here when they come back to do the itemising. They might think you're part of the furniture.'

Alexandrine could only stare at him, her face streaked with fury at his betrayal. 'We're through this time, Eduarde. Do you hear me? I never want to see you again.'

He shrugged. 'I understand.' Love for her was blazing in his eyes. Eduarde went into his study and closed the door.

On their way down the long flight of marble stairs, Polly wordlessly tried to comfort Alexandrine. She did not ask anything about the child called 'the bastard'. She guessed that her guardian would not – *could not* – speak of it.

It was only as they reached the bottom stair that Polly realised with horrific certainty what Eduarde had taken from the bureau. With it came an image she had never seen but had long imagined of her father's last moments on earth. She stopped dead, looking at the Comtesse. 'He's got a gun, Alexandrine . . .'

Alexandrine was confused. 'What are you saying, Polly?'

Polly took her by the arms, terrified. '*Eduarde has a gun.* He took it from the drawer – a little one. He slipped it inside his robe while we were talking. He's going to do something desperate – just like my father.'

Alexandrine's eyes went wide.

They turned to run up the stairs but then a gunshot rang from above, followed by Suzette's scream.

When the authorities had been and gone, and before the Germans returned to begin their cataloguing, Alexandrine and Polly went out the front door. It was evening on the Boulevard de Courcelles. The City of Light was all shadow. With bombing raids coming from England, Parisians had become accustomed to blackouts. The streetlights had no globes in them; the headlights of the German military cars were covered with material that let only a strip of light through. This new darkness meant a tentativeness when walking. Strange sounds could be heard in place of the Parisians' missing cars, sounds that were jarring and frightening in the unnatural quiet. Sudden shouts could give way to cut-short screams.

Making their way along the avenue, Polly could see nothing but the bouncing beams of other people's flashlights. They had no flashlight of their own, having left the Ritz when it was still daylight. This was just as well, for Alexandrine had the blood from her husband's skull on her dress. Rubbing at it, the Comtesse found herself filled by a brutal honesty that, once started, could not be stopped. 'I should never have assumed myself capable of mothering you,' she said.

Numbed, Polly felt these words like a slap. 'Don't say such a thing. You mean everything to me.'

The Comtesse was deaf to it. 'I have no mothering in me. I never have. I am cold and selfish. You are excused from your obligation to me, Polly.' She walked ahead of her along the pavement.

'Stop it, Alexandrine.'

She turned. 'You have Zita and Lana Mae left to mother you. You need nothing of me.'

Polly stared, uncomprehending in the gloom. '*Please* stop this,' she begged. 'I could never stop needing you.'

'But you must.' Alexandrine's voice rang shrill. Her eyes were stark with guilt. 'If you knew of the wrong that I've done to you – the lies.'

'You only hid the truth of the war from me because you were frightened yourself,' Polly fought to reassure her, 'it means nothing now.'

Alexandrine was tormented. 'That's not it at all . . .' She hid her face in her hands. 'Look at what I've exposed you to today? You, whose own father killed himself?' She was near to weeping. Only her aristocrat's self-control was holding her back. 'You're only sixteen. That I could have done such a thing to you . . .'

Polly clutched at her. 'No more of this. It's the grief and the shock.'

Alexandrine forced her off. 'I'm no mother to you, Polly, and no mother to the bastard. I'm not even going to *tell* the bastard what has happened today, do you understand that? I will have someone else break the news. That's my mothering for you, darling. That's the depth of the love in my heart.'

'Alexandrine!' Polly pleaded with her.

But the Comtesse was quickly walking away. 'Marjorie was wrong to thrust you upon me,' she threw over her shoulder, 'she was hopelessly deluded and wrong.'

The tiny tapping at his door stirred Tommy from a state that wasn't sleep, only something like it. He had still been awake, or thought he had, staring up at the moonless sky through the little dormer window from his bed. But he was not quite awake. The tapping came again; long, female fingernails on the door.

'Polly?' She knew that he lived in the Ritz. He had told her about the forgotten attic rooms.

The tapping stopped. Tommy slipped from the bed to open the door, remembering then that he wasn't wearing enough clothes. 'Wait a second.' He pulled on his threadbare tweeds and found his old undershirt where'd he'd thrown it on the floor. 'Polly?' He opened the door, pulling the shirt over his head.

But it was Blanche Auzello.

'Oh, Madame . . .'

Embarrassed, he pushed his arms through the grimy sleeves. 'I'm sorry, I didn't hear you properly.' He hoped his smile covered his disappointment. He never wanted her to know that there were times, like this one, when he didn't feel like seeing her.

'It's late, I know,' said Blanche. Alcohol hung heavy on her breath. She had spent the night drinking again, Tommy guessed. Her dark eyes bore into him, yet she struggled to keep them in focus. 'I need to talk to you, Tommy . . .'

He pulled back the door for her and looked from the unmade bed to the room's only chair. 'Where –' Nervous when alone with her, he didn't know how to finish the sentence.

'It's okay,' she whispered. He felt her hand touch his before she shut the door behind her. He knocked his uniform from the chair and straightened the bedcover. The only light came from the window above. Tommy went to turn on the lamp.

Blanche's hand found his again. 'Leave it. It's nicer like this.'

She stood there staring at him for what felt like minutes in the shadow. Tommy could see the gleam of feeling in her eyes. 'What do you want, Madame?' he whispered.

She seemed to remember herself. She sat down in the chair and opened her purse, rummaging for her packet of cigarettes. She found it and offered him one. He took it half-heartedly. Tommy watched from the end of the bed as she fumbled for the match, her hand shaking. He found his own matchbook first and lit the cigarette for her, not bothering to light his own.

'They hate me here,' Blanche said.

'Who do?'

'These dames. Lana Mae Huckstepp and Zita. They look at me like I'm some heap of dirt.'

'No, they don't.' Tommy said softly. 'You're a wonderful woman . . .'

She shook her head. 'I remind them of where they're from, you see. We're all phonies at the Ritz and they loathe me for rubbing it in their faces.'

'That isn't true – they're your friends.'

Blanche sniffed and pulled on her cigarette. 'The Comtesse, though, she's decent.'

Tommy wasn't sure what she expected him to say.

'I used to be an actress once.' She smiled. 'Did you know that?'

He didn't know. He didn't know why she wanted him to know it either.

'Back when the movies didn't have sound. I was in one with Zita. But my voice was too squeaky. When the talkies came they told me I was through in the business.' She exhaled a cloud of smoke and wine fumes. 'When that happened, I had to work on making new friends . . .'

'What is it, Blanche?' Tommy pressed her.

'You happy here?' she asked him.

He answered automatically. 'Of course.' Then he added, ever mindful of her, 'And grateful.'

'Being happy has nothing to do with grateful,' she told him. She took another drag and exhaled, the smoke rising to the dormer window. 'You're still very young – you've a right to know happiness before your life gets too thorny. While things are still simple, you *should* be happy.'

He smiled for her again. 'I am happy. I like working here. I think I'm getting better at it.'

'Good. Good for you.' Blanche started to cry.

He reached out for her from the bed. 'What is it, Blanche? Please tell me what's wrong tonight. You're making me worried.'

'Oh, Tommy . . .'

'You mustn't cry for me,' he told her, 'you've been my great friend. I owe you everything for what you've done. You've given me my life.'

'I've done nothing.' She sniffed and wiped her cheeks with her hand. She took another drag from her cigarette. 'Claude and me, we got paid for it, didn't we? Don't sucker yourself into thinking we're anything good.'

He said nothing at that.

She glanced long at his narrow bed. 'Sometimes, at night, I think of you all alone up here . . .'

'I'm not lonely, Blanche.'

'Is that because you're thinking of me?'

The air was loaded between them. 'It helps to know I have someone who cares,' Tommy offered her.

Blanche stood up abruptly from the chair. 'I'm drunk. I'm saying things I shouldn't be saying, instead of things that I should. I don't know *how* to say those, Tommy . . .' She began to cry again.

He stood up, too. 'Please, you've said nothing wrong, Blanche.'

'Oh, I have,' she said. 'It's because you're so young and so cute. It takes me back to when I was cute, too.' She pulled herself together. 'Well, I'm not cute anymore. I'm the mother of a kid who's going blind.'

'Blanche . . .'

'*There's been a death.*'

Tommy felt the words like a punch to his gut. 'Not Claude?'

Blanche blinked. 'What?'

'Monsieur Auzello is dead?' He felt sick. 'The krauts –'

'Not Claude. Oh God, Tommy, not my husband.'

He knew then why she had come to him. 'Who is dead, Blanche? Tell me . . .'

Polly had no way of knowing which of the attic rooms might be his. She had discovered that the fifth floor was kept in near-darkness after midnight, located as it was right at the top of the stairs. The Ritz was very different at roof level. The walls and floors had been left bare; the attic rooms were intended only for the people who served the guests.

Polly didn't know how she might locate Tommy, surely asleep at this hour, hidden somewhere behind one of so many closed doors. Yet, she had to find him. Tomorrow, Polly knew, would bring the distance of a night's sleep, and with it a weakening of certainty. It had to be tonight that she told him, so that her words of commitment could be spoken while they burned inside her, and once said, could not be taken back again.

'Tommy?' She whispered. The noise felt deafening in the depths of the quiet. 'Tommy, are you up here?'

Somewhere in the corridor she heard a door creak open.

With a rush of fear, it occurred to Polly there might be Germans on this floor. She heard footsteps coming towards her from the shadows. Polly pressed herself to the wall, knowing how hopelessly visible she must be.

The footsteps were those of a woman in high heels, unsteady, as if she was staggering. The steps stopped for a moment, and Polly held her breath. Then they began again.

Blanche Auzello loomed from the darkness, tottering towards Polly at the wall. She stopped in shock. 'You?'

Polly could smell the wine and knew Blanche was drunk. She felt a pang of sympathy for her before the sharper pang of disappointment. What reason could there be for Blanche to be here other than the same reason Polly had come? *Tommy.*

She watched as Blanche came to the same conclusion. The older woman's face softened. 'Oh girl. You like him, don't you?'

'Of course not!' said Polly.

'You *don't* like him?'

Polly stammered. 'He's a friend – nothing more.'

Blanche touched Polly's cheek, sad. 'I should warn you off him. But there'll be others who'll warn you, and they'll be doing it soon. So, all that I'll say is knock yourself out before they get to you, honey. You'll be cute together.'

Polly knew she had to make herself clear. 'It *not* like that, Madame, I promise you.'

Blanche was kind. 'Okay.' She made her way to the stairs, but as she turned to descend, she whispered, 'Watch out for him at least, will you? He needs his friends now.'

Polly didn't know what this meant. 'Yes, Madame.'

Polly moved in the direction Blanche had come from, knowing she hadn't heard a door close. She walked quickly, not caring for the sound of her own footsteps as she peered into the gloom.

She found the still open door. Tommy was inside his little attic room, seated on the edge of his narrow bed, in his threadbare tweeds and dirty undershirt, without any shoes. He was slumped forward, his fingers clutching fistfuls of his German blond hair.

Polly didn't have to say his name; he looked up when she came, sensing her.

She lurched straight into it. 'That paper you gave me – *Tips for the Occupied.* Why did you want me to read it, Tommy?'

He'd clearly almost forgotten. He stared at her in the light of the stars from the window. 'You were discovered with it?'

She considered lying, but then could see little point. 'Yes.'

He stood up. 'Oh my God.'

She stepped into the room. 'It's all right, Tommy, it doesn't matter now. I'm safe.'

His face was filled with remorse, far deeper than she had imagined he would be. 'I'm so sorry,' he said.

'Don't be.'

'But I put you at risk.'

'Perhaps I want to be at risk?' Then she said, 'After what's happened to me today, and after everything I've seen and experienced since the Germans arrived, risk seems more and more irrelevant.'

There was a moment's quiet. 'What happened today?' he asked, softly.

She paused. Her breath was shallow in her chest. 'Can I sit down, please?' She sat in the lone chair before he said anything.

Tommy closed the door. He sat on the edge of his bed and waited.

'A man died,' Polly told him, simply. 'I didn't know him, but he was a good man and he killed himself because of his fear of the Germans.'

He stared at her uncomprehendingly. 'That was also my day . . .'

She stared back. 'Someone you know took his own life?'

'Yes.' Tommy cleared his throat. 'My father . . .'

In the half light of the stars she could only see now how much he was fighting not to break down in front of her.

'I didn't know him,' he told her. 'I'd barely met him my whole life. He was ashamed of me, you see. I was his illegitimate son.'

Realisation crashed upon Polly. 'Your father was Comte Eduarde?'

He scraped a hand through his hair. He didn't need to answer.

Polly reeled. 'Listen,' she said, 'he was not ashamed of you. I was with him before he died. He spoke of you, he loved you, he wanted you safe – he was *not* ashamed, Tommy. I swear he wasn't.'

He clearly didn't believe this. 'You know all about me then.'

'Now I do. But I didn't before. I knew none of it.'

'Ah,' he sniffed and scraped back his hair. 'Then things are very difficult for you now. I'm sorry.' He stood up to open the door again.

'Wait,' said Polly.

'Your guardian Alexandrine despises me,' said Tommy. 'My mother was her husband's mistress. My mother is dead, but the Comtesse's hate for her lives on for me. I am her enemy.'

'Then why are you living here, where Alexandrine lives?'

Tommy took a deep breath. 'Because my father begged her to use her connections to hide me. Alexandrine had me taken away from my school because it would be targeted by the krauts. She had me hidden here where everyone, yet no one, would see me, because I'd be a mere servant. I think she loved this, in truth. She paid Monsieur Auzello to do it. She paid his wife, Blanche.'

The spectre of Blanche as Tommy's would-be lover receded for Polly forever. The woman was Tommy's benefactor. 'But why did Alexandrine do this – I don't understand.'

'Polly,' he whispered, 'it's because I'm a Jew . . .'

She felt ashamed of her naivete. 'Your father killed himself for being that.'

He looked at her defiantly. 'Maybe, but I will not. The krauts will have to do it for me.'

She stood up to face him. 'Then they'll have to kill me too.'

It was a moment before he laughed. 'Why would they ever kill you? A little rich girl living at the Ritz?'

The words stung her anew. Then she remembered her resolve: male disregard would no longer hurt her. Polly bit the hurt back. 'Little and rich is irrelevant. They'll want to kill me because I'll be just like you now,' she told him.

'Don't insult me. You're not a Jew, Polly.'

'No,' she said, 'I'll be resisting the Occupiers alongside one.'

There was a pause once she'd said this.

'I know why you gave me that mimeographed paper,' Polly told him, after a moment. 'You did it because you wanted me to feel the way that you feel: angry. Well, I do, Tommy. The adults are weak, and they've let us all down. They've forgotten what France even stands for – what the Republic was founded on: liberty, equality and fraternity.' For Polly there was something wonderful in speaking those three words aloud. 'The future is ours,' she said, 'so that means it's all up to us now if we want to see those notions mean something again.'

He blinked at her. 'But you're not even French.'

'Neither was my Aunt Marjorie. Why don't you ask me to show you her *Légion d'honneur*?'

He was astonished by this. 'So, what do you suggest?' he asked her, after a moment.

'We fight back,' said Polly. 'We *resist*. I know that's what you're doing already, Tommy, and I know there must be others who are doing it with you. Who wrote the leaflet – was it you?'

'I don't know who wrote it,' he said. 'The original we had was only a copy.'

'Who printed it then?'

He hesitated. 'My friend.'

'A friend with a mimeograph machine?'

He was reluctant. 'I don't know. I haven't asked. I'm not going to ask, either.'

Polly was incredulous. 'But shouldn't you know? This is so important.'

'It's also very dangerous,' said Tommy. 'It's better not to know anything at all.'

She tried to take this on. 'Then who else is part of this? Are there dozens by now?'

Tommy shook his head. 'There are only three. There's me. And now there's you . . .'

Polly found that her resistance dreams retreated a little in the face of reality. 'All right then. And who's number three?'

Tommy grinned at her. 'That's my friend. She's a blind kid.'

Polly was astonished in turn, realising this must be Odile.

Tommy paused for a moment, staring at Polly, before coming to a decision of his own. He wanted only to be honest with her. 'Listen,' he said, 'I gave you that sheet for a very simple reason, there were no high ideals behind it. Yes, I wanted to see if you felt as I did, and the *Tips for the Occupied* was a test of that, which clearly you passed, because you came and found me up here. But liberty and equality and the rest of it, they were not what was most in my mind, Polly.'

She hung on his words. 'What was, then?'

He seemed to drift in her eyes, as if she was suddenly to him quite beautiful. 'Your gun.'

Polly gave an intake of breath.

'It is precious – more precious than anything these days,' Tommy told her. 'I gave you that sheet because you have a weapon, and I hoped you might be persuaded to use it in a way it can do the most good.'

'The gun . . .' Polly felt the stab of past hurts. She hadn't been wanted for herself, only for what she owned – or had owned.

Tommy was sincere. 'You keep it in your handbag. Or perhaps you hide it somewhere safer these days. It doesn't matter – what matters is that you *have* it, Polly, and with a gun we can make a difference.'

If there was anything good to be had from his words, it was this: Tommy had not been the one who had taken Aunt Marjorie's gift. He truly believed she still had the gun in her possession.

Polly didn't know how to break it to him.

Naked, Metzingen tossed the Renoir onto the grand Imperial Suite bed where Zita could properly see it. She was naked herself, propped up on the pillows. While she stared at the ringleted girl, Hans tried to pull the cork from the fresh champagne bottle with his teeth. When this failed, he found his sabre and slashed at the

216

cork instead. It came off at the second go, spewing bubbles across the carpeted floor. He topped up their glasses.

'I know this one . . .' she told him. She blinked at the portrait of Alexandrine's mother and then looked away.

'The vintage?' said Hans. 'It is excellent, I believe. I gave a bottle to von Stülpnagel. He looked pleased.'

Zita's eyes were expressionless. 'The painting, Hans.'

'Ah.'

She didn't touch her drink. 'You promised me you would not hurt them.'

'Who?'

'My *friends*. This painting belongs to the Comtesse.' She seemed to be summoning all her strength to stop herself shaking. 'What did you do to her to get this?'

He went to tell her, but Zita held up a finger before he could answer. 'If I don't like what you tell me, I'll kill myself, Hans.'

He looked briefly gobsmacked at that, before bursting out laughing. Then he saw what she clutched in her other hand: a *Modèle* 1935. '*Liebchen*?'

She flicked the safety switch. 'But first I'll kill you.'

He sipped from his glass, studying her. 'Where did you get that weapon?'

'I mean it,' she said.

'All right . . .'

'So, tell me, what did you do to Alexandrine?'

Hans enjoyed her like this: unpredictably dangerous. Behind the one-liners and sass was a woman who had the means to arm herself – and smuggle a weapon into the very place of their love-making, without him even suspecting she would. He let the smile play at his lips, contemplating the endless surprises that came with his passion for the film star. 'But the painting is *kitsch*. Fit to print on a chocolate box. I had planned to give it to Göring when he comes. More his taste than mine.'

She waited.

'When you know what happened, you will thank me for it,' he tried teasing her. Despite the threat she posed, his loins were growing hard, anticipating. 'I saved the Comtesse's life.'

Zita didn't move. 'How?'

He shrugged. 'I erased the Jew.'

He loved that he could still make her reel at the ease with which he said such words.

'What – what does that mean?' Zita demanded.

He started stroking himself, wanting her to see the effect she had on him when she was like this. But she held only his eyes. 'The Comtesse began the day a Jewess and the very worst kind: one who had chosen to join the parasites willingly.' He lifted his other hand to drain the last drop from his glass. 'Well, she has finished the day clean – she is no longer a Jewess. All thanks to me.' He indicated the painting. 'As you can see, she was grateful for it.'

Zita pulled the trigger and the explosion was shockingly loud. The bullet flew past Hans' shoulder to smash into the boudoir wall. A puff of pulverised plaster merged with the smoking gunpowder. Hans nearly messed himself.

'I don't believe you,' said Zita, coolly, as if nothing had occurred. 'I can't believe you. You've hurt her in some way, Hans, when you promised me you would not.'

He managed to control his panicking bowel. His manhood was only engorged by the violence. 'I'm sure you will ask her,' he began again. 'And perhaps she will ask you where it is that you go so late at night?' He enjoyed what he imagined was shame he exposed in her face. 'Ah. I can see that both of you will choose an untruthful answer.'

Zita pulled the trigger again. This time her bullet pierced the incongruously placed armoire, sending splinters in the air.

'I am an excellent shot,' Zita told him. 'And next time I will prove it to you.'

She was half crazy, unhinged – and Hans wanted only to enter her. 'When you hear what the Comtesse tells you, *Liebchen,*

218

I encourage you to favour my account,' he said. 'Mine will be unemotional and accurate . . .' He waited, stroking himself, to see what she would do next.

When Zita did nothing, Hans moved slowly to the bed, holding her eyes with his own. With Zita's finger still on the trigger, he gently took the end of the gun in his hand and brought it up under her chin. 'Pull it,' he whispered. 'You could end it all now. Our great love could be over forever. Why don't you just pull it, *Liebchen*?'

She wouldn't, of course, and he knew it. There was Lotti.

'Good.' He took the French gun from her hands and rested it next to her head on the pillow. He liked the picture it made: the weapon side by side with the ringleted girl and his lover.

'Please let me see our daughter . . .'

'When you are better behaved,' he told her. He was ready to go inside her now, he was ready to start thrusting.

'But I've been so good – you know I've been good.'

'Shhh.'

'Please let me, Hans . . .'

Sex lost its appeal.

He sprawled beside her and shoved the Renoir to the floor. After a moment he said, 'I have two more bottles of that vintage. There is one to give to von Hofacker – he needs buttering up. And who for the other one, do you think? Speidel perhaps?'

Zita said nothing.

He released a sigh, giving in. 'All right then. When you see Lotti, we will do so together – as mother and father. Won't that be better, *Liebchen*?'

He watched as Zita read the implications of this, beginning a new navigation of his ever-evolving rules. 'All right then.' She nodded. 'We will go there together.'

He stretched his great arms behind his head and gazed at her fondly on the pillow beside him. Hans felt nostalgic. 'You remember how we found each other in Berlin again, *Liebchen* – all those years after we met here at the Ritz?'

'Here at the Ritz,' she whispered in echo, 'when you held the Vendôme door for me . . .'

'Yes.'

'When you gave me my lip rouge, which had fallen from my hand . . .'

'The sweetest night of my life.'

'Our life . . .' said Zita.

Not for the first time he wondered if she really did remember it, or whether it was only the story which had become the memory to her now.

'And then we met again in Berlin,' Zita finished, as if by rote. 'Five years after, in '27. On the film set.'

He scooped her in his arm, let her nuzzle at his massive chest. 'What a beautiful script that was.'

'The film?'

He chuckled. *'You and I.'* He wondered if he had the energy to grow hard for her again. 'Perhaps it is time to re-make it. And even better. After all, our setting is the Ritz now . . .'

She propped on her elbow to look at him. 'What is it with you and this hotel, Hans?'

He closed his eyes, tired suddenly. The Comte's looted champagne was relaxing him.

'Hans?'

'Hmmm?'

'What is it with you and the Ritz? Tell me. I want to understand it. Do you love it here – or do you hate it?'

He opened his eyes again. 'You really feel the need to ask me that, *Liebchen*?'

'Yes,' she said. 'I don't know the answer anymore . . .'

A smile played at his lips again. 'What does your heart tell you?' he wondered.

She looked in vain for the truth of him. 'That's just it, Hans,' she said, 'my heart won't tell me anything about you . . .'

*

When Hans left to luxuriate in the bathroom, Zita ran her fingers across the bullet hole in the side of the polished armoire. Even with the hotel blueprints she had stolen for Hans, he had not noticed the boudoir's apparent lack of built-in. Dazzled by the Imperial Suite as a whole, he had simply hung his uniforms inside the armoire, unrealising.

Zita tried to guess how weighty the armoire was. Could one tiny woman shift it, she wondered, just enough to crack the built-in door open to slip something inside? Perhaps it was possible.

Of course, Zita knew what Lana Mae had hidden in there: her seventeen furs. Zita decided she would hide other precious things from Hans, before Reichsmarschall Göring began his occupancy.

The ringleted girl, for example. Hans had no right to it, whatever he might claim.

And the *Modèle* 1935.

Zita had been shocked when she'd found the gun inside Polly's Hermès handbag – shocked because she had thought it long gone. It had been Alexandrine who had snatched it from Zita when she'd found it in her possession on that fatal day aboard the Riviera train. Alexandrine had not done as she'd claimed, which was hurl it out of the window. Instead, she had given it to Marjorie to hold, which was no doubt when she'd told Marjorie why they had come to her, and Marjorie had, in turn, for reasons that were perhaps understandable in the circumstances, given it to Polly.

Well, Polly had three guardians to protect her, and no need of a gun.

Zita had made a habit of telling people she loved that she wanted to kill herself. It was what she had told Alexandrine on the train. Only with the gun in her hand did anyone believe her. The weapon was Zita's again.

And if it all grew too much, Zita could make good on her promises.

9

11 November 1940

The sharp rap on the doors to the Imperial Suite by the Wehrmacht soldier who had accompanied Lana Mae brought an instant response. Her enemy opened the door to her personally.

'Darling Herr Metzingen!' she gushed as she saw him, willing away disgust from her face.

'Why, it's dear Frau Huckstepp,' said the Oberstleutnant. He was dishevelled and bleary-eyed. 'What an unexpected joy. Won't you come in?'

Lana Mae caught a whiff of the stale slick of sweat that lay beneath his dress shirt. He was still in his white evening trousers. 'Yes, I will,' she said, with apparent warmth. 'And you know the joy's all mine, honey.' The lying words stuck in her throat, but she was nothing if not pragmatic these days. She was prepared to say anything to gain what she wanted from him.

Lana Mae guessed that the guards had telephoned Metzingen from the Vendôme lobby while she was ascending the stairs with her escort. They had wanted to let him know she was keen to make another business call. Deliberately extravagantly dressed for what was only ten in the morning, she made a show of wiggling through the door Metzingen had opened for her, bouncing into the suite that once had been her own.

The Ritz, Lana Mae had come to learn, was the one Paris hotel that hadn't been completely requisitioned by the Germans. The Crillon, the Meurice, and every other famed establishment was now home to men of the Wehrmacht, the Luftwaffe, the Kriegsmarine, the Gestapo. Only the Ritz still had rooms for civilians, and among the newest guests were art dealers, eager to make sales.

The sight inside the first salon was startling. There were more paintings and sculptures and *objets d'art* than the late César Ritz would have conceived could be crammed in the room. Lana Mae peered into the dining room and the other salons beyond, and saw it was the same throughout. There was so much random art it was like being in the Louvre storeroom, she thought, before she had the sickening feeling that this could well be the storeroom's contents. Old masters rested casually on the floor in vertical stacks, arranged against every wall and chair back; classical statuary stood massed at the windows forming unlikely family groups. Lana Mae recognised a piece she had once admired in the entrance hall of the Comte's home on the Boulevard de Courcelles. She forced away thoughts of his death.

'Well, someone *has* had fun shopping lately, haven't they?' She winked to Metzingen. 'I guess that's a good omen for me today.'

High-ranking officers of the German command were slumped about bored and half-dressed in the chairs and divans. She recognised faces: von Stülpnagel, von Hofacker, Speidel. Some were playing cards; all of them were drinking. The stench of old cigar smoke was hideous.

'Good morning, fellas,' Lana Mae waved and wiggled some more. 'Is the party starting early?' Under her breath she added, for Metzingen's benefit, 'Someone should open a window.'

Von Stülpnagel nodded to her, Speidel as well; men she'd met and dined with at *l'Espadon*. The Vendôme salons and bars, initially forbidden to civilians, were now open again. The Germans wanted their fellow Ritz guests to know that they were here to enjoy themselves.

'It is still last night's party,' said Metzingen, strained. 'We have not yet retired.'

'Ah,' said Lana Mae, sympathetically. 'Well, they say war is hell.'

Metzingen gave into a yawn. 'Perhaps we will be luckier within the next few hours.'

'Well, I hope so,' said Lana Mae, 'for your sake, honey. You look dead on your feet.'

There was a little pause while she waited. Metzingen did indeed seem to be nodding off standing up. She rolled her eyes, privately loathing him and every other man in the room. 'Herr Metzingen?'

'What? Forgive me.' He rubbed at his cheeks.

'Will the charming Reichsmarschall see me today?' She smiled. 'Or has he already gone to bed?'

'He has not gone to bed,' said Metzingen, 'which is why our party has not ended.'

'That's lucky then,' said Lana Mae. 'Because I've got something real pretty for him this morning.'

He looked at her meaningfully. 'The Reichsmarschall is in the *bath* . . .'

Lana Mae swallowed, by now familiar with what this meant. 'Well, you Germans are so clean.'

Metzingen smiled grimly. 'Will you come this way, Frau Huckstepp? He will be pleased to see you.'

She steeled herself. 'I hope so.'

Metzingen took her through the grand boudoir. She barely let herself glance at the rosewood armoire, now scarred by a bullet hole, yet still placed exactly where she and Tommy had positioned it, hiding the built-in doors. The armoire itself was open. Inside she glimpsed vibrant, garden-like colours: lavender and pink;

a yellow silk kimono; a scarlet woollen cape. Lana Mae tried not to think of what they might look like upon the person who reputedly wore them.

The bathroom door was closed. She could hear male voices from within.

The look Metzingen gave her was deeply ironic. 'And so, the show begins, Frau Huckstepp.'

She looked back at him levelly. 'Lucky it ain't my debut, honey. I know all the cues.'

Metzingen knocked.

'Come,' said a throaty German voice from inside.

Lana Mae took a deep breath and Metzingen opened the door.

The master bathroom was no longer as Lana Mae had enjoyed it. Sodden towels lay in piles everywhere. The steam was so thick the mirror was useless. The original bath, which was by no means small, had been torn out and replaced by a tub of colossal dimensions, deemed suitably spacious for the fleshy proportions of Reichsmarschall Hermann Göring, who spent hours upon end submerged. Lana Mae had been apprised of his habits before her first visit, and while not every meeting with the Luftwaffe Chief had been conducted in this way, enough of them had for Lana Mae to have learned how to cover her revulsion.

Metzingen's manner when dealing with his superior was like a nanny's bright cheer with a child. 'Look, Herr Reichsmarschall! Here is a comely visitor for you.'

'Who is it, Hans?'

Lana Mae displayed herself. 'Am I interrupting you, Herr Göring? I can come back another time.'

Göring was wallowing, but he was not in the nude. He wore purple silk pyjamas which billowed about his bulk like flags in the bathwater. 'Frau Huckstepp!' he cried, seeing her emerge through the steam.

Metzingen at once abandoned her, leaving the room.

'You are always welcome. Come in, come in,' said Göring, waving her forward. In one fleshy fist he held a flute of champagne; in the other he clutched caviar on toast.

Lana Mae gave a longing look to the mountain of caviar heaped in a bowl on a table beside the bath, trying to recall the last time she had enjoyed any.

Göring recognised her weakness for fine food. 'Perhaps you would like some of this delicacy?' he wondered, indicating the bowl.

Claude Auzello was the bathroom's second occupant, sweating inside his pinstriped suit, his monocle as useless as the bathroom mirror in the fog. With sodden gloved hands, he scooped more caviar onto a tiny square of toast, placing it on a plate for Lana Mae. She and Claude exchanged brief but sympathetic looks as she accepted it.

The bathroom's third occupant was Göring's doctor, an obsequious quack from Cologne called Kahle, whose 'wonder cure' for morphine addiction was the reason for his patient's long baths – and insatiable appetite. Lana Mae paid him no mind whatsoever as he cleared away syringes and pills.

She perched at the bath edge, enjoying the caviar. 'And how is your progress today, Herr Göring?'

'Ah, it ebbs and flows,' he said. 'Kahle continues to work at his treatments but do you think I crave the dope any less?'

Lana Mae nodded compassionately.

'Not so – the Reichsmarschall's cravings are much reduced!' said the servile Kahle, his hands buried deep in his doctor's bag. 'They are a fraction of what they were.'

'Whose cravings are they, fool?' said Göring, kicking water at the doctor from the bath. 'He speaks out of his arse.' He stuffed the toast in his mouth. 'I rue the day I started on this tormented path, Frau Huckstepp,' he confided, dripping little black eggs.

Lana Mae adjusted herself to advantage so that more cleavage showed. 'Taking morphine for your pain?' Claude presented her with a second scoop of caviar on toast. 'But you can't be blamed for that. I'm sure the injuries you suffered in the last war must have been awful.'

'What are broken bones?' said Göring, dismissive. 'No, it was wrong to hide from the agony. I should have faced it manfully back in '17.'

Lana Mae knew better than to try equating 'manliness' with the creature before her in the bathwater. She stuck to her lies. 'You were so very young,' she said. 'You must forgive yourself for it.'

Göring shrugged and took a gulp of champagne to wash down the toast. 'I denounced the doctors who prescribed it to me, did you know that?'

Lana Mae now felt the caviar sitting heavy in her stomach. 'No. I didn't know.'

'Filthy frauds,' said Göring. Then he added pointedly: '*Communists*.'

'Oh heavens,' said Lana Mae, reacting appropriately.

'Well, they're not anymore,' said Göring, ominous.

Claude cleared his throat. 'Perhaps if Herr Göring has finished with me now?'

The Reichsmarschall threw a cold look at him. 'You're not going anywhere, man.'

Claude was too professional to sag. 'But of course, Herr Göring.'

'If there's a more important guest than me inside this hotel then I want you to show him to me,' said Göring.

'No one enjoys a higher rank than your own, Herr Reichsmarschall,' said Claude.

Lana Mae saw the doctor throw a look of disgust. Claude's effortless servility outshone his own.

'You're right,' said Göring. 'If I'd wanted to be served by low-level flunkies I would have asked for them. But I *didn't* ask.'

Claude refilled the champagne flute. 'No, Herr Göring.'

Lana Mae wondered how long he'd been trapped here. The corpulent Nazi returned to her. 'So then, Frau Huckstepp, how might I help you today?'

'Oh, well, it's just a little thing . . .' said Lana Mae. She placed her hands at the clasp of her purse but didn't open it, having become practised at drawing the ritual out. 'You know how badly I feel the suffering of those hurt in battle,' she told him. 'It's why I understand your pain.'

'We have talked of it often,' said Göring. His eyes were fixed at her bag.

'And the French, *well* –' she sighed, 'disorganised would be the kinder word for them.'

'And incompetent would be the truth.'

'We understand each other,' said Lana Mae. She avoided looking at Claude for her next words. 'The useless French simply cannot be depended upon to take care of their own boys – and so it's fallen to me to do so. It's the cross I bear, Herr Göring. But willingly.'

He chuckled at her theatre. 'I hear we should be calling you "the American Angel" these days?'

Lana Mae had the good grace to blush. 'If those poor French boys are ever to be useful to the Fatherland, then shouldn't they get well first?'

'The Führer is in your debt,' said Göring.

'But of course, it all costs money,' said Lana Mae, sadly, 'money I no longer have. Roosevelt froze my funds, you know.'

Göring did know.

She opened the clasp of her purse now but didn't yet show its contents.

Flatulence bubbles popped at the surface of the bath.

'Is it possible you are selling more jewellery today, Frau Huckstepp?' Göring's lust at the prospect was as naked in his face as it had been the first time Lana Mae had come to him. His avarice never diminished.

'Ordinarily, I would go to a jeweller, of course,' said Lana Mae, in seemingly bashful apology. She steeled herself for what she had to say next. 'But since all those helpful yellow signs went up in

228

the shop windows, well . . .' She whispered to him, 'I was shocked to learn just how many of 'em are *Jews*.'

Göring nodded. 'I wasn't.'

She reached the climax. 'So, I thought maybe because you so enjoyed some of my other gems, Herr Göring, you might consider this one . . .'

Lana Mae withdrew a ruby as large as a pigeon's egg.

'As I said,' she offered, demurely, 'it's only a little thing . . .'

Another burst of sulphuric bubbles hit the bath surface. The water now turned brown, pulling Göring from his reverie. 'Auzello, you cunt,' he said, seeing it. 'Why did you take a shit in my bath?'

Outside the bathroom door, Lana Mae took a big slug of pink bismuth from the bottle in her purse. Her belly ache was worse than ever – she blamed the pressure of holding her nerve against Göring for it. Then she had to wake Metzingen where he'd gone to sleep upright, slumped against the armoire. His shock at stirring from slumber brought down clothes from the hangers: lavish, full-figured gowns, trimmed in ermine and mink.

Lana Mae carefully hung them again as Metzingen returned to the bathroom to confirm the ruby's price with Göring. When he came back out, the price that he quoted was less than the one Göring had given Lana Mae. She knew the drill and didn't care. Metzingen was deducting his cut.

The Oberstleutnant opened the room safe, not caring if Lana Mae saw the lock combination. He took out handfuls of used Reichsmarks, counting them out for her. He handed them over and she stashed them inside her purse, relieved, thinking of what this would bring for the hospitalised soldiers. It was true, they were calling her 'The American Angel'. Never had Lana Mae known such self-worth. She was a different woman for her acts of sacrifice. She felt worthy of Marjorie.

When Metzingen escorted her to the Imperial Suite's doors, he paused as he delivered her to the hands of the Wehrmacht escort. 'Do you know, Frau Huckstepp,' he mused, sleepily, 'you and the Reichsmarschall are so much alike.'

Lana Mae had been made exhausted by her performance and had little energy to continue it. 'I really don't think that's so, honey,' she told him. 'We don't even take the same size in high heels.'

Metzingen chuckled. 'But that's where you have it. To some people he's ridiculous – effeminate and obscene – vermin daring to infest such an elegant establishment as the Ritz. They used to laugh at him, you know, behind his back.'

Lana Mae stiffened. 'People can be mean.'

'Don't the same people laugh at you?' he asked.

Lana Mae's lip curled. She would never forget the day he had humiliated her at *l'Espadon*. 'Once they did. But they don't anymore – not the Frenchies, anyway. And they're all that counts.'

Metzingen chuckled anew. 'Those same Frenchies who call you "collabo"?'

She stiffened.

'It is widely known, of course, that when you might have found yourself alternative accommodation, you chose to remain at the Ritz – along with many others. And it is widely known, too, that you wine and dine with us – and sell off your "assets" to the highest German bidder.'

Lana Mae was rigid. She looked to the face of her Wehrmacht escort. The young man was expressionless. She told herself that all that mattered was the cash in her purse. 'I wonder whether you think it should be you in that bath?' she asked Metzingen.

He held her eye some time before answering. 'The very idea.'

'Yet you wish it was, don't you?' she said. 'It niggles you something awful that you're not the one buying my jewels . . .'

To her immense satisfaction the comment hit home.

'Oh, *honey*,' said Lana Mae, feigning upset for him. 'You'll get your own rocks someday, I just know you will. All you've gotta do is say your prayers and eat your vegetables.'

He looked darkly at her.

'See you round then.' She giggled, preparing to go.

'You must introduce me to Zita,' he shot at her back.

She stopped. For months, Lana Mae had done her utmost never to let Zita enter her conversations with Metzingen. 'You haven't done that for yourself already?'

He shook his head. 'I have only admired her from afar. We have never met each other, sadly.'

Of course, she knew this for a lie. Lana Mae realised with surprise then that Metzingen didn't know that Zita had confessed what she'd done. He believed the secret of his lover's actions was just that, a secret, at least from Zita's best friends. That it wasn't made Lana Mae see she had the edge on Metzingen. 'Zita ain't backwards in coming forwards,' she said, playing her apparent ignorance, 'if she wants to meet *you*, then she'll see to it herself.'

'All the same,' said Metzingen. 'I put store by introductions. I'm sure that you will see to it as her friend . . .'

Lana Mae tried to calculate what he was up to and became fearful at the possibilities. Did he wish to take what existed in secret and expose it for all those at the Ritz to see? Zita would become a pariah – a 'collabo' in extreme – and by extension, they all would. 'You really don't need me for that,' she said, anxious now.

'And yet, I insist,' said Metzingen, 'and so, you will arrange it. Thank you, Frau Huckstepp.'

He kicked the door shut on her.

They now had a name for themselves: The Freedom Volunteers.

The spot that they'd chosen for their 'launch position' was not at the Ritz, obviously, for that would only risk bringing attention to themselves. Instead it was opposite the hotel on the rue Cambon, located in an apartment building whose elderly concierge had died in the exodus. The lack of a doorkeeper allowed Tommy, Polly and Odile the perfect opportunity to execute their plans.

Across a spate of days, Tommy and Polly had performed the reconnaissance. They took turns walking alone into the building entrance as if they were familiar with it, mounting the stairs. Tommy wore his Ritz uniform, carrying a covered tray as if he was delivering a meal from *l'Espadon* to someone who lived within. It worked in his favour that servants were simultaneously noticed, yet not noticed by most people. If he encountered someone on the stairs or the landings, he greeted them with a nod, and continued ascending. No one blinked twice. Polly took a different approach. If she encountered someone, particularly a male, she chatted pleasantly for a moment, without revealing her business, which only implied that she had reason to be there. Fortuitously, given the proximity to the Ritz, which was crawling with Occupiers, the apartment building was of no interest to the Germans.

One of the fourth-floor apartments was empty, its door left unlocked for new tenants. It had a little balcony off the sitting room, which looked over the narrow street – and the rear entrance to the Ritz. It was ideal for their purpose.

The contraption was ingenious, conceived by Odile. Owing to her dwindling eyesight, however, she could not be the one to place it on the balcony, and so this was Tommy's task. The day they had decided upon was the day of a mass student protest against the arrest of a prominent college professor. Rumour of its planning had reached them through Odile's network of school friends. Initially, they had intended to join the march, until good sense kicked in. If they were ever to succeed in what they had committed themselves to, then they must never allow themselves to be the objects of adverse German attention. The student march would draw the Occupiers like a magnet. It presented them with a distraction.

They had tested Odile's contraption often enough in Tommy's hotel attic room to know it would work. Crouching behind the apartment balcony's flower boxes, so that anyone looking out from the windows on the Cambon side of the Ritz wouldn't see him, Tommy first laid a modified rat trap. Then, in setting it, he placed an empty tin can with a hole punched into its bottom. He filled the tin can with water he'd drawn from the apartment's sink. Immediately the water began to seep from the hole, but not at any great speed, for the hole was deliberately small. Tommy then placed the little container of 'butterflies' that would in time be flung into the air, when the tin can had become light enough to release the trap's mechanism. With everything in place Tommy picked up his covered tray, which had the remains of a meal inside for added authenticity, and exited the apartment, softly closing the door behind him. He strode unhurriedly down the stairs, reached the rue Cambon, crossed it and returned to the Ritz.

Released at last from the Imperial Suite by Göring falling unconscious in bed, Claude kept fresh in his mind the one – the only – silver lining to be wrung from the cloud of the Germans' despicable treatment of him. He had all their names. Speidel. Von Hofacker. Von Stülpnagel. And all the others besides.

Reduced by the Occupiers to a position of such rank servitude, the likes of which he had not suffered since being apprenticed to a Nice hotelier in his youth, Claude relished the Germans' blind spot he had found in their glee at humiliating him. It had not occurred to them that for every hour they forced him to fawn on the dope-addled whale that was Göring, Claude was listing in his head the names of everyone he encountered there. New names and ranks, sometimes unclear in the frenzy of partying, always became clear in good time to be added to those he already knew.

As Metzingen himself had first told Claude: only the very highest ranked Germans were permitted to stay at the Ritz. They were the occupying elite. This was nice information for those who put store in tracking the bastards' movements.

Claude reached the Vendôme lobby, passing the pair of sentries at the bottom of the stairs. 'Good afternoon, Messieurs.'

They ignored him. Of course, they did. He was beneath their contempt, so why should they be mindful of him at all?

He reached his little desk with its ledger and white telephone, and at that moment he thought of Marjorie. He had to blink and pinch the skin at his wrist, telling himself that the hint of her favourite perfume in his nostrils was memory, not real. He would not believe in ghosts. Yet it was almost as if she was with him, right by his side, inspiring him to fight. Marjorie, a foreigner, had received the *Légion d'honneur* for sacrifices she had made for a country that wasn't even her own. How could he, a Frenchman, claim not to be shamed by that?

From the drawer Claude took out his 'shopping list', in full view of the sentries. They looked right through him. 'Ah me,' Claude sighed to no one in particular, 'It's always the dullest of tasks that we put off until last, isn't it?' He picked up the telephone receiver and dialled the number of a very old friend who lived in the Unoccupied Zone in France's south. If anyone asked, this man owned a farm; a reliable supply of black market vegetables, essential to feed German guests. Yet no one did ask.

The telephone rang at the other end of the line and was shortly picked up.

'Ah, Jean-Luc! How are you today?' Auzello greeted his friend heartily. The information Claude would now give 'Jean-Luc' would be passed on to a railway worker who worked near the Swiss border. This man, whom Claude did not know, and most likely never would, would then pass it further along to agents of the Free French Army working in the neutral territory.

With vengeful pleasure, Claude thought of the code name he'd assigned to Göring. 'Yes, dear Jean-Luc, it is time to place our orders again, if you can spare me anything you have. Let me see.'

He consulted his shopping list. 'A sack of potatoes. Yes, a great big fat one, if you have it for me . . .'

Revived by an hour or so's sleep, Metzingen, now in a freshly laundered uniform, was joined in the Cambon lobby by Jürgen. The younger man predictably had his camera around his neck, their plan being to view the magnificent stained-glass windows at Sainte-Chapelle, tucked away on the Île de la Cité. On the point of exiting the Cambon doors they saw the Comtesse Ducru-Batailley approaching from the street, accompanied by her pretty young ward.

'You see who it is, Oberstleutnant?'

'Of course,' said Hans, grinning.

'So beautifully dressed.'

'The Comtesse – always. When is she not? She was wise to secure her own money.'

But Jürgen's appreciation was for Polly.

'Ah,' said Metzingen. 'She's a little young for you, surely?'

The Hauptmann shrugged, fingering his camera case as he watched the women draw nearer. 'I'm still only twenty-five and the girl is blossoming of late. She is not the same girl you paid so little regard to at the Boulevard de Courcelles.'

'*I* paid?'

Jürgen winked at him. 'You ignored her. I, Oberstleutnant, saw her potential.' He studied Polly, the wide smile staying in place. 'Look how lighthearted she is. It's like the Jew's death never touched her.'

Metzingen got there first to open the door for them, showily sweeping his Oberstleutnant's cap from his head for Jürgen's benefit. 'My dear, Comtesse, how elegant you are today – and indeed every day.'

Both Germans enjoyed watching Alexandrine go through the motions; an aristocratic automaton. 'Dear Herr Metzingen,' she muttered, bowing slightly, 'you are so very kind.'

Metzingen turned to Jürgen as if the women weren't there. 'She seems tranquilised.'

Alexandrine winced as Jürgen nodded. 'There is nothing behind her eyes.' But Jürgen's eyes were for Polly. 'And little Fräulein Hartford.' He actually chucked her under the chin. 'You should be sweeter to your guardian – today you risk putting her in the shade.'

The girl was that much livelier, it seemed to Hans, refreshingly lacking in loathing or fear. Her eyes were quite beautiful, too, now he was watching her anew.

'Hello, Herr Jürgen,' Polly said to the younger man. She met and held his appraising look, before turning to Hans. 'Hello, Herr Metzingen.' She turned to Jürgen again, and both Germans knew then where her interest lay. 'It is much colder outside today,' she said to him. 'I do hope you're rugged up enough.'

They were all four paused at the doors, not quite outside or in. The only traffic in the street was cyclists.

'I'm sure I shall warm up with a good healthy walk,' Jürgen told her.

Metzingen turned to Alexandrine. 'And might I take this opportunity to remind you of the register, Comtesse?'

Her eyes were still lightless. 'The register, Herr?'

'Oh, you have not heard of it?' said Metzingen. 'It is for all Jews. For their own protection. They are to report to the police prefectures, so that it can be freely known who is who.' He smiled at Polly. 'Just as it is already so with non-interned foreigners.'

Alexandrine's unfocused gaze grew sharp. 'What an admirable administrative procedure.'

'Yes, isn't it?'

'Tell me,' asked Alexandrine, 'is the man who thought up this idea the same man who ordered yellow stars be glued to the windows of Jewish shops?'

'Of course,' said Hans, 'that man is the Führer.'

'Things move so quickly,' said Alexandrine. 'You're telling me this because I am a Jew?'

236

Hans tut-tutted. 'I am telling you this because of that old woman who looked after your late husband – what was her name?'

'I don't recall,' said the Comtesse.

Metzingen clicked his fingers as if prompting the correct answer to a quiz.

'It was Suzette,' said Jürgen. 'She was insolent.'

'Yes, that is the one.' Hans turned to Alexandrine again. 'Kindly remind *her* to report to her nearest police prefecture, Comtesse. She must be registered for her own peace of mind. Where is she living now? The Marais?'

'I have lost touch with the woman,' claimed Alexandrine.

Neither German believed that. 'Press the urgency upon her,' Hans advised, 'in case she has forgotten the authorities' directive. There are to be no exceptions to it, I believe.'

There was a long moment as both women remained looking at them, their respective expressions unchanged.

'As ever, the authorities have our better interests at heart,' said Alexandrine, eventually.

'So very true.' Metzingen went to return his cap to his head, which is when he saw the little slip of paper that had landed inside it.

'Look! How pretty,' said Polly, pointing upwards.

In the rue Cambon it was snowing. Tiny, toilet-paper-thin documents were floating and spinning through the air around the cyclists. There were hundreds of them. On the sidewalk, pedestrians snatched at the little papers in fun.

Metzingen left Jürgen holding the door as he stepped into the street, enraged. 'Put them down!' he ordered those who had caught them. 'Put that thing down!' Alarmed, people did as he said, but the wind had taken hold of those papers still airborne, spiralling them north towards the Boulevard de Madeleine.

A massive black Daimler, the only car in the street, was approaching from the same direction. With dismay, Metzingen and Jürgen saw whose it was. In the spacious back seat, fresh from

237

another 'shopping' expedition at the requisitioned mansion of a Jew, sat Göring. The car windows were damp from a rain shower. The little papers stuck all over them, obscuring Göring's face.

Metzingen turned to the Comtesse and her ward, who were still where he'd left them with Jürgen at the hotel door. They withdrew in unison.

'What do they say, Monsieur?'

Metzingen was jolted by a voice to his left. Auzello's sightless step-daughter was slouched in the entrance alcove, puffing on a cigarette. Had the unpleasant child been there all along?

'Don't let me catch you reading them,' he warned her. The girl flinched at his accent, as if she hadn't realised she had addressed the question to a German.

'But I can't read them, Monsieur, that's why I asked,' she spluttered at him.

Göring's Daimler slowly passed by the Cambon doors. The Luftwaffe chauffeur was trying to drive with one arm stuck out the window, scraping at the little papers on the windscreen. Metzingen retreated to the lobby, with Jürgen closing the door behind them.

They stared at each other in mortification for a moment.

Then they read the little butterfly that had landed in Hans' cap.

This little joke is a gift to you from the Freedom Volunteers.

Hitler is searching for the means to invade England. He drags in the Chief Rabbi of Berlin to help him. 'How did Moses part the Red Sea?' Hitler wants to know. 'If you can get me that information, dear rabbi, I will end my harassment of the Jews.'

The Chief Rabbi gives this some thought. 'That sounds like a pretty good deal, my Führer,' he says to Hitler. 'Give me a week and I promise to tell you how Moses did it.'

Exactly one week later, the rabbi returns. 'I have good news and I have bad news,' he says to the Führer.

'Get to the point,' says impatient Hitler, 'do you have the answer for me or not?'

'Yes, my Führer, that is the good news,' says the Rabbi, 'the answer is that Moses parted the Red Sea with his staff.'

'That's great!' says Hitler. 'So where is this staff?'

At this the Rabbi looks awkward. 'Well, that's the bad news, I'm afraid. It's in the British Museum.'

For Jürgen, once was enough, but Metzingen read and re-read the little butterfly for a long time. When he looked up at last, the Cambon lobby was still empty. If anyone had come in, they had seen them both, and understood from the Germans' bearing that they would be wise to retreat.

'You will not visit Sainte-Chapelle today, Hauptmann,' said Hans.

'Of course, Herr Oberstleutnant,' said Jürgen. 'I will go another time.'

Metzingen nodded. 'Instead you will find who is responsible. Is that clear?'

'Perfectly, Herr Oberstleutnant.'

'And when you have found them, you will do what is necessary with our friends at Gestapo Headquarters.'

'Of course. I know the procedure.'

Metzingen nodded again, grateful. He didn't care that the younger man could see the devastation in his face.

Jürgen was gentle with him; a friend. 'It is to be expected, Hans,' he said, formality dropped. 'A hotel of this size and renown. Of course, there must be one or two bad eggs. It'll be someone with an axe to grind from the last war – you see if it's not.'

Metzingen was touched. 'I see sense in that theory.'

'I will find them,' Jürgen promised.

'I know you will.'

'And when I have, it will be your Ritz again. There will be no repeat of this.'

Metzingen felt cheered. He tore the thin paper into shreds as Jürgen glanced into the glass and chrome Cambon bar; a room both men disliked for its ugly modernity.

'I will start the search there,' Jürgen told him.

In almost total silence, not daring even to risk the rustle of their clothes, Polly and Tommy found each other at the top of the stairs. It ached not to laugh with sheer joy at what they'd achieved under the noses of the Germans, as tiny as it seemed in the scheme of things.

'Did you see it go off?' Polly whispered to him.

He shook his head. 'I couldn't risk it. I went to the kitchen. Tell me what it looked like.'

'Like a miniature blizzard.'

'We're brilliant!' hissed Tommy. 'We pulled the prank off.'

'So, what do we try next?'

'We can't go back to the apartment. We'll have to find some-place else.'

'I wish we could look for somewhere *together*,' said Polly, before she realised how it sounded. She flushed with embarrassment. 'That's not what I meant.'

'What isn't?'

'What I just said.'

He was smiling teasingly at her. 'What did you just say?'

She crossed her arms. 'I meant I wish we could look for some-where together as colleagues in resistance.'

Tommy raised an eyebrow, still smiling at her.

Polly thought then of how easy it would be to become lost in Tommy's soft brown eyes. Then she remembered that it had been the gun that he'd hoped for, not her, when he'd made her part of his resistance, and how disappointed he'd been when she'd told him that someone had stolen it. She retreated to the safety of her old resolve about males, frowning at him. 'Please don't you start on this, too.'

'Start on what?'

'Imagining stupid things that simply aren't there.'

'What things?'

Polly punched him hard on the arm. 'Why is no one able to accept that without steadfast resolve and purpose we will never win this war?'

She saw these words land on him far more effectively than her punch had.

He was stunned. 'You say I have no resolve?'

Polly wavered. 'Of course not. You inspire me with your commitment. You inspire Odile.'

'You and Odile inspire me back – especially you, Pol.'

'Why me more than her? I'm nobody, Tommy. She's the inspirational one. Disability means nothing to Odile.'

Tommy just looked at her.

'Well?'

'I don't know,' he said simply. 'You just do, Polly.'

She started heading down the stairs again. 'I'm not contributing another word to this ridiculous conversation.'

'Wait –'

But she wouldn't wait. 'And if we ever have it again,' she told him, looking firmly ahead and not over her shoulder where he stood watching her, 'then I shall find someone else to inspire me – someone whose commitment is actually as strong as he claims it to be.'

The impact this exchange left upon Tommy's face was considerable, but such was the strength of Polly's resolve that she refused to let herself see it. Yet if she had glanced around as she descended the stairs, she would have recognised in Tommy's expression one that had so often been her own.

Tommy Harsanyi, sort of Hungarian, Jew, illegitimate son of a Comte, showed the devastation that came with disregard and rejection – something he'd experienced too much of in his seventeen years.

Although Polly would never know of it, her own resolve gained a twin in that moment in Tommy. As he watched the last of her disappear down the stairs, Tommy told himself bitterly that the last of his devastation went with her.

He would never allow himself to be crushed by rejection again.

Guy saw Jürgen approach through the Cambon bar doors and resisted the urge to look sideways for another barman to serve him. His tried-and-true bonhomie would have to sustain the encounter as it somehow sustained all the others he'd been forced to endure with the Germans. It wasn't as if he disliked them personally; he'd enjoyed a kraut lover or two when there'd been so many of them left broke and washed up in the city at the end of the last war. He'd found that Germans could be perfectly charming and surprisingly accommodating then. Yet this time around so many of them lacked any evidence of charm; charm having been ejected to make way for belief. And what they seemed to believe was highly troubling for someone like Guy, who loved men. His thoughts went then to his lover Baptiste at the Théâtre du Vieux-Colombier bar. The Algerian Baptiste not only had to conceal his sexual proclivity from the Occupiers, but his race: he was quarter-part black. Guy feared for him.

'Bonjour, Herr Jürgen,' he greeted the handsome German. 'How nice it is to see you today.' He resisted his natural urge to call him *'Cherie'*, as he would with any French man. Guy's compatriots enjoyed harmless flirting. German men largely did not. 'Would you like your favourite tipple?' Guy tapped his head. 'You don't need to remind me what it is – I keep it up here. I never forget a favourite drink.'

Jürgen sighed. 'Why not, Guy. It can only do good. Just like you, my friend.' He took the camera from its strap around his neck and placed it on the chromium counter.

Guy took down from the high shelf a little-touched bottle of kirsch and reached for a martini glass. 'You seem down in the dumps, Herr Jürgen. Having a bad day?'

'It could be better.' He fiddled with the camera case, distractedly.

'Cheer up. You're still here at the Ritz. You're still in Paris. Where else is it better to be?'

Jürgen smiled at that. 'True.' He considered what was weighing on his mind. 'Still, I am sorry to say that the Ritz has disappointed me today. Worse, it has disappointed the Oberstleutnant. And you know of the great regard in which he holds this hotel.'

Guy did know. It was impossible not to. Metzingen swaggered around the place as if he owned it. And in his darker moments, Guy fancied that owning the Ritz could well be Metzingen's intention. 'I cannot believe this is so,' he said.

'I would have said so too, had I not seen the disappointment for myself,' said Jürgen, sadly. 'The disappointment is great.'

'Ah.'

'I cannot let it drop.'

'Oh dear.'

'I really cannot. The Oberstleutnant's hurt is too deep.' He leant across the counter to whisper. 'He has been humiliated in front of the Reichsmarschall.' He winced. 'Soon they will all hear of it – von Stülpnagel, Speidel – it will be terrible for him.'

The hair on Guy's arms prickled. 'I see.'

He handed the German his summer fruit cup as he considered his next words carefully. 'Hurt and humiliation are of course not welcome at the Ritz, Herr Jürgen. So, tell me, as your humble barman, is there something that I might do to remove this unpleasantness?'

Jürgen sipped. 'All right. Why not.'

Guy smiled, waiting.

'If you had to enact the reprisal on someone, who would it be?'

Guy's smile froze. 'Herr Jürgen?'

243

'Someone at the Ritz is to receive the reprisal for the Oberstleutnant's humiliation – who should it be? Give me a name.'

'I'm confused.'

Jürgen placed his drink on the counter. He took his camera out of its leather case, admiring it. 'It's very simple, surely. You know everyone here. So, who should it be?'

Guy was bewildered. 'But – but who was it that hurt Herr Metzingen? Who gave him the humiliation?'

Jürgen shrugged. 'I wish I knew. It would make the task so much easier, of course.'

'But it was someone at the Ritz?'

Jürgen scooped a handful of nuts from a dish. 'Again, I wish I was sure. The outrage occurred in the street outside – I suppose I could find who it was, but why waste the resources? There are far more important things. No, in this instance, the Ritz will just have to do.' He dropped the nuts in his mouth.

Guy could only stare at him in horror as he chewed.

Jürgen swallowed and took another sip of his drink. 'So, tell me, Guy, who should it be?'

'Herr Jürgen, please –'

'Propose me a name.'

'I can't possibly do that.'

Jürgen took the cap from the camera lens and studied Guy through the viewer, pulling him in and out of focus. 'I will only ask you one more time, Herr Martin. *Please give me a name . . .'*

The pressure of keeping a straight face was agony, yet somehow, they managed it, every one of the diners, biting the insides of their cheeks if they had to, or the tips of their tongues. As one, without even the ghost of a smile, the *l'Espadon* patrons watched Reichsmarschall Göring make his entrance to dinner.

The Ritz restaurant was full. Easily half of the occupants were Germans, high-ranking officers of various commands. Regular uniforms were not permitted in the dining room, by German order, not French, and so the officers wore dress uniforms, mostly in white, which made differentiating the Wehrmacht men from the Gestapo even more challenging for those who comprised *l'Espadon's* other half: the civilians.

Tonight, Göring had a new piece of finery to display: a solid gold baton, made for him by Cartier, liberally studded with diamonds and other precious gems. He swung it in his arms as if he was an obese majorette; his pupils like pinpricks. The collective need of the diners to scream with hilarity at this display was almost over-whelming. Yet no one succumbed. There was only applause.

'I recognise those rocks,' spat Lana Mae to her friends, over the din of the clapping.

'Think of all the good they bought you, puss,' said Zita.

'I'd been friends with those rocks for years,' Lana Mae said ruefully. 'Horace T. bought 'em for me.'

Zita patted her hand. 'We know, puss.'

'That man is on dope again,' said Alexandrine of Göring.

Filed along with all the rest of Zita's culpability was the guilt she reserved for the fact that Alexandrine was drinking more than her friends.

'Shhh, honey,' Lana Mae warned. She took the glass from her reach.

'Well, he is,' said Alexandrine, 'look at the state of him.' She moved the glass back where she could get it.

Polly, seated next to the Comtesse, squeezed Alexandrine's hand. Zita could take solace from the rapprochement Polly had achieved there. Zita had not been privy to Alexandrine's words spat in the wake of Eduarde's suicide, but she had witnessed Polly's devastation afterwards. Polly had forgiven Alexandrine, but Zita knew the Comtesse was as haunted by the vicious things she had said as she was by the memory of her husband's head in pieces.

Alexandrine opened her purse on her lap and shook out a pill from a bottle. 'For my indigestion,' she said, before anyone asked.

'You haven't even eaten yet,' said Lana Mae.

Alexandrine indicated prancing Göring at the other end of the long, mirrored room. 'I'm getting in early, darling.'

Resigned, Zita watched Göring some more, weaving his way around tables of overly jocular Nazis, men who cracked every last joke but the obvious one. He knocked Colonel von Hofacker's wine glass to the floor, staining the officer's white trousers deep red. This set off another round of phony guffaws. 'He's as high as a goosestep tonight,' said Zita. 'Maybe he'll slip on his arse.'

'If he does then you'd better pretend you never saw it,' Lana Mae told her. She looked over to Polly. 'You're doing swell, honey. You keep up that poker face of yours like a pro.'

Polly smiled. Zita watched her gaze drift to Tommy waiting on tables among the Germans. Some of them slapped him on the back like he'd become an old friend. She thought of how well his hair made him blend in among them.

'Oh hell,' said Lana Mae, under her breath. 'Don't let that face slip now, Pol. See what's coming.'

Zita looked. Metzingen had risen from his table near Göring's boorish group and was weaving through the room in the direction of their table, greeting fellow officers and guests as if he was personally responsible for the evening. He stopped at one table and regarded the centre flower arrangement for a moment, taking exception to something. He clicked his fingers until a waiter approached. With a brief exchange of words, the flowers were removed. Metzingen looked satisfied.

Lana Mae hissed at Zita. 'Honey, there's something I might have forgotten to tell you . . .'

'What?' she said.

'He wants an introduction.'

'Who does?'

Lana Mae nodded apologetically in the direction of the approaching Metzingen.

Zita froze. What was he doing?

'Buckle up, baby, we're all here to protect you,' Lana Mae told her. She rose in her chair and called out to the Oberstleutnant. 'Oh, Herr Metzingen! Do you have a little minute to spend with us girls?'

Metzingen was greeting Speidel, but he looked up and beamed, before playing a little pantomime that he'd been going to a different table all together. 'But Frau Huckstepp! Of course, of course. How delightful you look this evening.'

'This old thing?' said Lana Mae. She clearly wanted to get this over with. 'I've a friend of mine here who's just been begging to meet you.'

Zita locked challenging eyes with Metzingen, acutely aware that Polly remained ignorant of any subtext. The complexities of Zita's secrecy grew daily more challenging. She steeled herself to pull this next performance off.

'Oh yes?' said the German, as if surprised. He pulled a chair from a neighbouring table and planted it crudely among their own, sitting directly across the table from Zita, so that he might appreciate her fully.

'I don't know if you're a fan of the movies?' Lana Mae began.

'Of course, of course,' said Metzingen heartily. 'I so enjoy the *Kino*.'

'You do?' said Lana Mae. 'Then you must have seen our very good friend on one of your little excursions.'

Metzingen frowned, apparently confused. 'The lady is a fan, too?'

Lana Mae laughed hollowly. 'Oh, Herr Metzingen, you really shouldn't kid. This is Mademoiselle *Zita*,' she said. 'Don't you recognise her face?'

Metzingen held Zita's cold eyes. 'I'm afraid I do not, Frau Huckstepp. I've never seen this lady anywhere but *l'Espadon*.'

Zita was glad Lana Mae chose silence at this.

Metzingen presented his hand across the table. 'Zita, you say? The pleasure is mine, *meine Dame*.'

Zita's 'Fräulein' retort didn't come. Instead she took his hand like it was something decayed. 'The movies have changed.' She sighed. 'It's a wonder we bother going anymore. Everything's German now, even the newsreels. And aren't we sick of the auditorium lights being turned up full? Why do they do that, do you think? To scare off those who might boo?'

She let herself seem impervious to the leaden pause that followed from Metzingen. Alexandrine took another pill from her purse and washed it down with her wine; her eyes like beads of glass.

'You must forgive me that I do not recognise you at all, meine Dame,' Metzingen offered to Zita. 'Perhaps I will place you if you remind me of the roles you have played in your films?'

She sneered at his conceit. 'I play upper-class virgins,' she countered. 'I've made a whole career out of them.' She leant forward on her elbows. 'Someone told me you Occupiers are opening a brand-new studio to make French films. But I didn't believe it. Why the hell would you make pictures people want to go see?'

Metzingen smiled at the provocation of being called an 'Occupier' to his face. 'And yet it is true, Frau Zita. This new enterprise is to be called Continental Studios. Why do you ask? Are you hoping for a walk-on part?'

Zita blithely lit a cigarette. 'Sure, puss,' she said, exhaling. 'Just show me the dickless rube I'm expected to screw and we'll all be in business.'

Alexandrine filled the next pause. 'Did you know that Herr Metzingen has been tasked with keeping Parisian culture alive?' she asked the table.

'Culture?' said Zita. 'Is that like cultured pearls? Never as good as the real thing?'

'Oh, I'm sure the dear Oberstleutnant won't disappoint us with anything fake, darling.' Alexandrine's glass clattered as she placed it unsteadily on the table. 'It must be a very big job for a very big man, Herr Metzingen?'

Polly looked alarmed and Zita saw her try to grip Alexandrine's hand under the table to warn her to stop, but the Comtesse evaded her.

Metzingen kept his eyes only on Zita. 'We all look forward to seeing your face on the silver screen, meine Dame. I'm sure with adequate rehearsal you will even be passable.'

'You can take a flying continental with your Continental Studios,' Zita told him.

Lana Mae gave a sharp gulp of breath. 'Please don't over-egg the cake now, honey . . .'

Metzingen's expression didn't change. 'And yet, I feel that you *will* appear in these forthcoming films, Frau Zita.' He tapped his nose. 'And I have a sixth sense for these things.'

'But what if your sixth sense is nonsense?' From the corner of her eye, Zita saw a German officer who was not in dress uniform approach Tommy from behind – and saw that Polly saw it too. This man's uniform was stark black against the white of his fellows. He tapped Tommy hard on the shoulder. Tommy turned in surprise, before Zita's attention was taken by Metzingen again.

'No, no. You see, I'm so often right,' he told Zita. 'I feel stardom is ahead for you at Continental.' He stood up abruptly, his chair clattering behind him. He scanned the crowded dining room. 'Jürgen! Where are you, Jürgen!'

L'Espadon fell into silence at his shouting. At the far end, Göring's table of cronies halted their sycophancy a moment to look at Metzingen with interest.

'Jürgen!' Metzingen bellowed at the room. 'Speak up, man – where are you in here?'

'I am here, Herr Oberstleutnant.'

The young Wehrmacht Hauptmann stood up from a little table near the terrace. Those at Zita's table now saw with surprise who it was he'd been dining with: Coco Chanel.

'Ah, Jürgen,' said Metzingen, pleased. Every eye was watching him, every ear was listening. 'Why don't you bring me that exciting new screenplay?'

'Screenplay, Herr Oberstleutnant?'

'Yes, yes. You know the one. It's very good. The one Doctor Goebbels most especially recommended for our new studios. You have it with you, of course?'

'Of course, Herr Oberstleutnant.' Jürgen's briefcase full of manila files was beside his chair. He bowed and clicked his heels at Chanel. 'Please excuse me a moment, Fräulein.'

The designer looked at no one, gazing coolly at the garden outside.

Jürgen removed a bound wad of paper from the case as he approached Zita's table and placed it in Metzingen's hand. His eyes wandered to Polly's and caught them. He smiled.

'Ah, yes, this is the one,' said Metzingen, thumbing through. He shut it again and tossed it onto the table where it fell at Zita's plate. 'Why don't you read it, Frau Zita? There's an excellent role for you.'

She could plainly read the words on the cover: *The Filthy Truth of the Jew Rothschilds*.

'The title is a little unwieldy,' Metzingen admitted. 'Still, it does catch the eye.'

'I'm illiterate, sorry,' said Zita, stubbing her cigarette. 'I've always preferred to feel my parts.'

Metzingen chuckled at her smutty joke. 'I'm sure that's not so. This role will be a refreshing departure. She's a poor little simpleton who knows nothing of how the world is run. The writer has called her *Lotti* . . .'

Zita stiffened – as did Alexandrine and Lana Mae. Zita glanced across the table then and saw it: Polly had reacted, too, frozen just like the rest of them were. She felt sick as she guessed what this meant: Polly knew about the child. Yet she had never confronted Zita with it. Why hadn't she? Zita arrived at the likely answer: Polly had not yet learned that the father was Hans. Polly alone took the conversation between Zita and Metzingen at surface value, believing that they were meeting for the first time. How much longer could Polly's ignorance last with Metzingen behaving as recklessly as this, Zita wondered.

'Ah, you like it already?' Metzingen noted. 'I agree, Lotti is a very charming name. And yet there are conflicting thoughts on what the ending should be. Does Lotti win over her captors and return to her mother's arms? That's the one I prefer. But others feel she should meet a different fate. Perhaps you will have your own ideas?'

Zita gave him nothing for a moment. Then she said, 'I don't believe that is the plot at all.'

'No?' said Metzingen. He chuckled again. 'Perhaps I have confused it with another storyline. I read so many these days.' He patted the screenplay in front of her. 'All the same, you will read this.'

The restaurant began to hum again as people returned to their own conversations.

'Thank you, Jürgen, that will be all,' said Metzingen. He took his seat again. The younger man saluted and winked at Polly.

Zita saw Polly gawp for a moment, unsure of what to do. Then instinct seemingly told her she must wink back, for she did so. Jürgen's face split into a wide grin before he returned to where he had been dining. Zita felt her heart thumping in his wake. In her mouth was an unpleasant metallic taste.

Metzingen signalled to a waiter that he wanted a setting brought for him. None of Zita's friends looked at each other.

'If our dear Herr Metzingen is looking to staff this new enterprise, perhaps he'll find an opportunity to encourage new writers?' Alexandrine wondered at last.

Metzingen raised his eyebrow at her.

'Particularly those with a gift for comedy.' She sipped from her glass. 'Such a funny piece I read today,' Alexandrine went on. 'The writer was so happy to share it with everyone. Did you chance to see it, Herr Metzingen? I seem to recall you were strolling the rue Cambon.'

Zita saw anxiety fill Polly's eyes.

'Oh, that writer?' said Metzingen. 'Yes, it was a very funny thing he wrote.' He waited while cutlery and crockery were laid before him by one of the other waiters. When the process was finished, he added, 'Yet, that writer is no longer available.'

Zita stared at their ward. Polly seemed to be willing herself to give nothing away. *She has secrets of her own*, Zita thought to herself. *It was impossible not to, for any woman keen to survive.*

'No?' said Alexandrine. 'That's disappointing.'

'My very sentiments,' said Metzingen. 'Disappointing, too, because he was resident at the Ritz. I had allowed myself to think otherwise of those who live here. A good lesson learned.'

Zita saw the silent panic that now hit Polly and prayed that Hans wouldn't notice it.

'I believe he is writing for the Gestapo boys this evening.' Metzingen shrugged. 'But as to whether he is still funny . . .'

Zita watched on as Polly forced herself to seem calm, casting a casual glance to where Tommy had been serving at the Germans' tables. There was no sign of him now. Polly gave a slow sweep of the room. Then she took a sip of her glass of water before carefully dabbing her lips with her napkin. Then she knocked the glass over.

'Oh, bother.'

Water dripped onto Zita's dress.

'Butter fingers,' said Lana Mae.

Polly looked bashfully at the oblivious Hans. 'Will you excuse me a moment, Herr Metzingen? I think I should change.'

'But of course, little Fräulein.' He stood up politely as she arose from her chair, smiling.

None of the Girls made anything more of the table accident – Zita most especially.

'I shall be back in a moment,' Polly told them.

Polly fled to the Cambon lobby, hot tears of dread stinging at her eyes. 'Tommy – oh, please, not Tommy.' She stopped uselessly, frozen with indecision as to whether she could risk looking for him down in the kitchens. How could she explain why she wanted him? Her mind ran with horrific possibilities and recriminations. What had they overlooked when they had laid their silly prank? What was it they had done to give themselves away so hopelessly?

She remembered her last image of Tommy in the dining room: the black-clad German officer tapping him hard on the shoulder, Tommy's look of surprise – or had it been alarm? Polly tried to remember which Germans had black uniforms. Was it the Gestapo? She was sure it was. 'It can't be true – it can't be.'

A little huddle of people was grouped near the entrance to the Cambon bar, visibly distressed. There was an air of fearful incomprehension and shock. Polly saw Mimi in the middle of them, weeping into her gloved hands while other crying people tried to comfort her. Claude Auzello was there, his face dark with grief.

Then a head of German blond hair.

It was Tommy.

He looked across to her. His expression bewildered, marked with something far worse: crushing guilt.

With sickening certainty, Polly realised who she had selfishly forgotten about in her fear.

The Germans had Odile.

Her own tears threatened to spill now as she thought of what must be happening to the schoolgirl who couldn't even see. Horrific images overwhelmed her.

Tommy was breaking away from the group, still looking across at her, imploring her without words to turn around and retreat. She somehow pulled herself together and took to the stairs. Polly reached the second floor, and then the third, with Tommy keeping one flight behind her. She reached the attic rooms with no one but Tommy to see it. Polly kept walking along the corridor until she reached the door to his room.

Odile was waiting there.

'Oh my God!' She threw herself at the girl, hugging her and kissing her cheeks. 'Thank God, you're safe, Odile. Thank God.'

'Keep it down, Pol,' Odile complained. She extricated herself from her arms.

Tommy appeared. Silently, he unlocked his door. When they were all inside, Polly started crying fully. 'I thought it was you – then I thought it was *you*,' she told them both. Her tears were those that came only with a miraculous reprieve. 'But it was neither of you. The Germans don't even *know*.'

Her co-conspirators didn't share her relief.

Tommy told her. 'They took Guy.'

It took Polly a moment to comprehend. 'But he had nothing to do with us?'

'It didn't matter,' said Tommy. 'They just took him anyway.'

Fresh emotion overcame her. 'But he's innocent – Guy's innocent!'

Tommy had to put his hand to her mouth to stop her screaming.

PART THREE

Insurrection

10

11 December 1941

It was already very cold for early December, but mercifully it wasn't yet snowing. The morning sky was clear, coloured the very palest of blues. For a moment Polly lost herself staring at it, then her mind went somewhere she didn't wish it to go, and she was pricked with anxiety for Tommy. He and Odile were conducting a butterflies prank today. How much longer before they – before any of them – made an error that would see them exposed? It had been more than a year since they had started on this path of resistance; more than a year since Guy had been taken by the Gestapo, never to be heard from again. Her mind full of his unknown fate as it so often was, and with it a fear of what her own fate might be, Polly glanced guiltily at Suzette standing in line with her in the narrow Marais street. As ever, it was as if the old woman could read her mind.

'What are you thinking about, Mademoiselle?' said Suzette, looking up at her, suspiciously.

Polly tried to shake the thought of what Tommy had planned for today. 'Nothing, Suzette. Or everything perhaps. *Queues.*'

Suzette grunted and looked to wordless Alexandrine. The three of them returned to waiting in the cold.

Polly had vowed never to eat at *l'Espadon* again after Guy was taken, and her guardians had seemingly understood, without understanding at all, Polly knew. They knew nothing of what she did with Tommy and Odile, just as she continued to know nothing of their secrets. Although, lately Polly knew rather more than she chose to let on. She was seventeen now and considered herself a young woman – more than old enough to harbour secrets of her own. She had a cast-iron conscience to guide her.

The wrinkled old housekeeper now lived in the apartment Eduarde had bought for her in the Jewish community she'd been born to in the teeming Marais. Suzette had made queueing her main daily activity out of sheer necessity. She needed to eat. When Alexandrine had discovered that Polly had joined her, queuing at shops and paying with ration tickets, just like an ordinary Parisian, her shame at her own flawed character had grown to become shame at her aristocratic entitlement. She in turn had rejected *l'Espadon*, and with it *La Tour d'Argent* and *Maxim's*. And with this rejection, she had ended her practice of slipping fifty-franc notes under dinner plates to ensure she received black market food.

The alternatives to queuing were few. To refuse to bribe waiters was to refuse the black market, which in turn was a refusal to fatten the 'BOFs'. These were the *Beurre Oeufs Fromages* – or the Butter Eggs Cheese – the name given to those who grew rich from black market racketeering. Some of the fabulous profits the BOFs made were blown at the very best fashion houses. To Alexandrine, who had seen BOFs for herself with their fistfuls of francs at Jacques Fath, the coarse language and manners were a very ill match for the tone of haute couture. She, like Polly, despised them. Yet only Polly and her guardians had heard the word 'collabo' hissed at them for continuing to live at the Ritz. But where else should they live? It was home.

The line inched forward again. More women exited the shop. The lone gendarme at the door, whose job it was to ensure the queue remained orderly, allowed more women to go in. There were at least ten women ahead before Polly, Alexandrine and Suzette would get their turn.

Suzette bemoaned her empty basket. 'Every patch of public land has been turned over to growing vegetables,' she complained to no one in particular, 'and still there's not enough to eat.' She gave meaningful glances to those in the queue behind and in front of them. 'I wonder why?'

A woman directly behind, as old as Suzette, was happy to join in. It helped pass the time. 'Oh, I think you know why, Madame,' she replied, grinning toothlessly. 'France is the food bowl for the armies of the Reich. Everything goes off to them now, while we're all stuck here on starvation diets.'

'There's a generation of babies growing up with rickets,' said Suzette, shaking her head.

Tommy returned with anxiety to Polly's thoughts. She tried to force him away.

'My neighbour sent off her youngest on her bike all the way to her husband's cousin in Picardy,' said their queue neighbour.

'Did she come back with anything good?' Suzette wondered, her interest piqued.

'A cauliflower and a couple of eggs.'

'A feast day!' Suzette cackled.

'The eggs broke in the basket.'

The two old women nodded grimly, warming to each other in deprivation. They introduced themselves.

'I am Suzette.'

'A pleasure. I am Alma.'

Surnames weren't necessary. Standing in queues removed so much formality.

'There're soup kitchens set up now,' said Suzette, 'if things get too bad. I hear you can eat for ten francs a day.'

'They're giving soup to us Jews?'

Suzette wasn't sure.

'No,' said Alma, cynically. 'Why would they?'

The slow and lengthy lines so often gave them time for contemplation, and occasional moments of revelation, too. Polly had come to see that the queues were intended to simulate the experience of being prisoner. To queue for hours in all weather was to have one's notion of time, space, and desire controlled utterly by the Occupiers. Yet the experience was not without benefits. The interminable periods, the forever lost mornings that stretched into long afternoons spent standing in lines some-times provided gossip more credible than the news from the German-controlled radio and newspapers.

Polly saw the toothless Alma looking at Alexandrine.

'That's a very nice outfit, Madame.'

'Thank you, Madame,' said Alexandrine, graciously. Her accent exposed her to the woman as upper class. She introduced herself. 'I am Alexandrine. This is my ward, Polly. Suzette is my friend.'

Polly smiled at Alma and watched as the old woman adjusted herself, knowing it was not with any intention of rejection. In the food queues all were made equal. Those who queued had licence to pass comment on anything.

'Make it yourself?' Alma asked Alexandrine.

Polly watched as Alexandrine suppressed a smile and Suzette stood just that little bit taller beside her. The old housekeeper was made proud by such interest in Alexandrine's fashion.

'If only I possessed such skill,' Alexandrine told their neigh-bour. 'I'm afraid I purchased everything I'm wearing today.'

The old woman didn't condemn her for it. 'I admire you for showing the Occupiers how these things ought to be done, Madame.'

Alexandrine was appreciative. 'I never dress down for the queues.'

'Quite so. What are we Parisiennes without our style? Lose that and we've lost it all, I say.'

Alexandrine nodded, clearly warmed by the words. She opened the voluminous bag at her arm. 'I have something I was going to give away today. Perhaps you might like it? I think it would look well on you, Alma.' She produced a Hermès scarf, patterned with horses.

The old woman's eyes lit up. 'Madame – you don't want it?'

'Not anymore.' Alexandrine draped it around Alma's neck. Polly remembered the unexpected pleasure the Comtesse had found when giving away the contents of her suitcase in the exodus. She knew this had fuelled her to repeat the largesse. 'There. Doesn't it suit her, Suzette?' She completed the knot.

Suzette winked at Alma. 'More money than sense.'

'You are very kind to an old woman,' said Alma. She planted a kiss on Alexandrine's cheek.

Polly's little group had reached the head of the queue, with only the young gendarme's say-so to come before they could enter the butcher's shop. Cold and bored, yet far better fed than any of the women in the queue, the man stared into space.

'I want to see Tommy,' said Suzette, from nowhere.

Ripples of reaction passed through Polly and Alexandrine. Both were all too aware of the gendarme. Alexandrine glanced at Polly, who tried to implore Alexandrine wordlessly. How could the Comtesse ever imagine she didn't know about Eduarde's son, Polly thought, even if she wasn't secretly resisting with him? Then Polly feared that she, in turn, was deluding herself. How much did Alexandrine know of Tommy's actions?

'He is safe and sound, you mustn't worry yourself,' said Alexandrine, at last.

'But I do worry. And so, I want to see him.'

Alma had tuned out, fluffing at the scarf.

'I told you,' said Alexandrine, 'he is safe and sound. Don't you think it's a good thing that he stays that way?'

'Did he put himself on the Jew register?'

Alexandrine kept her voice very low. 'How would I know that?'

'And that's your "safe and sound", is it? You should know, Madame. I only pray that he didn't.'

Polly watched carefully as Alexandrine reconsidered her answer. 'Of course, he didn't, Suzette. It would have exposed him. He knows why he's been hidden.'

'You know nothing,' said Suzette. 'He was writing to me, we had a secret system – hiding letters for each other in the Tuileries until I begged him to stop. It had become too dangerous.'

Polly guiltily recalled the letter to Suzette that she had read.

'I didn't want him outside in the streets. Now I don't hear anything at all from him.' There were tears in Suzette's eyes. 'You resent me because I helped raise that boy.'

Alexandrine said nothing, and Polly knew why. It was true.

'His mother died,' said Suzette.

'The Hungarian slut.' Alexandrine spat the words automatically.

'She was dead and he was just a tiny kid.'

'Eduarde's kid to his mistress,' Alexandrine reminded her. 'Not me.'

'None so heartless as the wronged,' Suzette said. But the look she gave Polly was pleading, before she turned to Alexandrine again. 'Where do you think this is going, Madame?'

'Where what is going?'

'Their *rules*. The krauts. What waits for us all at the end of it, do you think?'

Alexandrine seemed to hesitate.

'Well, waits for *me*, anyway,' said Suzette. 'You'll be all right, Madame. You're not a Jew, after all.'

Polly saw the old servant had skilfully pricked Alexandrine's Achilles heel.

'Please stop saying that. I converted.'

'For the jewels and the clothes. God wasn't fooled by your phony faith, even if the rabbi was.'

Alexandrine closed her eyes, vulnerable to Suzette's barbed tongue.

'No idea what's ahead for the Jews then?' Suzette prodded her.

Alexandrine had nothing to say.

'Let me know when you think of something,' Suzette said, turning her back on her. 'And when you do, you might even let me see the boy.'

The young gendarme signalled. It was their turn to go in. Suzette slipped her arm through Alma's and the two old women went inside together. Polly hesitated, poised to follow. Alexandrine remained where she stood, unable to move, ashamed.

'Alexandrine?'

The gendarme clocked her. 'What's wrong with you, Madame? Don't you want your pork sausage?'

The Comtesse bristled.

The gendarme thought himself a wit. 'But you're a kike, aren't you? You won't want your ham baguette either.'

'We are going inside, Monsieur,' said Polly, holding her hand out for Alexandrine.

But the aristocrat didn't take it, regarding the young gendarme as she would a social inferior. 'Forgive me, Monsieur, but your accent confuses. Are you French – or are you German?'

It was the uniformed man's turn to bristle.

'Are you deaf?' he challenged. 'I'm more French than you'll ever be, Jew.' He stepped forward and shoved Alexandrine towards the shop entrance. 'Buy your butcher's meat or go.'

Polly knew that Alexandrine had never been handled in such a manner by anyone. Paralysed on the shop step, she saw the Comtesse brush imaginary dirt from where his hands had dared touch her. 'That is not necessary, Monsieur.'

'This uniform says what's necessary, Jew.' He shoved her harder, and on the cold winter pavement Alexandrine lost her balance and slipped heavily to her knees.

Polly jumped to help her. 'Alexandrine!'

But the gendarme pushed her back to the door. 'Leave it.'

Alexandrine had grazed the flesh under her stockings. Those in the queue had fallen silent, watching in fear. She tried to right herself.

'Stay there, Jew.' The gendarme held his pistol on her. 'Now apologise.'

Polly remembered the confidence that a weapon could bring. Where was Marjorie's gun now? she wondered. Was it being put to a use any better than she could have put it to here? She fantasised about snatching the gendarme's weapon from his hands. How would he speak to them then, she wondered? Would he find his last shred of respect?

'For what should I apologise, Monsieur?' Alexandrine asked him. 'For the misunderstanding?'

Through the door, Polly could see Suzette with Alma, making their selections, oblivious.

'I regret I was confused,' said Alexandrine. 'The truth of your origins is so obvious to me now.'

The rough treatment had excited the gendarme, his enjoyment of it obvious. He had grown hard in his trousers. Yet Polly saw that he wavered, as if unsure of how next to proceed with a well-spoken woman he had felled on the pavement. He was no older than Polly was; new and inexperienced, over-reacting to tiny provocations – or perhaps the gendarmerie had been instructed to do whatever they liked these days. She doubted he'd had his pistol long. What would come now, she wondered, a rape overture?

'Please. The lady has apologised, Monsieur Gendarme,' said a voice from behind Alexandrine. Polly saw an elderly Jewish man take himself out of the line. 'She regrets her mistake, you can see that.'

Alexandrine allowed him to help her get to her feet, with Polly's assistance. When she was standing again, the gendarme regarded all three of them with open contempt. 'You think of yourself as some classy piece of tail,' he spat at Alexandrine.

Polly was shaking now. He would smell her fear. He would smell the fear in all of them and start firing his gun. Who would stop him? Polly wondered.

Alexandrine's aristocratic breeding compelled her to respond to him as a woman of the upper class. 'What I think is unimportant these days. What do you think, Monsieur?'

'I think I'll fuck your pussy off if I see you again,' he told her. 'I'll bring my mates along.'

As if the violence of his words hadn't occurred to her, Alexandrine hooked her handbag at her elbow and straightened her coat. Her leg was bleeding from where she'd struck it. 'I did indeed make a mistake, Monsieur,' she said, not to the gendarme, but to the elderly man, 'I know now exactly what nationality this officer is and I will not have reason to ask him again.' She turned to the baby-faced policeman. 'Heil Hitler.'

He frowned, stymied by this.

'Polly?' Alexandrine clearly had no intention of entering the store and now made to leave. She tried to walk with élan but found that her knee hobbled her.

'Here, lean on my arm,' said Polly. She knew it was selfish to think they'd have nothing to eat from this episode.

The old man reappeared at Alexandrine's left, supporting her other arm. 'Please go back, Monsieur,' she told him, 'don't lose your place in the queue.'

But he wouldn't. 'I know you, Madame,' he whispered to Alexandrine.

Alexandrine indulged this, as she always did, when someone recognised her face from a society page or similar.

'You wed the Comte Ducru-Batailley.'

Polly saw this surprised her. 'Yes, Monsieur, I did.'

'I sometimes help the rabbi at the Synagogue de la Victoire,' he told her. 'I was there on the day you converted.'

Alexandrine stopped still. Would he insult her now? Polly wondered. Would he call her guardian a fraud?

But the old man's eyes were glistening. 'It was so beautiful to see – I thought myself privileged for it. You were resplendent that day, Madame. The love that you had for God shone from your face like a sunrise.'

Alexandrine's voice nearly broke. 'Thank you, Monsieur. It was a very special day. I'm so honoured you witnessed it.'

He held tight on her arm, a quiet desperation in his eyes. 'What will happen to us, Madame?'

She glanced at Polly. 'Happen?'

He cocked his head at the hateful gendarme they had left in their wake. 'His kind are no better than the krauts these days. The things they once muttered behind their hands they shout openly now. What will it lead to, Madame? What do they plan for us?'

To Polly's mind, Alexandrine should have been made fearful by this. Yet she watched as her guardian's heart seemed to soar with the joy of inclusion. 'Whatever it might be, Monsieur, we will survive it as one,' she promised him, tender.

He nodded, comforted. 'Has it ever been otherwise for us?'

*

This little joke is a gift to you from the Freedom Volunteers.

A Parisian man reports to his wife some horrible news. At 9.20 the previous evening, a wicked Jew attacked and killed a German in the Metro. He even ate the German's entrails, starting with the heart.

The wife laughs herself silly at this, 'You'll believe anything you hear, Pierre!'

'But it's true!' her husband insists.

'No, my love, it's impossible.'

'But why?'

'First,' says the wife, 'Jews don't eat pigs; second, Germans have no heart; and, third, at 9.20 in the evening everyone is at home listening to the BBC.'

Smiling – always smiling – Tommy held his folded identification papers ready in his hand. But the pair of Wehrmacht sentries at the Barbès-Rochechouart Metro entrance didn't want them. They almost never wanted them, now. First, as they had come to do routinely with him, they looked at his hair, then they looked at his face. Then Tommy kept his easy smile in place as they drew further assumptions from his height and build, before finally reading him as German, or something like German, and thus something like them. Indeed, Tommy *was* just like them. For him, looking in the face of any Wehrmacht sentry was to look in a mirror.

Then the sentry looked at Odile on his arm.

On these excursions the younger girl left her shaded glasses inside her pocket and her stick at home. They had realised early on that nothing about her blindness should seem too theatrical to observers, in case it was doubted, and so Odile kept her eyes exposed for the world – and Wehrmacht sentries – to see them for what they were: milky and useless. It was hard to keep a good ham down, however. Odile enjoyed adding a tic to the spectacle.

'What's wrong with the kid?' the sentry asked Tommy in German. The other sentry started checking the papers of people standing behind them in the line.

At these times Tommy was thankful he'd learned German at school. 'She's simple,' he told the sentry.

Mouth gaping, Odile directed her sightless eyes to the German's voice. Tommy guessed she was going to dribble.

'Poor thing,' said the sentry, wincing, and Tommy read him as one of those Occupiers whose ideological foundations were shaky. There sometimes seemed to be more of those than fanatics.

'She's my cousin,' Tommy offered, softer. He put his arm around Odile's shoulder. 'She can't help how she is. She's only got me in the world to look after her.'

'I know how it is, brother,' said the sentry, sympathetic. He waved them inside.

Tommy kept his arm around Odile as they descended the stairs.

'You're cuddly,' Odile snickered.

'Stop it. Do you want to fall down?'

'No, I want to feel nice and safe in your arms,' Odile joked.

It suddenly felt to Tommy that there was more than a word of truth to this. He looked long at her sideways, seeing her anew, as Odile remained apparently oblivious.

'What?' she said.

'Your face looks different . . .'

'It does? How?'

He tried to find the right words. 'Not quite so . . . pouty.'

'That's a compliment, is it?'

Tommy didn't know what it was. He flushed his thoughts away. 'Just stop teasing. We're here now.'

The two of them reached the end of the stairs and began to make their way along the corridor to the platform. It didn't matter which platform they chose; the destination was always meaningless.

This Metro, like too many others Tommy had been to lately, was plastered with posters for a so-called exhibition the authorities had opened at the Palais Berlitz, in the 2nd arrondissement. Billed as 'The Jew in France', it promised to show how the evil depth of the Judaic influence leeched at the nation. Loudspeakers promoted the exhibition up and down boulevards, from the Opéra to the Place de la République. The image selected for the poster was unapologetically ugly: a woman on the ground, covered with the French flag, with a vulture perched on her belly. The caption read, 'Frenchmen, help me!'

'Has this place got any of those shitty posters?' Odile whispered.

Tommy grunted a disgusted yes.

'Perfect,' said Odile. 'It deserves what it gets then. How long 'til the next train comes?'

Tommy looked for the clock. 'About twelve minutes.'

'Even better. We won't have to miss one and wait. The next one will give us enough time.'

'Let's do it then.'

Odile squeezed Tommy's arm in resolve.

They now fell into the act they'd rehearsed. Tommy began to guide them to a spot he deemed suitable; somewhere neither too close to other commuters on the platform, or so far away as to lose all the benefit of witnesses. With an ideal spot found, and aware there were now lots of eyes upon them – him being a German-looking blond boy with a blind girl on his arm – Tommy stooped to tie up his shoelace, having deliberately untied it in the street. This left Odile 'unsupervised' to walk freely to the edge of the platform.

Odile began to sing, her voice full-throated and warm:

'Wait for me in this country of France
I'll be back soon, keep confident . . .'

'Monsieur!' A woman who was watching them pointed at Odile. 'Your friend?'

Tommy looked up from his shoelace to Odile's back. 'She'll be all right, Madame. She knows her way. She just likes to sing and listen for the trains.' He went back to tying the knot.

The woman accepted that, but still looked uneasy, her eyes fixed on Odile.

Odile was toeing at the platform edge. 'I wanna go,' she called to Tommy over her shoulder.

'We are going,' Tommy answered, 'as soon as the train comes.'

But he had apparently misinterpreted.

'Oh my God,' said the woman who had called out to him. She now pointedly looked away.

Others followed her like a wave, turning their faces from an unwelcome spectacle.

'Oh, my heavens . . .'

'That's too dreadful.'

Odile had turned around and hitched up her skirt, hanging her behind over the edge of the platform. She was urinating onto the tracks.

'Don't!' hissed Tommy. He leapt up. The pissing dribbled to a stop and Odile covered herself. 'I'm so sorry, Mesdames,' a mortified Tommy told the witnesses collectively, and then to Odile he said: 'I'll take you to the urinal, you're disgusting.' He began to drag the blind girl back the way they'd come in.

People looked acutely embarrassed for them.

'I'm so sorry, Mesdames,' Tommy repeated.

He knew no one had seen what Odile had dropped onto the tracks in the act of relieving herself.

There was the sudden rush of warm air that said a train was approaching from the tunnel. Tommy and Odile stopped. 'It's come early,' whispered Odile, horrified.

'Stay cool,' said Tommy.

The train rattled into the Metro station, and in doing so, set off the little device that Odile had tossed from the platform. A projectile shot forward from where the train's front wheel triggered it, and broke into dozens of tiny, flickering pieces of paper that rained onto the heads of commuters. New butterflies.

Tommy and Odile began calmly ascending the platform stairs.

A young German officer, little older than they were, rushed past them, heading down; he was a naval ensign, dressed in the whites of the Kriegsmarine. Tommy turned to look after him. The young ensign slowed down, making his way towards the first-class carriage at the centre, reserved for Occupiers. As he placed his foot on the threshold of the door, another young man, French, no older than eighteen, stepped forward from the group of commuters.

The Frenchman pulled a pistol from his overcoat and fired two shots into the back and head of the ensign. There was a vivid splash of red upon white and the German fell dead, as the train began to move off. The ensign's body was half inside the carriage and half out, now being dragged along the platform, boot caps scraping on the tiles. People on the platform were starting to scream.

The teenage assassin caught eyes with Tommy for a split second, from where Tommy gaped at him from the stairs. Tommy was horrified by the suddenness of what had occurred; the assassin's look was the same. Tommy guessed why: the other boy had never killed someone before. Then the assassin fled towards the platform's far exit.

Tommy got Odile moving up the stairs again. 'What's happened?' she said. 'Did the butterflies go off?'

Tommy knew they'd be dead if they panicked now. 'They went off,' he said, with a calmness he didn't feel.

'What's going on then – I don't get it.'

'A bit more than we'd planned.' He now found he couldn't stop grinning. 'A kraut just got shot.'

'What!'

'Keep cool, a guy like us did it. He was just another kid. But he had a gun.'

'But – but the stupid gag we put on the butterflies,' said Odile. 'It was about killing a kraut!'

Tommy had already realised it. The Freedom Volunteers had unwittingly put their name to a murder they hadn't committed.

Odile started laughing. 'We're completely screwed.'

'Looks like it,' said Tommy. He wanted to laugh, too. He only wished that he knew who the assassin was. If he did he could have thanked him for changing the way that the resistance game would now have to be played by all of them, Frenchmen and Germans alike. No one had killed a kraut in Occupied Paris before today. 'Yeah, we're screwed,' said Tommy. 'But first we'll be famous.'

Ahead on the stairs came the sound of the sentries, rushing towards them to get to the platform. 'Press tight against the wall,' said Tommy. Odile did so. The sentries barrelled past them to the chaos below.

Tommy and Odile reached the top of the Metro stairs. Tommy knew they had the tiniest amount of time to flee before the whole place was flooded with Germans.

*

On the makeshift film screen made from a hospital sheet hung from the rafters of the ward's ceiling, Zita glowered with sexy angst in cheap, off-the-rack clothes. And yet, being Zita, what was happening on screen had nothing to do with clothes, and everything to do with her electrifying portrayal of a tormented victim of blackmail. This was Zita's third film with Continental Studios, and Polly thought it her best. She had never seen Zita act so compellingly. The rehabilitating French soldiers who were watching the film with her from their hospital beds were clearly in agreement. Amputees many of them, others with terrible burns, they were as one in their love of the film star. Those who could whistle had long since stopped doing so every time Zita entered a scene. Now they watched her with silent fascination as she lived out her character's inexorable decline. Zita was so realistic, it was almost as if she had experienced the degradations of blackmail for real. Zita was the best actress Polly knew.

Polly tried to push what had happened with Alexandrine in the queue from her mind, together with her anxiety for Tommy. She had heard nothing from him and Odile and wouldn't know how they'd fared until she returned to the Ritz in the evening. She glanced to the end of the ward and saw Lana Mae struggling in the corridor, her arms full of folded clothes and blankets. Polly joined her outside to help. 'You look exhausted,' she told her over the clatter of the projector and Zita's one-liners behind the ward doors.

'Oh honey, I feel every last second of my age today,' said Lana Mae, off-loading some of the things to Polly. 'My *actual* age, mind you, not the one I "own up" to.'

Polly politely laughed, although she still knew better than to ask what that age really was. They hefted what they carried to a little office off the corridor, to which the hospital administrators had given a brass door plate that said '*L'ange américain*'.

'But it's *good* exhaustion, I've gotta tell you,' said Lana Mae, dropping folded blankets onto the desk with a sigh. 'God, the experience of being worked to the bone used to be a mystery to me, honey,' she said. 'Once upon a time, the end of the day meant the start of the cocktail hour, which was only the beginning of whatever came next, let's face it. Now, don't get me wrong,' said Lana Mae. 'I'm still very happy to mark sundown with a martini, but these days I don't last beyond the second sip. I can hardly keep my eyes open, yearning for bed.'

'Well, I think you look beautiful with it,' Polly told her, giving her a hug. 'Exhaustion becomes you, Lana Mae.'

'Oh honey, you say all the right things to your ancient guardian,' said Lana Mae, squeezing her with affection.

'I suspect personal fulfilment becomes you, too,' said Polly. 'The more you give, the more you glow from it. You *are* fulfilled, aren't you, Lana Mae?' she added, teasing her. 'It's written all over your lovely face.'

'I'm not doing anything that anyone else in my lucky position wouldn't do, too,' said Lana Mae, modestly. All the same, she glanced at the little mirror that hung on her office wall and was evidently pleased with what she saw.

Polly lowered her voice. 'Lana Mae, I don't see how you can possibly have a single jewel left. I know you're bankrolling the recuperation for all those poor soldiers in there, and I don't know how many other soldiers besides.'

Lana Mae patted the handbag on her desk. 'I owe France a great debt,' was all she said.

'Your friends Flossie and Babs owed France one, too, but they've gone back to New York,' Polly reminded her.

'Yeah, well, there's nothing for me there, remember,' said Lana Mae. 'New York had its chance, and it didn't want me. Paris *did*. So, I ain't going nowhere anytime soon.' She now made it Polly's turn to come under scrutiny. 'And while we're talking of glowing . . .'

'What?' said Polly, at once self-conscious.

'Lately you've got a certain *look* to you, baby. Don't pretend it's not so.'

'Me? Oh, you mean my new outfit?' Polly displayed her recent buy: a divided skirt ensemble in red, white and blue. 'It's by Lucien Lelong. He won a prize for it.'

'Oh, I know,' said Lana Mae.

'It's bicycling fashion,' said Polly. 'Essential nowadays.'

'And it just so happens to be in the colours of the French flag?' said Lana Mae. 'I'm surprised that he – and *you* – haven't been arrested for it.' Lana Mae held Polly's eye for just as long as she could before bursting into laughter. 'Oh, baby, I love it,' she said when she'd recovered. 'Fabulous Lucien. It's both chic and slyly defiant – and it looks so wonderful on a girl with your figure.'

Polly laughed, too. 'You'd have this figure too if you got out and rode a bike more.'

'Oh honey, do you know me at all?'

Polly struck a fashionable pose. 'It *is* a French flag,' she whispered, 'I honestly don't think the Germans have noticed. I've been wearing it for a week – and so have plenty of other girls.'

'There's more to your glow than just a new outfit, honey,' Lana Mae studied her quizzically. *'Tommy.'*

Polly froze.

'Ah-ha!' said Lana Mae, delighted by the look on her face. 'Guilty as charged.'

'I – I don't know what you mean,' Polly started.

'Do you think I was born yesterday?' Lana Mae retorted. 'I know he's your secret boyfriend.'

'He's not! We're friends.'

'Oh please. That old line.'

Polly found safety in umbrage. 'Why is an innocent friendship between a girl and a boy so difficult for people to believe?'

'Because he's as cute as a button and so are you.'

'Me?'

'God,' Lana Mae mused, 'he's more than cute. Tommy is *divine.*'

'I am *not* cute,' Polly insisted.

'Who says you're not?'

Polly was dignified. 'No one has to say it, I can use my own eyes: I am *plain*, Lana Mae, and don't go making silly platitudes claiming otherwise. I know what I am, and I accept it – and frankly, it's liberating. I don't need a boyfriend, because I'm perfectly happy with how my life is without one.'

When she dared to look at Lana Mae again, she was surprised to see a sadness for her in the American's blue eyes. Lana Mae blinked it away. 'All right. If you say so. You and Tommy are just friends then. So why haven't you told us about him?'

Polly had a believable excuse. 'I was scared Tommy might get fired for breaking protocol with a guest.'

'That's a nice way of wording it,' Lana Mae tittered. 'And if it was really a problem, half the staff would have gone thanks to Zita alone.'

Polly saw she needed another excuse. 'I was scared about Alexandrine.'

'Why? She's no Snow White herself.'

'I don't think she likes Tommy very much.' Polly hoped she needn't say more than that, testing what Lana Mae knew of Alexandrine's connection to Tommy.

The American chose to have Polly believe she knew nothing of it. 'Don't take her so personally, baby. She's not herself anymore and you know why. Tommy hasn't even entered her head.'

Polly nodded, having seen through Lana Mae's words. The American knew who Tommy really was.

Lana Mae seemed to catch a hint of something else in Polly's face. 'That is *all*, isn't it, baby?'

'All what?'

'Why you've been keeping things tight. Tell me there's no other reason why you don't want people to know about you two.'

Polly swallowed. 'What other reason would there be?'

'Like you're doing something stupid?'

Polly's shock was real, because Lana Mae's guess was so accurate. 'Like what?'

The older woman looked searchingly at her while Polly fought not to squirm. Finally, Lana Mae let the subject drop. 'Okay. If you say so.'

'See, there's nothing else to worry about,' said Polly, relieved.

Lana Mae was looking out her office door at something that had caught her attention. She went white. 'Oh hell.'

Polly turned and saw. Sweating Gendarme Teissier was at the end of the corridor, with several fellow officers, in tense conversation with some hospital staff.

'What is he doing here?' said Polly, thrown. 'I signed the Foreigners' Register this morning.' She looked down at her divided skirt and suddenly felt sick. 'Lana Mae, you don't think . . .'

The gendarmes broke away, heading down the corridor towards them.

Polly felt her heart quicken. 'Surely, I couldn't really be in trouble for it?'

Lana Mae put a steadying hand on her shoulder. 'Empty my handbag,' she whispered.

'What?'

'Tip it out. *Empty it.* Don't let them see you.'

'But Lana Mae?'

The American stepped out into the corridor, beaming. Teissier saw her emerge. The group of gendarmes stopped, surrounding her.

'Are you Madame Huckstepp?' said Teissier. He had documentation in his hand.

'Gendarme Teissier!' gushed Lana Mae, preening herself among the uniformed French men. 'Well, of course, it's me. What can I do you for?'

Inside the little office, Polly couldn't move for fear. Lana Mae's handbag sat untouched on the desk.

Teissier read from his papers. 'As of 1000 hrs this morning, Madame, Germany is at war with the United States.'

Lana Mae blanched. 'Well, Germany may be, but we're here in France, aren't we?'

Teissier just looked at her. He tapped his documentation. 'This is the order for your immediate internment, Madame Huckstepp. Do you understand what that means?'

One of the other gendarmes had his eye upon Polly through the door. She couldn't have moved to reach Lana Mae's handbag without him seeing her, even if her nerves hadn't failed her.

Outside, Lana Mae was polite. 'This must be some kinda mistake, Monsieur. Sure, I'm American but I'm no threat to Germany. How could I be? Ask Reichsmarschall Göring at the Ritz.'

The name-dropping had no impact. 'No mistake has been made, Madame,' said Teissier. 'I have the order.'

'But the order from who?'

'The Occupation Authorities. As of this morning you have been classified as an enemy alien.'

Lana Mae looked as if she'd been slapped. 'That a *Frenchman* should say that to me . . .'

Teissier looked away. 'I am sorry, Mrs Huckstepp, but that's how it is. We're at war now.'

She refused to hear it. 'France and America will never be at war – they're like brothers. You gave the Statue of Liberty to us. We share the same principals and ideals.'

He fixed a stare at her, in no mood for such statements. 'Your "principled" France was on the path to catastrophe, Madame. Too few people give the Occupiers their due for reversing that fate.'

Lana Mae gaped at him, incredulous.

'And so many of those who don't are behind barbed wire for it.' Teissier acknowledged Polly standing frozen, staring at him from the little office. 'You could learn from your ward, Mrs Huckstepp. One early moment of misplaced patriotism from Polly and there has been no repeat of it since. She is a blameless young person, exemplary in everything.' He smiled patronisingly at Polly. 'We are very fond of the girl.' He gave Lana Mae his full attention again. 'So, you mustn't worry for her while you are gone – she has the entire 8th Gendarmerie looking out for her welfare. We all know her well in there. How many other girls her age can boast such thorough protection? She will come to no harm, I promise you.'

From behind the ward doors came the sound of Zita's blackmail movie hitting its climactic scene. The French soldiers had started to cheer from their beds. At the far end of the corridor hospital staff were watching Lana Mae's exchange with the gendarmes in misery.

There was hurt in Lana Mae's eyes. 'Please don't do this to me,' she begged Teissier. She waved her arms uselessly at the closed ward doors. 'I've been doing real good in here – for the recovering soldiers. You must have heard about it.'

Sympathy cracked Teissier's veneer. 'It will not be forgotten, Madame.' He signalled a subordinate to secure her. 'However, you must be interned. This is our order.'

'Wait!' Lana Mae cried out. She glanced at Polly in the office. 'It's my time of the month. I need a sanitary napkin.'

A male, Teissier predictably quailed at this feminine need. 'All right.'

'They're in my office. Can I have a moment's privacy?'

Teissier looked to his colleagues. They were as squeamish as he was. 'Don't test our patience by taking long, Madame.'

'Of course, I won't.'

Lana Mae closed the office door behind her, her eyes meeting Teissier's through the little window before she pulled down the shade.

'Oh, Lana Mae!' Polly threw herself at her guardian, hugging her. Her guilt was terrible. 'They were watching me through the door. I couldn't get to your bag.'

'It doesn't matter.' Lana Mae looked at the drawn shade. 'They can't see in here now. I've gotta make this fast.' She opened her handbag and tipped out the contents. Among the detritus was a box of her sanitary pads, her pink bismuth, and another little bottle of pills. Lana Mae unscrewed the pill bottle cap. 'Fix me a glass of water, honey.' She was now very pale.

'You're ill?'

'Just my usual belly ache.'

Polly poured a small glass of water from a jug.

Lana Mae tipped the contents of the pill bottle into her palm: instead of pills there were six sizable gems, long ago prized loose from necklaces and bracelets; three diamonds, a ruby, and a pair of extraordinary emeralds. She stared at them ardently.

Polly's eyes were wide. 'Lana Mae, what are you going to do?'

'I wish I could leave 'em with you, honey, so you could go on helping those boys in my place. But I don't think I can now. I'm gonna need 'em myself. You understand, don't you?'

'Understand? What are you going to do with them?'

Lana Mae tipped the gems into her mouth. They rattled hard and sharp on her teeth. She reached for the glass of water and took a great gulp of it. She nearly spluttered. With effort she made herself swallow.

Polly stared at her guardian in horror.

Lana Mae took another deep gulp. 'Jesus Christ . . .' She placed her fingers to her throat, her face contorted, as she forced the gems down. When she was finished, there was blood in her mouth. She dabbed at her lips with a handkerchief, before placing it inside her purse, along with her sanitary napkins.

Polly was speechless.

Lana Mae then took a slug from her bottle of pink bismuth. She grimaced as it followed the jewels. 'That hand cream I gave you. You still got it, haven't you?'

'Of course,' said Polly. 'For when I've got dry hands?'

Lana Mae smirked. 'You're funny.' Her stomach made a loud groan of complaint. 'Oh Jesus.' She rubbed at it. 'Listen, I want you to know something, baby. Something bad.'

All Polly could do was nod.

'There's a letter from Marjorie,' she told her.

'Another one?'

Lana Mae's face was a picture of shame as she didn't quite answer this. 'Some day you might find it. And if you ever do.' She embraced Polly tight. 'Try to forgive us for it, baby, okay?'

'Forgive you for what?'

'You'll know.'

'I don't understand – forgive you for what?'

But Lana Mae couldn't answer. 'You'll know when you find it,' she whispered. 'But I also want you to know that I love you – with all of my heart. We all do.' She blew a kiss to her.

Her handbag on her arm, Lana Mae opened the office door.

11

13 December 1941

The Canadian Doctor Mandel, once resident at the Ritz, knew that as far as imprisonment went, things could always be worse. Indeed, they had been worse for him when first he'd been taken, within days of the Germans' arrival. He'd expected arrest, and French friends had begged him to leave in the exodus to prevent it, but two decades' service at the American Hospital of Paris was not something to leave behind lightly. And so, he hadn't left. They'd arrested him while he was doing his rounds on the wards. What rankled the doctor most was that it wasn't the Germans who'd taken him, but the French police. Their switch from enforcing the laws of the French Republic to enforcing the laws of whatever it was that was now in its place was seamless. He could only assume that laws were just laws to the gendarmerie; it didn't matter who was issuing them. It didn't matter about conscience.

Mandel's first months of internment were spent in a prisoner-of-war camp along with French soldiers, where conditions had been unspeakable. Blameless civilian men like himself had died pointlessly, along with countless uniformed French. There had been sore need of his medical skills, but no supplies and equipment to apply them. He'd done what he could. But when the British turned the tide on the Luftwaffe, winning the Battle of Britain, the Germans gave up all ideas of a quick victory. This necessitated a different solution for the interned. The British had apparently learned of the poor conditions the internees were being subjected to and, it was rumoured, threatened to send their own interned German civilians to the arctic wastes of Canada. Whether this was true or not, there had come a sudden change. Doctor Mandel, along with two thousand or so of his fellow internees, had been transported to the spa town of Vittel, east of Paris.

With the enticing name of 'Frontstalag 121', this camp consisted of requisitioned hotels grouped around a large park. Here, despite a barbed wire perimeter and patrolling armed guards, conditions were better. The internees could do their own cooking. The hotels mostly had heat and running water. People could send and receive mail. Red Cross parcels made it to them, delivered through neutral Sweden. This supplemented an otherwise monotonous diet and gave them items to barter with French civilians through the fence wire. They were not subjected to forced labour, mercifully. They organised classes and lectures for the young. Films were shown on weekends, albeit German ones. Most important of all, from Mandel's perspective, was that they had the very basics of a hospital. People could be treated, if not always cured.

Of course, it was all for propaganda purposes. It was said that Joseph Goebbels carried photographs of Vittel to show how well the Germans treated foreigners. Mandel didn't expect these conditions to last. If the war turned against Hitler, why bother caring for the enemy interned? He feared they were all of them living on borrowed time.

But for now, the hospital gave him purpose; something he clung to. He had been issued a hotel room of his own when he first came to Vittel, but he gave it up, sleeping instead in a cold, grubby office off one of the wards. It was a sacrifice he had gladly made. He only wished he could somehow make more. Purpose and sacrifice were notions he had not understood until he had served in the trenches at the end of the Great War. France had given him his understanding of what both notions truly meant, and for that he was eternally glad. It was why he had given himself to France in turn.

These thoughts were in his mind now, as they so often were, as he began his morning rounds. His English nurse, Fiona, a fellow internee in her fifties, once a doughty nanny for a family of wealthy Parisian Jews, apprised him of events that had occurred overnight. Rarely for Mandel, he'd slept right through. Patients had been admitted without him even stirring in his cot.

'There was an American woman admitted just before dawn, Doctor. She was in a great deal of pain.'

'The area?'

'Abdominal.'

Mandel saw the name on the admissions list. He looked hard at Fiona. 'But you know who this is, don't you?'

'I do, Doctor.' There was emotion in her face.

'Has her complaint been diagnosed?'

'I had thought appendicitis. But there is rectal bleeding.' She bent her head closer to his. 'Our morphine supplies are so minimal, as of course you well know, reserved for the worst cases.'

He waited.

'I gave her some all the same. Not because of who she is, but for all that she's done.'

He touched her arm. 'You did well, my old girl. Where is she then?'

Fiona led the way to a ward upstairs, where the woman was the only patient. When Mandel saw her he was almost overcome. His time at the Ritz seemed so long ago now, his life having changed so entirely. It seemed almost obscene, in truth, that he ever took such luxurious cushioning for granted. Now, faced with someone else who had lived in it, someone also brought low by the war, it was almost too much for the Canadian doctor.

There was a chair near the bed and he sat down in it. He looked to Fiona. 'She is a friend.'

Fiona understood. 'I'll return shortly, Doctor.' She left them alone.

Lana Mae's hand rested on top of the blanket. Mandel took it in his. The air in the ward was chilly, but Lana Mae's skin was hot to the touch. She had the remnants of a fever. He placed a palm to her forehead, brushing the henna-red hair. 'Mrs Huckstepp?'

She stirred, seeing him. She smiled in recognition. 'Why, it's Doc Mandel . . .'

He smiled back. 'Paul.'

She squeezed his hand. 'Are we home at the Ritz?'

He shook his head, sadly. 'Not this time. But you are safe.'

She closed her eyes, grateful.

'Are you still feeling pain?'

She wasn't for now, or not much anyway. 'That Fiona was kind.'

He stroked her fingers. Given all that he knew of her actions since the Germans had come, he knew he couldn't lie to her about what was most likely ahead. She had proved herself stoic. She would understand that if she was seriously ill then he could not save her in Vittel. 'I must tell you that our facilities are almost nothing, Mrs Huckstepp. I have not examined you, of course, but if surgery is required, as I fear it might, well then . . .' He trailed off.

She opened her eyes again. Her voice was painfully weak, but her good humour remained. 'I know what's wrong with me, honey, you don't have to fret.'

'What is it?'

She told him.

His surprise at the truth returned a humour of his own. He found himself chuckling.

'The cops didn't even realise,' said Lana Mae, grinning at him. 'My last six rocks, swallowed like a handful of uppers.' She felt her bowel churn. 'Oh God.' The effects of the morphine were beginning to wear off. She looked at him imploringly. 'Will the rocks kill me, Doc?'

He didn't think so. 'The bleeding is to be expected, I suppose, but I doubt they'll be fatal.'

She looked relieved, briefly, before a look of determination replaced it. She peered around at the ramshackle ward. 'This is what you call a hospital here?'

'We are interned at Vittel, Mrs Huckstepp. This is the best our hospital can be in the circumstances.'

'Vittel, Vittel . . .' The name meant something to her. 'You know, I took the waters here once. It cleared up a yeast infection.'

He chuckled again.

'What do you need? What sort of supplies?'

He gestured helplessly. 'Where do I start with that question?'

'Maybe let's start with some more goddamn morphine,' Lana Mae suggested. Her bowel churned again. 'Oh God.'

He bent closer to her. 'Mrs Huckstepp, this is delicate, I know, but have any of your jewels so far –' He made a motion suggesting the miracle of birth.

'No,' winced Lana Mae. 'I've had boiled English ox tongue that got out of me quicker.' The twisting in her guts was audible. 'I think the sextuplets are about to come home . . .'

Mandel stood up. 'Perhaps a bedpan.'

Lana Mae clutched at his arm. 'I mean it. What do you need for medical supplies?'

'You're in no fit state for this, Mrs Huckstepp.'

'Call me Lana Mae, for Christ's sake, and listen to me. When my rocks arrive, we'll have something.'

'You'll have something. They're your gems.'

Hurt, her eyes pricked with tears. 'Do you know nothing of me?' She reconsidered this. 'Maybe you don't, you've been locked up.' She looked at him imploringly. 'Please, Doc, listen. I've changed. I'm not the same stupid, self-centred woman I was before the Germans got here – that woman you knew at the Ritz.'

'I know of what you've done for wounded French soldiers. Of course, I know.'

She was pleased, then emotional. 'But you don't know *how* I've done it. My funds were frozen. Roosevelt left me broke. But I still had all my rocks with me, didn't I? So many damn rocks. And the Ritz is stuffed full of those greedy kraut pigs.'

He realised now how she'd achieved it. Mandel's notions of purpose and sacrifice came flooding back to his mind.

She pointed at her belly. 'So, when the kids show up again, which won't be very long, we'll put 'em to use, Doc. We'll get the supplies, the equipment, everything you need.'

He knew it was unethical, yet he suddenly felt a great desire to scoop the voluptuous patient from her bed and plant a kiss on her.

'But we're gonna need a real good plan,' Lana Mae told him. 'A serious one. To fool the goddamn krauts. Something that'll let me get in and out of here when I need to . . .'

Crouched in Tommy's attic room, on the floor, with the volume turned down as low as they could get it while still being able to hear something, Tommy, Polly and Odile pressed their collective ears to Odile's little radio, pilfered from Blanche.

It was not long after nine o'clock in the evening, and the radio was tuned, as were so many other secret radios throughout Paris, to the French language news broadcast across the English Channel by the BBC. The news so far had been enlightening, but not yet what the three of them half-hoped, half-dreaded to hear. They'd so far learned that Romania and Bulgaria had joined Germany in declaring war upon Britain and the United States. They'd been told that the Japanese destroyer *Hayate* had been sunk by American coastal defence guns. They had tried to comprehend that part of an Andean glacier had collapsed into a lake in Peru, causing a lethal landslide. Then the announcer moved on to a Paris item:

'From the German-occupied French capital comes news of the first seeds of civilian uprising sown among starving Parisians. A German naval officer was shot and killed while boarding the metro at Barbès-Rochechouart. The assassin escaped German arrest, but left a calling card, stating allegiance to the underground movement, the Freedom Volunteers. This group has previously been known for its distribution of anti-German leaflets. The killing marks an escalation in resistance activity in Paris, and with it an escalation in German reprisals. Occupying authorities arrested twenty French civilians from a Paris bread queue, mostly women. All have been executed by firing squad in retaliation for the killing –'

Tommy, Polly and Odile clutched each other's hands in learning of this brutality.

'– General Charles de Gaulle, leader of the Free French Army in exile, praised the actions of the Freedom Volunteers, while condemning the German atrocity. "The Freedom Volunteers grow in strength," said de Gaulle, "numbering not a few, but thousands. Their courage serves France. When the day of Liberation comes, I will be proud to shake every one of them by the hand."'

They listened to the rest of the news broadcast before turning the radio off. They spent some minutes saying nothing.

'De Gaulle thinks there's thousands of us,' said Odile, eventually. 'Maybe he could learn to count better.'

'Who says there's not thousands?' Tommy said. 'There's the assassin, and he must have some friends. We don't know what else is going on out there, Odile. People could be resisting in ways we haven't heard of.'

'I think Claude's doing something,' said Odile. 'I've heard his telephone calls. He thinks because I'm blind that I'm deaf too.'

Tommy was surprised by this because resistance seemed out of character for obsequious Claude. Then he reconsidered it.

'Claude's well placed to be doing something if it's true. He deals with more krauts than anyone.'

'Then we should join in with him.'

'We will not,' said Tommy. 'Block your ears to his telephone calls, Odile. You know it's safer if we don't hear about it. We don't want him discovering what we're doing either, even if we're all trying to do the same thing.'

Odile snapped. 'I'm sick of being alone in this!'

'You're not alone,' said Tommy. 'There's you and there's me and there's Pol.'

Odile said nothing, glowering. Tommy looked apprehensively at Polly, crouched in silence on the floor. 'We've never made you tell us who prints the butterflies, have we, Odile?' he pressed.

'Sometimes I want to tell. You'd be amazed if you knew.'

'And what if someone gets taken by the krauts?' Tommy threw back at her. 'The more resisters a person knows, the more resisters they'll name. We can't take the chance. No one can.'

'That's only if they force it from you,' said Odile, angry. 'How is a "bathtub" a torture weapon?'

The Gestapo's interrogation method had acquired a name, but only that. They knew of no one who had faced this bathtub and returned. If Guy had met his fate with it, no one had heard so. 'Just do as I say,' Tommy mumbled.

Petulant, Odile sat up on the end of Tommy's bed. She started bouncing on it.

'Stop it,' Tommy told her, hiding the radio away. 'Someone will hear the springs.'

'They've already been hearing them for months. Just not when it's me . . .'

He flushed with embarrassment at what she implied and couldn't look at Polly. 'It's not like that between Polly and me at all.'

'Isn't it?'

He hesitated a second too long. 'We're friends – colleagues in resistance. Like you and me, Odile.'

Odile said nothing. And in her silence, Polly thought she heard what Odile was not saying.

'What would you know about it anyway?' Tommy scoffed, self-conscious now, before playfully slapping at the back of her head.

Odile put her hand to the impression Tommy's hand left in her hair and seemed to be made wistful by it.

'I'm sorry,' Tommy said. 'Did that hurt you?'

She shook her head. 'We can't do any more butterflies,' she told him, eventually.

'No. We can't,' Tommy agreed. To Polly, still watching in silence, it was clear he was experiencing a sudden and overwhelming urge to sit next to Odile on the bed. Polly looked on as he now did so, Tommy trying to make it seem casual. The edge of his hand touched Odile's on the quilt. He let it stay where it was. Polly knew he was imagining Odile in ways he'd not done so before.

She felt a flare of jealousy and sprang from the floor.

'Where are you going, Pol?' Tommy looked up at her.

She had come to a decision. '*L'Espadon.*'

This startled him. 'You said you'd never go in there again.'

'That was before today happened. Now I see I shouldn't have stopped going.'

Tommy stood up from the bed. 'Please. It's a disgusting place. It's not safe in there. You know it's not, Pol.'

She did know. 'I let myself have the luxury of a conscience about it. That was wrong. And I've been a fool. I've got the perfect disguise right in front of me and I've not even thought of it in that way.'

'A disguise?' said Tommy, lost.

'Just like yours – just like Odile's. Both of you hide in plain sight from them. So, what do *I* look like?' she asked Tommy.

Tommy didn't have an answer.

'Remember what you called me that night I first came up to this room? Remember what you thought of me the day we first spoke in the Cambon bar?'

Tommy did remember. 'I'm ashamed of that.'

'You said I was a silly little rich girl.'

'But that's not who you are at all, Pol. I only said it because of your clothes.'

'Thank you, Tommy.' She was pleased. 'I should hope it's not me.' She took a deep breath. 'But I think, because of those clothes, it's who I *should* be.'

Tommy saw it now.

'Who'd be threatened by someone like me? A stupid feather-brain, thinking only of the latest fashions? It's time I start dressing like a BOF properly.'

He laughed. 'But not that flag skirt,' he warned. 'It's asking for the wrong kind of attention.'

She had to agree. She had taken an unacceptable risk with that outfit and would not chance wearing it again until the day the Germans fled Paris. Polly felt renewed in determination. 'I'm returning to *l'Espadon*,' she told them. 'I have thought of a way that the Freedom Volunteers can get hold of a new gun . . .'

Lately, in order to go on, Zita had rediscovered a little line of 'powder'. She'd been familiar with it back in the old days – the early '20s – when she was still very young. Back then, she had loved the lift the powder gave her, the firing up of her confidence, the charge to her sexual appetite. It had all been such fun, the means to enhance a good party. That was until she saw too many others discover that nothing came free of cost in this life. She'd been frightened enough to stop the powder cold. But now here she was back with an amusing old pal again, wholly aware of the consequences, and not giving a damn about them. The dope addict's life couldn't be worse than the life she had been living without it, she rationalised. And besides, she wasn't just doing it for *her* benefit.

She had a rapt audience in Hans.

Powder took away her conscience, or it mostly did. When the powder didn't quite manage the task, she found herself doing reckless things in a desperate effort to placate her shattered morality. That was what the blackmail film had been. The production had been lucky the krauts didn't have the brains to read between the lines – Metzingen chief among them. For a man who had been to the Sorbonne, he could certainly be dim. Zita had never been schooled past the elementary level, yet she had seen the sly truth of the screenplay the second she'd read it.

She knew they'd not be so lucky again. Better to stick with the powder.

Zita emerged from the ladies' room at *l'Espadon* just as the fresh effects took hold. It was her third little line of the night and it likely would not be her last. She felt glorious – and deliciously deadly. Dinner was over and done. Now it was all champagne and cognac until the Germans retired to their rooms, which was always long after midnight. The curfew never applied to them. Zita's eyes raked the tables as she decided who of the Ritz regulars to drop in on.

'Hello, Zita.'

She spun around in surprise at the voice.

'Polly!' A spark of Zita's conscience kindled – the girl shouldn't be here, shouldn't be seeing her like this. 'What are you doing in *l'Espadon*, puss? I thought you'd given it all up?'

'I was bored.'

She looked unaccountably mature to Zita, wearing a stunning gown belonging to Alexandrine.

'I wanted to see people. I wanted to see you. We hardly spend time together these days since you've been so busy at the new studios.'

Zita felt a violent surge of love for her. 'Mother Mary and Christ – you say all the right things.' She linked her arm through Polly's, beating her conscience back into the dark. 'I was looking for a partner in crime. I'm feeling *dangerous*.'

Polly laughed. 'Who's here tonight? I feel I'm hopelessly out of the loop.'

'Out of the noose, more like it,' said Zita, 'a lucky escape. But if you insist on having some fun with me, then let's see who's still awake.'

Together, they scanned the tables.

'There's Göring,' said Polly.

Distant alarm bells somewhere rang for Zita that Polly would even contemplate engaging with Göring, but she made herself deaf. 'Well, we *could* go say hello, I suppose,' she mused. Then something like sense kicked in. 'But even when I'm as high as a cloud his jokes are still stinkers.'

'High as a cloud?'

'I've had some champagne? That's a crime now?'

'Of course not,' said Polly, 'it's nice to see you so happy.'

Telling herself that if she looked that way, then she must surely be so, Zita considered other tables.

'The playwright Guitry's still here,' Polly pointed. 'Who are all those women with him?'

'Fawning actresses.'

'Friends of yours?'

'*Acquaintances*. From the Comédie-Française.' She turned up her nose as she said it.

'Let me guess,' said Polly. 'They resent famous film stars?'

'They're jealous. Bitterly. Someone must have let slip what I get paid.' She waved gaily to the table.

Arm in arm, they moved further into the mirrored dining room.

Zita locked eyes with Metzingen at last. He was sitting at a table full of the Wehrmacht high command. She thanked God for the powder now, and she wanted him to know she was using it. He would guess all the signs just by watching her. The re-written script between them had gained a new storyline: the heroine was being maddeningly, glamorously self-destructive, to match the recklessness of the love-struck hero.

She took unexpected strength from Polly; warmth from her arm.

'There's Jean Cocteau,' said Polly. 'He looks a bit strange.'

'He *is* strange. But we could go over if you like?' Zita knew the poet was as high upon dope as she was, but it was a different dope, one that flattened him out rather than flinging him up to the ceiling where she preferred to be. There was no fun to be had in that.

She saw the ideal table and let go of good sense entirely.

'Hullo, puss!' she called out. 'You look *embalmed* tonight. Is it true what *Vogue* says and you're dead?' She marched across to Chanel, leading Polly by the arm.

The designer beamed at them, although her wariness was obvious. 'Zita, darling. How very nice. Do you know, if these walls could talk they might tell us how many knee-tremblers you've had up against them?'

Zita threw her head back and roared. Helping herself to a generous glass of the designer's bottle of champagne, she fixed her eyes upon Chanel's Teutonic companion. She suspected they were screwing, which meant Chanel was no better than she was. 'Hauptmann Jürgen,' she purred, 'tell me I'm mad, but you seem to get younger every day.' She gave theatrical looks back and forwards between him and Chanel. 'Unless it's just the effect of the comparison?'

It was Chanel's turn to laugh, although less raucously.

'Fräulein Zita enjoys her teases,' said Jürgen, saluting her with his glass.

Zita winked and turned to Chanel again. 'So, what is it with you and those Jews?'

There was a pleasing ripple across Chanel's composure. 'Whatever could you mean by that, Zita?'

'Oh puss, it's all over town.'

'What is, dear?'

Zita turned to Jürgen. 'Coco has no head for business. It's sad.'

Jürgen chuckled. 'Now we *know* you're drunk.'

'But it's true,' said Zita. 'Overlooking for now that she threw her whole workforce onto the street when she shut down her shop as a "patriotic act", back in the '20s she sold off her famous perfume, didn't she? Well, it wasn't famous *then*.' She lowered her voice to a stage whisper, clicking her tongue. 'She sold it to Jews.'

Jürgen stiffened.

Zita felt Polly becoming uncomfortable, but she didn't see it as reason to stop. With the powder, there was *never* a reason to stop anything that was fun. 'Yes, she sold it to nice friendly Jews,' said Zita, reminiscing. 'And Christ, what they did with it, Hauptmann. What a smash they made of the stuff. They earned more money than God from that perfume. More money than poor old Coco did from it, anyway.'

Chanel's humour had evaporated. '*Zita . . .*'

'All water under the bridge now,' said Zita, placatingly, 'she's just got the perfume back in her paws again, haven't you, puss? Thanks to these new Jew laws. What was it you actually paid them for it? That's right: not one single, stinking red *sou*.'

Jürgen abruptly stood up. 'You take exception to the laws regarding Jewish property, Fräulein Zita?'

She resisted Polly trying to pull her away. 'Not me, Hauptmann – why would I? Not when Mademoiselle Chanel does so well out of them.'

Jürgen glowered at her and she could see his mind ticking. Then he turned to Polly. 'Fräulein Hartford, it is such a pleasure to see you returned to our evenings at *L'Espadon*.'

Polly was gracious. 'Thank you, Herr Jürgen.'

'Please let me extend to you my condolences for the news.'

'What news?'

'About poor Frau Huckstepp. It is so very sad. We were fond of her here.'

The unasked-for image of interned Lana Mae pricked Zita, her old friend suddenly embodying her banished conscience. She tried to force Lana Mae away, refusing to think of her behind barbed wire. Zita scrabbled in the brief onset of darkness for the light of the powder again and found it.

Polly was speaking. 'Of course, it is sad our good friend can no longer continue her charity work –' But the look upon Jürgen's face brought Polly to a stop.

'I see you have not heard.' He turned to Chanel, who was listening with wordless interest from the comfort of her chair. He clearly wanted her to appreciate this. 'There was a report today from Vittel. Frau Huckstepp has been diagnosed with womb cancer.'

The shock was total.

Yet the powder wouldn't let it feel real.

Zita looked at Jürgen. She looked at Chanel. 'That can't be right . . .'

'I tell you it is,' said Jürgen.

The girl at Zita's side crumbled. Polly sank to the floor.

Zita watched her as if watching herself in a film where she observed an actress playing Polly dissolve. She was utterly detached from it, completely unmoved. Polly's agony meant nothing. She looked to Chanel again, feeling that perhaps she should explain the girl. 'She is still only young –'

But the designer was stricken by what had occurred. Polly's weeping was terrible to hear. People around them had stopped talking, staring at the scene. Zita looked to Jürgen again. His nasty surprise had backfired on him. He was ashamed at drawing tears from someone so innocent.

He tried to help Polly to her feet. 'Fräulein Hartford, forgive me –'

Polly could only shake her head, unable to reply to him, unable to get up.

Zita glanced across the dining room and saw Metzingen staring at them. In the powder's grip, she was pleased.

Chanel stood from her chair, as ashamed as Jürgen was. 'I'm so sorry, Zita. We wouldn't have wished such a thing on Lana Mae, you must know that.'

'Do I, puss?'

Chanel didn't have a retort. 'I'm so sorry, Polly.'

Jürgen took Chanel by the arm as they left the restaurant together.

When Polly stood up of her own accord, she kept her hands to her face. Zita helped her sit down at Chanel's abandoned table. The other diners stopped looking at them, respecting Polly's distress.

'I'm sorry, that was lousy news.' Zita glimpsed beneath Polly's hands and thought she seemed somewhat dry-eyed. Had the weeping been real?

'I'll be all right in a moment,' Polly told her.

Zita slipped her a handkerchief from her purse. Polly pressed it to her face.

Zita's heart soared. Polly was up to something. The girl was enacting a deception in the face of a kraut, and he'd fallen for it. 'Feeling better now?'

Polly nodded. 'I'll sit here a while.'

Polly looked sideways at her, trying to tell if she'd bought the performance as easily as Jürgen and Chanel had. Zita tried not to let on, her love for the girl expanding in her chest until bursting point. 'I don't believe she's got cancer,' Zita told her. 'She was as healthy as a horse before they took her.' She stood up before Polly could read her face.

Zita saw Metzingen coming towards them. Empowered by Polly as much as the powder, she decided it was time to milk the reward for her own performance. 'I'll be back in a moment.'

She walked off at speed, diagonal to him, in the direction of the doors, forcing him to change path. She made it to the Cambon lobby before he did and stood there invitingly, looking up the stairs.

He gripped her by the shoulder, furious, spinning her to face him. 'You're on dope again.'

'So, what if I am?'

'You told me you'd stop this self-indulgence.'

'Did I? Turns out I lied. Took a page from your book, didn't I?'

She relished seeing his rage melt away, transforming into pathetic concern. *'Liebchen, please* – don't do this to us.'

'Us? I'm doing nothing to you, Hans. I'm not sniffing snow for two.'

'But how can you do it at all? How can you let yourself become an addict – like *him?'*

'Who? Göring?' She laughed. 'I do it so that I might feel happy.' She grinned at him. 'Sorry, but the dope is all that I have at hand.'

He clutched at her. 'Let *me* make you happy – please, *Liebchen*. The Ritz is all *ours.'*

She laughed at that, wild-eyed. 'Fuck the Ritz. You're welcome to it.'

He was shocked. Then angry once more – the angriest she'd made him this evening. She saw his hand pull back to slap her. 'Do it, Hans. Beat the insolence from me.'

His hand stayed where it was.

'What's the matter?' she taunted. 'Don't I deserve a beating for insulting your beloved Ritz?'

His hand fell to his side again.

'I hate to break it to you,' she told him, 'but you still don't actually own this hotel. And until you do, you don't own any of us who might choose to live inside it.'

He took in her words. 'Who says I don't own you?'

She knew what was coming next. She'd opened the door to it.

'I owned you the moment the whore became the spy . . .'

She held his look before the weight of her guilt became too much again.

He was remorseful. 'Please, Zita – I didn't mean that.'

She scrubbed a tear from her cheek. 'You want me to stop killing myself? Then give me the one thing I need to keep living for, Hans – the one thing you forever deny me.'

She watched him sag and give in to her, a familiar routine.

'All right.'

She believed none of it. 'So, say it then.'

'I will take you to Lotti.'

She dismissed him in disgust. 'So easily you always make those words, Hans, but I know you never will. In the meantime, I'll keep on taking the dope.'

She was pleased to see she was frightening him.

'I mean it, *Liebchen*. I'll take you to her. Just stop this self-destruction.'

'More lies. I'll be free of them dead.'

'It's the truth this time, I swear it is.'

She shook her head. 'It never is. I'll only believe you when I have our daughter in my arms.'

'We'll go the asylum together. You'll be able to hold her.'

'*When?*'

There was silence. He grappled for an answer. 'In a week.'

She snorted. 'Too vague. In a week it'll be another week, and then another week after that. I'll need all my dope just to cope with it.'

He clutched at her hand. 'I swear it, *Liebchen*. I'll need time to arrange it – but – but we will visit together in a week. You will see.' He so desperately wanted her to believe him.

Zita's kohl-rimmed eyes drilled into the very heart of her lover, past all the layers of clung-to ideals. She saw the rejected, humiliated man he once had once been. The man he claimed had held the door for her at the Ritz.

'All right, Hans.'

'Yes?'

She nodded. 'Yes. I trust you.' She felt the surge at her loins at the glimpse of vulnerability in his eyes – too rarely seen. If only she could find this in him always, she thought. If she could, she might even feel more than mere lust for him. But for now, lust was enough. Indeed, on the powder it was everything. Zita kissed him on the mouth, tender with longing, aroused by the drug. 'Just think of it, Hans – in one week's time we will be little Lotti's mama and papa again . . .'

His face was hidden from hers in the kiss. Zita knew she should look at him, knew she should see if his sincerity remained, or discover if it had been replaced by something that fit him better. But she didn't want to look at him.

Thanks to the powder, all she wanted was a handful of his prick.

Jürgen returned to *l'Espadon* without Chanel. He had deposited the designer in her tiny room high on the Cambon side of the hotel – her old Vendôme suite having long been taken from her – and resisted her entreaties to stay for a 'nightcap'. Ordinarily he would have done so quite happily. The famed designer's attentions gave him kudos among those colleagues who were aware of the trysts. Still, with Chanel easily three decades his senior, quite possibly more, despite being unarguably well preserved, sometimes he missed the pneumatic flexibility of a woman closer his age. For all his accomplished athleticism and rapid rise through the Wehrmacht ranks, people forgot just how young he was. Jürgen was still four years away from turning thirty, after all.

The Ritz dining room was emptier now, although revellers remained. Von Hofacker, von Stülpnagel and Speidel were in a huddle together, well away from the other tables – something he'd seen quite a lot from them lately. He half-suspected they were plotting something. Metzingen had gone, he was pleased to see. Jürgen scoured the room for the reason he'd rejected his evening with Chanel – and found it. He strode to the very same table near the terrace where he had left her fifteen minutes before.

'Fräulein Polly?'

The girl looked up at him, startled at first. Then her expression relaxed somewhat. He hoped that his smile had disarmed her. He was pleased to see that her tears had dried. Her face showed no evidence of the pain he had caused her – the pain he so keenly regretted now.

'Herr Jürgen? Have you forgotten something?'

'Yes,' he said. 'I have forgotten to properly apologise to you.'

She was surprised by that.

'Would you allow me to sit down to do it?'

'Of course.' She still seemed apprehensive of him as he took a chair, yet his senses told him that she was also attracted. In truth, how could she not be? They were both fine specimens. Jürgen knew they would make an excellent pair.

'I'm confused,' Polly told him, 'what is it that you feel you should apologise for?'

'Fräulein, please – I am ashamed of what I did.' He hoped she could see the sincerity in his ice-blue eyes. 'I broke the news of Frau Huckstepp's illness to you in an indifferent way.' He saw the pain in her face again.

'Oh. Well . . .'

'She is your guardian – you love her – it was very wrong of me.' He realised she was hanging on his words now. He dug deep in himself to speak with complete honesty. 'I am a man of the Wehrmacht. We are expected to lose our sensitivity in order to fight. But sometimes we forget when we need it again. *I* forgot. And so, I am very sorry for it.'

She looked long at him. For a moment nothing more was spoken between them. Then she said, 'I forgive you for it. Zita was being provocative.'

'Thank you, Fräulein.' He smiled at her; his very best smile. 'While we sit in these chairs – would you do me the honour of calling me Günther?'

She tipped her head. 'All right. *Günther.*'

There was still some champagne left at the table. But he saw that Polly wasn't drinking any and so he sipped from a water glass instead.

He cleared his throat. She was an innocent girl who deserved a more considered seduction than the perfunctory effort he'd made with Chanel. Such an enterprise could take months. He didn't mind. So much of the excitement was to be had in anticipation of the prize, after all. 'It might be possible for me to arrange for you to visit Frau Huckstepp.'

He saw the rush of hope this gave her. 'At Vittel?'

'Perhaps not there.' Now that he'd said it, he needed to give it proper thought. 'I have connections. Frau Huckstepp's internment was unfortunate but necessary – yet no one wishes her to suffer in her illness. She will be permitted to receive treatment in a Paris hospital.'

He was gratified by seeing Polly's hopes soar higher.

'Will you let me see what I can do, Polly?'

She beamed at him. 'Yes, Günther. That would be so wonderful.'

The late-night tap at the door to her suite roused the twin griffons first. They lifted their little heads on the bed and looked to Mimi, her head on the pillows, where she was dozing but not quite asleep. They whined but didn't bark, trained to show alertness but never alarm; a prerequisite for all who lived at the Ritz.

Mimi's eyes opened. 'What is it, girls?'

She heard the tapping for herself.

'Ah.' She lifted the book from her chest where it had dropped, and placed it on the bedside table, next to her favourite photograph of her late husband César; one taken when he was so handsome and young.

The dogs dropped off the bed, racing to the door, the clicking of their nails lost in the carpet. Mimi carefully rose from her pillows, feeling her age but refusing to succumb to the indulgence of 'old lady' noises. Mimi was not in the custom of adhering to the expectations that came with growing aged. She put on her peignoir over her nightgown and sought out her mules where the griffons had knocked them under the bed in their haste.

The tapping came again.

She made her dignified way to the entry, where the griffons were waiting, wagging their tails. She teased them affectionately as she opened the door. 'We know who it is, don't we, girls?'

Odile was on the other side, for all the world looking as if she'd spent the evening lying in dust. 'Hello, Madame Ritz. Am I disturbing you?'

'Never you, young lady.' She gave a theatrical look up and down the empty corridor. 'But if you were one of our German guests . . .' Then she remembered that theatrical looks were likely lost on Odile. 'Well, fortunately you aren't. Come inside, won't you.'

Never entirely sure how much or how little Odile could actually see, Mimi preferred to err on the side of caution with the girl, taking her by the hand. 'This is nice,' said Mimi, closing the door behind them. 'Would you like some hot chocolate? We don't need to ring for it, I can make it in my suite.'

The girl was uneasy, upset about something. 'Perhaps another time, Madame Ritz.'

'Call me *Mamie*,' she said, using the French word for granny, 'you know it gives me joy.'

'*Mamie*,' Odile repeated.

She led her to the divan. 'Take a seat then.'

Odile sat. Mimi took position by her side. 'What is it, Odile? You don't seem yourself.'

Odile had clearly prepared her words. 'I cannot use your mimeograph machine anymore, Mamie.'

Mimi took a long breath. 'I see. And why is that?'

'I'm not going to tell you.'

'All right . . .'

'I don't mean to offend you. It's just safer this way. Safer for you.'

'I understand, Odile. Since they took poor Guy . . .'

'That was the krauts' crime not ours. We can't let ourselves feel guilty for it. They are the monsters.'

Mimi only wished she herself could have achieved absolution for Guy's fate so easily. 'All the same, I do understand. The mimeograph can stay hidden. No one will ever know that I have it in here.'

Odile's young face was full of commitment.

'Perhaps we will think of some other way to put the wind up them, then?'

Odile nodded and then fell into silence.

The pain in the girl's heart was so transparent to her. 'What else is troubling you?' Mimi asked gently. 'Are you still in love?'

Odile's face folded with the emotion of it.

'Ah. And it is still unrequited, I see?'

She nodded, miserable.

'And still he doesn't know?'

The girl said nothing.

'Odile? What is it?'

Mimi had the sudden sense of Odile standing at the tip of a great precipice.

'Oh, Mamie . . .'

The old lady watched as Odile fatefully stepped off. 'It is not a *he*, Mamie,' she whispered.

'Oh!'

With it finally said, Odile couldn't stop herself crying.

As she comforted her, Mamie realised she had suspected it all along, but still her old heart broke for the girl. First love was always the most wonderful and painful love of all. She put her thin arm around Odile, stroking her hair.

'I'm so ashamed,' Odile told her, after a time.

'But why should you be? Do you think you are the first young lady who has ever felt this way about another young lady?'

Odile could only cry again.

'Well, I assure you, you are not,' said Mimi. 'I have known plenty of young ladies like you – and young men too. At the Ritz we applaud such love – why, we applaud any love. All love is worthy, Odile. One only has to think of the alternative.'

Odile took off her dark glasses to dry her eyes on her sleeve. 'Thank you.'

Mimi kissed her cheek. 'Maybe you should tell this girl?'

Odile shook her head. 'She loves someone else.'

'Oh.'

'A boy.'

'I see.'

'And because it's so much easier to lie I've been making out like I love him, too,' said Odile, 'which of course he believes – boys are such vain idiots.'

Mimi chuckled. 'And what does this girl believe?'

Odile sighed. 'She's got no idea. She's an even bigger idiot than he is.'

Mimi chuckled more but Odile wanted to reassure her. 'She is a very nice girl, Mamie. I don't just love her, I *respect* her. I couldn't cause her embarrassment or hurt.' Odile thought about this. 'She is *courageous*, Mamie. I admire her.'

'Well, you're remarkably courageous too,' Mimi told her.

Odile dismissed this. 'I don't know any better – I've got all my mama's craziness to blame for it. This girl's been brought up nice. You'd never guess the truth if you met her.'

A warning bell rang for Mimi. 'Are this girl and this boy in the butterflies venture?'

Odile stiffened. 'I cannot tell you that.'

Mimi knew then that they were, and of course, she knew then who they most likely were, too. She could hardly blame Odile for falling in love with a girl like Polly Hartford.

Then Odile added, 'And we're not doing butterflies anymore, remember.'

Mimi had to accept it, although her mind raced. 'Perhaps, you will simply fall out of love? It happens, you know. Then you might fall for someone new who can love you in return.'

But Odile fervently rejected the idea. 'No. I don't want to fall out of love with her, Mamie. I don't care if it hurts. I *need* my feelings. They make me be brave. Do you understand that?'

Mimi looked through the door to her boudoir and saw the little photograph of César; taken when he was barely older than Odile. When she'd pulled out the old mimeograph machine from the attic stores and given thought as to how she might do something useful with it, the memory of César had fuelled her. He would not have taken kindly to half a hotel full of 'guests' who never paid one *sous* of their bill. 'All right then.'

Odile stood to go. 'You're very kind to me.'

'How could I not be? You inspire this old woman.'

Odile blushed. 'Don't be silly, Mamie.'

At the doors to her suite, Mimi watched as the sightless girl made her way down the corridor, so confident of the hotel map she kept inside her head that she had no need of a cane when she visited.

Odile not only inspired Mimi, she shamed her.

12

Zita remembered when she saw it again: Lotti's home was both imperially magnificent and unexpectedly pretty. Steinhof Psychiatric Hospital had seemed at the time such a fearful name to give to a refuge in which they might place their little girl, but Hans had encouraged Zita to look beyond the forbidding title and see the Steinhof for what it was. She had tried to put her faith in him then, and he had rewarded it when they had visited the Steinhof in person, her hand in his, just like they did now. The hospital had looked beautiful, not at all the Gothic institution of Zita's fevered French imagination. Surprisingly, the Steinhof was not one vast building but many smaller ones, called 'pavilions'. These were dotted throughout an enormous park, at the centre of which stood a golden-domed church on a hill – St Leopold's – build in the Art Nouveau style in which the turn of the century Viennese architects excelled. The hospital had seemed perfect, blessed with the added appeal to both her and Hans of being nowhere near Paris or Berlin. Their Lotti would be kept safe here – and secret.

Returning to Steinhof now, so many years later, Zita was comforted to see that nothing of any lasting importance had changed. Yes, there were banners with swastikas everywhere, that was to be expected, but the eye became blind to the ugliness quickly. The gardens were still the same, although dusted with snow. The church was still lovely upon its hill.

If there was one difference, it was the large numbers of recuperating soldiers taking in the frosty garden air as the car had driven up the long drive towards the Children's Pavilion.

'Are these soldiers all patients?' Zita, swathed against the winter in her furs, had wondered to Hans as she viewed them from the window of the Benz.

'They must be, *Liebchen.*'

There were dozens of men, and men alone.

They reached the pavilion that for the past twelve years had been their daughter's home. If it had been spring, there would have been flower beds; bulbs poking their heads through the soil. It was still early winter, so instead there was a snowman to greet them from the lawn, and above the entrance lintel, Christmas holly. The Wehrmacht driver opened the rear car door for them and Zita alighted after Hans, her winter boots connecting lightly with the gravel while he clapped his arms in the cold. Through the pavilion doors she glimpsed a cheery Christmas tree in the lobby, sparkling with lights.

More men were taking exercise on the frozen lawn where the snowman stood with coal lumps for eyes.

'Good morning!' she called out to them in German, waving. Their wounds looked entirely physical – missing limbs and other injuries implied under bandages. What were the wounds to their minds, Zita wondered, that would have seen them sent here?

'I know who you are, sweetheart,' one called back to her. 'You're a kino star!'

His fellows searched her lovely face and saw he was right.

'You're Zita!'

'You're my favourite!'

She had expected as much; she would have been crushed if they hadn't known who she was. She looked to Hans apologetically, but he was indulgent of it. Six strapping young men surrounded her; excited to meet a real film star, yet scrupulously polite and articulate – perfect Germans. They were additionally respectful of Hans, of course, as he watched on from the steps in his Oberstleutnant's overcoat. They Heil Hitler-ed him.

Zita brought a fountain pen with her for just such occasions. She signed plaster casts.

'Why are you here, Fräulein?'

'To visit you sexy boys – why else would I come?'

They laughed at that, but wisely didn't believe it. 'Why are you really here? Tell us.'

She cast a private smile to Metzingen. 'To see a dear one.'

'Ah.'

They understood and liked her the more for it.

Metzingen ushered them on. 'Perhaps the Fräulein will charm you again when she leaves, lads.'

She well knew that she would; her heart would be bursting by then. The men Heil Hitler-ed Hans once more. He held the pavilion's door open for her. Inside, Zita stopped to take in the Christmas tree. She pronounced it the most beautiful she had ever seen.

Jürgen had not expected to feel anything like shock in bringing Polly to visit her American guardian – yet he was shocked deeply when he saw the extent of the woman's decline. That Frau Huckstepp had cancer was undeniable; she was stark and gaunt and had lost much weight. Her skin was drained of all colour and sheen; her once henna-red hair was now grey. Her face had acquired deep, scouring lines that made her look ancient. She was not the same woman who had lived at the Ritz; she was advanced on her journey to death. Jürgen knew that it could not be long before she reached her destination.

That Polly was clearly profoundly upset by how fast the disease had consumed her guardian was to be expected. Polly was female, after all, but Jürgen was made to feel vulnerable by his own reaction, and he disliked it. When the American woman shifted in her bed, lifting herself from the pillows to embrace Polly, Jürgen had glimpsed her wasted body beneath the blanket and seen the livid red stain at her lap. She was haemorrhaging. Jürgen had lived through carnage in the battlefields of Poland and France, and yet the sight of Frau Huckstepp's body corruption threatened to bring his breakfast up.

He held back near the door of the little private room at Pitié-Salpêtrière Hospital while Polly spoke with Lana Mae; all whispered encouragements and steadfast denial from the women of what was so obvious. There were tears, of course, feminine tears; the kind that could fall without halting conversation. And then there was gossip, at the commencement of which Frau Huckstepp noticeably lifted in spirit. She and Polly talked of people they knew at the Ritz, while Jürgen zoned out until he heard his own name mentioned. He looked up as Polly gushed words of praise for his kindness. At this he stepped forward, hoping the near-dead woman might guess of his intentions towards her ward and bestow her approval of them.

Lana Mae reached out for his hand. 'Herr Jürgen – we're so very grateful for you.'

He winced at the touch of her skin on his; clammy and cold. 'It is nothing, Frau Huckstepp.' He gave her his brightest smile.

'Please, call me Lana Mae.'

'If you wish – *Lana Mae.*'

'You must call him Günther,' Polly told her guardian. She lightly gripped Jürgen's other hand, before releasing it again. It was the first time she had ever touched him so intimately. The impression of her hand remained on his skin. 'He's a good friend to us,' she said, 'not like some other Germans.'

Jürgen frowned at Polly's words, but from Polly's perspective, he supposed it was true; he was not much like his comrades, especially those boors like Göring.

'Thank you, Günther,' said Lana Mae, weakly, smiling at him. 'I don't know how you did what you did so that Polly and I could see each other again – but honey, you're a gem all the same.'

The word 'gem' seemed to lift him from the moment as he remembered what Lana Mae was most known for at the Ritz. So meaningless is great wealth in the face of death, he thought to himself, and then, because he enjoyed the high esteem of women, he fell into his old trap of trying to think on the spot of new ways to please them.

'Perhaps,' he offered Lana Mae, smiling his most flawless smile again, 'perhaps there is a way to keep you interned here in Paris instead of Vittel. I have connections.'

Polly's face lit up bright with hope. 'Oh, Lana Mae – yes.'

He loved her like this.

But the American was oddly reticent. 'I don't wanna risk it.'

'Your illness is obvious – and you are no criminal. The authorities are not without compassion with such things.' He overstepped himself now with his candour: 'And really, to most Germans, the war with America is meaningless; a token conflict. No one expects any shots to be fired.'

She seemed to appreciate this. 'I agree. Thank you, Günther honey.' She closed her eyes a moment, cradled by her pillow. Then she added, 'The authorities have let me be brought into Paris when I need to get treatment. I don't want to push their patience any. I'll keep staying at Vittel in between times.' She looked pointedly to Polly. 'You understand, don't you, baby?'

It seemed to Jürgen that Polly clearly didn't, yet she nodded bravely.

'Doctor Mandel is at Vittel,' Lana Mae said, 'I told you that, didn't I, baby?'

'Yes. Yes, you did.'

There was a secretive smile now shared by the women.

Jürgen conceded to Lana Mae's wishes, patently relieved. In truth he would have been hard pressed to achieve any more than he had already.

Lana Mae seemed to be looking at her ward meaningfully. 'Baby, I'm feeling so parched,' she told Polly. 'Could you see if there's coffee to be had? Or maybe some tea?'

Polly stood up to leave the little room. 'Of course, Lana Mae.'

'Günther will keep me company.' Her guardian smiled, sinking deeper into the pillows. She actually winked. 'No need to rush . . .'

With Polly gone, Jürgen saw Lana Mae's demeanour change instantly.

'Günther . . .' She beckoned him closer.

He bent his head to hear better.

'I'm gonna *beat* this,' she whispered.

'Of course, you will,' he said automatically.

There was now a desperation to her eyes that she'd kept hidden from Polly. Her voice seemed a husk of itself, a dry leaf. 'When I started hurting and bleeding *down there*, I told Doc Mandel that I knew what was causing it . . .'

He blinked. 'You have medical training?'

'No.' She cleared her throat again. 'I'd *swallowed* something – something hard with sharp edges.'

He was alarmed. 'You tried to kill yourself?'

She was tittering. 'No, honey – I was trying to hide something; something those Frenchie gendarmes had no need to know about when they arrested me.'

Jürgen stared at her in confusion.

She uncurled the fingers of her right hand. A magnificent emerald sparkled against the sallowness of her palm.

Jürgen's jaw dropped.

Lana Mae snapped her hand closed on the gem again. 'It came out in due course – and don't worry, I sure washed it. But the bleeding didn't stop like it should have. That's when the doc diagnosed me.' She grinned at him wryly. 'It turns out I have uterine cancer. All those bottles of pink bismuth I used to drink – my belly always ached but I thought it was indigestion. What are the odds?'

He stared at her in incomprehension. 'Why are you telling me this?'

'It's like I said to you: I'm gonna kick this disease.'

'All right . . .'

Her sallow brow wrinkled. 'But nothing comes free in this world and that includes cancer.'

In the little pause that followed, Jürgen wasn't quite sure what was going to come next.

Lana Mae's other hand fluttered at her throat before she began again. 'You may have heard,' she started, 'that from time to time, in order to raise funds, I have been happy to accept offers for my jewels . . .'

He had certainly heard that.

'Respectable offers, of course,' she assured him, 'but all the same, nothing like they charge at Cartier. I'm not a greedy woman. And of course, with the Reichsmark's excellent exchange rate, I've not lacked buyers.'

'I see,' said Jürgen. He found himself unaccountably sweating.

'My most loyal customer – if that's the right word for him – has been Reichsmarschall Göring, as it happens.'

'Really?' Of course, he well knew it; everyone did.

'I was going to send a little message to the Reichsmarschall to see if he might be interested in this emerald,' said Lana Mae.

'Oh, yes?'

'I've no doubt he will be. He collects them, you know?'

'He does?'

Lana Mae giggled. 'He's got so damn many jewels – and not just from me. To him they're like candy almost. He keeps them in a bowl by his bed so that he can fondle them at night. Isn't that funny?'

Jürgen had not seen this bowl for himself but he had certainly heard of it. Such excess was not funny at all; it disgusted him.

Lana Mae was now looking at him hopefully. 'But I thought – and it was just a thought, mind, nothing more – that before I approached Herr Göring, perhaps I should offer you the same opportunity?' She opened her palm again.

Jürgen felt his mouth go dry. The emerald seemed almost to pulse in the room.

'Are you interested in jewels any?'

'I – ah.' Words temporarily failed him.

'It's a real pretty rock,' said Lana Mae. She angled it and the light from the hospital room window hit it perfectly. 'It belonged to a Russian grand duchess,' she went on. 'Olga her name was. Such a charming woman.' She shrugged in sympathy. 'She fell on hard times herself.'

Jürgen swallowed. 'Well – I don't know, Frau Huckstepp.'

'Perhaps there's a girl who'd like it?'

Her knowing blue eyes held his.

'A girl?' Jürgen felt like a schoolboy, exposed at confessional for having impure thoughts.

'There *must* be,' said Lana Mae, kidding him. 'Big, tall hunk of man like you.' She winked at him again. 'You must be beating them off with a pole.'

He blushed to the roots of his hair at this choice of words.

Her fingers snapped shut on the jewel again. 'I'm sorry, I've embarrassed you, haven't I? Forgive me.'

'No – no.' He so badly wanted that uncanny green glow now that she'd hidden it again.

'You can't afford such a thing – of course, you can't,' said Lana Mae. 'You're an ordinary man of the Wehrmacht. I'm so sorry, Günther. I forget myself.'

'But my family are landowners, Frau Huckstepp. We have owned land for centuries.'

'That's swell.'

'We are not *ordinary*.'

She looked him up and down in his uniform; his Luger in its holster by his side. 'No. I can see that, honey. Now that you mention it.'

'I have access to funds.'

She opened her hand again. 'Do you now?'

Jürgen felt calm washing over him at restored sight of the jewel. 'Perhaps there *is* a girl . . .'

She was beaming at him. For all her physical suffering her cornfed American teeth were quite perfect, as if nothing was wrong with her at all. 'How could there *not* be a girl for you, honey?'

She tipped the emerald from her palm into his. It was heavier than he would ever have expected it to be. Jürgen somehow managed to pull his gaze from the jewel to look in Lana Mae's eyes. 'What sort of offer would be acceptable to you, meine Dame?'

Zita and Hans took their seats in the director's comfortable office and looked through the tall windows at the snow-dusted Steinhof grounds. The director, they'd been told, would be with them shortly. Zita had given the assistant Lotti's full name. A large photographic portrait of the Führer watched over them from the wall behind the director's oak desk.

Zita shrugged out of her furs in the too-heated room and reached over to squeeze Hans' arm. He smiled at her but said nothing. It was as strange for him as it was for her, she guessed. Today they were to be happy families together as if those were the parts they'd played always. Zita knew she would not have to play it; the part was wholly real.

They waited.

On the low table beside her chair was a little pile of children's school books, no doubt belonging to patients. Zita picked up a mathematics textbook and opened it randomly. She read a math question:

The construction of a lunatic asylum costs 6 million Reichsmarks. How many houses at 15,000 Reichsmarks each could have been built for that amount?

The question struck an ugly chord. She shut the book again.

An inner door opened and a gaunt, authoritative woman, dressed unexpectedly in English-style tweeds, came into the room, wreathed in toothy smiles and cradling a porcelain vase in her arms. 'Herr and Frau Metzingen? I'm so sorry to have kept you waiting this long.'

Zita and Hans stood.

The woman clocked his rank and placed the vase on her desk to salute him.

'Heil Hitler.'

'Heil Hitler.'

'I am Director Anna Weber, won't you be seated, please?'

They sat down again.

The director smiled compassionately at them. 'I so commend you for being here. It is admirable.'

Zita flushed away her guilt at how little she'd been here before. 'It is not always easy – I live in Paris, you see.'

Weber needed no explanation from her. 'Of course, of course. It is even more admirable for that being so. You have come a long way.'

Zita nodded. She took Metzingen's huge hand. 'We have come together.'

'Commendable, as I said. We have seen so few parents since the program began.'

Zita bit back her guilt again.

'But I do not blame them,' said Director Weber, 'of course I don't. Nobody would. Such matters are not easy.' She sighed and looked from Zita to Hans. 'Still, we are fortunate to live under the Führer, are we not, Herr Oberstleutnant?'

'Of course, meine Dame. Fortune favours all Germans.'

'Indeed, indeed.' She flicked her eyes to Zita apologetically, before continuing again. 'In lesser countries, among peoples of inferior race, such acts of mercy are considered unthinkable.' She sadly shook her head. 'Sorry displays of weakness. Is it any wonder we're winning this war?'

'No wonder at all!' said Metzingen.

'Only our Führer can conceive of such necessary solutions. How lucky we are.'

'Indeed,' said Metzingen.

Zita had lost the thread of the conversation. 'Our daughter, Madame Director . . .'

Weber looked compassionately at her again.

Zita tried to order her thoughts of what needed to be said. 'Her birth, it was a terrible –' She rejected that path and tried another. 'We had hoped for a healthy child, you see.'

'What parent doesn't?'

'At first she *was* healthy.'

'At first,' said Hans. 'Only at first.'

Zita still held his hand. 'But then it became clear that she was not developing like other babies.'

Director Weber nodded. 'The imbecilic are never hidden for long.'

Zita flinched. 'Well, no. No. And so, we brought her here to the Steinhof. For the very best care she could receive.'

'Of course.'

'For the very best care I –' she corrected her narrative for Hans' sake '– we could pay for.' Zita had always paid for everything, but this was not an occasion for tallying. She took from her purse the photograph of Lotti that Metzingen had given her on the day he returned to the Ritz. She showed it to Director Weber. 'Here she is, see? Look at the smile on her little face. She's so happy. I can tell that the care she's received here has been excellent, Madame Director – the very best in the world.'

There was not a scrap of recognition on the director's fleshless face. 'The child was before my time.' She handed the photograph back to Zita.

The words registered to Zita without registering at all. She looked to Hans. His brow had creased as if he'd misheard something. 'Well, perhaps we might be permitted to see Lotti now?' Zita suggested.

Director Weber's own brow furrowed.

'Visit her in her room?' said Zita. 'Or perhaps she's in the common room this morning, playing with her friends? If so, we'll go there.' Zita showed what else she had in her purse: a gift-wrapped doll. 'I have a little present for her all the way from Paris.'

The director blanched. She looked to Metzingen. 'Herr Oberstleutnant – is your wife not familiar with the T-4 Program?'

Hans stared back at her. 'Meine Dame, *I* am not familiar with it.'

'But I thought – because of your Wehrmacht high rank?'

'Tell me, where is our daughter, please?'

Director Weber swallowed with difficulty. 'I fear we have been at cross purposes . . .' She gently pushed the porcelain vase towards him across the desk.

Zita felt her heart fall out of her. It was not a vase at all, but an urn.

Weber was grey-faced with the misunderstanding. 'These are your daughter's remains. As I said, you are admirable. Few parents come to collect them, you see . . .'

The conversation went on, and Zita participated without participating at all. Her mind had gone to a Steinhof of her own, a Christmas-themed sanctuary, from which she gave thought as to what she would now do. From here she heard the words of fury from Hans at his not having known of the T-4 Program, at his not having been told anything at all, and she wondered for whose benefit these words were intended, suspecting it was for her alone. She heard the denials from the director that such an oversight could ever have occurred with a parent of his rank. Then came patriotic claims from Weber, ideological justifications to which Metzingen listened in silence. These lives had been 'non-lives', Weber informed them; Lotti had been one of so many 'useless eaters' abandoned at the Steinhof, 'parasites' that had sucked the German state dry. The Steinhof was now a rehabilitation hospital for the Fatherland's superior troops. Only the Führer had such boldness of action. Only the Führer knew solutions to the wrongs that plagued the Aryan race.

Hans escorted Zita from the former Children's Pavilion through the Art Nouveau doors, to find the six soldiers were waiting, now joined by some friends. There was a crowd of strapping German boys, all of them wounded, not one of them hurt in their mind. If they had been, Zita knew now, they'd have been euthanised for it; the fate of all useless eaters.

Zita went through the motions, cracking one-liners, signing more casts, letting them flirt with the star. Hans had been given the urn to carry and when he tripped on the step and it slipped from his hold she didn't care. It smashed hard on the concrete, spilling Lotti on his shoes. The soldiers were mortified, but not Zita. She didn't even acknowledge the accident, leading them away from the mess. She looked over her shoulder just once and saw Hans on his knees, scrabbling in the ash. He had discovered something there.

When Zita sent the boys on their way, Hans wouldn't show her what he had found. She lost herself then, succumbing to hysteria, until Hans thrust the thing in her hands. It was the twisted remains of a child's little necklace; a cheap metal locket and chain.

Zita had never seen the necklace before; neither of them had. The locket's contents had been incinerated. The back of the locket was engraved. Hans had scratched at it to read what it said.

To Emma with love from Mutti

The ashes weren't even Lotti's.

They'd been given the remains of a generic deceased, something that was no doubt prepared in readiness to give to anyone.

In the big Wehrmacht car, as Zita listened to Metzingen's sobs without listening, and spoke comforting words without saying anything at all, she embraced rationality, picking over the inconsistencies in everything she had formerly half-believed to be real. When had her daughter been murdered? Was it recently, or had it been many years before? And was it even her Lotti in the photograph, or some other poor girl, so easily accepted because children with Lotti's condition all look the same? And had Lotti been alive at all when Metzingen had used Zita's shame and guilt at abandoning their daughter to make her his willing Ritz spy?

Zita decided that she would never ask these questions of Hans. She would never voice them aloud. She didn't want to hear the answers. She believed she already knew them in her heart.

Hans had made a spy of her, he had promoted her from being his whore. But with her daughter dead she had nothing left to be taken. She could kill herself, certainly, as she'd so often threatened to do, or she could take a different path – one that would only open for her if she accepted she was long dead already.

In the rear of the car, cushioned by her furs, Zita accepted it. With death she had freedom, if only she'd realised it before. She was still the spy. She was still the whore. She would use the skills of both to screw the bastard. It would be all the more beautiful because she loved him.

She fumbled at the catch of her purse and opened it. She rummaged around and found what she'd put in there when they'd left Paris. She marvelled at her foresight; it was as if she'd already known Lotti's fate. She took out a little enamel tin and prized the lid off it.

'What are you doing?' said Hans, looking up from his hands.

'What I need to,' Zita said.

The tin was full of powder. She had a little silver spoon for the purpose. She scooped up a mound of it but didn't place it to her nose. Instead, she offered it to him.

Hans stared at what she proffered. 'How can I possibly?'

She shrugged. 'It is like breathing in air – like breathing in happiness. It makes pain go away.'

'And when the happiness wears off?'

'You just snort more.' She regarded him with pity in her face. 'Christ, are you really such a rube?'

His pride trembled, as had been her intention. He stared at the spoon.

'Suit yourself then,' said Zita. She took the spoon away.

Hans grabbed at her wrist.

'Changed your mind now?' She watched him teeter at the edge.

'You'll tell no one of it?'

She smiled at him, lovingly. 'You keep my secrets, don't you?'

He couldn't return her smile.

'Well then,' she said, 'why ask me?'

Zita watched Metzingen take his first hit of dope. She had some herself then and very soon her brightest smile, as unreal as the movies she was famous for, was reflected in his.

Hans was smiling like they'd never even had a daughter.

Alexandrine had secretly feared they might find conditions icy in the uppermost reaches of the Ritz, high in the attic rooms, tucked under the mansard roofs, where guests never went. She'd been wrong. The Ritz fifth floor was pleasingly snug thanks to all the heated spaces below, which was a considerable relief, sparing her as it did Suzette's expected condemnation. Alexandrine was only glad the old woman was giving no thought as to what the temperatures might be in August.

Yet the Suzette on her arm was a very different Suzette to the salty old crone who had spent decades berating her madame. Here, she was lifted with love, a miraculous transformation that pricked Alexandrine twice: one, because she had so delayed in bringing Suzette to the Ritz; and two, because it only made her think of the love the old woman might have given Alexandrine's child, had it lived.

They reached the top of the final stair and Suzette paused, surely exhausted, catching at her rattling breath. But Alexandrine well knew she would never admit to it.

'Where is he?' Suzette asked.

'Down this corridor,' she said, feigning certainty. She had the room number at least, given to her by Blanche.

Suzette unexpectedly clutched at her.

She was alarmed. 'Suzette – what's wrong?' She looked worriedly around her, fearing there might be Boches nearby.

But Suzette had tears in her eyes. 'Thank you, Madame . . .'

The old grudgingness covered her relief. 'For what?' She well knew what.

Suzette didn't need to tell her. 'Just thank you.'

Alexandrine wouldn't let herself feel any of it. 'He lives down here,' she said perfunctorily.

They made their way down the gloomy hallway, Alexandrine alive to the grimness of it; the lack of paper on the wall, the lack of carpet on the boards. 'Guest servants were roomed up here long ago,' she felt obliged to explain.

'It's decent,' said Suzette, 'don't apologise for it. There are Jews living in much worse nowadays.'

Alexandrine flinched at the word. 'The boy isn't a Jew. His Hungarian slut of a mother was Catholic.'

'Not this again.'

'You of all people know how it is, Suzette. Jewishness is passed down maternally.'

'He was circumcised. I was there for the bris.'

'It's meaningless.'

'His father considered him Jewish. That's why you took him from school and hid him here, isn't it? That's good enough for me.'

'And yet *I'm* not good enough for you?' said Alexandrine.

Suzette glanced at her – then glanced away. 'Let's not fight. You're taking me to see the boy.'

'Very convenient for you.'

Suzette clutched at her again. The tears were there. 'I'm sorry, Madame. I mean it. I don't want to fight with you. I don't have it in me these days.'

In truth, neither did Alexandrine. She squeezed the old woman's hand. 'All right.'

But Suzette wasn't letting go, looking pleadingly up at her face, her abrasive manner fallen away. 'You're a Jew, too. You never faked it. God sees the Jew in you, Madame, just like He sees it in Tommy. Of course, He does.'

The flood of emotion that came to Alexandrine was almost as much as she could bear. She had to fight to keep herself together. 'Don't be so silly.'

'You're the daughter I never had,' Suzette swore to her, 'you always have been, Madame. That's the maternal line – from me down to you.'

'Suzette, please . . .'

The old housekeeper was kissing her hand. 'I say terrible things, I know I do, but it's just my way – I never mean them, you know that.'

Alexandrine stared down in awkwardness at the frizzled grey hair. 'You mustn't upset yourself so.'

'I'm not upset, I just want you to hear me, Madame: I never mean any of it. My life was hard before I met the Comte. Then everything changed. But I found it beyond me to let go of the bitterness of the past.'

'I know you don't mean any of it,' Alexandrine assured her. 'I know how good you are, how good you've always been to me.'

'People think I can't love. They think I'm too cold and too hard. And I've let them think that because it's easier to live with a closed heart.'

Alexandrine was thrown. Suzette could just as equally be describing Alexandrine herself. 'They're wrong – of course they're wrong. I know you're not like that at all.'

There was pleading in Suzette's look to her. 'That's why, when the boy was born, I had the chance to be different – to be a better woman – you understand, don't you, Madame?'

Alexandrine did understand. It was the same chance that Polly had given her; a chance she had squandered. She had let herself grow colder and harder than Suzette could ever be; she had made a life's work out of her own past bitterness.

She kissed the old woman on the head, forcing those memories aside. 'Let's find him now,' she whispered. Suzette felt warm and soft in her arms, and she had come to realise, frail. She had no idea of Suzette's real age, but knew it was well past seventy. The German Occupation had been cruellest of all upon the defence-less elderly.

Alexandrine looked at the numbers on the room doors. 'It is just down here.'

They located the right door number together.

'You knock,' said Alexandrine. She stood back a little so that the old woman would be the first one Tommy saw.

Suzette tapped gently.

They heard immediate movement from inside the room; a chair scraping the floor; someone getting up from the bed.

Tommy's voice through the door jamb. 'Who is it?'

'Little one?' Suzette whispered. 'It's only me.'

They heard the gasp of surprise from the other side of the door. '*Grand-mère?*'

Suzette pressed her lips to the jamb. 'Let me in, little one. Someone might see me out here.'

There was another short silence. 'Are you alone?'

Suzette was heartfelt. 'I'm here with the only one you can believe in and trust as much as you can believe in and trust me.' She looked imploringly to Alexandrine. 'You have nothing to fear, little one. *Nothing.* We have only love for you.'

Alexandrine told herself she felt nothing.

They heard the fumbling of a bolt being withdrawn at the other side of the door.

The door opened onto the dark attic room. Tommy was in his underclothes.

'Oh, Tommy – my boy!'

'*Grand-mère . . .*'

Alexandrine hung back in the shadows as the striking young man, with his shock of blond hair that came wholly from his mother, and his soft brown eyes that were so undeniably from Eduarde, took the tiny old servant in his long, lean arms.

Suzette gripped his arms in her hands. 'Are you safe, Tommy?'

'Yes.' He gave his first apprehensive look to Alexandrine. '*Yes,*' he repeated, acknowledging what she had done to hide him. 'No one suspects me here. No one ever asks for my papers. They see me without seeing me.'

'Good. Good,' said Suzette. 'And did you go on that filthy Jew Register?'

'Of course, I didn't.'

'Thank God. I prayed you'd stay smart – but I couldn't be sure that you would.'

'I don't leave the hotel much,' Tommy told her, 'and those times that I do, the krauts seem to like me. They never ask to look at my papers outside either.'

'Good, good – keep it that way. Don't take any stupid risks.'

'I don't, *Grand-mère.*' Tommy cupped her wizened old face in his hands. 'Please tell me you didn't go on the register, either.'

Alexandrine's heart lurched as she realised that Suzette couldn't answer him.

'*Grand-mère? Tell me.*'

Suzette was resolute. 'There was no getting out of it for me.'

Tommy was ashen. 'Yes, there was.'

Suzette shook her head. 'Not in the Marais, little one. The cops wanted every apartment occupant made accountable. I'm too visible there. I had to go along.'

Alexandrine couldn't bear the look of fear that washed over him. She turned her eyes away.

Suzette was quick to reassure Tommy. 'It means nothing. You mustn't worry about me, little one, I always get by. And I've had my time anyway.'

'Please don't say that.'

'It's true, I'm old and done – the future rests with you.' Suzette looked back to Alexandrine in the shadows. She beckoned to her. 'Please come closer, Madame.'

Alexandrine drew a deep breath as she did so.

There was a moment's quiet while she stared at the object of her hatred and resentment; this boy she'd so despised from the moment of his illegitimate birth; this boy who was so undeniably of her dead husband's blood. His hands, his mouth, the curl of his ear at his neck; all of it she remembered and knew so intimately. He was a Jew, just as she was.

Tommy was humble. 'Madame Comtesse . . .'

'Please, don't –'

He reached out to her.

Then her own tears came as her hand found his.

'Madame?'

She found herself saying what she had believed she would never say. 'Forgive me, Tommy. Oh God, please forgive me, for all that I've done to you . . .'

'But there is nothing to forgive.'

'There is – there is.'

He refused to accept it.

She stared into his eyes – Eduarde's eyes. 'Look what you have with Suzette – the love that is so unbreakable between you. I know it might have been mine, too, if only I'd let it, but I could not let it. I was stupid and wrong. Please forgive me for it, Tommy. I know how foolish I was.'

Her flood of words stunned him into silence. Then he stepped forward and embraced her as he had embraced Suzette; warmly and wholeheartedly, wrapping her in his hug. 'Love is all that we have, should the end come, Madame,' he whispered to her. 'It is the one thing that separates us from *them.*'

13

15 July 1942

While Alexandrine waited on a little gilt chair to collect the item made especially for her at Madame Lanvin's, she watched as Blanche Auzello entered the atelier from the rue du Faubourg Saint-Honoré, stamping raindrops from her shoes. The two women locked eyes for a moment but neither gave any sign that they knew each other. Paying no mind at all to the ill-mannered BOFs and frowsy German officers' wives putting the *vendeuses* through their paces further inside the shop, Blanche went to the counter and asked Giselle, the young assistant, whether Madame Hélène was in residence.

'The public relations director, Mademoiselle. I would so like to see her. She and I are old friends.'

'Of course, Madame,' said the young girl. 'If you will just bear with me a moment.'

Blanche waited while she dialled, her eyes travelling casually to Alexandrine's again, where they met a second time, before each looked away without a word.

'Madame Hélène?' said the girl to the receiver, when the connection was made at the other end. 'There is a lady here to

327

see you – a friend.' The girl looked to Blanche. 'Your name, Madame?'

'Madame Biélinky,' said Blanche, with no hint of the lie.

Giselle repeated the name into the telephone receiver. She listened a moment, then nodded. She turned back to Blanche. 'Madame Hélène will come down to the floor shortly.'

Blanche smiled. 'Thank you so much, Mademoiselle.'

The girl indicated the little gilt chair next to Alexandrine's. 'Will you take a seat as you wait, Madame?'

'Of course.'

Blanche sat next to her friend from the Ritz as if they were strangers.

They said nothing for a moment, each watching a corpulent BOF woman loudly complain in a rough country accent that the dress measurements the *vendeuse* had taken must surely be wrong.

'Of course, Madame knows best,' the *vendeuse* offered, patiently. She wrote down the woman's preferred measurements in a column next to the correct ones.

The BOF was smugly satisfied.

'What we'd do to know good ham and cheese as well as *she* does, Madame,' Alexandrine said to Blanche under her breath with a sigh.

Blanche nodded. 'Maybe someday these big fat imbalances will be tipped in our favour again, Madame.'

'Maybe,' said Alexandrine. 'Someday soon, God willing.'

Madame Hélène appeared from the offices above the shop floor, searching for the face she would recognise. She clocked Blanche with Alexandrine. 'Lily, darling,' she called down.

Blanche got to her feet, giving Alexandrine's knee a squeeze so light and fast that it was all but imperceptible. 'Hélène, my love!' she called across the room as the director reached the bottom of the stairs. The women showily kissed each other's cheeks in the middle of the shop floor. 'Darling, you can still make luncheon?'

'Of course,' said Hélène, 'but there's something I simply must complete in the next ten minutes, or my life will be miserable.'

Blanche looked stricken. 'But the table at *La Tour* – they might give it away.'

'You go ahead, darling. I'll catch you right up.'

'All right. Promise me you won't take too long.'

'You know I won't.'

Alexandrine now saw she had an envelope in her hand. 'This is for Geneviève – she knows what it is. You two can have a giggle over it while you wait for me to arrive.'

'What is it?' said Blanche.

Hélène winked. 'Something naughty. You'll both love it.'

Blanche slipped the envelope into her coat pocket. 'I'm sure we will.' She waved goodbye. 'Please don't take very long – I'll order a cocktail for you.'

Hélène waved as she headed back up the stairs. 'I'll be there in a tick.'

Blanche met Alexandrine's eyes for the final time as she put her hand on the door. She called out to the assistant. 'Thank you, Mademoiselle!'

Giselle waved at her gaily.

Alexandrine knew: there would be no luncheon, for there was no reservation at *La Tour*, and indeed no Geneviève. This jolly little exchange, seen by everyone on the shop floor at Jeanne Lanvin, and yet seen by no one at all because it was just like any other exchange between friends, was really about whatever was inside the envelope.

Somehow, Blanche and Hélène had found the means to resist. They had discovered an unsuspected courage within themselves that they never would have thought possible before the Germans had come. Whatever it was that they were doing, Alexandrine would never ask them about it and neither woman would ever tell. This was, Alexandrine had come to understand, the unspoken rule when it came to the conduct of clandestine activities under the noses of the Boches. And Blanche and Hélène were not alone in being clandestine. *She* had done it. She had saved Eduarde's son by hiding him.

In recent months, Alexandrine had come to suspect that others she saw daily, friends at the Ritz, had also developed such nerve. She strongly suspected Claude Auzello of it, and Mimi as well; even Blanche's poor sightless daughter was engaged in some secretive fight. Alexandrine had drawn these conclusions because those Ritz friends and others had acquired a certain change to how they walked into a room; to the very way in which they held up their heads – and such change spoke of a secret resurgence of pride, a return of self-worth, an emboldening through learning what was – and was *not* – worth fighting for.

Alexandrine understood this change, because she had experienced it too.

And lately, Zita had also acquired it.

And now, Alexandrine was more than sure, Tommy had it, too.

It was as if they all had a fire raging inside them; a shared commitment to something greater than themselves. Alexandrine's certainty about this both terrified and re-inspired her. If she could see the change in them all so clearly, how long until it was seen by the Boches?

For anyone who resisted, the consequences of exposure were chilling. Yet the consequences of not resisting, of staring dully down the barrel of a future life no better – and likely far worse – than life endured now seemed more chilling still.

This was why she had set upon another means of resistance.

The scent of Arpège reached her nostrils.

'Madame Comtesse?'

Alexandrine looked up, startled. The exquisitely dressed, elderly Madame Lanvin herself was before her, a vision of chic, wearing her signature scent. 'Jeanne?' She stood up from the chair and kissed the old lady.

'Alexandrine – bless you.'

Alexandrine looked about her. The ignorant BOFs hadn't even realised it was Lanvin herself here among them. She saw the little wrapped package Jeanne had for her in her hand. Madame Lanvin stood close by her.

'You look worried, darling.' Alexandrine hoped her smiling confidence would dispel Jeanne's doubt.

Madame Lanvin indicated the package. 'How else should I be, Alexandrine? If you intend to wear *this*?'

Alexandrine tried to hold onto her confidence, but it wavered under the couturier's unfailing eye. 'Perhaps I won't put it on *every* day.'

'Perhaps not at all. Why bring trouble upon yourself?'

Alexandrine held the couturier's look. 'Perhaps I want the trouble, Jeanne?' She thought of a better riposte: 'Perhaps I *deserve* it?'

Her old friend's concern was painful. 'No one deserves it.'

Alexandrine had no more to say on it. 'How much do I owe you, darling?'

'Nothing.'

But Alexandrine had already opened her purse. 'Don't be silly. You made it for me especially – it's haute couture after all.'

Jeanne clutched at her wrist. '*Please* don't wear it. You're too good a friend for me to knowingly place you at risk like this.'

Alexandrine teetered then, until she thought of Blanche and Tommy – and Zita and Lana Mae, and everyone else she suspected had already gone down the path ahead of her. She held firm, kissing Jeanne on the papery skin at her cheek. 'I'll be all right, darling.' Then, as she turned to go she added: 'I'll leave forty francs for it with Giselle at the counter.'

'If you do that I'll never speak to you again.'

BOFs and German officers' wives' heads turned at the tone of her voice. There was an obvious reply that didn't need to be spoken by Alexandrine: if she did wear the contentious item they might never speak again for wholly different reasons.

'It's *complimentary*, Comtesse,' Jeanne told her, wanting them all to hear now. 'For being a loyal client to the House of Lanvin for so long.'

Alexandrine knew she'd have to accept this. She slipped the package into her open handbag. She would keep it in there, she decided then, until the occasion came when she would take the wrapping off and put the garment on for everyone to see.

'And you're a very loyal couturier,' she whispered.

She blew a kiss to Madame Lanvin as she stepped out into the rue du Faubourg Saint-Honoré. The rain shower had stopped, and the summer sun was shining.

'Hullo, puss.'

Patently lost in her own little world, Alexandrine looked up with a start at the sound of Zita's husky voice. 'Darling – I didn't see you there.'

Zita well knew she hadn't. She'd been watching Alexandrine from the other side of the café for some minutes, thinking upon what it was that she needed to do, before she decided on a plan of action and came over. Her beloved friend had been in total ignorance of her the whole time, which was fortunate. Alexandrine was distracted, and Zita hoped she'd stay that way, at least for a few minutes more. 'Want some company?'

'When do I not?' Alexandrine tapped the back of the empty chair at her table. 'It has your name on it.' She removed her open handbag from the seat, placing it on the floor between them. Zita glanced inside the bag as she did so and saw a Lanvin package.

'You've been shopping.'

Alexandrine shook her head. 'I had meant to,' she said, 'but Jeanne didn't want my cash today.'

Zita was incredulous. 'Not good enough for her now? Christ, she's turned into Chanel.'

'No, she just wouldn't let me pay.' Alexandrine's distraction remained; she seemed rather wistful. 'She's a very good woman really.'

'No one's denying it,' Zita watched as Alexandrine now made an effort to be more engaging.

'I think Jeanne double-charges all those dreadful Boches wives,' said Alexandrine. 'Loyal old clients like ourselves have not been forgotten, darling. Perhaps she'll give you a freebie, too?'

'Sure,' said Zita, looking up again. 'Why not? It'd make a nice change to start *saving* my money.'

Zita bent in her chair to scratch at her ankle, and slipped something of her own inside Alexandrine's handbag. It was all she could do to warn her friend, and still she feared it was doomed to failure. If she told Alexandrine outright what she'd learned, she knew she'd unravel in front of her, making Alexandrine want only to save her. Zita couldn't be saved. What's more, she didn't want to be. All that mattered was the information. When Alexandrine learned of it she'd waste no time on Zita. She'd use the time that remained to save who mattered most.

'You're terrible with your funds, darling,' Alexandrine was saying. 'What'll you do the day they stop paying you so much?'

'Start sponging off you.'

Alexandrine laughed. Then she looked at Zita with uncharacteristic emotion.

'What is it?'

Alexandrine shook her head again, and the emotion was gone. 'It's nothing.'

'It's something.'

'No, it's not, I'm just happy, that's all.'

'Half your luck – what's your secret?'

Alexandrine just smiled enigmatically at her.

Zita considered her dear friend. 'You *are* happy, aren't you, puss? Don't think I've not noticed it before. A change has come over you.'

Alexandrine sat up at once. 'A change?'

'Yes. A distinct one.'

Alexandrine looked uneasy.

'You've got a new lover, haven't you?' Zita fished, slyly.

Her friend was now oddly relieved. She made the face of a mock-coquette. 'I couldn't possibly say.'

Zita took that as a yes, and then, in a moment of sheer reck-lessness for what it could so easily expose in herself, she added, 'He's not some sexy kraut, is he?'

Alexandrine's disgust made it clear he was not. 'As enjoyed by Mademoiselle Chanel?'

Zita took a gossip segue. 'I don't think she's screwing that Hauptmann Jürgen anymore.'

'No?'

'She's got herself another one. This one's been out of the cradle longer.'

'One day she'll regret who she sleeps with.'

Zita hid her wince at this by puffing on her cigarette for a moment. 'Who knows,' she mused, 'perhaps she even spies on them?'

Alexandrine gave her a searching look at that. 'In the last war,' she said, 'the women who slept with the Boches had their heads shaved.'

Zita closed her eyes. 'Yes. I remember that.' She opened them again. 'It was terrible.'

'And terribly deserved.' Alexandrine looked long at her friend, on the cusp of asking her something.

Of course, Zita knew what it was. 'Go on,' she said, 'it's all right, puss.'

The Comtesse took the plunge. 'You and *him*,' she started, at a near whisper. 'That's all over between you now, isn't it?'

It was as if the friendship of a quarter century meant nothing to Zita anymore, such was the apparent ease with which she broke the rule most precious to the friends: the burden of a secret must be shared. 'Of course, it is,' she lied.

Zita watched as the Comtesse processed this and hated herself for it. 'But what of Lotti?' Alexandrine asked.

Zita reached for the shreds of her own soul – and crushed them in her fingers. 'She is healthy and well cared for. Almost a young woman these days.'

Alexandrine nodded, reassured. She plucked her handbag from the floor.

Zita nearly jumped at this action, her heart in her mouth, but her friend merely clasped the bag shut. 'Perhaps that Jürgen is not so bad,' Zita offered, blowing smoke to the café's ceiling to calm herself. 'He was the one who took Polly to visit Lana Mae that time.'

Alexandrine had read nothing in that. 'He's young and polite – the latter only when he's nowhere near Metzingen.'

Zita winced at mention of Hans' name again. 'You don't think she's sweet on him?'

'I do not.'

'He's pretty good looking. I bet he's hung like a beast.'

Alexandrine didn't laugh. 'Stop that at once. Polly is not in some love affair with that Boche. I *know* she's not.'

'You seem very sure.' Zita was regretting everything about this conversation but didn't care. All that mattered was that she'd hidden the thing inside Alexandrine's handbag and her friend hadn't discovered it yet – or anything else.

Alexandrine placed a coin on the table and stood up to go. 'I should be off, darling.'

'I've had a new letter from Lana Mae,' Zita told her, suddenly.

This stopped the Comtesse.

'The Swedish Red Cross passed it on. The krauts don't seem as fussed about the internees these days – they can't be if they're letting more letters go through. Must have bigger things to worry about. You'll get something from her next.'

Alexandrine's eyes were sparkling. 'How is she?'

Zita gave her a blank look. 'For a woman with a terminal disease she's a stinking long time getting dead.'

'Zita!' Then Alexandrine was laughing, 'What Polly claimed is absolutely true?'

Zita was comically careful. 'I don't *want* to think that Lana Mae might be lying . . .'

'Neither do I!' Her friend dabbed at a joyful tear. 'But still, she might be,' she mugged.

Zita and Alexandrine looked delightedly at each other. 'It's all a ruse!'

'I miss her so much,' said Alexandrine.

'Me too.' Zita puffed her cigarette. 'Somehow, she's still funding all her big-hearted stuff for the soldiers. Of course, we both know her too well not to guess that her so-called "cancer" is playing a part – we didn't need Polly to confirm it.' Then she added, 'Doctor Mandel's still in there with her.' She now made a comic rise of her eyebrows. 'In this letter Lana Mae only mentioned him *three times.*'

Alexandrine chuckled again. 'God bless our dear friend,' she sighed. 'We'll all be together again one day.' She blew a kiss to Zita as she left. 'See you back at the Ritz, darling.'

Zita felt as if she'd turned a ship around. The conversation had ended on a better note than it had threatened to. Alexandrine had looked happy again and Zita now recognised a sliver of the old emotion in herself, however fleetingly it lasted.

She suddenly had a longing for champagne and looked around for the waiter. It was then she saw Blanche Auzello at a table on the other side of the room. It was a testament to Zita's own distraction that she hadn't even noticed her.

She felt a sharp pang about Blanche, remembering her afflicted daughter. Then Zita thought of Lotti again and had to blink back tears about it.

Zita had gained the waiter's attention. 'A bottle of bubbles,' she told him. She nodded to Blanche's table. 'For her over there – two glasses.'

'Of course, Madame.'

'*Mademoiselle.*' She winked at him.

Zita watched as the bottle was opened and prepared at the counter – then delivered to Blanche. Informed of who it was from, Blanche looked over to Zita's table in surprise. Zita raised her empty hand as if she had a glass in it.

Blanche cocked an eyebrow.

Zita had received that signal enough times in her life to know that a conversation could accordingly ensue.

She sat down with Blanche. Before the American could say anything, Zita put out a silencing hand. 'I just want to say, puss, that all those years ago – back in 1924 – when you and me were on that film set at the Château de Vincennes, I was a goddamn bitch to you, and now I'm sorry about it.'

Blanche blinked in astonishment for a moment. Then she started to titter. 'You sure were one nasty broad, Zita.' She sniffed and took a sip from the champagne glass. 'But the trouble was I just couldn't *act.*'

It was Zita's turn to giggle. 'Want to talk about old times?'

'Always,' said Blanche.

Zita settled into the seat next to her, readying for a nostalgic half-hour.

Alexandrine slipped into the Ritz through the Cambon doors, finding the lobby welcomingly cooler than the street outside, which had now grown humid, thanks to the summer rain that had hung over Paris all day. She fanned herself with her hands for a moment, weighing up which had the greater appeal: a cocktail in the Cambon bar or an hour resting in her suite. The former won out; she still felt buoyed by the day's interactions and wanted to extend this rare experience of being so unaccountably happy.

She walked into the chromium-plated interior and at once regretted it.

'Alexandrine – please come and join us!'

She plastered a smile over her inner dismay. A colourfully dressed, middle-aged woman of Greek heritage was seated with a tight-faced Mimi, together occupying the most prominently positioned table in the bar, making avoidance impossible. 'Madame Breker, what a nice surprise,' Alexandrine lied.

'You know very well that it's *Demetra*, darling,' said the Greek woman, patting the chair beside her for Alexandrine to sit down.

'Of course – darling Demetra.' She glanced at Mimi and correctly read the latter's relief at the opportunity of escape that Alexandrine had just provided her.

Alexandrine looked longingly towards the bar. Tommy was behind the chrome counter serving a group of patrons. He saw her and nodded.

The Greek woman was anxious to include her. 'I have just been telling Mimi all the changes we require now that our stay has turned out to be so long.'

Alexandrine saw Mimi flinch.

'You must know how Arno's career's taken off?'

'Since he joined the Nazi Party?' Alexandrine mused, pleasantly. 'All Paris knows that, so how could I not?'

Demetra chose not to elaborate on her husband's political affiliations. 'He gets more sculpture commissions today than he ever did,' she said, preening. 'He can barely keep up.'

Alexandrine signalled her desire for a drink to Tommy as if he hadn't seen her while Demetra began running through her list of requirements with Mimi.

'*Lamps*,' said Demetra, 'there are simply not nearly enough lamps in our Vendôme suite. Arno stumbles about half-blind. How is he ever to work?'

Mimi had heard enough. 'Oh, there's Claude in the lobby – I shall take your wishes to him at once.'

'But that's not everything!'

Mimi tapped at her temple. 'It's all in here, Madame Breker – I never forget.'

Demetra watched exasperated as Mimi made a hasty exit. There was no sign of Claude in the lobby at all. She turned to Alexandrine. 'She forgets who's paying.'

'Who *is* paying?' asked Alexandrine. Perplexingly, she had found an envelope she didn't recognise inside her bag, next to her still-wrapped item from Lanvin.

Demetra waved the enquiry away. 'It doesn't matter.'

'Ah, so presumably it's not you and Arno settling the bill. That *is* fortunate.' The envelope was blank, sealed; there was a folded letter inside it.

Demetra fixed a cold look at her. 'Tell me, Alexandrine. We've not seen you at the Musée de l'Orangerie. Why would that be?'

'Sorry – what's that?' She worried at the envelope in her hand, trying to understand how it might have found its way inside her bag. She held off opening it for a moment.

'To Arno's exhibition,' said Demetra, 'down at the Tuileries. It's been on since May and yet we've not once seen you there.'

'We?'

'Arno and I, of course.' She leant forward on the table, danger-ous. 'Or do you find yourself quite unable to agree with what constitutes the art of today?'

Alexandrine dropped the letter into her lap. 'Of course, I don't, darling, what a thing to suggest. I've visited Arno's lovely sculp-tures several times. You must have missed me.'

Demetra raised her eyebrow, rightly sceptical. 'Is that so?'

'I prefer to drop in when it's quiet,' she said. 'And good riddance to all that progressive muck I say – trying to take art forward, the cheek of it. Arno keeps art firmly running on the spot, doesn't he? No troubling newness there. And those towering, muscular figures that he sculpts these days are so much more *nationalist*, aren't they? So comfortingly Teutonic. It's no wonder the Führer pays your way.' She flicked Demetra a deliberate look, up and down, before glancing awkwardly away.

'And I suppose the years when *you* were Arno's muse are such a long way behind us now?'

Tommy made his way to the table once the patrons monopolising him at the bar had dispersed. Demetra Breker had by now departed, and Tommy had enjoyed her testy exchange with Alexandrine from afar, unable to hear what was being said, but knowing from the look upon Demetra's face that Alexandrine was easily getting the better of her. He brought a negroni to Alexandrine upon a tray, expecting to discover an expression of amused triumph upon Alexandrine's face, but instead he was thrown by her fear.

'Madame?' Shocked, he glanced around the now emptier room, ensuring no one was listening. 'Madame – did that traitor threaten you?'

She shook her head. '*Tommy . . .*' She couldn't finish.

An opened letter was on the table before her.

'What is it?'

Her hands were trembling so much she couldn't pick the letter up to show him. Glancing around again, Tommy placed the cocktail before her on the table and picked up the note, laying it flat on his tray. He read it as he stood there. It was childishly scrawled in a tried and true method: the correspondent had used their unfavoured hand in an effort to disguise their handwriting.

Save a friend.
Belleville, Saint-Paul, Popincourt, Poissonniere, and the Temple will all be crying tonight. The neighbourhoods around and including the Marais will be swept of all Jews. They'll be loaded into buses and driven off before dawn. First to the Vélodrome d'Hiver, because they can be locked up inside it, and then they'll be taken to Poland. And it won't be the krauts doing this – it'll be the 'French' cops.
Save a friend.

Tommy felt his throat close tight, like he was struggling for air. 'Where did you get this?'

'My bag. It was slipped inside.'

'When?'

'I don't know. Sometime today.' She tried to order in her mind where the day's tasks had taken her, but she could barely remember any of it. 'Perhaps at Lanvin.' She thought of Blanche and the coded conversation they'd held where it had been as if they hadn't known each other. She thought then of how it was always better *not* to know. 'Yes. I think it was at Lanvin.'

'Who gave it to you there?'

She wouldn't tell him. She wouldn't risk Blanche. 'It could have been anyone.' She looked up at him with tears in her eyes. 'Is it real, do you think?'

He didn't need to answer her.

'Suzette,' said Alexandrine, helplessly. 'What will I do?'

'*We*,' said Tommy.

'You can't risk it,' she told him, 'you see what it says. All Jews will be taken. It has to be me.'

'*We*,' Tommy repeated. 'The question is what *we* will do.'

'Tommy, please.'

'I will not argue,' he said, 'because there is no argument. Suzette is my *grand-mère*.'

A tear escaped from her eye and she dabbed it with a finger lest anyone notice it. 'All right.'

Tommy was silent for only a moment, his thoughts racing, before he gave her his plan. 'We will go to her in the night and take her from the Marais – we'll go early, well before dawn; before the cops come.'

'But where will we take her? Here?'

Tommy shook his head. 'Too dangerous. She stands out. We'll take her to the Left Bank – the Latin Quarter.'

'But there'll be patrols.'

She watched him wrestle with revealing something he obviously knew well. 'There's a route you can take – through the *guichets* of the Louvre. You can make your way to the Pont du Carrousel and from there cross the Seine. There are never patrols along that way.'

She heard this with astonishment. 'Never?'

He nodded. 'And there're a lot less krauts on the Left Bank, too,' said Tommy, 'it's too disordered for them. And in the Latin Quarter there are some trustworthy friends.'

'*Friends?*'

The look he gave her told her not to ask, but her worry was too great now not to. 'But how can you know of such "friends", Tommy, when you live hidden away here?'

'Please don't ask me this.' He came to a decision. 'I've changed my mind. You will *not* be involved.'

'I'm sorry?'

'You heard me, Madame. It's best this way.'

She bristled. 'I will not be kept from Suzette.'

'Why not? You kept her from me long enough.'

It was as if she'd been winded.

The silence between them ended when Tommy's face creased with shame. 'I'm sorry.'

'No, I'm sorry.' And she was. She knew she'd have to plead. 'I can never make up for my years of coldness towards you, Tommy. But I still need to try.'

'I should never have said such a thing.'

'But it was true.' She reached for his hand. No one saw. 'My conscience torments me. I *have* to help her.'

He squeezed her hand. 'We'll go together then.'

Alexandrine sagged with relief.

Then he looked at her thoughtfully. 'Dress up. Tonight it's essential. Dress up as you would to a party.'

She considered, although it seemed bizarre. 'All right. But why?'

342

'If you're caught you can make it look like you've been out having fun and you lost track of time. You're a Comtesse, you live at the Ritz, they'll believe you – especially if you act a little drunk. You might spend the rest of the night in some police cell, but they'll let you go in the morning.'

Again, she was made nearly speechless by the depth of experience he seemed to have in conducting clandestine activity. 'But what about you?'

He scraped a hand though his shock of hair. 'Don't worry about me.'

'But I do worry.'

The truth of such a statement, one he had so hopelessly longed to hear from her for so much of his life, and now said so easily, moved him. They had come such a great distance in such a short time, Tommy and his dead father's wife, with all the lost years to make up for. 'I have a disguise of my own,' he told her, after a moment. 'And I know already that it works.'

When Polly knocked on the door of Alexandrine's suite, the Comtesse admitted her, having just been delivered a letter stamped by the Swedish Red Cross.

'It's from Lana Mae!' cried Polly.

'Zita got one, too,' said Alexandrine, beaming, as happy about it as Polly was.

They tore open the thin envelope together, to find an even thinner sheet of paper inside.

Polly hesitated. 'Perhaps you should read this alone, Alexandrine. She addressed it to you.'

'Don't be silly, darling – she'd want you to read it, too.'

'Would she though?' said Polly, thinking of the impenetrable ties that bound her three guardians.

'There are no secrets between us,' said Alexandrine.

The absurdity of this statement hit Polly at once. But it was only when she said nothing in reply that Alexandrine looked up at her and realised it, too. She at once grew uncomfortable.

'Sometimes I think there are more secrets between us than there are stars in the sky,' Polly said. 'Why is that, Alexandrine?'

The Comtesse seemed to be forming an acceptable answer in her head. Then Polly's own look made her abandon it. 'It is the habit of lifelong friendships,' she said, simply.

'We have known each other – we have *loved* each other – for more than two years, Alexandrine. When will I be let in?'

The Comtesse blanched. 'But we let you into our hearts at once – when your Aunt Marjorie died.'

Polly again said nothing. She knew she didn't have to.

Alexandrine grew defensive. 'Some secrets simply cannot be shared.'

'Really?' said Polly 'Or do you mean they cannot be shared with me?'

Lana Mae's letter lay on the bed between them, unread.

'Perhaps I can break this habit,' said Polly, 'by telling you some of my own secrets, Alexandrine. Are you ready to hear them?'

The Comtesse's eyes widened. 'What secrets could you possibly have at your age?'

Polly looked hard at her. 'This one for a start: Aunt Marjorie gave me a loaded gun – just before she died. It was hidden in the green Hermès handbag.'

The Comtesse gasped.

'Someone stole it,' said Polly. 'Was it you?'

She had made Alexandrine speechless.

'Don't worry,' said Polly, 'I think it was Zita.'

The Comtesse was pale. Then she gave Polly a single nod of confirmation. 'Then it most likely was, darling.' She filled her lungs. 'It was hers in the first place. I took it from Zita on the train. I told her I'd thrown it from the window – but I lied. I gave it to Marjorie. She said she would throw it from the window herself. Now I know that she didn't either.'

Polly saw. The beginnings of trust were being built at last. 'Why did Zita have a gun at all?'

'To kill herself,' said Alexandrine.

Polly was horrified. 'But why?'

Yet trust proved incremental. The Comtesse's shutters came down.

Polly tried again. 'Here's another secret then: Tommy and I are colleagues in resistance . . .'

She'd expected a more forthright reaction but didn't get it. This startled Polly. 'Did you hear what I said?'

Alexandrine had. 'Are you in love with him?' she asked, simply.

Secrets proved tenacious on both sides. 'We are *colleagues*,' Polly stressed.

The Comtesse seemed to accept this. But whether this acceptance was for what Polly had claimed – or because Alexandrine had gleaned the truth in Polly's heart – Polly could not have known.

Alexandrine kissed her. 'Let's read Lana Mae's letter now,' she said.

They did so. Together.

Dear crazy old Comtesse

So, as cancers go, mine's got golden eggs with it, and they're all being served 'over easy'! And if that sounds sorta cryptic, honey, then I'm sorry for it, but I gotta speak a lotta hooey if I ever want this letter to get through to you, even with them swell gals from Sweden. But if you put your pretty head onto it you'll most likely guess why. Worked it out yet? Jesus, honey, you sure are dumb! Lemme give you one last hint: this type of cancer I got rhymes with 'cake', and if you wanna put an F at the front of it, then I ain't gonna stop you.

Phew.

Listen, honey, you mustn't worry about me. Camp Vittel sure ain't the Ritz, and you know what? I couldn't give a flying fig tree about that. My life's never been richer, and I don't mean in pennies, because, baby, I ain't got none of those left – another thing for the fig tree. I've reached the bottom of my rock pile now, honey, but Jesus, what I got for it. It's let me SAVE LIVES – lives that would have been yet more casualties of this lousy war otherwise. Just imagine that? If not for what I've done people would be dead right now. This makes me so happy.

I wouldn't mind betting you've been working on plans of your own in this area. Shoehorning all that wealth and position into something that gives something back. You've never been flashy, God knows, so whatever it is that you're up to I'm sure the volume's down low. Good. That's the best place to keep it. But if I'm somehow all wrong about you, baby, and you're <u>not</u> on the path to make great, then lemme say this: you should be. We Ritz Girls have long had it lovely, honey. Ours ain't a fair share. So, go spread yours around some. Use what you got to save others.

It was humiliation that fuelled me – it's got more zoom to it than gasoline. If I met that kraut Metzingen now, I'd thank him for it. But getting called a dumb whore in *l'Espadon* is nothing to what you've experienced at kraut hands. That's some mighty fuel of your own you've got there. I reckon you could fly to the moon on it.

I gotta go now, baby, I'm getting tired. I'm a better actress than old Zita these days, and sometimes I even fool myself. I get actual pains! I've still got my lucky pink bismuth.

I think about you Girls always, and all the fun we had – and all the fun we're <u>gonna</u> have just as soon as this lousy war's done itself.

And remember, no matter <u>what</u> happens, baby, put on your best frock for it.

Your ever-loving Lana Mae xxx

*

When Polly had gone, Alexandrine marvelled at her old friend's exquisite timing. If Alexandrine had harboured even a scrap of a doubt about what she had to do, Lana Mae would have obliterated it with her letter. Yet as it was, the big-hearted American had still planted fresh seeds. Alexandrine began to give thought as to what else she might do to resist once Suzette was safe. The only surprise about Polly's confession of resistance activity with Tommy was that she, Alexandrine, was not surprised by it.

It felt right. Why should either of the young people Alexandrine loved not seize opportunity to fight for France, too?

On the other side of the tissue-thin letter paper was an extra message, scrawled not by Lana Mae, whose handwriting was distinctive, but by someone else's hand. This handwriting was atrocious, near to illegible – like a doctor's prescription, Alexandrine thought. She stared at it a moment, trying to decipher it, only making out single words here and there, but no sentences. In the end she gave up, too distracted for such a trying task. Alexandrine placed the letter upon her bed again, with the intention of coming back to it when everything was done at the Marais. Her mind would be at peace by then, she knew. She'd have a much better chance of understanding what on earth the extra bit said.

Alexandrine opened her built-in wardrobe, where gown after gown met her gaze. It took her a while to decide on something appropriate to wear, with Tommy's insistence that she dress for a 'party' both guiding and confusing her, given how un-celebratory was the occasion.

When at last she settled upon the ideal dress it seemed ridiculous she'd not chosen it at once for its great significance.

Alexandrine decided upon a Lanvin gown.

From somewhere in the blacked-out Paris streets between the Marais and the 1st arrondissement they heard a clock tower strike two o'clock, and Alexandrine felt that little bit more reassured that they could actually make it to the *guichets* – the narrow-arched entryways that led to the courtyards of the Louvre – without anyone demanding to see their identification papers. Suzette was sandwiched between her and Tommy, her arms hooked through their own so that they could hurry her along and catch her if she stumbled. Suzette wore a coat thrown over a summer dress, even though it wasn't chilly; her yellow star had come loose at a corner, but they were all so used to seeing them – and in Suzette's case, wearing them now – that none of them thought to remove it.

Suzette had let them take her from her apartment without complaint only because she was half asleep. They'd given her little explanation. All that had registered with the old servant was that there was some imminent danger and, together, her would-be daughter and her would-be grandson had come all the way from the Ritz to spare her from it.

Yet now that Tommy had led them through a bewilderingly indirect route comprising back alleys and rear courtyards, entrances, and even staircases of apartment houses, the once familiar city had come to seem like some cunning nocturnal trap.

An alley had ejected them onto the rue de Rivoli near where it connected with the avenue de l'Opéra – the only major thoroughfares it had been impossible to avoid. Across the curfew-imposed emptiness stood the tantalising *guichets* of the Louvre. Suzette was now awake enough to know that she'd been taken far, and at a very early hour, on a dearth of information. They waited in the shadows until Tommy felt absolutely certain they could dash across the road to reach the gloomy safety of the arches without being seen.

'You're very dressed up,' said Suzette to Alexandrine, taking advantage of their momentary stillness to appraise what she was wearing.

Alexandrine retained her humour. 'Let me guess – I look like a tart.'

'I would never say such a cruel thing, Madame,' Suzette protested. 'You look very elegant.'

Alexandrine raised an eyebrow. 'Thank you, Suzette.'

'Have you been to some *soirée*?'

Alexandrine looked to Tommy and decided it was easier to lie. 'Yes.'

Suzette turned to Tommy now. 'You look handsome, too – I've never seen you in such shiny duds.'

Tommy, dressed in a showy blue serge suit, was a visual match to Alexandrine's beautiful Lanvin gown.

'You almost look like one of the krauts,' said Suzette, teasing him, 'splashing his phony exchange rate dough on the first thing he tries on at Printemps.' Then the accuracy of this observation hit her. 'That's *just* what you look like, little one,' she said, staring at him in incomprehension. 'That suit's so shiny you could pass for one of the bastards.'

He glanced uncomfortably at Alexandrine. 'Shhh, *Grand-mère*.'

'Why shhh? Where are we going?'

There was no movement to be seen along the inky black rue de Rivoli or up the deserted avenue de l'Opéra.

'We can chance it now – let's go,' said Tommy.

'Wait –'

But Alexandrine and Tommy had Suzette secured by the arms, and they pulled her into the street, across the two narrow lanes and safely into the archways of the Louvre. They paused again as Tommy peered into the great Louvre courtyard for any sign of Wehrmacht patrols. As he'd predicted, there were none.

'We'll stick to the sides of the courtyard where the shadows are deepest,' he told them, pointing at where he meant, 'and make our way around to the opposite *guichets*.'

'Wait,' said Suzette, panting. 'I need to get my breath.'

'Of course, darling,' said Alexandrine. 'You take as long as you need.'

The old woman took longer. 'Now tell me where we're going,' she demanded, releasing herself from their hold.

'We told you, *Grand-mère*. The Latin Quarter,' said Tommy.

'You told me nothing at all.'

'Yes, we did – there's danger if you stay in the Marais. We're taking you to safety with a friend.'

'Every night's a danger,' said Suzette, 'what makes this one any different that I can't spend it tucked up inside my own bed?'

They had already decided between them not to tell her what they'd learned of the imminent round-up until she was hidden.

'Please trust us, darling,' said Alexandrine. 'We wouldn't be going to this trouble just to make a joke.'

But Suzette was too canny. 'I can tell you're not giving me the whole story, because I'm not a fucking fool. So, I'll ask you again, Madame: what makes tonight different?'

'Please keep your voice low, *Grand-mère*,' Tommy pleaded. 'Someone will hear us before we can make it to the Seine.'

The rumble of approaching vehicles frightened all three of them.

They threw their backs against the narrow passage walls, while the glow of approaching headlights threw a dull illumination into the reaches of the archway. They watched in shared anxiety as the dim blue light licked its way along the walls, while the vehicles drew closer along the rue de Rivoli, headed east towards the Marais. Then the first of the vehicles passed: a familiar green and cream Paris bus.

'Cops,' said Suzette, in amazement, 'dozens of 'em, did you see inside? They looked like they were going off on their summer holidays.'

A second bus passed, and Alexandrine saw a gendarme she even recognised: the fleshy face of Teissier, unmistakable even in shadowy profile through the bus window. A third and a fourth bus passed; each one filled with policemen, and not only those from the city gendarmerie, but young men wearing varying *kapi* on their heads signifying rural constabularies.

'It doesn't make sense,' said Suzette, 'half of them are country boys. What are they doing bussing them all here?'

350

More buses followed, but these became emptier, until the final vehicles had no one inside at all save the drivers. A chill fell over the three of them, hidden in the archway, as the last bus disappeared east.

Suzette turned to them, angry. 'You *know* what those cop buses are about, don't you? And that's why we're here.'

'Suzette,' Alexandrine began.

'Don't fob me off because you think I'm so old – tell me what's going on right now if you want me to go one step more.'

Alexandrine looked helplessly at Tommy. She made an attempt. 'I received an anonymous note.'

Tommy stepped in. 'The cops – the krauts are using them to conduct a round-up.'

'A round-up of what?' But Suzette knew the answer before she'd finished asking the question. She went weak in her legs. 'Oh God.'

'Suzette!' Alexandrine had to steady her in her arms.

The sound of two sets of feet rapidly nearing from the rue de Rivoli sent fresh alarm through them. Tommy looked desperately into the vast courtyard, knowing they couldn't make a run for it without giving themselves away. He gestured for them to press themselves tight against the passage walls again.

Two figures appeared at the archway entrance, silhouetted against the night sky. They stopped, peering in. Alexandrine, Tommy and Suzette held their respective breaths. One of the new arrivals was slim, not especially tall; the other was unmistakably a young child. Clearly believing they were safely unobserved, the two newcomers came into the passage, breathing hard with fear and exertion.

Suzette gasped, recognising them in the gloom.

The two nearly cried out.

Suzette stepped forward. 'Don't be scared, Anaïs, it's only me – old Suzette from the Marais – don't you recognise my wrinkly face?'

They did. Then they gaped at Alexandrine in her beautiful gown.

'Madame Suzette?' said the older of the two, Anaïs, a girl in her early teens, who was dressed in what seemed to be a makeshift uniform.

'Yes, that's right.' Suzette looked to the younger child. 'And I know you, too, don't I? It's little Vidette.' She turned to Alexandrine. 'She's Alma's grandchild. Her mother died of consumption.'

'Alma?'

'Alma from the queues – you gave her that old Hermès scarf, remember?'

Alexandrine did remember. Then she realised that the tiny girl was wearing the item at her throat.

'What are you doing here so late?' Suzette asked the older girl. And to the little one she asked, 'Does your granny know you're out?'

'Granny woke me up and told me to go with Anaïs,' said Vidette. 'She wanted me to have her nice scarf.'

Tommy had recognised the teenager's tatty uniform. 'You're with the *Eclaireurs Israelites*,' he told her, before explaining for Alexandrine's benefit, 'they're the Jewish boy scouts.'

'I know what they are,' said Alexandrine.

'Girl scouts, too,' Anaïs corrected him. She looked wary. 'What are *you* doing out so late, Madame Suzette?'

Suzette looked askance at Tommy. 'My grandson was about to tell me that, sweetheart.' She looked to the children again. 'He's a good Jewish boy, despite him looking like a kraut – we can trust him, girls.'

Anaïs smiled with relief at Tommy. 'I'm taking Vidette to the Left Bank to hide her, Monsieur. Are you doing the same with your *grand-mère*?'

'Yes,' Tommy told her, after a pause.

'Hide Vidette from what?' asked Suzette.

'From what's going to happen tonight,' said Anaïs. 'We received a tip-off at our *Eclaireurs* troupe. So, each of us went in to the Marais to try to save someone.' She saw Alexandrine's fearful look. 'Don't worry, Madame. Our troupe is from Mont-parnasse. It's not being targeted tonight. That's why we're taking the risk.'

When Alexandrine could speak, her voice was tight with emotion. 'You're a very good girl . . .'

Anaïs shrugged this off. 'Screw the cops. They've betrayed our France.'

No one disagreed.

'*What* is going to happen tonight?' Suzette asked, getting terser now.

Anaïs looked to Tommy.

'I'm asking *you*, sweetheart,' said Suzette, 'I don't think my grandson is too happy to tell me.'

It was clear that Anaïs wasn't sure of who she risked upsetting by answering. 'The cops are going to round up everyone in the Marais, Madame.'

Suzette was ashen. 'Everyone?'

'Everyone who's a Jew. That's what the tip-off told us.'

Suzette turned accusingly to Alexandrine. 'And that's what your "tip-off" told *you*, was it, Madame?'

Alexandrine could only lower her eyes.

'And even little kids will be caught in this round-up?' Suzette asked.

Anaïs's silence was the answer.

Alexandrine watched as Suzette battled her panic. 'But what will they do with all the Jews?'

Alexandrine stepped forward. 'They'll be taken to the Vélodrome d'Hiver.'

'And then what?' Suzette demanded.

'And then to Poland . . .'

Suzette stared at her uncomprehendingly. Then Alexandrine saw a change come over her face. The old servant looked to the children again. 'So, who's with Granny Alma now, sweetheart?' she asked Vidette, gently.

The little girl was distressed. 'She's all alone, Madame. She wouldn't come with us.'

Suzette nodded. She looked to Tommy. 'My grandson will take you where you need to go,' she told the children. 'He knows what he's doing – I don't know *how* he knows but he knows. He'll get you there safe. I promise.' She glared at Tommy. 'He promises, too, don't you, little one?'

Tommy objected. '*Grand-mère –*'

'*Don't* you, little one? Say it.'

Tommy was made shamefaced. 'Of course, I will.'

'Good.' Suzette wiped a stray tear from her cheek. 'My daughter will go with you, too, girls.' She now looked to Alexandrine. 'Make sure you listen to her. She's a very good Jewess, my daughter – the best I've ever loved.'

Alexandrine held Suzette's eyes with hers.

'You'll all get there safe together, you'll see,' Suzette said, her voice breaking.

'But what about you, Madame?' asked Vidette, worried.

The old servant was resolute. 'You told me Granny Alma's got no one to talk with. Well, I can't be having that.'

Alarm rang for Alexandrine. 'Suzette, no –'

She turned on her. 'You think I could live with myself otherwise?'

Alexandrine saw what was coming. 'Darling, *please –*'

'You think I could still get up in the morning? You think I could hold my fucking head up?' She turned to the children, apologetically. 'Forgive my bad language, girls.'

Tommy tried to take hold of her hands.

'Leave off,' Suzette spat at him. 'Try to make me come with you and I'll jump in the Seine.'

He was desperate. '*Grand-mère*, please – we must save you.'

She pressed her palms to his face, tender. 'You already saved me the day you were born.'

Alexandrine saw how close this brought Tommy to breaking down.

Suzette smoothed the yellow star that was still pinned to her coat. 'It's not a bad night for a wander, all up.' She walked unsteadily up the passage towards the rue de Rivoli.

'Suzette!' Alexandrine screamed out at her.

The old woman stopped, shocked by the noise, silhouetted in the archway. She waited.

Alexandrine placed a hand at Tommy's back as he hid his face against the wall. 'Darling, listen.'

'They'll catch her. They'll catch her.'

'You don't know that. And these children need you.'

'I can't let her go. *I can't.*'

'Of course, you can – and you will,' she told him. She smiled at the wide-eyed girls. 'Anaïs and Vidette are the future now.'

She waited as Tommy pulled himself together.

'Good.' She kissed him on the cheek. 'Good boy.' She looked into his face for a moment. 'There's something I'd like you to do for me, darling. There's something I'd like you to tell Polly.'

He looked up at her. 'Polly?'

'You know who I mean – Mademoiselle Hartford. You've spoken to her before, haven't you?'

She was testing what she already knew. Tommy nodded, guarded. 'You can't tell her yourself?'

She shook her head. 'Tell her only when you feel she can cope with it.'

'When I feel?'

Alexandrine elaborated. 'Use your good sense. Don't tell her at once. You'll know when the time's right.'

'But what is it?'

She took a long breath. 'There was a letter,' she said, 'from her late aunt. I want you to tell Polly I wrote it.'

Tommy rightly looked lost. 'What letter?'

'It doesn't matter. Polly will know. It will devastate her, but she has to hear it. Just tell her it was me and that I was sorrier for doing it than she will ever understand.'

Alexandrine had to steady herself, feeling suddenly lighter as a burden had lifted. 'And also add this,' she said, 'Polly never needed any letter at all – from Marjorie, from me, from any of us. Her life is her own and she's living it quite beautifully. Her aunt would be very proud of her.'

Tommy stared at her in dismay. 'But we have to go.'

Alexandrine fiddled at the clasp of her handbag. 'Indeed.' She looked to where Suzette had remained at the passage entrance, listening. 'You mustn't worry about your *grand-mère*, darling. I will take care of her tonight.' She withdrew the package from her handbag, wrapped in its paper from Lanvin.

He read her intention. 'Are you going to go back there with her?'

Alexandrine nodded. She started tearing the paper off. 'You heard what she said. I don't much fancy a dip in the Seine. I'll take her to Alma's. Vidette's granny is very good company.'

He stared at her, stunned. 'But Alexandrine . . . the round-up.'

'It's all right.' She revealed her unpaid-for purchase from Lanvin: an haute couture star, made from appliqued silk in saffron yellow; the word '*Juif*' beautifully embroidered in a graceful black copperplate, the painstaking work of Madame Lanvin's own hand. It came with a pretty gold pin, which Alexandrine used now to attach the star to her gown between her breast and her shoulder. 'There,' she said, patting it neatly in place. 'Now *I* can hold my head up with her.'

Tommy could only gape as he saw what was happening.

Alexandrine smiled at the children. 'Tommy here is very handsome and brave – he's done courageous things for the sake of France, and he's going to do more, and more even still, until one day, girls, thanks to his courage – and the courage of others like *you* – France will be ours again, and it will be France as it should be.'

'Oh, Alexandrine . . .' Tommy whispered to her, helplessly.

She pressed a finger to his lips. 'We'll be all right.'

She turned back to the children. 'Now, should you ever be frightened, girls, should you ever find yourselves feeling scared and alone – don't be. Just think of Tommy, think of his courage, and let him inspire you. As he inspires me.'

In her tattered scout's uniform, Anaïs looked up at Alexandrine with awe. 'Is Tommy your son, Madame?'

Alexandrine placed her hand at Tommy's cheek. 'Yes, darling, he is. And perhaps tonight I'll be something like a mother to him.' She leaned in to kiss him again. 'We'll all meet again, Tommy,' she whispered. 'I *know* it.'

With that she moved swiftly to Suzette at the rue de Rivoli. The old woman turned to look at Tommy one last time with her eyes shining. 'We love you, little one,' she called to him.

Then the two Jewish women were gone.

Unable to sleep with her stolen knowledge of what had been planned for the Marais, Zita found herself wandering the corridors of the slumbering hotel. She passed Polly's suite and saw from the thin band of light that glowed from beneath the door that she was not the only one awake. She gently tapped and Polly opened and invited Zita inside. Neither discussed the reasons for their insomnia. Then another tap came at the door while they sat, and Polly reacted with a mixture of excitement and dread.

Zita knew all the signs: Polly had a lover. It was he who kept her awake. Perhaps it *was* Jürgen, despite Alexandrine's conviction that it was not. The perverse part of Zita hoped that the Comtesse was wrong. If Polly was romantically entangled with a handsome kraut, then perhaps Zita's own filthy compromise wouldn't seem quite so wrong.

'Are you going to answer the door, puss?'

Polly seemed frozen with indecision.

Zita guessed the reason for her state. If she let her lover inside, then Zita would see him, and a secret affair would be secret no more. Yet if she left him standing outside in the corridor, he'd likely go away, and whatever it was that he'd come here to tell Polly would be gone, too, unsaid.

'Let me run into the bathroom,' Zita whispered to her, smiling. 'I'll cover my ears while he says what he wants to say, and then you can tell him to come back in five minutes while you make yourself lovelier – and that'll give me time to run away.'

Polly looked exposed. 'But – but I don't know who it is out there.'

Zita shook her head at her, indulgently. 'Cling to that if you want to, but I think you should stop wasting time.' She winked at Polly as she went into the bathroom, pulling the door shut behind her.

For a moment, Zita did indeed make a show of covering her ears – a show for her own benefit – before burning curiosity got the better of her and she uncovered them. Zita perched on the lavvy for some minutes as she heard the sound of the door to the hallway opening and someone being let inside. There was a low murmur of voices, one of them Polly's and the other undeniably male. Zita craned to hear if she recognised Jürgen's baritone, but the sounds were too indistinct to make out from where she sat, until suddenly they weren't. Zita realised that Polly was weeping.

Zita stood up alarmed. She crept to the door and tried to listen, until she felt too ashamed and went back to the lavvy again. When this only proved to be more tormenting, Zita steeled herself.

She tapped on the inside of the bathroom door. 'What's going on out there, Polly?' she called out. 'Are you in trouble?'

Zita took a deep breath during the abrupt pause that followed and then carefully opened the door. The identity of Polly's visitor was both wholly unexpected and completely understandable: it was Comte Eduarde's bastard son. He was seated on Polly's bed in an attitude of urgency. Zita gazed approvingly and thought of how easy it must have been for Polly to fall for someone with hair like his; Zita would have done so, too, had she been younger.

And then she thought of Hans and remembered that long ago she already had.

'Hullo Tommy,' said Zita. She gave him a comic look, hoping the ice might break between them. 'So, I guess those phony rumours about you and old Blanche fooled no one?'

He gaped at her and stood up.

'*Tommy,*' Polly implored him, 'we can *trust* Zita. She knows who you are – Alexandrine tells her everything.'

He shook his head in bewilderment. 'We can't trust anyone.'

'We *can,*' Polly insisted, 'we have to now.' And then she added, 'Zita loves them both, too.'

Certainty flooded Zita that something was indeed very wrong between them – far more than a lover's tiff.

'I know what you're thinking about Tommy and me,' Polly whispered to her. 'But it's not what you think.'

'What is it then?'

Tommy's face fell with indescribable grief.

Zita knew then, without knowing anything of how Tommy was part of it, that the crisis involved the horrific plans for the Marais Jews, and the gutless anonymous letter she'd left in Alexandrine's bag to warn her of it. These things had been bought with her spy whore's wages, earned with her love for Metzingen.

Zita went very still. 'What has happened, puss?'

Tommy looked to Polly.

'We can trust her,' Polly said again.

So, Tommy told Zita everything.

Afterwards, as Zita wept there with both of them, promising she'd protect them, promising she'd never betray what she'd learned, her mind travelled straight to the powder, untouched for too long while she'd diverted herself digging for useless secrets.

Those secrets had claimed her friends – friends that were good as dead now, like she was.

Polly's emotion receded, Tommy's guilt-ridden grief. All that mattered now to Zita was the powder, and she told herself that as soon as she could she would embrace it again with all the blinkered fervour with which one embraced an abuser.

Much later, when the door to Alexandrine's suite was opened for her by Claude, Polly found the letter from Lana Mae where the Comtesse had left it on her bed.

When Polly turned the paper over and saw the additional message on the back, she was confused by it; not only because it was practically illegible, but because Lana Mae hadn't written it. Why would someone else put an addendum to Lana Mae's letter?

She showed it to Claude, who, to Polly's surprise, recognised the handwriting at once. 'That's Doctor Mandel,' he said.

'You can read what it says?' Polly asked him.

Familiar with the doctor's near-indecipherability, Claude could. With Polly seated beside him on the bed, they picked through what had been written there together.

Afterwards, when all that Doctor Mandel had told them was clear, Polly found she had no tears left. She knew she should have cried at what the message revealed – and so badly she wanted to – but nothing came. It would have been easy, she thought, when trying to explain this reaction to Tommy, to say that she had simply gone numb – but that would be untrue. Numbness implied that she had felt nothing, when really it was as if she felt *everything*, every emotion there was, and had felt it for everyone who had been crushed by this war. Yet this too seemed nonsensical when put into words, so in the end, once Alexandrine's suite had been locked again and Polly went up to see Tommy in his room, what she told him was far simpler.

Doctor Mandel's message had made her feel certain that the path they had chosen was true.

Comtesse Alexandrine. It is with the very deepest regret that I must inform you of the death of your friend, Mrs Lana Mae

Huckstepp – an extraordinary lady who, over the course of the months that we shared in internment, I had come to love utterly. So utterly, in fact, did I love Lana Mae, that I asked her to marry me. To my joy she accepted. When she went to her rest, she went as my wife, Mrs Mandel.

Lana Mae died of uterine cancer. She experienced great difficulty in accepting the truth of her illness, and the reason for this, I believe, was because lately her life had acquired rich purpose. Where once she'd been selfish, she was driven to serve. Lana Mae wanted those who most cared for her to believe that her illness wasn't real – that it was somehow put on, an elaborate theatre that would allow her to sell her last jewels to the Occupiers. She did sell her jewels, and many lives in Vittel benefited from the medical supplies she bought with the proceeds. But Lana Mae's cancer took her from us.

Among those she spoke about fondly in her final hours were yourself, my dear Comtesse, and Zita, her great film star friend, and young Polly Hartford. At the very end, Lana Mae's last lucid words were for the girl. I fear they'll mean as little to you as they did to me but they may well mean more to Polly, so here they are:

'Tell Polly I guessed what she's up to with Jürgen – and tell her I think it's swell.'

Please give my own regards to the girl. Until we meet again, Comtesse, I am your servant.

Doctor Paul Mandel

14

1 August 1942

O ver the happy run of months during which Polly had given him signs she was willing to be formally courted, Jürgen had experienced something like an epiphany. It was not of the religious sort, for he had no religion, blind faith in the Führer having replaced his once blinder faith in God. Nor was it the epiphany of love, even though Jürgen *was* very deeply in love with Polly, in a way he'd not known with any other girl that he'd been with before. Rather, Jürgen's epiphany was one that had come as a slow dawning of truth. He still had faith in the Führer but it was his faith in those who were subordinate to the Führer that had crumbled to dust. It had become impossible for Jürgen to work in proximity to a degenerate like Göring without seeing such a man for what he was. In a similar way, it had grown unendurable to see the other great princes of National Socialism in the soft pink light the Ritz cast upon them. Heinrich Himmler; Reinhard Heydrich; Adolf Eichmann; Martin Bormann, the Führer's secretary. And with this enlightenment had grown a nagging fear deep in Jürgen's conscience that he was quite unable to turn off.

It was only when talking with Polly that he found a semblance of peace; a return to the comfort of certainty that had once seemed unbreakable. Jürgen's new certainty was a simpler one: the conviction of love. When spending an hour with Polly, an untouched girl, Jürgen's mind often wandered to a time he believed could not be far off, a future when he and Polly shared domesticity. Love gave Jürgen the certainty that this bliss would come soon.

These thoughts were uppermost in his mind as he wandered the exhibition hall of the Musée de l'Orangerie, ostensibly looking at the sculptural supermen created by Breker, but really looking only for Polly. He had something for her in his jacket; something precious. They had arranged to meet – the Ritz being difficult for the conducting of love affairs that were anything other than lust trysts – and they had chosen the Breker exhibition because, while it was no less public, it was unarguably blameless. He had seen it four times; the first at the opening night *soirée* when the crush of sycophants had blocked out the art. He had returned when the crowds were less and was startled to find the experience of viewing the sculptures akin to catching himself in the mirror when stepping out of a bath. Breker's subjects were Aryan titans; specimens of physical perfection. Jürgen saw himself in all of them and could just as well have been a model for Breker, so close was the resemblance, he thought. Indeed, if Polly had been a lesser girl, of the sort he had known in abundance before her, Jürgen might have claimed that he *was* the model, just to boost himself that little bit more in her eyes. He knew he could never tell such a bald lie to Polly, of course, and yet the choice of the Breker exhibition for their rendezvous had still seemed ideal for the reflected appeal the sculptures might cast upon him. Breker's supermen were nudes. Perhaps, Jürgen hoped, the sight of his marble doubles would instil desire in Polly. He and she had been intimate for months but their relationship was not at all sexual. Polly's chasteness was nourishing, his love for her thrived in its soil. Yet still he was a man of needs.

The arrest of the Comtesse and her servant in the Marais round-up had upset Polly, coming as it had barely six months after the internment of Frau Huckstepp. Lest Polly labour under the falsehood that the Wehrmacht had been part of it, Jürgen had been at pains to make clear that the entire initiative had been that of the French Government – the gendarmerie had enforced it, after all. Polly had accepted this without conflict, which had been a great relief for Jürgen. He only wished that the rest of the city might have spared the Occupiers blame as well. The screams of Jewish children being shoved onto the green and cream buses before dawn had pulled non-Jews from their beds to stare down from their windows in horror. A change had come over Paris as a consequence. No longer did the city feel like a vacation spot to Jürgen's compatriots. Once, their shows of politeness, their sharp, crisp uniforms, their blond and blue-eyed sex appeal had made for an easy time of it when out on the streets. Now, this was markedly less so. In response to new provocations from Parisians the authorities had upped reprisals.

He saw Polly now among the sculptures and a smile came instantly to him. 'Polly.'

'Hello Günther.' She was dressed beautifully; her smile matched his own. 'You wore your uniform for me.'

He was bashful; a boy. 'Of course. You asked me to.' She was inspecting every inch of him in it. He made himself stand taller next to the towering nudes. 'I have a new suit I had thought I would wear, though,' he said, 'bought from Printemps.' He knew she liked shops. 'You would appreciate it.'

'Is it shiny?'

Was she teasing him? 'I suppose it is. It is still very new.'

'I'm sure it's very nice but I do like your Wehrmacht uniform best. That's why I hoped you would wear it for me.'

'Then how could I not?' His heart was soaring. She slipped her arm through his, mindful of the holstered pistol at his side.

They proceeded to look at the sculptures in companionable silence; the hall full of stark naked Aryans.

'That one looks like you, Günther.'

He blushed scarlet as if *he* was the virgin.

'He really does. He has your face.'

'We Germans all look the same,' he joked. Unconsciously, he assessed the sculpture's bunched genitals before flicking his eyes to hers. She was assessing them, too. His scarlet cheeks went crimson. He moved her on, ever conscious of the precious item he carried inside his jacket. 'There is something I should like to talk to you about tonight, Polly.'

'That's funny,' said Polly, 'there's something I should like to talk about with you, too.'

'Oh, really?'

'Yes.'

A moment's pause. 'There is no hurry for it, of course. We are looking at the sculptures.'

'I have a confession, Günther.'

A moment's alarm. 'What is it?'

'I have seen them before.'

He chuckled. 'So have I. Three times at least already, perhaps four.'

'I certainly like them,' said Polly, 'especially the one that looks so much like you.'

He resisted the near-overpowering urge to turn back to check it again.

'It is such a nice evening outside,' said Polly, 'why don't we walk by the Seine for a while instead?'

He thought of the nocturnal privacy afforded by the Right Bank quays. In the daytime they were choked with sunbathers; by night they were alluringly still. 'That would be nice,' he said.

Her arm still in his, they left the gallery together and strolled down a path in the Tuileries gardens. The summer air was heavy and scented. It was already past dusk and the last of the birds were reaching their symphony crescendo in the plane trees. 'I hope I never leave Paris,' he told her, spontaneously.

She turned in surprise. 'But don't you miss the Fatherland?'

He was losing his head to her, but how else should one be with the love of one's life except honest? 'Not so much lately, no.'

She smiled. 'But your family in Saxony?'

There'd never been love there, only land. 'I doubt they miss me.'

'Oh, Günther, I'm sure they do.'

He didn't want her troubling herself with it. 'They say Paris ruins you forever once you've seen it. So, what does it do once you've lived in it then?' he wondered.

'It transforms you,' said Polly, sagely.

'Exactly,' said Jürgen. 'This is why I wish never to leave.'

They had reached the road at the riverside and could see the steps by the Pont Royal that led down. 'Let's take those to go to the lower quay,' suggested Polly, 'right by the water, it'll be lovely.'

Jürgen felt his heart quicken. 'All right then.'

They crossed the carless road and strolled along the pavement that led to the Pont. Jürgen felt Polly's fingers press his bicep, the touch unaccountably erotic. They passed another German on the flagstones; a slim-hipped youngster with a shock of blond hair and a blue serge suit just like the one Jürgen had purchased from Printemps. It too was shiny.

'I think we Germans might lack imagination,' he joked.

'Hmm?'

She hadn't seen it. He patted her hand.

They reached the Pont Royal. Down the flight of stone steps lay the lower quay, so inviting in the last light of dusk. The Seine gently lapped at the edge. There seemed to be few other strollers out.

They began to descend. A figure stirred. A girl was slumped on the stairs. As they passed her, Jürgen saw she had a begging bowl before her; the girl was sightless. Recognition stirred. 'I know that kid.'

'Who?'

'The blind girl – she lives at the Ritz.'

They had passed her by now and so Polly had to turn to look. 'No, she doesn't.'

'Are you sure? She looks like her.'

'But how would she get all the way here when she can't even see?'

He had no answer to that question, and within a second had forgotten it anyway.

They reached the lower quay. The night air was cooler, trees rustled overhead. 'And has Paris transformed you?' Polly asked.

'Ah.' Where to begin on this count, he thought.

'I suppose that's a yes?'

He stopped now. Took both her hands inside his. The gift he had in his jacket pocket was begging to make itself known. 'Polly . . .' he started.

'Describe it to me, Günther?'

'What, my love?' He had called her that without even thinking.

She didn't flinch. 'Your Paris transformation – what has changed about you in the two years that you've lived here?'

His thoughts had become scattered. He wanted to talk about other things. 'Let me see . . .'

'Do you believe still?'

'Believe what?'

Her eyes raked him. 'In what you're supposed to believe as a German?'

She'd thrown him. He saw flashes of his masters at the Ritz; fat pansy Göring the transvestite with his bowl full of jewels and his pupils like pinpricks with dope. Jürgen tried to blink these pictures away, tried to think of the Führer, so remote, so unknowable – it was better not to know; ignorance meant stainlessness in the end. 'Of course, I do, my love – why would I not believe?'

'Because of the Jews?' she wondered.

There was movement on the steps, but he was blind to it, caught in a conversation he'd not wanted. He reached into his uniform jacket. 'Polly, I want to tell you something – *ask* you something, really.'

'I know. And I want to tell you something, too, Günther.'

His hand gripped the little box, fingering the hinge of the lid. 'All right. But who should go first?'

She glanced where his hand bulged expectantly in his jacket. 'I will,' she told him. 'It won't take very long. You see, this is for Alexandrine.'

He blinked. 'What is?'

'And Suzette. It's for both of them, Günther. It's for all of them, all the Jews.'

He was confused. 'What is, Polly? What are you talking about?'

The sudden scuffle of feet on the quay stones made him glance behind just as he received the first hammer blow. He didn't feel pain, only annoyance that someone had interrupted the interlude. With the second blow to his temple he had a déjà vu vision; his assailant was the same shock-haired German in shiny blue serge. The third and fourth blows brought pain to him now, and the awakening of instinct; he went to reach for the Luger at his side, but his trigger hand was still thrust inside his jacket, gripping at the box. Instinct clashed with instinct until another blow came, then a fresh assault: a breath-stopping punch to his groin. He looked down to see that it was not a punch, but a knife wound; the blind girl from the steps had stabbed at him.

Jürgen fell to the ground, an artery severed. More hammer blows rained upon him. 'Stop –' he tried to tell his fellow German.

Polly slipped the gun from his holster; the ammunition magazines.

'Stop it, my love.'

The last blow took the light from his eyes.

It was only as they pushed his body into the river – Polly with Tommy and Odile – that Jürgen's trigger hand came free from his jacket. The little Cartier box that he clutched in his fingers had opened in the violence.

Lana Mae's emerald, now set into a ring, glittered for a moment on the surface of the Seine, before it sank, disappearing, never to be given in love.

PART FOUR

Interception

15

21 July 1944

Polly's discipline of maintaining resistance had almost taken on a meditative quality in the two years that had passed since she and her friends had killed Jürgen. The Occupation had entered its fifth year. Polly had been a girl of sixteen when she'd began fighting back, and now she was twenty, her girlhood gone. She had acquired an air of circumspection to her bearing – a steady heart and an ordered mind. As Polly's commitment to resistance had deepened, so had the need to disguise it.

And so, Polly experienced victories as if she'd gleaned them from a newspaper, stripped of emotion, scattered among seemingly inconsequential things. Among these trivial triumphs was the attack where grenades had been tossed inside a hotel entrance in the German-favoured 9th arrondissement. There was a similar incident at the exclusively German restaurant at the Porte d'Asnières. There was the grenade that was thrown at a Wehrmacht patrol crossing the Boulevard de Courcelles – a privately gratifying act for being close to the house of the late Comte. Then there were the derailments of trains leaving Gare de l'Est on the horrific ride east to Poland.

With every resistance victory, Polly thought of Lana Mae and Alexandrine. Her private thoughts took on the tone of a chatty letter to them; a letter never to be sent. Of Alexandrine's fate, Polly knew nothing, which was both agonising and energising. So much of what Polly did in resistance was fuelled by her rage and grief for the missing Comtesse.

Polly knew her guardians would have grimly enjoyed dissecting the details of daily life in Paris now. There was the chronic soap shortage, for instance, that had made riding on the Metro in the warmer months beyond endurable. There was the fashion of dressing shabbily which had become chic in some circles. There was the mania for women wearing trousers, not just because it made cycling easier, but because these clothes so often belonged to men who had been killed or made prisoner. There was the French Government's response to this trend – condemnations of the trouser-wearers for their moral turpitude – which was universally, hilariously, ignored.

It was with her lost guardians ever in mind that Polly observed 'dry' Paris three days every week, when the cafés could not serve alcohol. The city was without gas; electricity was unreliable. People cooked as best they could over ten-gallon cans welded together, yet everyone was constantly hungry. Diets were supplemented by rutabaga, a variety of turnip once thought fit only for cattle. Each day's new dawn brought a cacophony of rooster crows to the city; people tended their undeclared poultry in back alleys, rooftops, garrets and broom closets. Others stole outside before sunrise to chop protected blades of grass from the few remaining parks for the rabbits they raised in their bathtubs.

With both her lost guardians uppermost in her thoughts, Polly embraced with particular passion the year's greatest publishing sensation, *Autant en emporte le vent*, a translated American novel, originally titled *Gone with the Wind*. There'd been an obsession for this book among the women of Paris. Polly had read and re-read it and had cried at it often. The spirited heroine's hardships in another, far-off war in the past, somehow made the sufferings experienced by women in this one even more poignant.

The Belgian griffons stirred only seconds before Mimi did: the air raid sirens had started; a nightly event in Paris now that the tide of the war had seemingly turned against Hitler. Mimi lifted her head from her pillow and fumbled for her spectacles in order to glance at her trusted Swiss wall clock. It was just on 02.15. The Allies had become as punctual as the Occupiers. Mimi patted the heads of her griffons and told them to stay at her heels. She slipped out of her bed, found her mules easily on the rug where she'd left them, before wrapping herself in her old peignoir. She moved to the entrance of her suite without pause, opening the doors to let herself and the dogs into the corridor, and pulling the doors softly shut behind her.

Taking care to stick to the carpeted parts of the stairs, through fear of the noise she might make on the boards, Mimi descended the two flights to the lobby. The area was deserted: the Cambon bar closed; *l'Espadon* long done for the evening. Satisfied, Mimi continued her descent to the basement level, all the way to the kitchens. The sirens cried on in the streets, unignorable even below ground. Mimi's memory for every last detail of the Ritz was unrivalled; she picked her way through the eccentric maze of storerooms, cellars and hallways, until she reached the Vendôme side of the hotel and entered the basement kitchen there.

The kitchen was wrapped in darkness. Yet Mimi went smoothly to the wall box that housed the electrical switches and waited, holding her breath for a moment, while she muttered a simple prayer. The shriek of the sirens was joined by the distant rumble of aircraft; the Allied bombers were now very near. Mimi knew exactly which switch did what, and so she flicked the one she needed.

Outside, in the Place Vendôme, the beautiful seventeenth-century façade of the world-famous Hôtel Ritz was abruptly floodlit: the perfect means for the Allied planes overhead to orient themselves above darkened Paris and find their intended targets. Mimi had no fear at all that the Ritz might be bombed; everyone knew that the planes sought German military facilities, far from the Place Vendôme, somewhere out by the railway yards in the suburbs. No one in central Paris even bothered with air raid shelters these days, preferring to put pillows over their heads and sleep through the attacks.

Mimi left the lights on for as long as her nerves held. Tonight, this was exactly five minutes before she flicked them off; long enough for the Allied planes to fly past overhead; long enough for Mimi to hear the first of their bombs detonate.

When Mimi traced her way back through the basement rooms, the little griffons paused at the closed door to a storeroom, sniffing at the threshold.

'What's there, girls? What's so interesting?'

She tried the door handle: locked.

'There's nothing, no one – let's go back to our bed.'

Mimi was well prepared with an explanation should she have actually encountered someone. The dogs needed to relieve themselves, she would have claimed, but the street was too dangerous; and so, she had placed a litter box for this purpose below stairs. She had even trained the dogs to use it, should proof be required.

When the griffons and their mistress had begun their ascent of the Cambon stairs, the storeroom door was unlocked from inside. Metzingen stepped out, only partly satisfied. The mystery of who was floodlighting the façade had been answered; the basement would have sentries from now on. But the answer brought no good solution. It wouldn't do to see the elderly, celebrated owner of the Hôtel Ritz given over to the Gestapo; such a move might risk making a martyr of the woman, and Paris was already too prone to uniting behind such figures as it was. Better, thought

Metzingen, to gift the Gestapo with someone else from the Ritz – someone already suspected for their clandestine activities, and only tolerated in the hope that continued surveillance might reveal greater things.

Hans badly missed Jürgen at moments like this. The young Hauptmann would have known who best to choose, and what's more he would have organised it. Metzingen would have reaped the rewards while his hands were left unsoiled. But Jürgen was dead, another casualty of war.

Hans felt the familiar itch in his nose – his first for the morning. Or was it still night?

When he reached the Imperial Suite, and before he picked up the telephone, he snorted a line of what he thought of these days as salvation. Then he dialled the Ritz lobby.

'Put me through to Gestapo Headquarters,' he told the operator.

He waited, salvation coursing through his veins, making him feel superhuman.

His call was patched through. 'This is Oberstleutnant Hans Metzingen at the Hôtel Ritz,' he told the voice at the other end. 'I have uncovered a resistance operative – yes, another one.' A trickle of blood left his nostril, touching the top of his lip. Hans wiped it away. 'This one is a girl – a child, practically.'

He waited for the Gestapo man to respond with interest, and when this didn't come, he attempted to sweeten it. 'But you'll be amazed by this one,' he promised, 'the sorry little bitch is sightless . . .'

The sunny summer's day was divine – pleasingly warm without any humidity – and Polly was happy to walk all the way to the Left Bank. She left the Ritz beaming, as if she hadn't a worry in the world, so apparently frivolous was she, with her Hermès handbag swinging just so at her elbow, and a brand-new copy of *Autant en emporte le vent* nestled in the crook of her arm. She was seemingly just one of so many beautifully dressed BOFs and German officers' girlfriends, who continued to pop in and out of the luxury shops around her as if the Allied forces weren't advancing at all. She kept heading east until the ruined Tour Saint-Jacques loomed through the trees, which was when she turned right onto the Boulevard du Palais. This route took her across the Seine and onto the Île de la Cité, where she came to a halt outside the Police Headquarters. She had no intention of going in, she merely wished to move beyond it, but of course there was a queue at the Wehrmacht sentry box first, as she'd known there would be. Polly took her identification papers from her handbag in readiness as she joined the long line.

She became aware of someone making disparaging tongue clicks. Polly glanced behind her and saw a dark-haired girl, younger than herself, condemning her with a glare.

'Something wrong, Mademoiselle?' wondered Polly.

The young woman wore trousers, which Polly quite envied her for. 'Who me?' She made a laboured point of looking Polly coolly up and down.

Polly smiled and turned around again.

'They say only collabos wear haute couture these days,' shot the young woman to her back.

Polly tensed. While disgusted looks were not uncommon when she went out in the streets, insults were harder to bear. She turned around again. 'And who are "they", Mademoiselle?'

'Anyone with a breath of patriotism left inside them.'

The two held eyes. 'You shouldn't judge a book by its cover, you know.'

The girl in trousers glanced at the book in Polly's arm and shook her head. 'You don't even read French books, so what I see is what I get with you, collabo.'

'Have you even read this?' said Polly.

'I wouldn't soil my hands,' said the other girl. 'Clearly you've not heard the day's news.' The girl sneered at her.

Polly resisted looking back. 'What news?'

'Why should I be the one to shatter your little dream world? You'll hear it soon enough.'

This was too much, and Polly turned around. 'What news? Tell me,' she insisted.

The young woman savoured it. 'They tried to assassinate Hitler. They failed but they came mighty close.'

This development sent a current of electricity through Polly.

'Aren't you going to ask me who "they" are?'

Polly stared. 'Tell me.'

'The krauts themselves. Just fancy it . . .' The girl leaned close to Polly's ear. 'The day of reckoning is coming fast, Mademoiselle. The day when all the collabos like you get shown to the wall.'

'What wall?'

A mocking grin on her face, the young woman made the silent actions of holding and firing a machine gun. This briefly caught the attention of the Wehrmacht guards at the sentry box ahead. The girl dropped her arms at once and cast her eyes to the pavement.

Polly leaned in to her ear in turn. 'This news is encouraging,' she told her, 'and I'm as sorry as you are that they failed, hopefully next time they won't. But the Allies aren't here yet – and if you keep carrying on, you'll be dead long before they make it.'

The young woman's eyes flicked at hers, angry. 'I'm not taking "advice" from some kraut's whore.'

Polly looked at her imploringly. 'What is your name?'

'Why the hell would I tell you?'

Polly held out her hand. 'Mine's Polly.'

Unexpectedly, the name seemed to register with the young woman. Polly saw the girl's face soften in surprise, although still she didn't say anything.

'Don't tell me yours then,' said Polly.

'It's Anaïs.'

They shook hands.

'Nice to meet you,' said Polly. She kept her voice even lower. 'Your papers – fake, I suppose?'

Anaïs said nothing, just staring at her.

Polly took that as a yes. 'They must be pretty good fakes then, if they've got you this far.'

Anaïs gave a small nod.

'Well, here's my final bit of advice,' said Polly, 'find a better "disguise", I beg of you. Not trousers. Dress younger – ankle socks. Let them think you're a kid. Then they'll see you without seeing you. Then perhaps when General de Gaulle gets here, you and I will fight side by side.'

She had robbed Anaïs of further words. Then, as Polly was about to turn around again, Anaïs whispered, 'I was *there*.'

'What?'

'I was there. When the Comtesse sacrificed herself for Suzette – I was there.'

Polly's eyes welled.

Anaïs touched her hand. 'She was a heroine.'

Polly wouldn't let herself cry.

'I'll never forget what she did,' said Anaïs. 'And someday, neither will France.'

Polly was only a dozen people away from the guards now, and she turned to face forward again, saying nothing more.

Polly made it through the checkpoint without incident, her papers checked cursorily, as they always were when she dressed like a BOF. As she neared the Pont Saint-Michel to cross over to the Left Bank, she glanced behind her once and saw that the trousered Anaïs was still detained with the sentries, her papers being examined in forensic detail.

Polly continued along the Boulevard until she came at last to the leafy Place de la Sorbonne. The storied façade of the great university's chapel lay at the end of the narrow square, the two streetscapes on either side lined with some of the Latin Quarter's beloved bookshops. Polly slowed down her pace, dallying by the fountain for a moment while she steadied herself for what would come next. She looked at the names of the bookshops on the shop awnings, finding the one she wanted: *Librairie Rive Gauche*. She spent a minute or so examining the books placed upon trestle tables in front of two other store windows, before she got to her intended bookshop's offerings. She thumbed through what was there with a feigned show of interest: German books mostly, for that was the bookshop's specialty, both in original printings and French translations, plus books written by French writers who were sympathetic to National Socialist ideals. Polly placed her copy of *Autant en emporte le vent* upon the table while she flipped through other books. In the act of putting one German book down to pick up another, she switched the little metal catch at the side of her book. The device inside the hollowed-out cavity clicked into motion. Polly knew she did not have very long. As casually as possible, despite the speed with which her heart was now racing, she strolled on to the next bookshop's trestle. Then she gave every appearance of giving up on book browsing, as she walked purposefully through the great wooden doors of the chapel.

The book bomb exploded without her seeing it. The *Librairie Rive Gauche* front window blew inwards, peppering customers and staff with glass. Flames quickly took hold in the well-stocked bookshelves and soon the ground floor was ablaze. While students around her ran out to the square to see what the commotion was, Polly kept going, enjoying her walk through the Sorbonne grounds, mostly unnoticed and entirely unsuspected as someone who had just destroyed the Occupiers' favourite source of Fascist literature. It had been easily done, Polly marvelled to herself.

Scarlett O'Hara would have well appreciated it.

*

To the BOFs and collaborators with francs to spend at the Bon Marche department store, they were just another Parisian couple succumbing to a public display of affection. No matter how grim things became, the city still had the same affect upon lovers. Their lips pressed together, two bicycles pressed tightly between them on the curb, Claude drew the nameless woman even closer to him, running his fingers through her long chestnut hair. As he did so, her fingers slipped her tiny bicycle pump from her bicycle to his. The kiss was over then, and Claude had to adjust his trousers at the pocket. He was still a man, and a kiss was a kiss, even if he had never met this woman before.

Her eyes flicked to his trousers and sparkled. *'Au revoir*, my Jean-Paul – I shall see you next week.'

'Au revoir, Lisette,' he grinned. They had christened each other on the spot. Although it was madness, he could have happily kissed her again.

Claude mounted his bike and smoothly joined the stream of other cyclists, heading away from the cluttered mishmash of the Left Bank and home to the ordered Right Bank again. From the direction of the Latin Quarter he heard the sirens of fire trucks. In the sky was a pall of smoke. Good, he thought, the more distractions the merrier.

Claude made it back to the Ritz without incident, stopping only briefly at the Wehrmacht sentry box that had been placed at the Pont Royal since Hauptmann Jürgen's murdered corpse had been found under it, two years before. The guards waved him through, brows creased with other concerns. There was pleasingly so much more going on than a fire in the Latin Quarter, Claude thought, having heard from his own sources about the assassination attempt upon Hitler. It was a delicious rarity to see guards looking worried.

With his bike stashed in the basement, Claude took the Cambon elevator to the floor where his suite lay, and once inside, with the doors locked carefully behind him, he went into his library and took down a red leather-bound volume on painting from the Napoleonic era. He thumbed through the book until he found a colour print of Jacques-Louis David's great masterpiece, *The Intervention of the Sabine Women*. Pinching the page between his thumb and his forefinger, Claude slipped a piece of tissue paper out from under the colour plate.

'Afternoon, Papa.'

He turned with a start. Odile was at the door. 'You're home. I didn't realise.' It was a relief the girl couldn't see what he was up to.

'Have you heard the news?'

Claude had. 'We mustn't go letting off fireworks just yet.'

'You're not excited?'

Claude considered. 'I'm cautious.'

'You olds are unbelievable,' said Odile. 'What's that you've got there?'

Claude froze in the act of unscrewing the base of the little bicycle pump the woman had attached to his ride. Once again, he wondered whether Odile could see more than her doctors claimed that she could. 'What's it look like?' Claude wondered, testing the water.

'Don't know – that's why I asked you.'

Claude knew Odile's tactics. 'It's an art book,' he told her. 'I'm looking up something for a guest.'

Odile came properly into the room. 'Boring.'

Confident the girl could see none of it, Claude reached into the pump with his finger and drew out another piece of paper. 'Haven't you got something better to do?'

'Better than watch you with your spy work?'

Claude lurched, dropping the pump pieces to the floor.

Odile laughed. 'Don't worry, I'm only having a lend of you, Papa.' She sat down in the library divan.

But Claude had suffered enough of these sorts of exchanges with Odile. 'If I really was a spy, do you think you'd show more respect to me than you do?'

'Only if you were a good one.'

'I see.'

'Or if you were my dad.'

This only made Claude feel sad. 'Then I fail on both counts.'

'Who says you do?'

'You, obviously,' said Claude.

'Not me – you've passed with flying colours in one of them.'

This brought Claude up short. He felt a surge of warmth. 'That's very nice – but I'm not your father, which of course you well know. But you are very much like a daughter to me, Odile. My life is only the richer for having you.'

'I don't know what you're talking about,' said Odile, flatly. 'My dad's some drunk on a film set. It doesn't mean anything to me. Where you pass with flying colours, Papa, is spying. You've got courage and smarts.'

Claude spluttered. 'Odile!'

'I killed him.'

There was a moment's quiet.

Claude recomposed himself. 'I'm busy, Odile, there's no time for this stupidity. There are guests waiting.'

'I know your secret,' Odile said, 'you can know mine. Me and two others, together we killed him.'

Claude's temper flared. 'I said I'm not playing silly games with you.'

'I stopped playing games when the krauts arrived,' said Odile. 'I do just like you do, Papa, and for real.'

'Odile, please.'

The telephone on the library desk rang. Claude picked it up and put it straight down on the receiver again.

The girl stood up from the divan, trembling with intensity. 'I'm telling you this because the day of liberation cannot be far away. Me and two others killed that kraut Jürgen. I stabbed him in the guts.'

Claude's stomach had knotted.

'You believe me?' asked Odile.

Although it seemed incredible, Claude actually found that he did.

Odile was relieved. 'We did it to get hold of his gun.'

There was another long moment as Claude sat with this. 'And you have it still?'

Odile nodded. 'Soon we will need it, Papa.'

Blanche appeared, framed in the library door. 'I'm on my way out.'

Both Claude and Odile jumped.

Claude glanced at the open art book, the pieces of paper, the bicycle pump parts on the floor but Blanche just turned to her daughter. 'You have *not* got a gun, Odile – so stop playing silly games with your step-father like a child. You're nineteen.'

There was a pause as Odile caught her breath. 'Yes, Mama.'

The weight of the paper Claude had pulled from the bike pump felt like a stone in his hand. 'And where are you off to, my sweet?'

'To the Théâtre du Vieux-Colombier.' Blanche fluffed at her hat. 'With Zita. We're seeing that guy Sartre's play.'

'Ah. I hear it's very good. Very original.'

Blanche shrugged. 'It's about three people stuck in some room. I just hope it's got laughs.' She blew them both kisses. 'See you later then.'

After she had gone, Odile said, 'She's probably lying. Mama does stuff of her own – resistance stuff. She thinks that she's hiding it.'

'Maybe,' said Claude, 'but I don't want to know. I don't want you to know either, Odile. It's safer.'

The girl nodded. 'Sometimes the pressure of not telling the truth is unbearable. I was weak and I'm sorry. I shouldn't have said what I said. Thank you for listening to me, Papa.'

'That's all right . . .'

Odile surprised him by kissing his cheek. 'I'll never betray you. I love you.'

Claude's step-daughter left the room.

The telephone rang again. Claude picked it up. 'Not now,' he said into the receiver without hearing who was at the other end. He hung it up once more.

After a moment, Claude smoothed out the two pieces of paper on his desk. Lettered on the sheet he'd taken from the art book was the code cypher used by members of the Gaullist Underground. This afternoon, once he'd uncoded the message from the bicycle pump, Claude would pass the information to another man on a bicycle on the Quai Voltaire. Where the message would go next, Claude didn't know, which was as it should be. He was part of a complex chain which relayed communications from the Occupied capital to the Free French Army headquarters in London. Resistance had thrived in the dark because no individual member knew anything other than the links in the chain immediately before and after them.

In the habit of reading without comprehending the messages he coded, Claude ignored this one, too, as he began the process. Then, once it was done, he decided he needed a nip of cognac before he set out on his bicycle to deliver the coded message. It was just now occurring to him that Odile's confession – and his own acceptance of it – had shaken him.

The telephone rang again just as a heavy knock came at the door. Claude shouted to Odile in her bedroom. 'Get the door, will you?' He picked up the receiver. 'Yes, what is it?'

The heavy knocking repeated. From the library, Claude saw Odile moving to answer it. He tried to make sense of what the footman in the lobby was telling him. 'Odile should expect a visitor at the suite – what visitor?' He glanced at the door. 'Odile – Odile, wait a moment.'

But his step-daughter didn't hear him, already turning the handle.

*

Zita had secured them front row dress circle seats at the Théâtre du Vieux-Colombier, but when the bells rang for Act Two at the end of interval, and the other theatregoers around them began to stream back to their seats from the bar, Zita gave Blanche a cock-eyed look and proposed they go home to the Ritz.

'Yes, please,' Blanche said,' I don't care how it ends anyway.'

'Here's my guess,' Zita offered, 'they stay put in that stinking damn room.'

'God, what a bore of a show!' Blanche laughed. 'And this being Paris, of course we all claim it's a masterpiece.'

'A piece of masturbation,' Zita cracked.

But on the walk home Zita admitted to herself that the play had badly unsettled her. She suspected Sartre had hidden a metaphor in it – and why wouldn't he? The Germans had proven themselves blind to metaphors. But Sartre's play about three self-indulgent sinners facing judgement and consequences in a room they can't flee from had echoes for those who'd collaborated. All Paris was a locked room – especially the Ritz – and how much longer before everyone inside it faced a judgement of their own? Zita shuddered and predictably felt the stirring of her itch. When she and Blanche were once more ensconced in the Cambon bar, she glanced at Blanche sideways. 'Want a little powder, puss?'

Blanche's eyes sparkled. 'I shouldn't.'

'Yes, you should.' She leaned closer to her. 'It'll give us the laughs the play didn't.'

'You're a bad influence, Zita.'

Zita chuckled, reaching into her purse for the little enamel tin she kept the powder in.

Blanche looked around them with unease. 'Right *here*?'

'No one cares,' said Zita. 'They expect it of me, I'm a "film star".' She clocked a barman she didn't recognise at the counter and waved.

'But where the hell do you get it from? We can't even get ourselves lambchops at the Ritz, and here's you with a can full of snow.'

Zita smiled and put a finger to her lips as she dipped her little spoon into the contents of the open tin. She offered it to Blanche, who hesitated for only a moment before snorting it up her nose.

'Oh hell,' said Blanche, reeling. She rubbed at her nostrils.

'Seeing stars yet?' Zita joked. She indicated herself self-deprecatingly. 'Well, *me* obviously, but what about the celestial type?'

Blanche couldn't quite order her faculties enough to speak, so Zita helped herself to a heaped spoonful. 'Manna from heaven,' she proclaimed, once done.

'Odile killed a kraut.'

There was a pause before Zita did a double-take. 'What?'

Blanche had found the words she'd not intended to speak. 'She says she did. She's never been an untruthful kid. I believe her.'

The buzzing in Zita's head threatened to become a pounding. 'That's crazy. She told you this?'

'She told Claude. I overheard it.'

'I know it hurts you to hear it, but she's blind. How could she ever kill a kraut?'

'Nothing stops her.' Blanch pondered her daughter. 'I think she's a lesbian, too.' This suddenly made her emotional. 'Poor sweet kid. How's she gonna find a nice girlfriend for herself if she can't see what the hell they even look like?'

'Why are you telling me this?'

Blanche blinked. 'I don't know.' Then she did. 'It's the snow. I come out with everything and then forget I said anything.' She found this unaccountably hilarious. 'Just like you do!'

'I don't do that,' Zita protested.

'Sure you do! Every goddamn time.'

Zita was paranoid. Was this true?

Blanche also became panicked. 'Promise me you won't tell anyone.'

'Of course, I won't. It's not even true. How can it be?'

'But it is. It was Jürgen.'

'Blanche! Stop it.'

Blanche tried. 'The pressure not to tell is too much for me sometimes.'

'I know.'

The barman brought two glasses of wine to their table, his eyes on stalks at the sight of the tin full of dope.

Zita gave him a hundred franc note. 'You're new, aren't you, puss?'

'Yes, Mademoiselle.'

She appraised him. He was pleasingly athletic. 'What should we call you then?'

'Baptiste, Mademoiselle.'

'Baptiste,' she repeated, savouring the sound of the name. 'And where were you working before here?'

She watched as he suddenly realised who she was. Zita batted her eyelids.

'In the Dress Circle bar at the Théâtre du Vieux-Colombier,' he told her, awed.

Zita and Blanched laughed.

'I don't blame you for chucking it in,' Zita told him. 'Their latest show stinks.'

But he was staring at her intently. 'I had a friend – Guy Martin – who used to be barman here.'

She saw the meaning behind the word 'friend' and felt sad. 'A good friend, was he?'

He nodded.

'We all loved Guy – didn't we, Blanche? Shame how it went.'

He bent closer to her ear. 'That new film you're in,' he said, keeping his voice low, 'the one that's set in a theatre just like the Vieux-Colombier, but a hundred years ago?'

'Yes?' said Zita. He had a fine set of muscles and an excellent tan.

'The one where the actors can only do plays that don't have any words in them because some stupid rule says so – and then

387

they go and break the rule.' Baptiste leant closer. 'I know what it's really about,' he whispered.

Zita was poker-faced. 'Sure you do, it's about some tart – just like all my pictures. Don't go searching for the secrets of King Tut's tomb in it.'

He looked taken aback, until he seemed to comprehend.

'Keep on going to the movies, puss.' Zita winked at him. She gave him another one-hundred franc note.

'Christ, the cost of a drink these days,' she muttered as Baptiste left. She took a gulp of the wine and grimaced. 'And not even vintage.'

Zita eyed Blanche lost in her powder-charged thoughts. 'Do I really blurt out crazy stuff, too?' she asked.

Blanche stirred. 'Sometimes. Not really.'

Zita tried to hide her rising unease. 'So, what have I said and forgotten about?'

Blanche looked at her. 'Things about Tom.'

Zita suddenly felt very cold. 'Who's he?'

Blanche put her hand upon Zita's. 'Don't worry, girl. I *know* Tommy. I knew him before you did.' She lowered her voice to a whisper. 'We're Jews.'

Zita panicked. 'Stop it, Blanche. I shouldn't be hearing stuff like this.'

'You know I'm a Jew.'

'I do not. *I do not.*'

But Blanche had gone still, looking to the entrance of the bar. 'Oh fuck.'

Zita turned to see Metzingen posed there, dressed in a blue serge suit. Grinning, he'd clearly been waiting for her to notice him. Her head throbbed. 'For God's sake, keep your shit in you, Blanche.'

'He's coming over here.'

Zita gulped at the wine. 'Don't listen to anything he says. He's a liar. Especially anything he says about me. He plays games with women.'

Blanche was perspiring. 'Oh fuck. Oh fuck.'

'Did you hear what I told you?'

'Yes.'

'*Stay calm.*'

Blanche whimpered. 'How can I stay calm with a head full of snow?'

Hans arrived, beaming at their table. 'Hello *Liebchen.*'

Zita feared he would kiss her, but he didn't. He had a fresh gardenia in his lapel, she could actually smell it. Her acting kicked in a beat too late when she looked around as if he'd addressed someone else.

Hans pulled out a seat, smiling at her indulgently. 'Your timing is off. Does your comedy grow tired?'

She now did her routine of 'noticing' him. 'Oh, Herr Metzingen. How very nice to see you here.'

Hans looked to Blanche, long-sufferingly.

'You know Madame Auzello, of course,' said Zita.

Hans smiled and directed his gaze to the still open tin on the table. 'I see you've been enjoying some of Fräulein Zita's vice?'

Blanche stiffened.

Zita frowned at him. 'I'd mind those accusations if I were you – it's talc.'

Metzingen chortled. 'Oh *Liebchen.*' He dipped the little spoon into the powder and brought it up to his nose. He looked to Zita, dangerously. 'Should I?'

Her eyes narrowed at Hans. 'I use it for athlete's foot, but sure, why not? Go for your life.'

Metzingen snorted it. At the bar, Baptiste was frozen.

Blanche watched, mortified.

Hans rubbed at his upper lip. 'Did she tell you how she manages to get her hands on it these days?' he asked Blanche.

Blanche looked sharply at Zita. 'She wouldn't say.'

'Ah.' He indicated himself as the source. 'She much prefers company when she takes it, you see. And I much prefer *her* company.'

'That's a lie,' Zita said. 'You hardly know me.'

Hans went on. 'Fräulein Zita and I are such old friends that we've become predictable to each other. Dope brings surprises. That's why I joined in.'

Zita looked desperately at Blanche. 'None of this is true. None of it.'

'Isn't it?' said Metzingen. He spooned some more powder up his nose. 'Yes, a pleasure shared is a pleasure doubled.' He reached across the table and brushed a speck of powder from Blanche's lip. He licked it off his finger. 'Or tripled today, Frau Auzello. There's no end to the fun.'

The strain of suppressing her terror at what else he might say only made Zita angry. 'Why are you always found here at the Ritz? You need to get out more. Blanche and I can recommend a shitty play.'

'The one by Sartre? But you were looking forward to it.'

Zita's eyes flashed. 'You had no idea I was seeing any play.'

'But you told me you would be.'

Zita's paranoia bit her. 'I did not.'

'But how do you know you didn't?' Hans asked her. 'You come out with everything when there's dope inside you.' He turned to Blanche. 'Doesn't she, meine Dame? It is something we must all be mindful of – those of us who indulge. I hope your own tongue is held tight.'

Blanche was shaking. She pushed back her chair. 'I've had enough of this.'

'Enough of what?' said Hans.

'*This* – whatever this is. Intimidation. Terror tactics. It's all gonna end.'

Hans laughed at her. 'I don't think so. The Third Reich is eternal.'

The powder proved recklessly emboldening to Blanche. She stuck a lacquered fingernail into his chest. 'Have you *heard* the damn news, kraut? Or have you spent the whole day with your head up your ass?'

Zita closed her eyes.

'Can you mean the Allied advance?' Metzingen wondered.

'What else would I mean, kraut?' said Blanche. 'You've got a fight on all fronts. There's the Yanks coming up the boot of Italy, and the Reds over there in the east – and now you've got God's own damn army coming at you like hellfire from the coast. Very soon it's gonna be a kraut sandwich.'

Metzingen said nothing for a moment as he and Blanche stared at each other.

Zita placed a hand on his thigh. 'Don't mind her, puss,' she whispered. 'It's just the dope talking. You said so yourself – we all say anything when we've had a sniff of the stuff, but it's bullshit in the end. She means none of it.'

Metzingen patted her hand, appreciative. 'Your own dope talk has solved so much for me today, *Liebchen*.'

Zita pulled back. 'What do you mean?'

Metzingen's huge hand cupped Zita's face. 'You're invaluable to me.' He looked over to Blanche. 'And to the Gestapo.'

Zita stood up in horror. 'What's that supposed to mean?'

He kept his eyes upon Blanche. 'Defiance of the air raid blackout has brought this upon you, Frau Auzello.'

Blanche gaped at him. 'Upon me?'

'Well, upon your unfortunate daughter,' said Hans. 'Zita told me so much of it.'

Zita went white. 'Don't believe him.'

'Yet still there are gaps,' said Metzingen. 'I wonder who her accomplices are, for instance? Well, we will soon know. While you've been here, Odile has been arrested. There is much for her to discuss with the Gestapo.'

Zita felt the very last atoms of her soul disintegrate.

Blanche snapped in terror – and made a run for the doors.

'Oh dear,' said Metzingen, watching her go. 'I hope her girl didn't respond in that way. Yet the Gestapo lads love a chase. Entitles them to bring out their "exemplary" measures, I'm told.'

He sniffed at the air. 'Not such a bad thing really. Odile always looked in need of a bath.'

Zita slipped to the floor and vomited under the table.

When she sat up again, Metzingen was helping himself to more powder.

'I know nothing of any of this,' she told him. 'I never said a damn thing.'

He rubbed at his nostrils, loving her like this: debased and half mad. He felt himself beginning to tent in his blue serge trousers. 'Are you sure of that, *Liebchen*?'

She wasn't, of course. 'Why arrest her daughter, Hans – are you inhuman?'

He placed her hand on his pants as he shrugged. '*Liebchen, Liebchen . . .*' he muttered pityingly.

Zita watched on as more of the dope went up his nostrils. Then he offered the spoon to her. She began to sob. 'Oh Jesus . . . oh Jesus, help me . . .'

'But it is nothing,' said Metzingen, waving the implement of her own destruction at her. 'It is like breathing in air, just as you once told me – like breathing in happiness. It makes your pain go away.'

Zita tried to shut her eyes to it, but the pull of the powder was relentless.

'And what's that, *Liebchen*, what's that you ask? What happens when the happiness wears off?' he taunted her. 'Well, that's when you snort some more of it.' He was laughing at her now. '*Liebchen*, are you really such a rube?'

Polly had enjoyed an untroubled afternoon. Her circuitous route home from the scene of her bookshop attack had taken her through the Jardin des Plantes, where, as she wandered between what was still left uneaten of the botanical specimens, she found that her conscience was not burdened. When Jürgen had died in the deception she'd initiated, she'd been haunted by nightmares. His splattered blood, his shattered skull, the desperate love in his eyes that he'd felt for her just as he died; these images stayed with her, seared into her heart. She knew she would never be rid of them. None of the many resistance acts she'd contributed to since had scarred her in the same way.

Yet at times of triumph like these, Polly's memory returned to that day of the very first butterflies prank when she'd stood at the top of the stairs at the Ritz and stopped Tommy from saying what it was that he'd been on the cusp of confessing to her. She'd seen in his eyes – Tommy's soft, brown eyes – that there was so much more to be said between them. But she'd used her commitment to resistance as the excuse to keep him from saying anything. Now, as she had on so many other occasions since, Polly wondered what might have happened had she not been so scared of rejection.

Polly entered the Cambon lobby, glad to be out of the heat. She saw Tommy inside with Mimi, and she knew from their faces that something was badly wrong.

'Pol . . .' Tommy was stricken.

'What is it? What's happened?'

Mimi put up a warning hand. 'Not here,' she said. She put a key in the door of a tiny office that opened off the lobby. Polly saw she'd been crying.

They went inside, closing the door behind them.

'Tell me what's happened please,' said Polly.

Tommy and Mimi passed a tormented look. 'The krauts have taken Odile,' he said.

Polly remained calm but it was a moment before she could speak. 'Gestapo?'

He didn't know. 'We saw Blanche going up to their suite – Metzingen had told her of the arrest – she was hysterical.'

'Metzingen?' Polly had to sit down in a chair. '*Why* did they take her?'

'I don't know.' Tommy looked more exhausted than she'd ever seen him, yet, like her, he appeared calm. 'It could be for things that we know of – it could be for things that we don't.'

Polly was thrown by the openness with which Tommy was speaking in front of the Ritz owner.

Mimi understood this without Polly saying anything. 'There is very little that goes on in this hotel that I do not know of, my dear.'

Polly looked at Mimi anew. Then she turned to Tommy again and saw now how desperately he was fighting his emotions, forcing himself to appear pragmatic. 'We always knew this day might come,' she whispered to him.

He stuck his chin out. 'We can't expect Odile to withstand interrogation for very long, Pol.' He was trying to seem stoic and failing.

'She's tougher than any of us,' Polly said, desperately. But she couldn't convince herself. Her heart had shattered. 'Oh God, Odile . . .' She started weeping in front of them.

Neither Tommy nor Mimi said anything more for a while.

'What should we do then?' said Polly, after a time, trying to pull herself together. 'Take tail and run like bunny rabbits?'

'Run where?' said Tommy, softly.

'Underground? We have friends. We could hide if we wished to.' She looked from Tommy to Mimi. '*All* of us, if needs be.'

'There are too many fighting the Boches from the cover of this hotel for us all to run,' said Mimi. 'Far more than you know, Polly. Far more than you need to know.'

Although their situation couldn't have been worse, Polly actually felt hope at learning of this. 'Is that really true?'

Mimi nodded. 'And I, for one, will never run from the Ritz,' she said. 'Which I'm sure does not surprise you.'

It didn't.

'Nor will Claude,' said Mimi. 'Despite what has happened. The fate of this great hotel and his own are too inextricably linked.' A tear rolled down her soft cheek.

Polly was buoyed by this too. 'Then don't expect me to run either.'

'Don't be so reckless,' Mimi snapped. 'You could escape them still.' She looked to Polly. 'You both could.'

Tommy was silent.

'I won't do it.' Polly looked defiantly to them both. 'Not in the face of Alexandrine's example. Or Lana Mae's courage – or Suzette's sacrifice. How could I possibly run with the memory of any of them?'

'Not even to fight?' Mimi challenged her. 'Stay here, my dear, and you're wasted for France. Run and the two of you might still join the fight for our victory.'

Polly clenched her fists. 'You can't make me do anything, Mimi.'

The old lady was cold. 'Don't you think you owe me a debt for your time here?'

Polly stood up from the chair, crushed. 'Madame – you can't mean that.'

'Why not?' said Mimi. 'The one thousand and one night's accommodation paid by your aunt's legacy ran out long ago. Am I just an endless fountain of charity?'

Polly was ashen. 'Is running away really what you want me to do, Madame Ritz?' she asked quietly.

There was a long moment before Mimi lowered her head, ashamed. 'I'm sorry – it's the shock of it. Odile was like a grand-daughter to me . . .' She sobbed.

Now Polly struggled to hold back more tears. 'Madame – since Alexandrine was taken, it's become so difficult to access my aunt's funds.'

Mimi was at Polly's side, kissing her hands. 'Oh, my dear – no explanation is ever needed.'

'But my continuing to stay on at the Ritz has weighed so heavily on my conscience.'

'You're not a guest – you're *family*,' Mimi insisted.

'One day, I'll make it up to you.'

Mimi fiercely waved this away. 'You have every right to resist to the last with dignity,' she told her. 'And I have no right to take that from you.' She looked back to Tommy. 'And what about you, my boy? You have not said what you will do.'

Tommy looked up from where he'd been staring at the floor. He was resolute. 'I would have thought it was obvious.' He glanced to Polly. 'We will both stay here.'

Polly nodded.

'But we will not stay here and *wait*.'

Polly knew what was coming.

'We will find a way to get Odile back,' Tommy vowed.

Mimi closed her eyes against his youthful idealism. 'Oh, my boy . . .' she whispered. 'What you propose is impossible.'

'We *will*,' he insisted, 'we will find a way to succeed. There will be a way.'

'There is no way.' Mimi was drained of all fight. 'Was there a way to save Guy?'

Tommy bit back his guilt at the memory. "We knew nothing then. The krauts have grown decadent and weak. We can defeat them if we stay strong. We *are* defeating them.'

'Odile is lost to us,' said Mimi. 'You must accept it.'

'No!' Tommy shot back at her. 'Just like we accepted all the rest? *No*, Madame. Not Odile. Not with everything she's done – and not while we still live.'

Mimi could only stare at him. 'Do you do this because you feel love for Odile?'

Polly saw Tommy falter at the question.

'Why, can't you answer me?'

He doubled down. 'Of course, I love Odile. How could you doubt that?'

'You love her as a friend, I'm sure – but as something more?'

He was flustered. 'Madame . . .'

'All this time you've never told her you love her – why is that?'

396

Tommy squirmed. 'Please, Madame . . .'

'Why?'

'Because there has been no time for love,' he insisted, 'no room for it. We've been filled by our purpose, our commitment to resist – haven't we, Pol?'

Polly heard her very words from that day on the stairs thrown back at her.

'It's all we've ever thought of,' Tommy went on.

Mimi looked at her hands. 'You speak about love without knowing anything about it,' she said. 'The commitment you feel only seems like love because it unites you – but true love is different. If you truly loved Odile, you would have told her so long ago. You wouldn't have been able to stop yourself. You wouldn't have been able to ignore your heart.'

And Polly thought then: to ignore one's heart is all too easy when life is full enough to distract from it.

'I think you've told yourself that you love her because it is easier than acknowledging love elsewhere,' said Mimi. 'Love with Odile is conveniently impossible and that's why you've chosen it.'

Tommy's defences went up. 'I don't know what you are talking about.'

'I think you do.'

'I do not,' Tommy insisted. 'We are above such things.'

A searching look passed between Mimi and Polly.

'No one is above love,' Mimi said. 'Free yourself from this burden.' She pleaded with them both. 'You do not know Odile's heart as well as you think you do.'

Polly couldn't hold Mimi's eye any longer.

'We will save our Odile,' said Tommy. 'You'll see that we will.' He looked urgently to Polly. 'Won't we, Pol?'

She smiled back at him warmly, willing what she felt inside from her face.

*

Polly was overcome with fear, but gave no hint of it, the experience of which was surreal. She felt as if she was standing at a great distance away observing herself through a telescope. Returning to the Cambon lobby again, she didn't look back at Tommy or see where he went. Instead, she glanced in the bar and saw Zita alone at a table. The Art Deco room was near empty.

The film star looked up and spotted her, her eyes raw. She at once looked away, shocking Polly with this reaction. Zita was overwhelmingly ashamed. At that terrible moment, Polly guessed what had happened to Odile had a connection to Zita. As if still watching herself from a distance, Polly stepped inside.

'What is it, Zita?' she called across the room.

Zita stared at her hands in her lap, deaf to her.

'Please – what's wrong?'

The film star turned and glared as Polly approached the table. Polly now saw how dilated her pupils were. 'Are you all right?'

Zita grimaced. 'I don't want you talking to me anymore, Polly.' There was spittle on her lips. 'Have you got that?'

Polly took an unconscious step back, frightened but determined to persist. 'All right.'

'I mean it. Don't test me. Fuck off from now on.'

The words stabbed Polly. 'I said all right.'

'Good.' Zita turned her back to her.

Polly just stood there.

After a moment, Zita said, 'You still waiting?'

'Yes,' Polly said. 'Yes, I'm still here.' Her voice broke in her throat.

Then Polly heard the sound of Zita weeping.

Polly went to her. 'What is it?'

The film star shook her head.

'Please tell me,' said Polly.

But Zita could not.

'Zita,' Polly begged her, 'there is only you and I – there's no one else anymore. So, who else loves you like I do? And who else loves you like I always will?'

'Oh, puss . . . you don't know what you're saying.'

'You can tell me anything, and still I'll love you,' Polly whispered, 'no matter how bad you think it might be.'

Zita stared at her, desolate.

'And I will say this always – you can tell me any secret, any secret at all.'

Zita mocked her. 'Yeah?'

'*Anything* . . .' said Polly.

For a long moment it seemed to Polly that Zita was on the cusp of telling her something unimaginable. Then a different instinct kicked in and Zita threw her attentions towards a middle-aged man who was passing the table.

'Bonjour Monsieur – it's Doctor Kahle, isn't it?'

Polly knew him then, too: Göring's old specialist, once lauded now rejected. He had remained at the Ritz long after the Reichsmarschall had left him to it. Now he was looking as nerve-racked as Zita was. Kahle gawped first at Zita and then at Polly.

'I'm Mademoiselle Zita,' she reminded him, presenting her hand, 'and this is my ward, Mademoiselle Hartford. Don't you remember us from so many nights at *l'Espadon*?'

'My God – of course.'

Zita gestured comically.

He grabbed her hand. Zita winced at the sweat slick he left on her fingers. 'It's a fine idea approaching them of your own volition, meine Damen – a fine idea,' he told her. 'It shows good faith to the Gestapo.'

Zita pulled back her hand like he'd bitten it. 'The Gestapo?'

Kahle nodded effusively. 'To choose fleeing instead is just fatal.'

Zita was thrown, refusing to look at Polly. 'Someone you know has been taken for questioning?'

'Someone I know?' Kahle echoed.

Zita leaned forward a little. 'I have heard that relatives and friends are treated with courtesy when making enquiries.' She lowered her voice. 'Perhaps you could tell the Gestapo that you believe a mistake has been made with your friend?'

The doctor was bewildered. 'I'm sorry, meine Dame – but don't you *know*?'

Zita was frightened. 'Know what?'

'Oh my God . . .' New nervousness crashed over him.

Polly's own nerves intensified. 'Doctor Kahle,' she asked him, 'what is it that we *should* know?'

The doctor stared back at her. 'The Führer,' he whispered. 'The attempt that was made to assassinate him.'

Zita had a sudden intake of breath. But Polly had already heard this news.

'Don't fear, he lives,' Kahle reassured them, 'but at cost . . .'

Zita seized on this. 'He is injured?'

'Yes,' said Kahle, 'but nothing so serious, thank God. The cost is not to his health.'

Zita stared at him levelly. 'Can you tell us what is happening please?'

The doctor looked around him as if fearing hidden listeners. Yet the bar was near deserted. 'The assassins were *Germans*, meine Damen.' He let the shock of that sit as Zita absorbed it, before delivering the next: 'And the assassins' conspiracy was born at our hotel.'

'You mean right here in Paris, Herr Doctor?' said Polly.

'I mean here right at the heart of the Ritz.' A sweat droplet fell from his nose to the floor. 'General von Stülpnagel,' he whispered, 'along with Colonel von Hofacker and General Speidel – they've been exposed as the ringleaders.'

Zita's mouth fell open.

'Stülpnagel tried to kill himself last night on the road from Paris – he blew out his own eye in the attempt but not his brains, the poor fool.' He gestured hopelessly. 'They have him now . . .'

'Oh Christ,' Zita said, quailing.

'Von Hofacker and Speidel are on the run still.'

Polly looked from Zita to Kahle and back again, trying to grasp what it was that wasn't being said. 'But I don't understand,' said Polly, 'why are *you* so frightened, Herr Doctor?'

'All of us – *all of us* – are under suspicion in this,' he insisted. 'The Führer said he'd be merciless in his reprisal . . .'

Polly now saw Zita's unmistakable flash of fear.

'All of us?'

'Everyone at the Ritz. None will be spared in discovering the full extent of accountability.' Then he saw how badly he was misinterpreted. 'Oh, meine Damen, do not worry yourselves,' he added, seeking to reassure them. 'I do not mean the *French* guests.'

'But why not, Herr Doctor? We live at the Ritz, too,' said Polly.

'Yes, of course, but this is a *German* outrage.' He took a long breath, contemplating. 'Just consider the boldness of it, the breathtaking ingenuity – how could a French mind ever lend itself to such an audacious attempt? No, no, the conspirators are born of the Fatherland.' He pulled at his collar, loosening it. 'Which means that it falls to those of us who are already considered guilty to take the initiative in proving we are not.' He meant himself. 'I am giving myself to them. Just as soon as I've had a drink or two for courage.'

Polly felt a sudden, tremendous exaltation at this. With the Allies advancing from the west, the Occupiers were consuming themselves.

'This bar is usually full of Germans,' Kahle said, indicating the empty room.

It was only now that both Polly and Zita realised the truth of this.

'You mean the Gestapo have been arresting people?' Zita whispered.

'Arresting *Germans*,' Kahle reminded her.

Polly watched as a great weight lifted from Zita.

'No French citizens have been taken from the Ritz today?' said Zita.

Kahle shook his head.

'None? Not one French citizen today at all? You swear it?'

Kahle looked at Zita in puzzlement. 'Were you expecting such an arrest to occur?'

Zita batted this question away. 'Of course not.'

Polly knew then that Zita was lying. She had expected Odile to be arrested. Yet here was Kahle telling them that this could not have occurred. So, had Odile's arrest even happened? It had only been reported by Metzingen – no one trustworthy had witnessed it. Polly put her own confusion aside in order to watch Zita intently.

'Who among the Germans then –' Zita pressed him. 'Who has already been taken – and who is still likely?'

The doctor gave her some names. 'I have no knowledge of any of them. And those who are still free I name only as conjecture.'

'Hans?' Zita whispered. 'Will they arrest Hans?'

Polly's eyes widened.

'You mean Metzingen?' Kahle asked, astonished.

Zita stood on a cliff edge. 'Will he be arrested?'

The doctor threw his head back with mirth.

Polly watched Zita's hands shake, brushing at her dress.

'Oh God,' Kahle said, trying to recover himself, 'that's a good one.'

Zita had gone very still. 'Why is that so funny?'

Kahle wiped at his eyes. 'Forgive me, meine Dame – it was just the surprise of it.' He cleared his throat, his fingers pulling creases from his coat sleeves. 'Of course, Oberstleutnant Metzingen will not be arrested. You have no reason to fear for him, if that is indeed what you feel.'

Zita clearly believed she betrayed nothing. 'But why will he be exempt?'

'Because Metzingen couldn't conspire his way through breakfast.'

Polly was quietly devasted by the wound these words made upon Zita. She shut her eyes to it, realising now everything it meant.

'But how can you say that?' Zita whispered. 'He is a powerful man.'

'I can say it because he is drug addict, meine Dame. Everyone knows it. He is hopelessly hooked on the dope. The power and responsibilities he once had are long taken from him. He's an embarrassment to the Reich, a bad joke. So pitiful is our Oberstleutnant that even the Russian front has no need of him. He's been left here in Paris to drift – and to drown. No one will arrest him, meine Dame, because no one will get sense from him.'

Polly made herself watch the tear that fell from Zita's kohled eye.

The doctor watched, too, and was compassionate. 'There is a love affair between you?'

Zita said nothing. She didn't need to. The truth was so obvious.

'I advise you to abandon it, meine Dame,' Kahle told her. 'It is only sensible. After all, he has already abandoned himself . . .'

When Kahle had moved off to the bar to order a drink, Zita stayed where she was, staring into space. Then, when Polly spoke to her gently, Zita rose from the table, but needed Polly to guide her to the doors. It was Polly who bid farewell to the doctor, offering certainty that all would be well, even though she didn't care if he was shot.

It was Polly who knew she had lost Zita somehow – the woman by her side was a phantom. It was Polly who clung on fiercely to her guardian's arm, wanting to cry, but not letting herself do so as they entered the Cambon lobby. As they began to cross the floor, they saw Blanche coming down the stairs – her arm linked through Odile's.

She had not been arrested.

Zita stopped still then, staring at her friend's sightless daughter.

It was Odile who spoke. 'Hello, Pol,' she said, somehow knowing she was there. 'I hear you met my friend Anaïs today?'

Polly blinked. 'Anaïs?'

'Yeah,' said Odile, 'she was visiting here earlier – wasn't she, Mama?'

Blanche nodded, her eyes cold upon Zita.

'You and Anaïs are friends?' Polly asked, surprised. 'I didn't realise that.'

For the first time in the four long years Polly had known the remarkable girl, Odile blushed.

Blanche patted her daughter's hand, protectively. 'You're real good friends with Anaïs, aren't you, sweetheart? She's a very nice girl. I like her.'

A secretive smile came to Odile's face. 'Anaïs came to visit especially today, so Mama could meet her,' she confessed. 'And Papa, too. She came up to our suite and surprised me. If we'd known you were around, Pol, we would have invited you, too, for some tea and some cake.'

Polly glanced at Zita. 'It's been busy today.'

'And weird,' said Odile, meaningfully, 'all the kraut guests have checked out . . .'

Zita shuddered.

'Come on, Odile,' said Blanche, 'let's go get some air.'

'See you later then,' said Odile, grinning.

But as they passed by, Blanche was unable to stop herself attacking Zita. 'Your kraut boyfriend was full of so much bullshit.'

Zita shrank from her.

'Letting me think Odile had been arrested – when she was fine! She was sitting upstairs giggling with her girlfriend!'

'I'm so sorry . . .' Zita began.

Polly saw Tommy and Mimi appear in the lobby – both looking up at Odile and her mother on the stairs in bewilderment.

'Sorry won't cut it,' Blanche spat at her friend. 'I think you're a collabo, Zita.' The word sliced through the air, nicking at the ears of all in the lobby. More faces turned to stare at them. 'You hear that, everyone?' Blanche screamed at this audience. 'The fabulous Zita is a filthy collabo kraut whore!'

*

When her accusers had gone, Zita disengaged herself from Polly's arm to approach the corridor of vitrines. She let Polly watch her walking away, the girl saying nothing.

Then Zita turned around to cast a last look at her. 'Puss?'

The look on Polly's face told Zita her heart had broken for her collabo guardian. 'What is it?' Polly said.

Zita's body felt like lead. 'That time when Lotti's ashes weren't even her ashes – and me and Hans were left sitting in that car?'

Polly had no idea of what she referred to. 'Yes, Zita?'

'I saw how I could end him then.'

'You did?' Polly whispered.

Zita nodded. 'I saw how I could do it – how I could destroy my Hans and be free of him for good.'

'I see,' Polly said. Yet Zita could tell she didn't see at all. Or rather, was it that Polly was only just now seeing what had been so long hidden from her with secrets?

Zita pushed back her hair. 'Now I learned that it worked.'

'Good,' Polly whispered. 'You did good then, Zita.'

But Zita's lashes glistened with tears. 'You know what they say: be careful what you wish for . . .' She gulped back a sob. 'The worst was being told he's not powerful.' She shook her head to rid herself of this. 'That I will never believe.'

'Wait,' called Polly.

Zita stopped again.

Polly took a deep breath, filling her lungs. 'Did you kill Aunt Marjorie?'

Zita fell still.

'Did she find out about you? Did she threaten to expose you?'

Zita tried to make sounds of denial, tried to brazen it out. But her mind went only to where it too often did, on board the Riviera train, where she and Polly's Aunt Marjorie perched on the gangway together between the two carriages, as they enacted their final exchange:

First there came Zita's shame that she'd spied for the Germans. Then came Zita's greater shame that Marjorie had been told. Then came her desperation to kill herself in atonement for everything. Then her pitiful fury that Alexandrine had snatched the gun from her things.

Then there was Marjorie's assurance that, together, the four of them would face Zita's nightmare and end it, just as they always would in such times, because they were friends. Then came Marjorie's own confession: she was working for the French Secret Service again and Zita's act of compromise – even Marjorie couldn't call it betrayal – meant that, really, given the crisis that was facing the nation, Zita had but one option. She should hand herself in. She should tell the authorities everything. And then she might turn what she knew of the Germans against them – and become a double agent for France.

She should fool her precious Hans.

Then came Zita's promise, heartfelt: she would do this. With the support of her friends she would do what was right.

Then came Marjorie's loveliest words: she forgave Zita. She forgave Zita everything. She would always do this because without such forgiveness friendship was meaningless for women in wars.

Then Zita had thanked her. Overcome with emotion, she had thanked her for such unconditional love. Reaching out, she had made to embrace her friend Marjorie – until Marjorie was racked by great pain.

Zita had pulled back from her. What was it? What was happening to her friend?

Marjorie had tried to tell her the answer, but the words wouldn't come. Her fingers had clutched desperately at her malfunctioning heart.

And Marjorie had slipped, lifeless, from the train . . .

'Please Zita,' Polly pleaded. 'I'll forgive you for anything. You're all that I have. Just tell me if it's true. Did you kill Marjorie?'

Zita blinked, the memory vanishing.

'Zita,' Polly begged.

Marjorie had forgiven her, but Zita had not forgiven herself.

'Sure, I did,' she lied to Polly, 'finally you worked it all out . . .'

The idea to kill everyone at the Hôtel Ritz came in a waking dream. That this dream was dope-driven didn't lessen its majesty any. Hans knew well that, for him, dabbling in the drug came free of ill consequences, thanks to his Aryan constitution. For those of unquestionable Teutonic ancestry like himself, dope brought not the fast road to debasement but the opposite: the *autobahn* to enlightenment. This, Hans explained to himself, raving in front of the mirror, was why Göring had so pathetically succumbed to it. The Luftwaffe chief had squandered the constitution that the purity of Aryan descent had given him. Göring was obese, effeminate, a pervert, and so, predictably, the dope had claimed him. Hans was as physically perfect now as he had been at twenty, which was why dope was never his scourge but his saviour. He could harness the enhanced awareness it gave him and profit, while lesser types slumped in the gutter. Göring was unmissed at the Ritz. The degenerate's absence had freed up the Imperial Suite – an absence that Hans had all too happily filled.

It was *his* Ritz, after all. It always had been.

'We must kill every last one of them!' he shouted to Zita from the boudoir bathroom mirror where he had been studying himself. 'From the very highest to the lowest – scour every floor, every room – we must scrub the place clean! Vermin has infested here. Why didn't I see this before, *Liebchen*?'

But when no reply came from his lover he pulled himself away from the mirror to investigate her silence. She was out cold, naked, face down in their bed, a relief to him. Sometimes he hallucinated her, raving away at her form only to be met by a ghost. This Zita was real. He was sure of it.

'Wake up, *Liebchen*, wake up and listen to me,' he pulled the covers from her and slapped at her bare rump. 'We should have made it *completely* our own from the start – don't you see it? It's not enough just to waltz in and take over – the Ritz must *become* us, *Liebchen*. And for that to occur we must kill them – French and German alike. Don't you see it?'

But Zita was unresponsive. He contemplated screwing her then and made a token attempt until his prick disappointed him, which it too often did of late. He saw the open dope tin upon the bedside table and re-charged himself with a new spoonful. Then his thoughts of sexual entitlement evaporated as the massacre idea resurged.

He picked up the telephone and expected the connection to the Vendôme lobby to be instant. Instead, it rang out. Hans struck at the telephone cradle with the receiver as Zita stirred in the bed beside him.

Doubt pricked. 'You *are* real, *Liebchen*, yes? You wouldn't trick me like last time?'

Still she didn't answer him.

Hans dialled again, and again the call threatened to go unanswered, until finally it was caught just as Hans was considering smashing the device to pieces.

'This is the Vendôme lobby,' said Auzello's voice.

The man sounded shattered despite the polish of his words; an appealing quality that Auzello could only have acquired since Hans had caused his step-daughter to be arrested. Hans only wished he'd been witness to it. 'Auzello, you turd,' he purred down the phone, 'how dare you not answer me at once.'

'Herr Oberstleutnant, please forgive me.'

'I will not – get up here right now. After I've kicked you in the balls for it I wish to discuss liquidating the entire hotel. It is well overdue and I'm sure you agree with me. It requires my personal stamp and it disgusts me that you, of all people, Auzello, have not thought to mention it.'

408

Hans enjoyed the long pause that followed until it became *too* long. 'Auzello! Do you hear me?'

'That sounds like both an excellent prospect and a dire omission on my part,' said Auzello down the phone. To Hans his voice seemed so broken he could visualise the pieces. 'But I'm afraid it is not possible for me to leave the lobby at present.'

Hans had the uncanny experience of flares being exploded inside his head. 'That you should say that to me will earn you a second kick. If you say it again I shall cut your balls off once I've sunk my boot into them.'

'Herr Oberstleutnant knows best, of course,' said Auzello from the lobby, 'and despite the risk to me physically I am afraid I must repeat that I am unable to leave the Vendôme lobby now, or I suspect, for some time longer. It is because we are seeing to our next wave of visitors.'

Hans snatched the lamp from the bedside table and hurled it into the bathroom where it shattered against the bath. 'Did you hear that, Auzello?' he said. 'That was the sound of your puny frog nuts disintegrating. Don't bother coming up here, I shall come down to you to sort out this ineptitude.'

Auzello remained smooth. 'Of course, Herr Oberstleutnant – and perhaps you will be pleased to greet our new visitors personally?'

'What visitors?'

'Has the Oberstleutnant looked outside his Imperial Suite window?'

'How much time do you imagine I have at my disposal, turd? Of course, I have not. The Führer has our victory to clinch.'

'The Oberstleutnant knows best,' said Auzello. He hung up.

Hans stared at the receiver, incredulous. The urge to smash the thing surged once more, then passed. Hans helped himself to another heaped spoonful of dope. Then the remnants of his fury disappeared altogether. He tried to remember what it was he'd been talking about. He recalled it and sneered to Zita. 'That I should be expected to look out of my own window, *Liebchen* – that's what we use others for!'

But there were no others.

Hans crept to the window and flicked at the muslin curtain.

What he saw in the square filled him first with panic and then with unaccountable hilarity. This was short lived. When he turned to the bed again, Zita was gone. *'Liebchen?'*

Her side of the bed was unslept upon. She'd never even been there.

Hans' eyes filled with dread. These hallucinations were starting to unnerve him.

Just then Zita let herself quietly into the Imperial Suite from the corridor, fully clothed. When he saw her, he was overcome no less.

'What is it, Hans?' But the look on her face told him she already knew.

'The Gestapo,' he hissed, 'they are out there in the square . . .'

She nodded, bleak.

'They have come for the blind girl?'

She moved gently towards him. 'You know they haven't, Hans . . .'

'But I reported the girl. She's a Resister.'

Zita had taken his hand. 'They are not here for Odile, my love. They're not interested in Resisters today.'

He gaped at her. 'Then who are they here for, *Liebchen?*'

She kissed him, eyes open, filled with great sadness.

'Who?' he repeated. 'Who is it they want?'

She led him towards the boudoir.

'Please answer me, *Liebchen* – you're frightening me!'

She placed a finger to his lips. 'They want Germans . . .'

Hans felt like a tiny child with her now; a boy with his *Mutti*. It was comforting. He watched as Zita now ran soft hands along the smooth, polished surface of the great rosewood armoire, once pierced by her bullet.

'I'm not going to let them get you,' she whispered, 'you're too powerful to be insulted by their hands. I'm going to hide you . . .'

'Hide me? Hide me where, *Mutti?*'

Zita kissed him again. 'Safe and secure in the womb . . .'

410

16

25 August 1944

Polly watched with supreme satisfaction as the last of the mimeographed handbills rolled off the once-secret machine. She glanced out the high windows of Mimi's suite and sighed with pleasure at the dawn of a breathless, blue summer morning. Then she grinned for sheer joy. 'Well then. The day has arrived, Madame.'

Mimi beamed back. 'Not one cloud in the sky to mar the dawning of this day of glory, my dear – not one.'

'It is so, so beautiful out there,' said Polly, 'the most perfect of days.'

'Nature and history would seem to have cooperated for Paris,' said Mimi.

'Still, the day is not quite with us, yet,' said Polly. 'There's work to be done before we start any celebrating.'

Mimi didn't need to be told.

Polly took the stack of purple-inked papers from the press: instructions on how to make Molotov cocktails.

Mimi took up the other pile: instructions on making barricades. 'God willing, my dear, this will be the final time we need to print such things.'

'They've served us well,' said Polly, proud. 'They've served Paris well.'

Mimi clutched them to her chest. 'The distributors will be waiting downstairs,' she said. 'Best we join them at once.'

With Mimi's griffons at their heels, they stepped into the corridor. 'Most of these will go straight to the pharmacists' network,' said Polly of her Molotov cocktail papers. 'They're the ones running lowest because everyone's been coming to them for potassium chlorate.'

'Good,' said Mimi, 'but hold some back for the emergency clinics – they've sprung up all over the 1st arrondissement like mushrooms. Those volunteer stretcher-bearers and medical students are so young. I fear they are hopelessly underprepared for today.'

Polly gave her a dry look.

'Or not,' said Mimi, corrected.

'Most definitely not,' said Polly, amused. 'They've all been resisting for years, Madame!' She patted the paper pile. 'Still, it will be very buoying for them to learn that others are just as well organised and that we are thinking fondly of them.'

Mimi agreed.

They passed the open doors of a neighbouring suite in the corridor. Inside they saw a frantic Doctor Kahle dashing between two blazing fireplaces at the opposite ends of his rooms. Polly and Mimi cast a contemptuous look at each other.

'Are you feeling a chill, Herr Doctor?' Mimi enquired from the doors. 'A rare thing in August.'

Kahle stopped with a shout, spilling his own pile of papers across the carpeted floor. 'Madame Ritz!' He looked pitifully exposed. 'I am disposing of rubbish – you understand, meine Dame. Nothing of value. Nothing of consequence.'

Polly glanced at the papers that had fluttered to her feet. She picked one up. 'But this is a medical document about Reichsmarschall Göring. Do you mean to tell us your most cele-brated patient is no longer valued?'

Kahle snatched it from her. 'Please, I beg of you – I have been an exemplary guest – unlike all the others.'

'All the others who were arrested by the Gestapo?' Mimi wondered. 'Or all the others who subsequently fled?'

'You're just about the last German left at the Ritz,' said Polly. 'They've all gone now.'

'Even Oberstleutnant Metzingen,' said Mimi. 'He vanished in a puff of air. Not one person saw him running down the rue Cambon – if that's where he went. A shame, really. I, for one, would have much enjoyed seeing it.'

Mimi glanced at the tiny watch at her wrist. 'Some might see this as cutting it rather fine now, Doctor Kahle.'

He looked stricken. He ran to the window and looked out on the square. 'Don't tell me they're here so soon. Where are they, meine Dame!'

'They're not here yet, but we're expecting them imminently,' Polly informed him, now smiling at him brightly.

'I shall ask Monsieur Auzello to prepare your bill at once then, Herr Doctor,' said Mimi.

He stumbled. 'But the French Government will take care of that.'

'What French Government?' said Mimi. 'Not the one that fled Paris days ago?' She made a show of looking deeply apologetic. 'If you're hoping Marshal Pétain will assist you, then I'm afraid he's disappointed both you and France, Doctor Kahle.'

The German had to feel his way to a chair.

'Perhaps the new French Government will listen to you with a kinder heart?' Polly suggested.

He looked up, hopefully. 'The new one?'

'Led by General de Gaulle . . .'

They left him among the ashes of his Göring files.

When Polly and Mimi, escorted by the griffons, reached the Vendôme lobby, they were in time to see a beaming young messenger bound through the doors from the square to throw a hastily wrapped bundle on Claude's welcome desk. The force was enough to knock the ivory telephone to the floor. 'Long live France!' the boy declared, elated.

'Long live France!' returned every person inside the hall. The crush of people was considerable – ordinary folk from every walk of life – each one of them a fighter for the resistance. Polly and Mimi gave the piles of mimeographed papers to those who would see to their distribution across the 1st arrondissement.

'Give priority to the pharmacists,' Polly shouted above the din to the uniformed schoolgirls who were overseeing this task. 'And save plenty for the emergency clinics, too.'

'Yes, Mademoiselle Hartford,' returned their leader, before adding, shyly, 'We all like your outfit – it looks just like the flag!'

Polly grinned and did a little twirl for them in her divided skirt, ignored and unworn since the day of Lana Mae's internment.

'Is it by Lucien Lelong?' the girl wondered.

At the welcome desk, Claude had opened the wrapped bundle. There, still smelling of printer's ink, were copies of the first flimsy newspaper of the dawning era: *Libération*. He seized one of the sheets, holding it up so that everyone in the packed lobby might see the headline. 'Do you all read what it says?' he beseeched the room. 'It's a war cry as old as the very paving stones of Paris!'

Splashed across the front page were the perfect words to inspire all Parisians: *'To the Barricades!'*

'Long live France!' Claude declared, tearfully, and again the whole room returned the cry.

'They're a little late, aren't they?' Blanche had appeared at his side bearing a heaving platter of asparagus spears drizzled in Hollandaise sauce from the kitchens. 'We've had the barricades up since Saturday.'

'It's symbolic, my sweet,' said Claude, kissing her. He started tossing newspapers into the hands of those milling around him.

Blanche spotted Polly in the throng. 'Help me, sweetheart –
this thing weighs a ton.'

Polly stepped in to help her with the enormous plate. 'We're
still doing room service today?'

'Not today,' said Blanche, with a smile. 'This is strictly barricade service – it's going outside.'

Polly stuck a tantalising spear in her mouth. 'Oh, my goodness –
it's divine.'

Beaming Mimi was holding the doors open for them.

'I can't believe the Ritz actually *has* asparagus,' said Polly, as she
passed. 'I'd even forgotten what it looks like, let alone how it tastes.'

'The Hôtel Ritz has a great many nice things,' said Mimi, enigmatically. 'And today we share them with all Paris.'

Capped with enormous, defaced portraits of Hitler and Göring,
the two Place Vendôme barricades, placed at opposite ends of the
square, were like so many others that had risen spontaneously
across the capital. Constructed with the intention of impeding
the Germans in their anticipated battle with the arriving Allies,
everything and anything that could be moved or carried had
been heaped into their creation. Paving stones had been ripped
up from sidewalks and stacked across the two roads that fed into
the Place Vendôme – just as they had been in all major squares
and boulevards across the city. The sandbags of the Civil Defence
had been lent to the task, along with sewer gratings, cut down
trees, burned-out German military vehicles, and even a massive
grand piano. In the rue de la Paix barricade that Blanche and Polly
headed to first, mattresses, furniture, and a rusty, ancient pissoir
had been put to new purpose. An old sign promoting the National
Lottery Draw had been placed alongside the Nazi leaders' portraits
in a fine example of dark French humour.

Polly smiled with happiness at those she recognised along the
way. The handsome Baptiste from the Cambon bar. The eccentric

Mr Wall, with his chow dog, Pepe, who today wore a tricolour scarf. The industrialist's forgetful wife waved to Polly from where she led a group of women preparing bandages. Monsieur Lefèvre, the chilly sommelier, was today anything but cold, as he led a class of giggling children in games of hopscotch. Seeing all these old friends from four years at the Ritz, Polly couldn't help but think of those who were conspicuous in their absence. Where was Monsieur Guitry, the flamboyant playwright? Or Serge Lifar, the Russian ballet star? Where was Monsieur Cocteau, the fashionable poet, who everyone said dabbled in drugs? Where were any of the collabos?

Where was Zita?

Polly blinked her troubled thoughts of the film star away. The whereabouts of her guardian, at least, Polly knew.

As she and Blanche reached the barricade, an old man with a handlebar moustache and a collection of medals pinned to his jacket was teaching a group of eager sixteen-year-olds how to fire a pistol.

'Won't you let your pupils take a little break to enjoy the hospitality of the Hôtel Ritz, monsieur?' Polly asked him with a smile. She spotted Tommy with Anaïs, perched in sentry positions near the top of the barricade; Anaïs in a too-big Wehrmacht helmet. Odile was among the crowd of people below, as ever showing negligible evidence of her impediment.

The moustachioed old man stood ramrod straight as tears welled in his eyes at the sight of the food. 'Asparagus – my God.'

'Had you forgotten what it looked like?' Blanche asked him, kindly.

'Oh, Madame – what a day is this. What a day.'

'Just wait'll you taste it,' said Blanche. 'There'll be *fois gras* to follow – and *profiteroles au chocolat* for dessert!'

The teenagers swooped on the cuisine.

Polly left Blanche to it, and looked to the barricade, her eyes resting upon Tommy. They'd spoken little since the day they'd believed that Odile had been taken by the Gestapo. Polly knew he was embarrassed – ashamed even – although she couldn't have quite said why. Certainly, Mimi's words that day had been mortifying, but Polly felt as if she had been the one intended to be humbled by them, not Tommy. It had been Polly, after all, who had long ago failed to act on her heart and had ever since lived with the emptiness. Tommy's feelings were unknown to Polly – or at least, that's what she persisted in telling herself. Yet still she longed to speak with him properly, if only to return their relationship to something like colleagues in resistance again. But in the few weeks since Odile's non-arrest, Tommy had avoided such overtures.

Someone had brought a phonograph to the barricade and was playing a collection of French songs forbidden by the Occupiers. A gloriously ugly Parisienne danced a wild *carmagnole* to the music, while over her head she flourished a personal trophy for the occasion: a pair of Wehrmacht officer's trousers, with the proud red stripe down the seam. Polly guffawed at the outrageous woman, and joined the others around her, clapping and cheering her on. She saw Tommy look over from the barricade, and for a moment their eyes met.

Whether Tommy did it as an unconscious gesture, or as a deliberate means of connecting with her again, Polly couldn't tell, but in the second it happened her heart sang: Tommy gave his little head toss at her and Polly, while his eyes were still upon her, gave her own head toss in return.

They broke out in grins at each other.

'I'm coming over!' Polly called out to him, waving.

But before she could, two beautifully dressed women, tugging at the handles of a huge laundry basket wrapped with a white tablecloth, appeared in front of her. She knew them both from Lanvin. 'Why, Madame Hélène!' exclaimed Polly, delighted to see her. She kissed the woman on each cheek. 'What on earth are you carrying in there?'

'Molotov cocktails,' said Hélène, gratefully letting the basket drop, 'we followed all the instructions. And might I say you look gorgeous, Polly – yet you're not in Lanvin today?'

Polly laughed and kissed Hélène's companion. 'Hello Giselle,' she said to the young Lanvin cashier. 'I'm afraid my Lelong won the toss.' She struck a fetching pose. 'I'm sure you see why.'

'I would have worn my own Lelong,' Hélène confided, 'but I dreaded what Madame Lanvin would say of disloyalty.'

A voice behind Polly entered the exchange: 'Well at least *I* knew the right thing to wear.'

Hélène and Giselle frowned and Polly turned around to see.

It was Demetra Breker, the sculptor's wife. She postured grandly in an elegant outfit: a pale beige shantung suit topped by a chestnut cape. 'One of Madame Lanvin's finest,' she purred.

None of them said anything.

'Have you been in the rue Cambon?' Demetra asked them. 'Mademoiselle Chanel has re-opened her boutique.'

Polly's eyes narrowed at this news.

'She's put up a big sign in her window,' said Demetra, 'she's offering free bottles of Chanel No. 5 for all American GIs when they get here.'

'She can't be serious,' said Polly.

'Oh, but she is!' crowed Demetra. 'What a masterstroke.'

'What on earth can you mean by that, Madame Breker?' said Hélène.

Demetra lowered her voice. 'Well, surely you know she slept with those Nazis?' she tittered. 'Yet who'll harm a hair on her head for it now, with a city full of grateful GIs on her side?'

'They're not here yet,' Polly reminded her.

A thick wad of spittle hit the front of Demetra's shantung suit. With a shock, Polly realised who had spat it: Giselle.

'You think to place yourself above the collaborators, do you, Madame?' asked the girl. Her face was twisted with hatred.

Demetra was ashen. 'How dare you insult me!'

Giselle reached out and slapped Demetra's face hard. 'You're no better than Chanel – you're no better than any of them.'

Hélène watched on, perfectly composed.

'How many years have we put up with your filthy disgusting-ness?' Giselle shot at Demetra. 'Well, it all ends now.' She began pushing her away. 'Get back to Berlin, you stinking collabo, and get there fast. You and all the Führer's other favourites have got your days numbered.'

They watched with satisfaction as Demetra scuttled away.

Polly rubbed Giselle's shoulder. 'Very nicely done,' she told her.

Giselle was trembling with rage. 'I never knew I could be so *rude*,' she confessed. She looked back at Polly, askance. 'And do you know, I think I quite liked it.'

Polly laughed.

Then they all felt it.

Low, right at their feet, the Place Vendôme rumbled.

The phonograph needle skipped.

'What was that?' said Hélène, looking around them.

The square rumbled again, deeper and louder. From some-where at the top of the rue de la Paix came the sound of metal tracks scraping upon stone.

'Tank!' cried a voice from the barricades. Polly looked up and saw it was Anaïs. 'It's coming this way!'

'It's the Americans!' cried someone from the crowd below.

'It might be the Free French!' called out someone else. 'Long live France!'

The cry rang through the square. 'Long live France!'

But Polly kept her eyes on Anaïs and Tommy, watching the looks on their faces. Suddenly they were clambering from their perch.

'Take cover!' screamed Anaïs to the crowd.

'It's a German tank!' Tommy yelled at them all. 'Protect yourselves!'

No one panicked. Everyone in the square was too fuelled by courage and optimism. Polly caught eyes with Tommy again and found herself running in the same direction he was heading with Anaïs.

'Wait – where is Odile?' called Tommy.

Polly saw Odile in the crowd. 'She's up there – she's with Blanche.'

All three of them flung themselves into a jeweller's doorway, behind the barricade, near the corner of the rue de la Paix and the square. When Polly collected her wits, she found Tommy's arm around her.

He at once took it off.

'It's definitely a German tank?' she asked him.

'A Panzer,' he said, 'just like the ones that were here in 1940.'

They heard it draw nearer and then actually saw its turret above the top of the barricade – along with the long barrel of its gun.

A dapper little man with a goatee and an antique hunting rifle stepped into the line of fire.

'What's *he* going to do?' said Anaïs, incredulous.

Shouldering his ancient weapon, the old man pulled on the trigger. A smoky blast sprayed the tank barrel. Then, his weathered old face glowing with happiness, the dapper gentleman fled towards the doorway from which he had just appeared.

The three of them laughed.

'Cheeky old coot,' said Tommy.

'I adore him,' said Polly, hugging her Hermès handbag.

The retaliatory blast from the tank blew the barricade to splinters. Mattresses, furniture, the ancient pissoir, all disintegrated with the impact. Crouching in the jeweller's doorway, the three of them covered their heads with their arms as shrapnel and debris rained upon them.

'This is all theatre,' cried Tommy, when he looked up again. 'That tank could have easily driven over us – they're just putting on a show.'

'Is there only the one tank out there?' Polly's ears were ringing.

Anaïs nodded. 'They must be really desperate. They've got nothing left to win this war.'

The tank rolled in through the hole it had made in the barricade and proceeded to begin lapping the square. It didn't fire a second shot.

'Is that all it's got for us?' cried Polly with contempt.

On the opposite corner in another shop doorway they saw a fellow resistance fighter's face they recognised: the now legendary Denis, who was twenty-two, and had once gunned down a young German officer in the Barbès-Rochechouart Metro station. With his dirty white shirt open to his chest and a tricolour band on his arm, he gripped an aged Mauser in his hand as he skirted along the wall opposite them. They watched him reach the next alcove where Blanche was crouching. The tank continued its intimidating rotation, with everyone who had been at the barricade now watching on intently from the sides of the square. They saw Blanche shove asparagus at the young fighter.

The young man swallowed the handful of spears and kissed her hand without a word, before moving on.

'What is he planning?' said Polly, watching from across the road.

'He's going to make a dash for the tank,' said Tommy.

'But it'll fire at him!'

'He's taking a punt they don't have any more ammunition,' said Tommy. 'And I think he's right. All this is just to bully us.'

Armed with his Mauser, Denis set out to cross the Place Vendôme. Seconds later there was a burst of gunfire. They watched, horrified, as Denis hit the ground, a vivid red stain oozing from under his white shirt.

'Oh no.' Polly closed her eyes to it.

Anaïs pointed to the façade above. 'It wasn't the tank that fired – it came from up there.'

'A sniper?'

But Tommy realised what had been amiss in Blanche's doorway. 'I thought you said Odile was with Blanche.'

'She was,' said Polly.

On the ground, Denis was still moving. They saw another young resistance fighter crawling towards him along the pavement. A new shot fired from above and the second fighter froze.

'He's up there,' cried Tommy, identifying a window high in the façade. 'I can see the bastard.'

'We've got to kill him,' said Anaïs. She snatched up her pistol.

'You can't go,' Tommy told her. 'He'll shoot you from above.'

'Want to see me try?' said Anaïs.

Tommy pulled his own gun from inside his shirt – the gun that had once been Jürgen's. 'Then I'll go with you.'

'Neither of you can go!' cried Polly. 'You'll both be shot!'

A rapid burst of gunfire came from a different side of the square. The window Tommy had pointed at shattered and the body of the sniper slumped across the sill.

The three of them looked in amazement at each other.

'This day's going pretty well,' Anaïs cracked.

In the square, the crawling resistance fighter made it to Denis. The tank did nothing, continuing only to roll slowly in a wide circle. 'It's all right!' the fighter shouted to the crowd. 'He landed on top of a tomato!'

A fresh cheer of hilarity rang out from all sides.

'I still can't see Odile . . .' said Tommy, worried.

'Sing,' said Polly.

He looked confusedly at her.

'That song she loves, you know the one – let's sing it for her. She'll hear it and she'll know that it's us – and we'll know where she is.'

Tommy was stricken. 'I – I can't remember it.'

'Yes, you can – how can you ever forget it?' But Polly struggled to remember it herself.

Anaïs had the tune: '*Wait for me in this country of France . . .*'

'Yes – that's it,' said Tommy.

'I can't remember what comes next,' said Anaïs.

Tommy joined her repeating it. *'Wait for me in this country of France . . .'*

The three of them sang it again, louder. *'Wait for me in this country of France . . .!'*

From somewhere across the square came the completed verse. *'I'll be back soon, keep confident!'*

'Oh my God!' cried Polly. 'She heard.'

The four now sang in unity:

'Wait for me in this country of France, I'll be back soon, keep confident!'

'But, where is she?' said Tommy.

They craned to see but there was no sign of their friend.

'Stay brave, Odile!' Tommy shouted into the square with his fist in the air. 'Stay strong! We're with you!'

Then, from a position nearer the Ritz, Odile stood up from the scattered debris she'd been hiding behind and gave a perfect impression of Tommy's characteristic head toss.

Tommy stared in astonishment. 'Where the hell did she get that from?'

Still crouching with them in the doorway, Anaïs shut her eyes to the sight, blinking back tears. When she opened them again, Tommy was looking intently at her.

Anaïs was momentarily surprised. Then, summoning her courage, she said. 'You might as well know: I love Odile.' And then, as she watched Tommy interpreting what this meant, she clarified it: 'And Odile loves me. We're together, you see. We're lovers.'

Polly watched the scales falling from Tommy's eyes. She almost wanted to laugh – almost. Instead she just marvelled at Tommy's blinkered naivety.

'She didn't like people to know that we're more than just friends,' Anaïs told them. 'But I don't think it matters much now, do you? Given the day.'

Tommy was silent with amazement, so Polly stepped in. 'I'm so very happy to hear this lovely news, Anaïs,' she said, and she truly meant it. She kissed Anaïs on the cheek, and as she did so, she stage whispered, 'Thank you for taking her off our hands.'

Anaïs blushed, squeezing Polly's arm. Then she turned to Tommy with a pitying look. 'If only you'd realised it long before now, Tom.'

He looked affronted.

Anaïs turned her pitying look upon Polly. 'Some boys really are just clueless, aren't they?' But before Polly could comment on that she added: 'Almost as clueless as some *girls*.'

Now Polly and Tommy couldn't look at each other.

Anaïs rolled her eyes. 'God, what a moron,' she muttered.

Polly flinched. 'You should stop niggling him,' she warned Anaïs. 'Tommy's got a very short fuse for insults.'

'I mean *you*.'

Polly's jaw dropped. 'What have I done?'

'Absolutely nothing,' said Anaïs, 'which is why you're the biggest fool here.'

Polly huffed. 'Anaïs, I think you'll find I've a short fuse for insults, too.'

'Good. Then why don't you blow your top? Might be nice to get some passion for a change.'

'What on earth are you talking about?'

Anaïs folded her arms. 'You don't even realise how you *look* at him.'

Polly felt exposed and was all too aware that Tommy was daring to cast his eyes at her again. 'What do you mean by that?'

'With those bloody great cow eyes – you've got lovely eyes, by the way, Pol – but when you turn them on Tommy I just want to scream.'

'Stop!' Polly cringed. 'This is ridiculous, Anaïs.'

'It's because your feelings are so pathetically obvious – you adore the dumb lunk. You just want to jump on him and have your wicked way.'

Polly blushed scarlet.

A burst of activity further down the square gave a welcome distraction. A young woman was crawling over a pile of barricade debris, her saffron-yellow skirt swelling around her like a summer flower. She clutched a champagne bottle in her hand.

'That's Giselle from Lanvin,' said Polly, watching on in amazement.

'What does she think she's doing?' said Tommy, uttering his first words in some time.

They realised together. 'She's making a run for the tank!'

The Lanvin cashier dashed barefoot across the flagstones of the Place Vendôme to where the menacing tank was completing an arc outside the Hôtel Ritz.

'Oh my God,' Polly cowered, 'it's going to blow her to pieces!'

She barely noticed when Tommy took hold of her hand. 'I told you, Pol, it's got no more ammunition left – and Giselle thinks so, too.'

'This is no way to put it to the test!'

Across the square, Giselle made it to the tank unimpeded. The crowd on all four sides began to cheer. As nimble as a cat, she started to climb, champagne bottle in one hand, just as the lid on the turret began to rise.

'The kraut's coming out – he must still have a pistol with him,' Anaïs said.

But the German was too slow. Reaching the top of the tank, Giselle's arm swept up, with the green champagne bottle poised in her hand for a second in the air, before she smashed it into the turret. A geyser of flame spat out of the hole.

The Place Vendôme crowd went mad with approval.

Giselle leapt from the tank and ran back to where she'd come from. But a few feet away she dropped with a thud, her yellow skirt spreading over the pavement like a blossom struck from its stalk.

A terrible hush fell upon the Place Vendôme.

Anaïs had her hands to her mouth. 'She's been shot – there's another sniper.'

But Giselle had merely tripped. She got up again, with the flames from the burning tank now framing her beautifully in her saffron Lanvin skirt, as she chicly posed to the ecstatic reception of the crowd.

Sometime afterwards, in the hullaballoo as everyone ran to hug the girl, Polly realised that Tommy was missing. 'Where's he got to?' she asked Anaïs.

'He said we needed a tricolour flag – a really big one that we can hang from the front of the Ritz. And he said he knew where to find one.'

'Where?' said Polly, surprised.

Anaïs told her.

As the joyous residents of the 1st arrondissement surged laughing and singing around her, Polly found herself standing still, struck by a terrible sense of foreboding.

'What is it, Pol?' Anaïs asked her, shocked.

But Polly had already started running towards the Ritz.

Unexpectedly, the Imperial Suite was unlocked. The handle turned easily when Tommy tried it and the door swung inwards, without him needing the master key he'd lifted from Claude. Tommy peered into the opulent salons, once choked with looted art in the Göring days, and now strangely empty with only the hotel furniture left.

It was dim. The muslin curtains were drawn across the windows, diffusing the summer sunlight from the square. The rooms looked grubby and untidy, as if no one had been let in to clean them for weeks.

Tommy tried a light switch at the door. Nothing. The city's electricity was still off.

He stepped inside, mindful of his dusty tennis shoes on the carpet. 'Hello? Mademoiselle Zita?'

He listened for a reply but there was nothing. Instinct told him that somewhere deep in the luxurious labyrinth of rooms he would find her. Tommy walked further into the reception salon, leaving the doors open to the corridor. 'Zita – are you here?'

He heard a muffled, far-off sound of something metallic dropped on a hard-tiled floor – it had come from a bathroom. Tommy peered into the grand boudoir. The bed was in chaos; the linen looked stale. There were choked ashtrays on the side tables, jostling for space with empty bottles of wine. Tommy saw the open enamel tin on a pillow, with its dainty silver spoon. Both were empty. 'Mademoiselle Zita?'

There came the sound of chair legs scraping on bathroom tiles. Zita was inside the boudoir's bathroom – the one with Göring's specially constructed bath. Tommy went softly to the door. 'Zita?' he whispered. 'Are you in there?'

There was a pause. 'Who is it?'

'It's me, Tommy. Are you all right in there?'

'Tommy . . .'

It seemed his name didn't register with her.

'Tommy the waiter,' he reminded her, 'Tommy the barman. Tommy the guy who sometimes brings you breakfast.' He almost wanted to add: Tommy the son of Eduarde.

'Oh puss,' Zita said from behind the closed door. 'Tommy with the hair . . .'

He ran his fingers through it, scraping it back from his forehead. 'That's right,' he confirmed. 'They always say I look like a kraut.'

There was another pause. When it seemed like Zita had forgotten about him, he tapped on the door.

'Don't come in,' she called out.

He stepped back a pace. 'I won't. Don't worry.'

He looked at the rosewood armoire he had once helped Lana Mae shift to conceal the built-in. He marvelled that not one of the German occupants of the suite had ever twigged to it.

'Tommy?' Zita called to him. 'What's happening outside?'

A wide smile came to his face. 'It is the happiest day in memory, Mademoiselle. A girl from Lanvin blew up a tank. The Free French Army are imminent. It will not be very long now. This is our Liberation Day.'

'It has come then,' she said quietly. 'I had thought that it must have. It is good I have made myself ready . . .'

'Mademoiselle?' Tommy asked tentatively. 'There is something I would like to request from you –'

'Do you love Polly?' she asked, interrupting him.

He was taken aback.

'Well, do you?'

'Mademoiselle . . .'

'Answer me,' she demanded. 'It's a simple question. And we shall not talk at all if you can't.'

Tommy sensed she was standing on the other side of the door. 'We are colleagues,' he told her, 'companions in resistance. You know that, Mademoiselle. You've known it since the day of the round-up.'

Tommy thought he heard a sob break in her throat, but when she spoke again she gave no sign of it. 'That's not what I asked you. Do you *love* Polly? Yes or no? It's very important to me to know this today.'

Tommy shifted, uncomfortable. 'This is not a conversation I came here to have –'

'So, you're a coward then?' shot Zita behind the door. 'I expected much better from you, puss.'

He was hurt. 'Mademoiselle – please.'

'Do you love her? Tell me!' she screamed through the jamb.

Tommy stepped back in shock. Then he closed his eyes. Gently, he pressed his palms to the door. 'Clearly, you know already that I do . . .'

He waited.

'Do I now?' said Zita, softly. 'How much do you love her, then?'

He tried to use the truth in his heart to form words. 'With all that I am capable of loving, Mademoiselle, with all that I have to give –'

Zita cut him off again. 'Yes, what pretty words, and yet nothing has ever come of it? Your love sounds like worthless shit to me.'

He felt this like a punch.

'You either love or you don't,' said Zita. 'And clearly you don't because you've never once said those sweet words to Polly. Instead, you've saved them for me.'

Tommy started to say that once, some years ago, he had tried to say them, but Polly had stopped him, making it clear that resistance was everything and that love was worth nothing in light of it. And because this had hurt him, he'd channelled his courage into everything *but* love – or at least, love that was true – and he had never dared speak of it with Polly again.

'Gutless,' said Zita with disgust, as if reading his thoughts.

Then Tommy's mind went to what Anaïs had exposed in Polly as they'd crouched in the doorway – and how, after he'd learned of it, he'd taken Polly by the hand without even thinking to ask first. 'It – it's been very complicated,' he started.

'What lies,' said Zita. 'People are complicated maybe, but not the feelings we have for them . . .'

He sensed her mind wandering, as if she was having a conversation with someone she'd lost.

'Why, my Hans is the most complicated man that I know,' said Zita, 'a man of such inconsistence he drives me half mad. And yet I know that I love him, despite everything. I've always known it. Since that day when he picked up my lip rouge . . .'

Tommy was saddened. 'But your Hans is long gone.'

There was a silence from Zita. Then she said, 'It's all over now anyway. Or it will be very soon. When the Liberators find us . . .'

The skin prickled at the back of Tommy's neck. 'Find *us*? Are you alone in there?'

She laughed without mirth. 'There's no one but me and the bath ring.'

Tommy knew he should try to keep her talking – thinking that this is what Polly would have done. 'You're right, Zita,' he whispered, 'love is not complicated – people are, definitely, but not the feelings we have for them. We either love or we don't, just like you said.'

She was quiet.

A sense of impending doom came over him – something that seemed impossible on such a day, and yet it was there. Tommy shivered, the skin now prickling his back.

'I want to marry Polly,' he told her. He imagined – hoped – that Zita might like this.

There was emotion in her voice when she finally replied, 'That's good news, puss, real good . . .'

Now that he'd voiced it, Tommy knew that it was indeed good. 'When all this is over, maybe even before, I'm going to ask her.'

She chuckled. 'Do you think she'll be surprised?'

He thought of himself and Polly crouching together in the doorway. 'She might call me an idiot, but I don't think she'll really be surprised . . .'

'That makes me so happy. Thank you.'

Tommy returned to his task. 'Zita, there is something important hidden inside this suite.'

'Hidden?'

'Long ago. I helped Mrs Huckstepp hide it.'

There was a silence as she processed this. When she spoke again, she sounded relieved. 'What is it then?'

'A tricolour flag – an enormous one. Big enough to hang from the front of the Ritz.'

Zita seemed to lose interest. 'Sure, puss . . .'

'Will you give me permission to retrieve it? I know exactly where it is, and I will have no more need to disturb you once I have it again.'

He sensed she'd moved away from the door. 'Whatever you wish,' she told him. 'I don't care about any of it now. I just want them to hurry up and get here . . .'

He listened at the door for another moment, but she had nothing more to add. 'Thank you,' he said to her. Then he turned to the massive armoire. In the four years since Tommy had helped Lana Mae move it, he'd grown physically stronger. He didn't need anyone's help to shift it.

Polly pushed her way through the crowded lobby looking for Claude.

'Monsieur Auzello,' said Polly, 'has Tommy been to see you?'

'I saw him but there were too many people,' said Claude. 'If he wanted something from me then he's gone off to find it on his own.'

'He wanted to get inside the Imperial Suite.'

Claude's composure rippled. 'But no one's been in there since Zita took it. She's not been well lately . . .'

'Tommy says there's a hidden French flag in the suite.'

'Well, he won't be getting inside without the key.' Claude reached into his pocket to show Polly the master, only to realise it was gone. 'He must have lifted it from me . . .' Claude said, dismayed.

Polly was already running up the grand staircase. 'Wait!' Claude called after her. Then he was swamped in the crush once more.

Polly took the stairs two at a time and landed, breathless, upon the first floor. She started sprinting down the carpeted corridor, her Lelong divided skirt flapping at her shins, her Hermès handbag swinging from her arm.

Then she saw that the Imperial Suite doors were ajar, and she slowed. Polly fought to quieten her breath for a moment, as she strained her ears, listening. She approached the rooms, knowing that something wasn't right.

'Tommy?' she whispered. 'Tommy, are you in there?'

She heard a rumble of voices from deep in the salons and Polly's instincts sharpened. In the two years since she'd help push Jürgen's corpse into the Seine, Polly had experienced many crises, some of them terrifying, and yet with each one she had only grown calmer. Now, Polly felt hardly anything at all as she peeked carefully inside each room.

She was seized by an unstoppable rush of warmth. Her long-held desire for Tommy surged in her heart before merging with an irresistible feeling of affection as she looked for him. This collision of feeling created a perfect blend of sentiment that Polly recognised finally was love. She knew now without question as she searched for him: she loved Tommy utterly; she could never and would never love anyone more. Polly told herself that as soon as she saw him again, safe and unharmed, she would confess that she loved him, and that she had always loved him, since the day they'd first met in the Cambon bar. Then she would ask him to marry her, and if this affronted his masculine propriety too much, then she would suggest he ask her first.

The electricity returned with a pop. Lamps snapped on in all corners of the rooms and from somewhere came the noise of a radio.

'Parisians rejoice!' cried an announcer's voice. *'We have come on the air, thanks to our brothers in the power stations, in order to give you the news of our deliverance. The Free French Army has just entered Paris! We are mad with happiness!'*

It was the sight of Tommy's hair that took Polly's attention, just as it always did.

He stood with his back to her inside the grand boudoir. Polly's eyes were then seized by the extraordinary sight of the furs, hanging in splendour in a cave that had opened in the wall. Polly's mind went to the oddness of this, before she realised it was not a cave but the built-in, which had somehow been shielded by an armoire. Then Polly found herself focusing upon a ring-leted girl before she realised that the lost Renoir portrait had been stashed in there, too. And then Polly's attention went to the other person in the room, and she found herself blinking as she finally recognised who it was.

Metzingen's hair had turned ashen and sparse on his skull; his once powerful frame had shrunk. He looked skeletal, cadaverous, his skin like parchment stretched on his bones. The stench of him was disgusting. Metzingen must have been hiding for weeks in this cave and hadn't run away at all.

Tommy had set him free.

Hans was near naked, wild-eyed, and holding Jürgen's gun. Somehow, he'd wrestled it from Tommy.

Tommy had his hands in the air, but the words he was saying to the last of the once-proud Occupiers were not in any way placatory.

'What did you expect would happen to you, kraut?' Tommy challenged him, simmering with rage. 'You've been living in a dream world.'

'Stop it,' Metzingen hissed. 'Just stop it . . .'

On the radio came the opening chords of 'La Marseillaise'.

'But why should I stop it?' Tommy taunted him. 'What do you even know about this war? You've experienced nothing but degen-eracy while you've lived at the Ritz – and what has happened to your Fatherland while you've indulged yourself?'

The bathroom door creaked open, and Polly saw who now emerged.

'Stop it!' screamed Metzingen. The gun was shaking in his hand. He took a step closer to Tommy. 'Just stop it, I say.'

From the square came the sound of dozens of radios, all switched on, their volumes being turned up high. 'La Marseillaise' pulsed out from each one of them, filling the Place Vendôme and beyond.

'You've lost this disgusting war,' Tommy spat at him. 'And better still, kraut, this war has lost you. You're a casualty now. You're no better than those whose lives you stole.' His breath caught in his throat. 'You're no better than Comte Eduarde . . .'

Metzingen staggered forward. 'You dare compare me to that dead Jew?'

Polly saw Tommy's unbreakable pride. 'I am his son,' he whispered.

Metzingen's fingers pressed upon the trigger.

'Herr Oberstleutnant!' Polly shouted at him.

The pistol swung from Tommy to her.

'Fräulein Hartford?'

'If you let Tommy live, I will give you something.'

Outside, people flung their windows open and rushed to their balconies. From sidewalks, boulevards, barricades and rooftops, the whole city began to sing along with the radios, joyous and alive.

Metzingen had trouble focusing on her. 'Fräulein Polly . . . Jürgen was so fond of you . . .'

Polly watched Zita creep nearer, clutching at a metal object in her hand. In the madness of the moment, Polly saw without comprehending that Zita had done something disfiguring to herself. She was bleeding.

Polly opened her Hermès handbag. 'I have something for you, Herr Oberstleutnant, if you want it. And I think that you will want it. It is something you'll very much like – but only if you spare Tommy for it.'

Metzingen's eyes had no white to them, blood red. 'You think you can negotiate with *me*, meine Dame?'

'Why not?' said Polly. 'Reichsmarschall Göring negotiated with anyone – and he had so many *jewels* . . .'

Metzingen's bone dry tongue licked at his bottom lip.

'He had *bowls* of jewels,' Polly whispered. 'So many he lost count. He had all the jewels in Paris it must have seemed like to you.' Polly's look was all sympathy. 'How galling that would have been. How very unfair. You are such a better man than he ever was. You *deserved* what he had . . .'

His mouth was gaping, mesmerised by her.

Polly took out a little jar of face cream, always kept safe in her handbag. 'Where were *your* jewels, Herr Metzingen?' she wondered. 'What did the greedy Reichsmarschall leave *you* in the bottom of the trough?'

'Nothing . . .' rasped Metzingen. 'Nothing at all. What I have is so pitiful . . .'

Polly opened Lana Mae's jar. 'Why not get something nice now?' she suggested. She tipped the contents into her palm. In the scented crème a sapphire sparkled, blue like the evening star.

Metzingen reached for it.

'Uh-uh.' Polly snapped her hand back. 'Let Tommy live.'

The German swung the pistol at Tommy's shirt. 'He's a kike.'

The weapon exploded as Tommy lunged at him – at the very moment a second weapon flashed in Zita's hand: the *Modèle* 1935. A spray of viscera spattered her face, before Metzingen fell forward.

'*Liebchen*?'

She shot him again.

Zita kept pulling the trigger and firing until the final breath spluttered from her lover's lungs.

She smiled at Polly. 'I couldn't let them have him, puss . . .'

Polly only saw now what Zita had done to herself. She had sheared off her famous curls in great hunks, leaving her scalp red raw.

'Oh, Tommy . . .' Polly stammered, staring at the ruins of the film star.

He was shielding her from harm, having snatched Jürgen's gun. 'It's all right – it's all right now, Pol.' He pointed into the built-in. 'Look. There's the flag . . .'

Outside in the Place Vendôme, and everywhere on the radios, 'La Marseillaise' reached its end. It was answered by the peal of cathedral bells.

The Free French Army was here.

Tommy let the gun slip to the floor as he crumpled beside it.

Polly screamed. 'Tommy!'

His fingers clutched uselessly. A dark red stain ran across his shirt. 'I should have dodged that one, Pol . . .'

Polly clung to him. 'Tommy, no – not like this – not today.'

Zita had the *Modèle* 1935 in her fingers, returning to the bathroom she'd come from.

'Help him,' Polly cried after her. 'Help him, Zita, please . . .'

'You'll be fine, puss,' she threw over her shoulder, 'he's gonna ask you to marry him . . .' She was already closing the door.

Polly pressed her hands to the bullet wound in Tommy's abdomen, trying to stop the flow. Tommy's blood pooled on the carpet around them.

'Oh God. Oh God, no . . .' she sobbed.

'You heard her, Pol, don't worry,' said Tommy. 'And I *am* gonna ask you to marry me.'

But his eyes were already closing as the gunshot rang from the bathroom.

Suddenly Polly was pressing her lips to his with such hunger his eyes opened again. It was too late to go back, too late to pretend, and the two of them kissed as naturally as if it had happened between them hundreds of times – and in each of their minds it long had. Tommy's lips were soft and warm. His breath was sweet on her cheek. His long arms encircled her, and when the kiss ended, they were both left breathless with the rush of it.

Polly didn't let him go.

EPILOGUE

14 July 1962

An eager young woman gliding into Tommy's orbit only to monopolise him was a spectacle Polly had grown used to. It was a testament to the great bond between Polly and her husband that she never felt jealous when witnessing it. Tommy was not one to stray and Polly knew the cause of the phenomenon anyway: his hair. As startling upon his head at age thirty-nine as it had ever been when he was a teenager, Tommy's neon bright thatch mesmerised women just as Polly had been mesmerised by it so long ago. Yet this evening's young monopolist was different – or rather, Tommy was. As Polly looked at them from across the Consulate's reception room, the young woman wore the same expression as all those before her: an enraptured gaze, awestruck even, punctuated by nods and preening. The difference now was that Tommy was mirroring it. He was as enthralled by his companion as she was by him.

Puzzled by this, Polly ended her own conversation with what she hoped was not unseemly haste and made her way through the throng of Australian notables. Then it was she who was struck. Tommy and the girl had been speaking in French but when Polly neared, Tommy called out in English.

'Pol – this is incredible – I want you to meet someone.'

The young woman's smile beamed from Tommy's face to hers, guileless. She was no would-be seductress, Polly saw. 'Madame Comtesse,' she began, also in English, 'it is such a very great honour . . .'

But the words had already fallen away for Polly, unable at that moment to process anything other than the young woman's scarf. 'That's so beautiful.'

The young woman's fingers brushed at the silk at her throat.

'It's Hermès, isn't it?'

The scarf was patterned with horses. The girl's eyes glistened. 'Yes, it is.'

'Polly,' Tommy began again.

But she couldn't move past it. 'I know that pattern, it's a very old one, isn't it, from long before the war? I once knew someone who wore a scarf just like that.' She shook her head as old memories came back. 'I could never forget how lovely it looked upon her – just as it looks upon you.'

'Was it Alexandrine?'

Polly stared at her, dumbfounded. How long had it been since she had heard anyone say that name out loud?

Tommy wound his arm around Polly's waist, and she automatically wound hers around his, fingers finding the ridge of his old bullet scar. 'Polly,' he said again, softer now, 'please let me introduce you.'

Yet she was still too caught in the moment. 'But how could you possibly know that name, Mademoiselle?'

Tommy shook his head, shrugging at the young woman.

'Because she gave it to my grandmother Alma, Madame,' the young woman told her, 'and my grandmother gave it to me.'

Words fled Polly. 'I – what?'

Tommy turned her face towards him so that she would listen. 'Darling,' he said, 'this is Vidette Carpenter.'

'How do you do,' said Polly, presenting her diplomat's hand.

'Before I came to live here in Sydney I was Vidette Benoir,' the young woman said, taking Polly's palm.

The name meant nothing. 'I don't understand,' Polly started.

'It's incredible,' said Vidette. 'Such a coincidence. I'm a journalist, you see, I write the social pages for *The Australian Women's Weekly*. I only accepted tonight's invitation because I had nothing else on.'

Polly had to laugh at that.

'Just listen,' said Tommy.

Vidette continued. 'You'll think it sounds silly, Madame, but I recognised the Comte's hair. I couldn't take my eyes from it. And when I was properly introduced to him, there was something about his face that struck a chord with me, too, although I couldn't quite name it.'

As if further proof of her French origins was needed, Vidette displayed an inherent flirtatiousness. 'He's very handsome, of course, but not in a movie star way; he's too French for that.'

Polly looked at her husband with one eyebrow raised.

'And like so many Parisian men of his class, he is exquisitely if somewhat *personally* dressed. His style is his own –'

'Mademoiselle,' said Polly, feeling a swell of impatience. 'You mentioned Alexandrine?'

The young woman remembered herself, and to Polly's surprise her eyes welled with tears. She fanned at her face. 'I had thought I was doing fine in holding these off . . .'

Polly was concerned. 'What is it?'

Tommy was about to tell her but Vidette stayed his words. 'The previous Comtesse was a very great woman – she sacrificed herself. And your husband is a very great man. He saved me, Madame,

439

on the night of the Marais round-up, when I was only five years old . . .'

Then the floodgates opened.

All three of them found themselves clutching each other and crying, there in the middle of the French Consulate; tears that were both happy and sad.

Polly told herself she didn't believe in fate, having long decried horoscopes and the like, and yet sometimes – at near-magical moments like tonight – she would hear the long-stilled voices of the Girls, who had each believed in fate so utterly, calling her a fool. Tonight, it felt as if she was watching herself from a great distance, perched in heaven, perhaps, accompanied by her guardians' wry ghosts. She watched on as Polly-on-earth went through the motions, waiting for where fate would deliver her.

Polly observed herself tell Vidette the old stories. They rolled off so easily, told at functions wherever she and Tommy travelled in the world. The stories started with the Liberation, of course, and then moved to the years afterwards, when all the deeds of the Resistance had come out. Polly and Tommy had been awarded the *Croix de Guerre* by President de Gaulle. That had led to a friendship with the great man, a meeting of hearts and minds. From there, in the startling speed with which things seemed to happen in the post-war reconstruction, the now Comte and Comtesse Ducru-Batailley had joined the French delegation at the United Nations. They had no children – by choice, not misfortune – because they were devoted to their work. Yet they had many children in their lives; disadvantaged children mentored and supported through the Ducru-Batailley charitable foundation. When in Paris, Polly and Tommy still lived at the Hôtel Ritz, their only home. They had a deep and lasting emotional connection to the famous establishment.

The evening drew on. The Consular function began winding down and Polly and Tommy were eager to bring Vidette to their suite at the Hilton so that stories might go on being told into the small hours. For Polly the sensation remained that something greater was at play, that the coincidence of meeting Vidette wasn't chance but the machinations of destiny.

At the Hilton suite, more champagne and yet more tales; the indulgence of nostalgia. Now came the story of Polly the orphan who was sent off to France and her aunt, the great Australian soprano, Marjorie Tighe. Then Polly being "given" to her aunt's three friends: Alexandrine, whose terrible end as a Holocaust victim was well known in France, if not in the wider world; Lana Mae, lately immortalised by Hollywood in *The American Angel*, even if they got the details wrong; and Zita, the symbol of insouciant defiance thanks to the Resistance messages in her films – and whose troubling death was swept under the carpet by her fans.

So many other people from that time to talk about – what had happened to them? Blind Odile had become a rabble rouser for the French Communist Party. Odile's beloved Anaïs, the girl scout who helped save Vidette, and whom she never saw again, now a journalist herself in the sphere of French politics. The loathsome Gendarme Tessier who went out in his civilian clothes to buy the first issue of *Libération*, only to be seen reading it by a fleeing SS officer who shot him dead on the street.

Then, right at the end of the evening, fate showed its hand.

Polly brought out the medals awarded in the earlier war to her Aunt Marjorie. She travels with them everywhere, Polly tells Vidette, these medals more important to her than the medals she won of her own. Vidette was honoured to hold them, but as she takes the case from Polly's hands a ghastly thing happens: she drops it. Right there on the floor. Vidette could just die at her clumsiness and blames the champagne. Yet as she is about to descend into shamefaced apologies, she is struck dumb by the look on Polly's face. Then she sees what has caused it. The medal case, upon hitting the hard floor, has fallen in such a way that the satin insert has dislodged, exposing something long been hidden behind it.

A letter from Marjorie to Polly – a letter never received.

A remarkable confession comes from Tommy then, but Polly only half hears it; a story about something Alexandrine had told him to reveal to Polly on the night of the round up; something Tommy never did because Alexandrine said Polly would be devastated by it. And so, he'd forgotten. Another spark of memory comes to Polly now that Lana Mae once revealed something similarly cryptic – and then comes Polly's realisation that nothing stays forgotten just because we say it is.

The letter was determined to reveal itself – or rather, Marjorie was, through her lost words.

Tommy and Vidette don't read what is there and nor do they ask to. It is private. But as Tommy leads Vidette to the door, thanking her for her company and bidding her adieu, Vidette can tell that what has been written in the letter moves the Comtesse profoundly.

Vidette is glad beyond words that she has played a small part in uncovering it.

1 December 1939

My treasured Polly,

So many drafts I have started, then abandoned, of this letter – so many by now I've lost count. This letter, Polly, more than any other I've written to you, means everything.

There's a war going on. It hasn't come to France yet, but it will, and soon. The timing, as my great friends might say, is lousy. I've got a death sentence hanging on top of me. I wish I didn't. Not only because it means I'll be robbed of seeing what you, the niece I so love, will grow up to become, but because I will have no chance to have sway upon this new conflict. I'm a woman. I can't fight in men's wars, at least not in the way men do, but I know I can do what I can to lessen its worst, however minutely, in places that men overlook. That's what I did in the last war. That's what I'd have done in this – if not for my heart. It's let me down badly. But you haven't.

So many times, in these weeks since the doctors gave me the news, I've thought of you, Polly, so far away in Australia. I've read and re-read your letters and seen in them a reflection of myself. It's uncanny. We're so very alike. We don't much resemble each other physically, but beneath our skins, in our beating hearts, we're the same.

I <u>know</u> you wish to do something good with your life. Not for you, I suspect, is domesticity's comfort – you want something much more. So did I. Sometimes at night I've laid awake fearing this war will rob you of the future's possibility. My fear of what might come – not for me, but for you – has made my usual optimism ring hollow. I know that it has, and I know that you've felt it, even if neither of us have yet had the courage to say so in what we've written to each other. But I know you've *got* courage – far more than me. You just haven't harnessed it yet. When you do, it will be the making of you.

Whatever war brings, whatever it throws at you, face it front on. As bad as things might get there will still be a need for decency – and loyalty, and friends. I'm 'giving' you some friends in my legacy. Three of them to start off with, marvellous girls: Alexandrine, Lana Mae and Zita. You'll know their names already for I've written of them often.

My hope is to bring you to Paris someday – with your father's permission – and sooner rather than later. I doubt he'll object much. He adores you but he's so luckless with money. I shall bring you to the Hôtel Ritz. I have paid for a thousand and one nights' accommodation for you – a standing arrangement that begins whenever you might arrive. When you get there, however, you must remember to look past the surface. It's a trap. Madame Mimi, the Ritz hotelier, once told me there's two types of guests who stay there: there are those for whom the Ritz is entirely surface – and there are those who can't see the surface for the heart. Which one will you be? I think I know already.

If I die before I can bring you to the Ritz, then the Girls will make it happen for me. Trust them. We are all of us peas in a pod.

Don't let this war stop you. Do the very opposite, Polly, let it help you become. Never feel hampered by your youth or your gender in the face of its horror – be empowered by these things you can't change and instead exploit them. They're both so very precious. Find a way to fight for what matters the most, and keep on fighting, until those things are in sight again.

And don't be blinkered to love.

Too often when purpose grips us we lose sight of why we need purpose at all. It's there to nourish the good things life throws at us – and this includes love. Nourish doesn't mean shut out. It means remembering that goals aren't single but several.

You will win your fight, Polly, but to savour your victory, you must treasure your heart.

In a life lived in wonder, you are the most wonderful thing that I've gained.

I'm so grateful for you.

Aunt Marjorie xxxx

The real characters
at the heart of
The Heart of the Ritz

The path to this book was paved by the books of others –
wonderful books by wonderful writers – and it was only
after I had read the third of what grew to be many that
I realised the joy of discovery I was feeling had purpose: I was
researching. The books were linked, even though I hadn't seen
them as being so to begin with. In retrospect, I must have been
blind. Actually, I was dazzled. I had read these books because that
was what I was seeking to be. Bedazzlement begets diversion, and
there were one or two things I was happy to be diverted from.

At the time of my reading, I had been feeling very troubled, as
were so many millions of people around the world, by the assaults
against institutions of democracy being waged in countries where
democracy had previously seemed unassailable. This unease was a
constant in the back of my mind. Coupled with it was a growing
sense of unfairness at the manner with which my generation,
Generation X, was treating the generation to which our children
belong, the so-easily disparaged Millennials. Perhaps the most

cherished by-product of my day-job as a university lecturer is the number of these so-called Millennials I have in my life. I know more people in this age group than I do in any other, and unlike many of my own generation I am not dismayed by them. Far from it. I am continually and marvellously inspired by young people – and I hate how they are so often disregarded. This, too, was a constant in my mind.

And so, it was, with these two concerns engaged in a dialogue in my creative subconscious, I was reading, I thought, purely for diversion. Except that I wasn't. I was unwittingly seeking the means to channel my brain-buzz into the thing I most enjoy writing: historical fiction. And that, I believe, is why I ended up choosing the books that I chose. What linked them was time and place: the late 1930s and early 1940s in France; a period when that most iconic of democratic nations not only betrayed a generation of its young people, it slipped loose from democracy to embrace Fascism, thanks to the Nazi invaders. That France returned to democracy at all was due in no small part to the same young people it had sidelined. French teenagers formed the backbone of the Resistance movement, stealthily fighting back against the Nazis and French collaborators, and doing so side by side with others who had found themselves marginalised through no fault of their own: patriotic French women.

But back to those books. The first one I read was *The Riviera Set: 1920-1960: The Golden Years of Glamour and Excess*, by Mary S. Lovell, a book I picked up for its promise of hedonistic escapism. It delivered. And while not remotely about the French Resistance, it did provide my introduction to a wonderfully seductive milieu, where bohemians and celebrities, and wealthy expatriates, and decidedly unconventional aristocrats intersected. The second book I read, several months later, examined that same milieu in Paris, away from its favourite pleasure grounds. *The Hotel on Place Vendôme: Life, Death and Betrayal at the Hotel Ritz in Paris*, by Tilar J. Mazzeo, was a revelation, providing a history of the famed hotel across the decades, but most particularly during World War II. I was astonished by what I read of the Resistance activities conducted by guests and staff under the noses of the Nazis. By this point I was starting to get an inkling that there was fine material for a novel here. The third book I read confirmed it. *Les Parisiennes: How the Women of Paris Lived, Loved and Died in the 1940s,* by Anne Sebba, provided me with compelling portraits, at turns both inspiring and heartbreaking, of the women of Paris during the Occupation. I knew by the time I'd finished it what my own book would be. So did my publishers, pleasingly. I sent them a proposal for what evolved to become *The Heart of the Ritz,* and they said yes within half an hour of receiving it. If there is a paradise for novelists, it will be wallpapered with such happy emails. Other excellent books joined my reading pile, all of them further inspiring me no end. The best of them were, *When Paris Went Dark: The City of Light Under German Occupation,* by Ronald C. Rosbottom; *The Paris Ritz,* by Mark Boxer and Pierre Salinger; *Is Paris Burning?,* by Larry Collins and Dominique Lapierre; and *Nancy Wake: A Biography of Our Greatest War Heroine, 1912-2011,* by Peter FitzSimons.

To all disparagers of historical fiction, should I ever have the misfortune of meeting any, I am ready to defend the form. The key to appreciating it, and indeed to writing it, is in embracing the meaning of the confluence: 'history' is presented 'fictionally'. Historical fiction is not non-fiction but is inspired and informed by it. Nowhere in the historical fiction writer's manual, should there actually be such a document, is artistic license precluded. If it was, then we'd all be in trouble, writers and readers alike. Some of the characters in *The Heart of the Ritz* are based directly on real people, and thus have been given their names. Other characters are composites, built from various aspects of one or more real people, and thus they have been given fictional names. It has been my intention to create an absorbing, emotional, and hopefully inspiring story about the Resistance movement at the

Paris Ritz, and then explain the real-life characters behind it. All the characters in my book were in some way drawn from the excellent non-fiction works named above.

Maxine Elliott, the early-twentieth century American star of Broadway and the West End, who gave away the stage to live in the South of France as a society hostess and philanthropist, provided me with the inspiration for Polly's beloved Aunt Marjorie. Aspects of another great star of the era, the Australian soprano, Marjorie Lawrence, also aided me here.

Alexandrine, whose act of self-sacrifice was among the very first story ideas to enter my head for this book, was inspired by several aristocratic French women of Jewish faith, who acted with both heartbreaking courage and naïve foolhardiness during the Occupation. The two women most influential to me were Élisabeth, Baroness de Rothschild, and Béatrice Reinach (née Camondo), both of whom died in the Holocaust. Anne Sebba's *Les Parisiennes* contains stories of many upper-class women who did extraordinary things for their country, and I acknowledge the inspiration their heroism also gave me. Alexandrine's husband Eduarde was inspired by aspects of Philippe, Baron de Rothschild, once husband of Élisabeth, who survived the war in exile and served in the Free French Army.

Lana Mae was directly inspired by the colourful life of Laura Mae Corrigan, the American millionairess and long-term Ritz resident dubbed, like Lana Mae, 'The American Angel' for her work with wounded French soldiers. Many aspects of Lana Mae's story are derived from Corrigan's adventures, although I also found inspiration in the internment experiences of another American, the actress Drue Leyton. The would-be cancer scam was Leyton's cleverness, although unlike poor Lana Mae, it really was a scam.

Zita was inspired by the once celebrated French film star, Arletty, who set a trend that Cher, Madonna and Bono would follow decades later for mononyms. A fabulous Ritz denizen, Arletty epitomised the treachery of one's own heart with her misfortune of falling in love with a handsome Nazi. As she so famously said, 'My heart is French, but my ass is international.' Arletty's lover was Hans-Jürgen Soehring, from whom I partly drew in creating both Metzingen and Jürgen, although the former's downward spiral of dope addiction was entirely artistic license on my part.

Arletty survived the war in body if not in career, sadly for her, although the power of her screen presence in the films in which she starred remains undiminished. I allude to three great French films in *The Heart of the Ritz*. Zita's fleapit hotel film is *Hôtel du Nord* (*Northern Hotel*, 1938, directed by Marcel Carné), which I made silent (and filmed in Berlin!) for my plot purposes, although it was neither in actuality, of course. Zita's blackmail film is *Le Corbeau* (*The Crow*, 1943, directed by Henri-Georges Clouzot), and her film set in a nineteenth-century theatre is *Les Enfants du Paradis* (*Children of Paradise*, 1945, directed by Marcel Carné), which starred Arletty. The latter two films, both glorious, are additionally revered for their subversive Resistance messages. I was a little loose with their production dates, again for plot purposes. The Jean-Paul Sartre play that Zita and Blanche fail to warm to was *Huis Clos* (*No Exit*, 1944), which debuted at the Théâtre du Vieux-Colombier, with its sly warning to collaborators, just ahead of the Liberation.

Other Nazis provided aspects of their lives to Metzingen, including Hans Speidel, who had responsibility for maintaining 'Parisian cultural life', centred at the Ritz. Speidel, along with Carl-Heinrich von Stülpnagel and Caesar von Hofacker, was among the high-ranking Nazi conspirators of the failed 20 July 1944 assassination attempt against Hitler, which was partly hatched at the Ritz. I kept this plot well to the periphery of *The Heart of the Ritz* – it's so complex it warrants an entire book to itself, which it already has, numerously, as well as informing the storyline of *Valkyrie*, the 2008 film starring Tom Cruise.

Speaking of Toms, *The Heart of the Ritz*'s Tommy was directly inspired by a truly heroic teenage Resistance fighter named

Thomas Elek. My biggest conceit was to place this character at the Ritz and make him the illegitimate son of a Comte. The real-life Tommy was neither aristocratic nor resident at the hotel, although many other aspects of his life are shared with his fictional self. Tommy Elek was a Hungarian-born Jew, whose mother ran a restaurant in Paris which was very popular with the Occupiers. With his Aryan good looks and shock of blond hair, Tommy was popular with them, too. What began as schoolboy pranks like the 'butterflies' grew into a far more dangerous resistance. Polly's book bomb was one of Tommy's real-life acts of anti-Nazi terrorism (he used a copy of Karl Marx's *Das Kapital*), along with many other reckless deeds, including grenade attacks and train derailments. Tragically, Tommy Elek did not survive the war. His teenager's false sense of invincibility brought him to grief. Along with a number of his young Resistance colleagues, Elek was arrested by the Gestapo and shot in 1944. He had not long turned nineteen.

If the idea of a near-sightless Resistance fighter seems somewhat far-fetched, it was in real-life, too, and thus was another perfect disguise. Odile was inspired by Jacques Lusseyran, a blind teenager whose disability proved no impediment when it came to fighting Nazis. Because his remarkable ability to navigate the streets of Paris carrying weapons and messages between Resistance cells so impressed his sighted colleagues, Jacques Lusseyran became a leader of the movement. Like Tommy Elek, he was eventually brought undone by his activities. Unlike Elek, he wasn't executed for them. Instead, also aged nineteen, Lusseyran was sent to Buchenwald concentration camp where, astonishingly, he actually survived to be liberated in 1945. My character Odile started out male, and thus more like Jacques, until she evolved along with the story, and eventually became female. Artistic license again. Her defiant spirit is very much Lusseyran's though.

Ritz husband and wife, Claude and Blanche Auzello, and the hotel's Swiss owner, Marie-Louise 'Mimi' Ritz, are direct portraits of real people, and thus have been given their real names.

The Auzellos have been well documented for their extraordinary Resistance work, which included relaying messages for the Free French Army, and hiding Jews and Allied airmen in the Ritz attic rooms. Both Auzellos were highly active, although, and perhaps surprisingly, they worked independently of each other. Neither seems to have let the other know of the true extent of their respective activities, presumably to protect their spouse. They did not have a child. I added Odile to their union purely to serve my story purposes.

None of the research material I read specifically names Mimi as working for the Resistance – she was exceedingly discreet by nature, like all great hoteliers – but none of it names her as not working for the Resistance, either. Because Mimi so successfully created her own myth of being across everything that went on in the Ritz, I found it hard to believe she wasn't wise to at least some of the Resistance work being carried out by her staff and guests. And given how outrageously the Occupiers exploited her establishment with the non-payment of bills, it's no great stretch to imagine Mimi wishing to settle the score somewhat. So, again, Mimi has benefited from my artistic license, but I like to think that my version of her is not beyond the bounds of reason.

Other minor characters mentioned among the hotel guests were also real people, like the disgusting Hermann Göring and his quack doctor, Kahle; the drug-addled poet, Jean Cocteau; the sculptor, Arno Breker and his wife Demetra; and the actor and playwright, Sacha Guitry. All the fashion houses, labels and designers mentioned in the book are, of course, real, and many of them are still icons of French haute couture today. Sebba's *Les Parisiennes* mentions the employees of a house that were active in the Resistance while their Nazi and BOF customers remained wholly unaware – yet it doesn't say which house it was. So, I decided to make it Lanvin, whose determination to stay in business I admired rather more than I did Chanel's decision to close.

My treatment of Coco Chanel in this book may be a surprise to some readers, because it jars with so many other depictions of the great designer. Few fashionistas have been better at cementing their own legend. Sadly, a rather different picture of Chanel emerges in the cold light of history. As with Arletty, I feel some sympathy with Coco for having fallen in love with one of the handsome Occupiers (her lover was Hans Günther von Dincklage), but I feel no sympathy for the actions she took in exploiting the anti-Jewish laws to regain control of her perfume business. Coco Chanel's Occupation history is very muddy, yet unlike Arletty, she paid no price for following her heart. In the fallout of the Liberation she successfully called upon the protection of friends in very high places, including Winston Churchill. Luckless Arletty found she no longer had any friends to call upon.

Characters like Suzette, Anaïs, Guy and others, weren't drawn from specific people so much as they were derived from the 'spirit' of so many courageous French women and men whom I read about and absorbed. Gendarme Tessier was drawn from what I learned of the inglorious history of the French police during the Occupation.

It is perhaps ironic that the character most important to *The Heart of the Ritz* is also the most fictional. Polly's circumstances are entirely my own creation, although many of her actions were drawn from the Resistance activities of real people. The idea that haute couture might serve as a disguise was one that seems to have occurred to several upper-class women mentioned in *Les Parisiennes*. The real-life person most like Polly is a woman whose name is still highly revered in France and in her country of birth, Australia. Nancy Wake was a young Sydney woman whose sense of adventure took her to France in the early 1930s, where, of course, she fell madly in love with the country – and with a dashing French man, Henri Fiocca, whom she married. Nancy's egalitarian contempt for authority, her belief in equality, her championing of the rights of the individual, and of course, her natural warmth and good humour, found immediate reflection in the culture of France. She took to the French and the French took to her – like glue. When the Nazis came, Wake did not hesitate to stand up and fight for her adopted country. Peter FitzSimons' biography details her Resistance activities in passionate detail and is an excellent read. Nearing her thirties when the war broke out, Wake was older than I wanted my character Polly to be, and she conducted her Resistance in rural France, not Paris, so I didn't use her as a direct inspiration. But I did draw greatly upon Wake's personality in *The Heart of the Ritz*. Polly's idealism and courage, her outrage at injustice, her refusal to give in, her steadfast feminism (before the word even existed), her ability to see and do what needs to be done, no matter how much danger it brings upon herself, are all Nancy's. These are wonderful qualities to find in a young person – qualities I know are still to be found in young people today.

We are so very lucky that the times aren't as grim as they were in France, mid-1940, when all that the French held dear was made so much more meaningful with the arrival of a regime that despised such values. Things aren't quite that dire now, but as I look at some democratic countries around the globe, I see the same signs that the people of France were blind to back then. Democracy is so fragile, and history is cyclical, after all. It could happen again. But one thing is certain: it'll be to our young people that we'll turn to step up and fight back should we find we have lost what matters most to us.

Acknowledgements

I 'm very lucky to have a network of support when it comes to writing. So many family and friends remain enthusiastic about me doing it, which is lovely. My partner, Andrew Brown, the yin to my yang, would happily put my novelist's aspirations out with the rubbish, I know (and should I depart this world before he does, I encourage scholars to examine our recycling bin for my archive), yet remarkably, he continues to endure me. Perhaps it's because, despite everything, we both know we're doing something right. In 2018 we clocked up twenty-five years together. Our secret is humour: a quarter century of making each other laugh.

My agent, Lyn Tranter, for whom the passage of this book was somewhat smoother than the book that preceded it, remains a shining jewel. Likewise, Roberta Ivers and the editorial and promotional team at Simon & Schuster Australia are utterly wonderful to their authors – I'm very grateful for the kindness. Deonie Fiford is a truly sublime editor; her every deletion felt like a masseuse's caress from heaven to me.

Richard Nylon, one of my oldest friends, proved very valuable in an area of research I initially knew little about: French fashion. One of Melbourne's great fashionistas, Richard's emails and texted replies to my questions were a joy to receive. As is always the case with my work, however, the necessities of plotting and pace forced me to whittle away excess historical details during the drafting process. The published book has a little less 'fashion stuff' than I started with, but I still enjoyed the exploration.

My colleagues at the University of Melbourne, particularly Nicolette Freeman, Annabelle Murphy, Meaghan Rodriguez, Sandra Sciberras and Zachary Dunbar, were brilliantly accommodating when I took off a whole semester to write the first draft of this book. The freedom of having nothing to do except write for four months was divine.

Luke Devenish

About the Author

uke Devenish has written plays and historical fiction, and worked as a writer, editor and script producer for long-running Australian television dramas. His previous three novels, *The Secret Heiress*, *Den of Wolves*, and *Nest of Vipers*, have been translated into multiple languages. A lecturer in screen-writing at the University of Melbourne's Victorian College of the Arts, Luke is as fervent about teaching as he is about writing, and is enjoyed for his lively, genre-loving classes. Luke lives with his partner and pets in historic Castlemaine, Central Victoria.

Visit www.lukedevenish.com

At Simon & Schuster we know there is nothing quite like discovering a really special book. Those books that make thinking a pleasure; put a smile on your face (or tears in your eyes); reignite your daydreams; and transport you to somewhere entirely new. This is exactly what we want to give you with our **Guaranteed Five Star Read** selection.

However if you're not completely satisfied with one of our books which features the Guaranteed Five Star Read sticker on the cover, simply complete this form and return it to us with your copy of the book and your original receipt:

Name: ....

Address: ....

....

Email address: ....

Phone number: ....

Please post to
Simon & Schuster Australia Guaranteed Five Star Read
PO Box 448 Cammeray NSW 2062 Australia

This offer expires 31 August 2020.
For full terms and conditions please visit www.GuaranteedRead.com

Visit **www.simonandschuster.com.au** or follow us online for great book recommendations, free chapters, author interviews and competitions.

SIMON & SCHUSTER
AUSTRALIA
A CBS COMPANY